The F
by L

GW01403053

The Halfblood War
Copyright © 2018 Liz Colter
Second Edition

ISBN: 978-1735354422
Cover design by Melinda Timpone
Cover artwork images by Adobe Stock

Tam Lin
Publishing

Published by
Tam Lin Publishing

To Martin, who always believed this would happen. I wish you were here to see it.

The Great Desert

Eanor

Arrend

Ishlin

Wildcat River

Lockgar Hold

HESH

Col

BASHEEN

White River

Bern

Pauden

Beneya

Fieryd Hold

Wayden

Fent

Fangtooth Mountains

The Great Road

Mistry Village

Hadash

San

Marshe

Relendel

Hassan

Chapter One

"It's too soon to risk it," Erimar said.

Tirren stood, anticipating the rest of the objections his father would raise. It was an old argument but past time to revisit it. He paced to the library's hearth and leaned an elbow on the fireplace mantle. "We've held off an extra year already. What will more waiting accomplish? It won't alter my son's heritage." The heavy, gray stone of Thiery Hold seeped cold into his arm, despite the fire. Outside, a chilly, spring rain pelted the leaded windows with a sound like small pebbles hitting the thick glass.

"He would have more time to mature," Erimar insisted.

"He's seventeen," Tirren said, striding back to the middle of the room, his volume increasing, "a year into his manhood." Escalating this would accomplish nothing. He took a breath and began again. "The more we emphasize his differences, the harder we make this for him. Chayan has enough to overcome already. He has to be ready to be Beodan by the time he's twenty, to be Bealdor when you and I are gone."

"Gods, Tirren! Don't you think I've thought of that every day since that woman brought him to us?"

That woman. Erimar had never once referred to Chayan's mother by name.

Tirren had intentionally steered the conversation away from Yslaaran, as much for his own sake as to avoid his father's bitterness, yet even the harsh and impersonal invocation of her triggered

1

memories: his first sight of her through the open gate of the Hold eighteen years ago, as she stood at the edge of the woods that Winterfest night. A woman, nearly of a height with him, wearing a single, flowing gown that had shimmered in the dark like opals, so different from the layered, high-cut dresses of Heshan women. Her thick, red hair loose, spilling down her back to her hips. He asked if she was well, titling her "Iden," as her graceful elegance bespoke a highborn woman. He hadn't realized at the time how much he debased her.

Tirren dragged himself from the memories. "I'm sure you've thought of her daily." He didn't bite back the resentment that seeped into his words. Unfair of him, he knew, to criticize his father's objections to her when he'd never reconciled his own conflict at loving the woman who stole his will and his seed for reasons he'd never understood, leaving him with the complications of Chayan's heritage heavy on his shoulders.

Their ancestors watched the argument even now, from tapestries covering the stone walls of the library. Men paused forever in the bloody battles that had won Thiery in the Conflicts, and paved the way for it to become the wealthiest of the four regions comprising their country of Hesh. Tirren's father would have continued the family's strong line, but his wife's frail body had given them only one child. And Tirren had failed more grandly still; one bastard child, born to the Elven woman who had abducted and seduced him eighteen years ago. A halfblood heir for a land that hated and feared the Elves.

"Don't twist my meaning, Tirren. You know I love Chayan. I've raised him as my grandson despite his blood and his illegitimacy. But to let him travel the region, see the people, meet with the councils. We have no way to know the effect it will have."

"We'll never know if we keep him prisoner in the Hold."

"Prisoner?" His father snorted. "Chayan has never been *kept* in the Hold and you know it. I'm saying we can't let our plans outrun our caution." His father stared into the fire. "The two of you are all I have," he said, quietly.

In nearly twenty years since Tirren's mother died, his father had never remarried, pinning his hopes on his son instead. Tirren had failed him there as well. He had been twenty-two the last time he saw Yslaaran, that following Winterfest eve, when she brought Chayan to him as an infant. At thirty-nine, he still couldn't bear the thought of another woman. His obsession with her was wrong, and guilt plagued him for it, but year after year the feelings refused to fade.

"I know we are," he said at last. "And I know the part I've played in that."

His own conflicted feelings extinguished the last spark of his anger. He moved back to the chair opposite his father and sat leaning forward, elbows on his knees, hands clasped. The silence that followed drew them in, drew them together.

"I appreciate everything you've done for Chayan," he said. "If not for your protection, he might have been murdered as a babe, even here in the Hold. You kept us both safe, helped him become accepted. I can never repay that. You are my father and my Bealdor and if you say not to go, we won't go."

The collapse of tension on his side left no wall for his father to push against. Erimar sat back with a deep sigh. "I'm not saying you can't go. I'm saying it frightens me."

His father had aged quickly in the past few years. At sixty-three, the brown hair and eyes of a Heshan had faded: the hair to gray, the eyes to a slight bluish cast. His olive skin had dulled and his trim muscularity looked almost skeletal, but he was strong and stubborn still.

"I promise you this, Tirren." Erimar's voice regained its conviction. "If you rush things and this plan fails, I'll see you married by the end of summer. Our line *will* continue to rule." The ultimatum had metal behind it this time, though the thought of marrying any but Yslaaran made Tirren's guts twist. "My own guilt has swayed me too often," his father continued. "No more. You had best be sure you are right about this."

He was sure Chayan could win out over the prejudice. The people of Thiery would surely come to accept him in time, despite his Elven blood, just as the community here in the Hold had done. He felt certain the magistrates wouldn't challenge Chayan's right to rule once they became familiar with him. He was gambling much on his son's readiness for this trip, though.

"Chayan has been preparing a long time. I don't want to tell him he has to wait another year or more." Tirren leaned back and watched the rain pound at the window, blurring the garden to steel gray. He was tired of the argument and they were returning to the crux of it again. "I think my status as Beodan and a couple of swordsmen at our backs will get us through the initial reactions." He met his father's eyes, willing him to agree. "The region expected to see the heir a year ago, when he turned sixteen, and the heir needs to see the region. If Chayan is different than the people anticipate, all the more reason for them to meet him, see his diplomacy, his humanness."

"The two of you and two swordsmen, and you think you'll be safe?" Erimar's grunt said eloquently what he thought of the idea.

"It's traditional," Tirren said, knowing that was not a strong enough reason for his father. Not even sure himself it was a good idea. "If we go with a show of force, people could be more frightened of him."

"They'll be frightened of him if he unleashes some wild magic on them, that's a sure thing. The two of you, trained soldiers that you are, and a couple of swordsmen won't save you from a mob. Or from an arrow in the back." Erimar waved one arm emphatically. "And as for the magic Chayan inherited, it's more likely to harm than help if you get in a bad way."

"It's been a long time since anything has happened. Chayan has worked hard on his control."

"He doesn't even understand what it is he's trying to control, Tirren!"

"How could he?" The sharpness returned to his voice with the painful memories. "There was no one to learn from. I certainly was no help, though the gods know I tried. But you've seen how maturity has changed him. The fevers are long gone and nothing untoward has happened in years. We can travel when neither of the moons are full, for extra caution."

Erimar stayed quiet. Tirren pressed his point. He leaned forward, as if moving closer could help him reach his father's emotions. "Even as a boy, he never meant to hurt anyone. He's a man grown now, and he tells me it won't happen again. I believe him. Chayan needs us to have faith in him. He can't succeed if we never give him the chance."

He held his breath, watching his father consider. He could see his thoughts dancing a razor's edge. "How many men would make you feel safe?"

"The whole gods-sworn army!" Erimar steepled his fingers and considered Tirren over the top of them. "Ten. Take ten good men with you, go at the dark of the moons, and be gods-damned careful in the Southlands."

Tirren woke to deep and nearly moonless darkness. He rolled onto his back, reorienting, trying to shake off his vivid dream of Yslaaran. In the five weeks that had passed since his father relented, the twin moons had waned concurrently, an event that wouldn't occur again until summer. Today he and Chayan would begin their journey. A cock crowed in the distance, heralding the approaching dawn, but his thoughts drifted back to his dream.

It had started as it always did, as things had started that night, eighteen years ago. Leaving the Winterfest celebration to take some cold night air in the courtyard and shake off the muzziness of the heavy mead. Seeing her at the edge of the woods; the heat of her touch when she took his hand as he approached to check on her. Leaving Thiery's snowy evergreens behind and entering a grassy meadow surrounded by beech and ash. Though the two full moons remained the same, the summer glade and the foreign stars overhead should have sent fear crashing through him, but nothing mattered except her. He would have walked through the gates of the Land of the Dead with her had she asked it of him. His mind had been cocooned in cobwebs, desire the only coherent thought. His memory of that night, though, remained as sharp as if it had been yesterday. Unfading, all these years, and bringing the frequent dreams, which in turn strengthened the memories. The most bitter torment she could have bestowed on him.

By the time the first sliver of dawn wrestled with the dark outside, Tirren closed the door to his apartments, saddlebags over one shoulder. He entered the hallway and saw the back of a soldier also heading for the stairs; from his size, it could only be one man.

Shen turned, hearing someone behind him. He filled the opening to the narrow stairwell as he waited for Tirren to catch up. Heavily muscled and nearly a head taller than most men, even Tirren came only to his eyes. The front of Shen's hair was tied up into a high ponytail, the same as Tirren's and every other swordsman's, but the rest of it hung nearly halfway down his back. It had kept growing a hand or more than most men's, just as Shen himself had.

The spiral stone steps were too narrow for them to go down abreast. Shen stepped back to let Tirren go first. "Are you leaving soon?" he asked at his shoulder as they descended.

"As soon as possible. I want an early start so we can take our time on the road."

"How is Chayan? Still nervous?"

Tirren nodded. "I think so, but he puts on a good face."

They reached the main floor and made their way to the great hall, the rows of long, heavy tables and benches nearly empty with the early hour. Tirren scanned the room for Chayan, not finding him, and he and Shen took a table to themselves. A wisp of a girl attended them a moment later, one of the many granddaughters of the Hold's eldest cook. She set out wooden bowls and pewter plates, with a large bowl of porridge and a platter of ham and warm bread. Tirren learned from her that Chayan had eaten before first light.

"He must either be packing or already at the stables waiting for me." He reached for the ham first, knowing his friend's appetite too well. The girl returned with two mugs of dark, watered ale and a bowl of fresh butter.

"I hope you know how much I wanted to go with you," Shen said.

He nodded. "I heard you asked to be in the escort. I also heard you drew first spring patrol. Just because you're a regiment leader now doesn't mean you'll get your way with Jaron." The captain of the swordsmen had never been a sentimental man.

Tirren was glad Jaron had promoted Shen early; he'd deserved it. Hard to believe it had been so many years since Shen first came to the Hold, arriving the same year that Yslaaran first appeared. He'd been sent from one of the better families up north, and Tirren had been impressed with the tall, athletic boy. He'd claimed him to squire as his personal uthow, which Shen did for six years, until old enough to join the ranks of the swordsmen. Since then, he'd become a good soldier and an even better leader.

"It must be nice to be out of the barracks and have your own rooms finally." Tirren smiled, but Shen remained serious.

"I'd give it up to protect you and Chayan."

"I can't go over Jaron's head to reassign you, not when Jaron himself is going with us." He looked down to saw at a thick piece of ham. "Besides, a giant like you would just scare people." He grinned, still looking at his plate.

Shen laughed. "You're in rare form today. It's good to see you smile, though. You should try it more often." He drained half his mug and wiped his mouth. "Well, I suppose you'll be safe enough without me."

"Gods, ten men," Tirren said. "I still think we might have been better off with just the traditional escort. I want so much for the people to accept him, not fear him."

"He picked a hard place to begin, starting off with the Southlands." Shen ladled a generous portion of porridge. "Why didn't he start up north, or better still, here in the Midlands? Thiery Village and Fent have been familiar with him for years."

"He didn't want the Southlands hanging over his head while he visited the other districts. I suppose I can see his logic."

Shen scraped the rest of the ham and bread from the platter to his plate. "Do you think people in the south really still see Elves, like they say? It's hard to believe when people in the rest of the region—probably all the rest of Hesh—have never seen any. Not these days, anyway."

Tirren shrugged. He often wondered the same himself, but the Southlanders were a suspicious and closemouthed lot. He had sent men there, years ago, to try and ferret out information about the Elves. They'd come back with nothing.

He'd never seen any of the Elven folk other than Yslaaran, and he'd only seen her the two times: that first night when she took him to the meadow, and the following Winterfest night—one year after she'd abducted him. He'd evaded the men his father had assigned to watch him and went to the woods looking for her. She was there, just as he'd hoped she would be, but Chayan had been a surprise. She'd passed the infant to him, naming the boy and, at last—when he'd begged—giving her own name. She'd never returned.

"I suspect they're just more superstitious in the south," Tirren said. He shrugged and his mouth crooked in a wry smile, "but I'm hardly the one to gainsay them."

Their first night together had felt to him like a single night, but he'd returned to find that search parties had been looking for him for three days. In legends, mortals abducted by the Elves usually vanished for years; when they returned, they had no memory of their abduction and their wits were often addled. Tirren's wits and memory had been intact, but he'd endured the whispers that followed him through the Hold for some weeks, and the looks the villagers had given him in town for months. Considering what he'd been subjected to, it was hard to imagine what Chayan saw in people's eyes every day.

Shen toyed with a piece of bread. "Do you still dream of her?"

Six years as Tirren's uthow and a dozen more as his friend had made Shen privy to more than most.

The memory of her emerald green eyes looking up at him returned to him from this morning's dream. The scent of her skin—jasmine, gardenia, and spice. Her deep red hair with tiny white flowers caught in it, wrapping about his bare forearms as he topped her.

He lowered his eyes, as if Shen might see the erotic images there. "Not as often now." He wasn't sure if he was glad of it or not.

"I notice that fewer of the camp followers are dying their hair red these days." Shen gave him a wicked smile. "Even they must be giving up on you finally." He bit off a hunk of bread.

The unexpected remark pulled a short laugh from Tirren in spite of himself, knowing it for truth. His vivid and sensual dreams had led him occasionally to those women, but the experience was such a coarse and disappointing shadow of his memory that he swore each time he wouldn't yield to it again.

"My patrol's gone fat and lazy over the winter," Shen said, recognizing when to change the subject. "It's good they'll be getting out of the Hold soon."

Shen was always anxious to start patrol. The man loved to travel. Tirren shoved his half-eaten plate of food aside and debated with Shen what the spring roads might be like. When Shen wiped his plate with a last piece of bread, Tirren stood and gathered his things.

"I'd better check the stables. Chayan's probably pacing the courtyard waiting for me."

Shen stood and came around the table to him. "Fare you well, both of you," he said earnestly, gripping his shoulder. "My patrol leaves later this week. We'll be out longer than you, but I'll see you when I return. Be safe." He clapped him on the back as they parted.

Tirren planned to do everything in his power to see that they were. He left the hall with breakfast sitting uneasy in his stomach, wondering if maybe he had been wrong to push for this.

He would find out soon enough.

Chapter Two

C hayan tied his bow and supplies behind the saddle of his stocky, tan gelding, Southern Star. The escort was milling about the stables with their horses packed and ready. Even Jaron would be going with them today.

Chayan wondered if everyone in the Hold was talking about the number of men his grandfather was sending with him. He spent a wasted wish that he could travel like any ordinary person. While he was at it, he might as well wish he looked as human as everyone he knew, making his green eyes brown or his pale skin olive. Wishing brought nothing but wanting, as his father said, and he staunched the thoughts before they gained the weight of fear or self-pity. For now, he just felt glad to finally be allowed to make this trip.

The soldiers were dressed in full patrol gear: hooded chain mail shirt and chain mail chaps, light quilted padding under the mail, and leather jerkins and breeches over it. The sky-blue diamond in the center of their jerkins proclaimed them soldiers of Thiery, though to whom Chayan couldn't guess. Except for the traders, hardly anyone in Hesh traveled outside their own region.

Like all swordsmen, the men rode heavy horse and carried long, double-bladed swords. Chayan had never been able to wear mail or carry a sword—the metal made his bones ache—but for this trip, neither he nor his father would go as soldiers. On this journey they would be diplomats.

A stable boy jogged past him to a stall and un-tethered Midnight, his father's gelding. Chayan turned to see his father and grandfather approaching. The boy led Midnight next to Star and held the reins. Midnight was taller than Chayan's draft, as black as his name, with heavy white feathering over the great hooves and eyes as blue as deep ice. His father came around to Midnight's near side and threw his saddlebags over his flanks. He flashed Chayan a quiet smile.

"Ready?" he asked, tying his saddlebags on and strapping his sheathed sword into place.

"Ready," Chayan replied. *Ready or not*, he thought.

His father looked around, doing a quick head count. He gestured to Jaron and mounted up. Chayan followed suit.

Erimar reached up to Chayan's father and clasped forearms. "It seems hard to believe twenty-three years have passed since you and I traveled the region together."

"It does indeed," his father said.

"Fortune favor you. We'll expect you back before the moon turns full again." Chayan knew he meant Hrar. Tlaas, larger, slower, and more distant, strove ever to catch his quicker sister.

Erimar turned to him next. "The gods watch over us, Chayan. Be careful, and perhaps the road will be easier than you think." Despite the words, he looked worried. Chayan nodded to his grandfather, hoping his own face held more confidence.

He turned Star to follow his father across the courtyard, to the gates of the Hold that he had so seldom passed through. The escort fell in behind them, the sound of a dozen horses ringing loud on the cobbles. They rode under the tall stone arch and Chayan's chest tightened with an eagerness and dread that filled him in equal parts, though they wouldn't reach Marshe until the next evening and they wouldn't truly be in the Southlands until the end of the week.

Chayan rode next to his father as they wound down from the Hold and turned east, riding above Thiery Village to the Great Road. The village lay to his right, flowing down the hillside in a clutter of timber and plaster buildings, spreading out into the level farmland below. Beyond that was evergreen forest. When they reached the Great Road, the wide dirt highway lay before him like an invitation, north to Thiery's border with Lacedar and south to the village of Relendel at the ocean's edge. Chayan had been to Thiery Village many times, west to nearby Fent a few times, and across this road to hunt in the mountains with his father and his men. Never in seventeen years had he turned south. Until now.

His muscles tightened again and he willed them to relax, chiding himself mentally that he wasn't even out of sight of the village.

"Do you still think the weather will hold?" his father asked, shaking him out of his thoughts.

Chayan looked at the hazy spring blue of the sky, then to the Fangtooths in the east. No heavy clouds massed above the giant mountains, but Chayan only looked at the sky out of habit. He'd always possessed a good weather sense, born of what he felt, not what he saw. "It may not hold in the north, but I think it will for us in the south."

They turned onto the wide road, and the soldiers with them fanned out in front, to the sides, and behind. Not a coincidence, he was sure. As the sun rose higher in the sky, the few travelers they passed stared at the large group of soldiers and missed him entirely. After the second wagon passed by, he asked, "If this is a trip to meet the people I'll rule someday, shouldn't they see me?"

"This trip is to meet with the magistrates and councilors of the towns."

Chayan nodded and said nothing. His father rode a few paces in silence, looking at him. It was the same look he had given when

Chayan had been teased as a child for his differences by others too young to respect his rank. The same look his father had given him in his early teens, as he sat by Chayan's bed, cooling his brow with wet cloths when the strange fever boiled his blood. That mix of sorrow and worry that always made Chayan feel guilty.

His father nudged his horse closer. "You're right. An heir would usually take this opportunity to let the people see him. It's as important to know the people you'll come to rule as it is to know the local administrators. But for this first trip, if we can limit your exposure as much as possible to just the officials, I think that'll be a better start. We need to be patient, introduce you slowly."

"I understand."

Chayan understood too well. He was ever the exception.

As a young boy he'd experienced the flights of fancy that all children do, imagining himself one of the powerful Elves, or other fantasies that painted him the hero in every new portrait in his mind. But as he grew, he wished nothing so much as to be like his father—human, respected, loved by his people.

Except for being tall, lean, and quiet—and thank the gods for the brown hair he had inherited—he was little like his father. His green eyes and pale skin were enough to set him apart, but there was a quality to his features that made people stare. His skin was smoother than any human's, the bones of his face finer, giving them almost a different set. He moved more fluidly, no matter how he tried to imitate the heavier tread of other men. Even his leanness was different from his father's, as if he had less bone, less substance.

"We'll be staying at inns, though," Chayan said.

"What we can control, we will. What we can't, we'll make the best of." His father gave him that half-smile of his, like he had all the faith in the world in him. Chayan hoped he could live up to it.

They entered the forest and rode leisurely for the rest of the day through the tall pines. Chayan breathed in their familiar, pitchy smell. He'd spent a lot of time alone in the forest near the Hold when he was young, and loved the height and color and smell of evergreens. They camped that night, well off the road, and reached Marshe without incident before dusk of the next day.

He'd known it was small but still felt surprised to see it wasn't even a tenth the size of Thiery Village; more a way station in the road than a town. They rode to the inn where they would be staying, and the innkeeper's wife showed them to their rooms, while one of the swordsmen asked the innkeeper to send for the magistrate. The innkeeper and his wife both snuck furtive looks at Chayan, but he was still largely screened by the swordsmen and bustled, unceremoniously, to his room.

It had been decided for him that Chayan would share a room with his father as a precaution. Jaron would have the room next door, and the soldiers would rotate the guard, two outside the inn and three outside the rooms, with the rest sharing one room until their turn at the watch. He'd just set his saddlebags on one of the two beds when there was a knock at the door. His father opened it. Jaron looked serious, which told Chayan nothing. The man always looked serious. "Tarn died six days ago," he said. "A tree split wrong and the butt of it kicked back and killed him." Like most of the workers in Marshe, their magistrate had been a woodcutter. "Three men and Tarn's widow are vying to be the new magistrate," Jaron continued. "Some came to blows over it downstairs in the common room two nights ago, trying to reach a decision before you arrived. The innkeep says, like as not, they'll come by one-by-one tonight to try and convince you to choose them over the others."

"It's not my decision to make," his father said, "or Chayan's either. I don't want him in the middle of this. Tell them to send word to the Hold when they've decided. We'll meet with no one until then." Jaron nodded and strode away. Tirren closed the door with that look in his eyes they so often held, distant sorrow and mild worry.

After mentally preparing all day to meet his first official, Chayan realized he would be spending an uneventful night in his room. Uneventful except for the thoughts spinning in his head. Relendel would now be his very first diplomatic experience.

Starting in the south suddenly seemed like a very bad idea.

———— ⟲⟳ ————

They left Marshe early, traveling through wooded and quiet country where Chayan saw few other travelers. There were no villages to speak of between Marshe and Relendel, and they camped out that night. By mid-morning of the following day the evergreens diminished, opening onto a flat, spare land that dropped toward the ocean. He had passed into the true Southlands, and was now farther from home than he had ever been. His unease of that first morning returned with redoubled intensity, and Chayan focused nervously on reaching the coast.

The bleak expanse left him feeling as exposed and vulnerable as the weather-beaten farms and tiny communities they passed. He endured the shocked stares of the few who saw him as they rode by, but he had spent seventeen years abiding the facts of his differences. He had learned long ago to make his peace with people's reactions to him. He kept his body relaxed as he rode, centered on keeping his mind calm but alert.

The responses to his Elven appearance became more pronounced the farther south they traveled. At one small farm, a woman drew her child forward to see the soldiers and caught a good look at him. She grabbed the girl and ran, shrieking, for the safety of the house. He would have found the response comical if it wasn't so disheartening.

"Doing all right?" His father's soft words cut through his reflections.

Chayan gave a small smile and nodded. "Fine."

Tirren looked hard at him. "We could still change plans and go north. Finish Relendel and the rest of the Southlands later. You'll have to deal with prejudice everywhere, but I'd be surprised if any other villages prove as difficult."

"No." He met his father's look with all the confidence he could muster. "I don't want to spend my time in every other town wondering how much worse it'll be here. I'd rather just face it now. I've been curious about Relendel for a long time anyway."

"All right." His father said no more, but his look spoke volumes.

"It'll be okay." Chayan tried to sound reassuring. Maybe if he said it often enough, it would be true.

By late afternoon they came to the outskirts of Relendel. A man and a teenage boy riding toward them slowed at the sight of the group, more than twice the size of a normal patrol.

"Ho, Kesum," the man hailed Jaron, who was riding at the front. "Is the Beodan coming today?"

Jaron gave a short nod. "He is."

Messengers had been sent to the villages they were scheduled to visit, to allow the councils to make a list of issues and prepare for the guests they would receive. Word would have spread. It had only been stated in passing that the Beodan's son would accompany him. His halfblood status had not been mentioned.

The man scanned the party, looking to see if this was a vanguard or if the Beodan himself was among them. His eyes fell on Chayan. "Gods be good," he whispered. He grabbed the near rein of the boy riding with him, jerking the horse around as he spun his own and wheeled back toward Relendel.

Jaron looked back at Tirren, unsure what to do. Tirren shrugged. Chayan thought if the whole town reacted like that, it would be a very short visit.

They soon passed through the scattered farms on the outskirts and came to the village proper. It was larger than Marshe, but still small compared to the villages with which he was familiar. The village square lay in sight just ahead and Chayan's belly tightened. He took a deep steadying breath, inhaling the unfamiliar salty sea air. His father looked about, wary as a cat. The soldiers mirrored his alertness.

The village square turned out to be a circle really, or rather a series of concentric ones. The shops and businesses formed the outer perimeter. They looked poor and ramshackle compared to Thiery or Fent, Chayan's only frame of reference. The center ring held the village well, with a broad round coping. Between the well and the shops ran a wide, circular, cobbled road.

On the left side stood a proper inn, judged against the tavern rooms in Marshe anyway. The brown wooden sign over the door had weathered to the point that Chayan strained to make out the name, The Bull and the Bear. A faded image of the two beasts head-to-head had been drawn in gold paint below the lettering.

People in the street stopped to stare, and Chayan noticed folk appearing at windows and doors as well. They were pointing to the group and muttering; not the excited buzz of people glad to see the swordsmen or their Beodan, but a low, disturbing grumble.

"Beodan," one of the soldiers near the rear said, just loud enough to be heard.

His father looked back and so did Chayan. A group of four or five men were walking toward the rearmost soldiers, staring hard at him. He watched as another man jogged to join them. It was the man they had seen on the road.

"See? There. In the middle," he pointed to Chayan.

The soldiers at the back spun their horses to face the men. His grandfather had been right to insist on ten men, Chayan admitted. Perhaps he should have sent more.

"Is it a prisoner?" the largest man in the group called to the swordsmen. He had the beefy red face of a drinker and a wide, crooked nose. "'Cause if it is, we don't want it in this town. Take it to the Hold."

Soldiers reached for their weapons, loosening the swords in their scabbards. A tingle ran up Chayan's back. He recognized the sensation and panic coursed through him as sharply as the magic beginning to flow into him.

No. No, not this. Not now.

The reaction intensified. It spread until every inch of him felt electrified, as if lightning had struck him. He'd been in Relendel only moments and already he was losing the battle to contain his magic. He fought to suppress it, focusing on the fact that he had controlled it for years; that he had promised his father.

"Hold!" Tirren called out to his men. Oblivious of Chayan's struggle, his father rode slowly from the middle of the group to the cluster of men.

Chayan's physical unease continued to grow. His senses heightened until it was almost too much to bear—too much to see and smell and hear all at once. Colors intensified, becoming so sharp and rich, they might have been freshly painted on his surroundings.

When he had terrified the young boys with visions of monstrous things, when he had ... done what he did to the girl, it had been over before he'd known what he was doing. He couldn't let it happen again. He had to focus.

"I am Tirren an Erimar a Balawen es Thiery, the Beodan of Thiery." His father's voice was calm, commanding. "The one with us is no prisoner. He has ridden here to meet with your council and he is no concern of yours. If you interfere with the business of the Hold, you do so at your own peril."

With an effort, Chayan closed his eyes on the danger his father faced. He turned all his attention inward, to the instinct for defense raging through him. Slowing his breathing, he tried not to think about this turning into his worst nightmare: a mob scene, a whole village overpowering the soldiers, killing them all.

Control warred with panic. Slowly, very slowly, he pushed all thought from his mind. He forced his muscles to relax and imagined himself encased in dark, cool stone, where he could see, hear, and touch nothing.

The heightened senses ebbed, diminished ... vanished.

Chayan took three deep breaths before he dared to flick his eyes open. It felt like he had battled the power inside him for ages, but only a moment had passed. His father's hand sat casually on his sword hilt, as if just resting there. Most of the soldiers had ridden to Tirren's side, while three watched the other directions. Chayan remained safely in the middle.

The village men were raising empty hands, taking a step back, looking at the ground. They had the sense to respect their Beodan and knew they were not a match for twelve armed soldiers, especially as no other villagers had come to join them.

"Beodan?" a tentative voice asked, from somewhere near the well.

Tirren twisted in his saddle to find the speaker. Chayan, still facing forward, saw a portly middle-aged man standing on the cobbles near the inn. His hair was pulled back into a ponytail. He wore a dirty white apron over dirty brown breeches, and a graying linen shirt with rolled sleeves.

"I am he," Tirren answered.

"I'm Councilman Beeson, Beodan. We've been expecting you. I run the Bull and the Bear." He waved a shaky hand in the direction of the inn. "Won't you and your men come inside?" Before anyone could answer, the innkeeper craned around the soldiers to address the man they had passed on the road. "Louden, you'd better get back to your farm." His voice was firm now. "It's near milking time. You too, Jance."

The big man, Jance apparently, nodded once, but didn't move. He shot another glance at Chayan, but his allies were backing away. Swordsmen stayed facing the men until the group reluctantly dispersed.

The windows of the houses and buildings near the village center were still filled with watching faces. The people who had gathered outside their shops and stalls stood transfixed by the spectacle of the swordsmen, the Beodan, and the showdown that had just taken place, but most of all, by Chayan as he dismounted with the others.

Chayan heard the whispers, saw the pointing fingers, and tried to ignore the scrutiny. He still felt shaky from wrestling with his magic. The soldiers scanned each face as they led their horses to the hitching post outside the inn, but no one else seemed willing to say or do anything provocative.

The innkeeper waited in the doorway with a nervous smile, his eyes flitting between Tirren and Chayan. His attention shot to Jaron when the captain spoke unexpectedly.

"How many entrances are there and where?"

Chayan understood why his grandfather had sent Jaron along; besides his rank, he was a measured man, thoughtful, intelligent, and never rash. He didn't look as commanding as he sounded, late-middle years with average features and not a tall man, but he was fit for his age and brooked no nonsense. He had been Captain of the Swordsmen as long as Chayan could remember.

The innkeeper answered his question and Jaron pointed out men to guard the doors.

"If you have any patrons in there," Tirren added, "please ask them to leave." Chayan thought it likely that once he went inside they would leave, regardless.

The man bobbed a quick bow. "I believe they all came out when Louden ran by. He brought the whole town out shouting about ... shouting, uh, that you were coming, Beodan."

Jaron pushed past the man and inside the inn. He reappeared a few moments later. "There's a serving woman, a cook, and her son. No more unless there are any in the rooms upstairs."

"No, Beodan," the innkeeper said. "We have no guests at the moment. We have kept the rooms clear for your party."

Tirren nodded. "Perhaps you have a private dining room where we might talk?"

Where I'm less likely to be seen, Chayan thought.

"Of course," the man said.

Beeson stood aside as two soldiers entered behind Jaron, followed by Tirren, Chayan, and the rest of the escort that was not left on guard outside. The innkeeper stared openly at Chayan as he passed.

When the group stopped, waiting for the innkeeper to show the way, Beeson came back to himself with a start. He sent the kitchen boy at a run to bring the other three members of the council and headed to a pair of wooden double doors at the back of the common room. A middle-aged woman with a dirty cloth stood wide-eyed by a table, her eyes locked on Chayan. A fat, yellow cat, lying on another table, yawned. The cat, he thought, might be the only one in the village that wouldn't stare at him.

"I hope this will do, Beodan." The innkeeper pushed the double doors open and watched warily as Chayan passed him again.

Chayan was surprised the inn had a private room. It wasn't likely many travelers or highborn would pass through here. Relendel was a coastal town but, like everywhere in Thiery, there was no port. The moons pulled too strongly on the tides for boats to put in at the rocky shores. Fishermen all along the coast could do no more than cast nets from the cliffs.

"This will serve us fine," Tirren said. The guards took up posts on either side of the doors as Chayan and his father stepped inside. "Do you know why we have come?"

"The message said only that the Beodan would be visiting the region ... with his son." The last word trailed off as the innkeeper stared at Chayan again, having at last put the pieces together.

"Yes, my son. This is Chayan an Tirren a Yslaaran es Thiery." Tirren recited his proper name with no inflection, showing neither of pride nor embarrassment at his uncommon first name nor at his mother's unmistakably Elven name. Chayan appreciated the "es Thiery" now more than ever, even if not strictly true. If any had known the place where he was born, his name would have been more foreign sounding by far.

The innkeeper blushed and stammered and finally bobbed a short bow. "I apologize for the roughness of the men you encountered, Beodan, Kesum." He addressed them rightly, as Chayan would keep the common highborn title of Kesum until his twentieth year, when he would also become Beodan. "The ... uh ... Kesum Chayan surprised them." The man turned red as a beet, but couldn't seem to pull his eyes from Chayan's face.

"Your help dispersing them peacefully was much appreciated," Chayan said. He did what he could to keep the musical lilt out of his voice and speak calmly, reassuringly.

Beeson's mouth hung open. Chayan thought the cat on the table might as well have spoken to him. In the end, the man could only bob his head again.

The other three council members arrived in short order. The innkeeper scuttled out of the room to meet them and Chayan could hear the low mumbles as he prepared them for what they were about to encounter. When they entered, Chayan breathed a sigh of relief to see none of the angry men from the street were among them. The councilmen huddled together like old women as Beeson introduced their guests.

Chayan stood quiet and relaxed, and let the men inspect him. He was more than used to stares, though it had been a while since he'd provoked as much reaction as he had today. Nothing about the council appeared to be remotely threatening and no magic tried to bubble to the surface, warring to take over his mind.

The innkeeper's hands trembled as he poured the wine, but so far, his father had been right. The Beodan's presence—and a contingent of armed swordsmen—seemed enough to moderate any overt hostility. Chayan began to have hope that the council would be more restrained and reasonable than the people they presided over.

He and his father seated themselves at the large table; the council remained standing until they sat. His father began the meeting and the village council remained deferential throughout, but fear danced in their eyes on the rare occasions they were forced to address Chayan directly. Something else hid within those looks, too, something clear in their faces every time they looked at him. Strange, but if he had to name it, Chayan would call it guilt.

He knew they would have heard the rumors before today that the Beodan's son was a halfblood, no matter how hard his father and grandfather had worked to minimize gossip about him. Perhaps they assumed the tales exaggerated ... or perhaps they had known and simply hoped never to encounter him in person.

His father kept the meeting short, just enough to ask the customary questions about the needs and concerns of the village and the financial matters. Chayan admired how well he guided the talk, diplomatically ignoring their reactions to his Elven appearance. He led them smoothly into issues that were points of contention between the council members, and moderated the resulting discussions.

For his part, Chayan spoke little but tried to be helpful and reassuring when he did. No mention was made of his heritage by anyone, though it loomed like the inn's mascot bear come to life and sitting in the middle of the table; something everyone chose to talk around rather than look at directly.

When the meeting finally concluded, Chayan gratefully escaped the claustrophobic room. They had, of course, been invited to stay, but the relief when his father declined the offer had been considerable, no less for himself than for the council members, he was sure. The plan had been to spend the night at the inn, but after his welcome by the villagers, Chayan would have rather spent the night in the Land of the Dead. His father must have felt the same.

He stepped out the front door behind the soldiers and stopped. It seemed the entire village was gathered outside the inn. He experienced a brief jolt of fear at their numbers. The fear tingled through his body, but he held his apprehension firmly in check. The swordsmen moved to the fore and dispersed the crowd with little trouble. None of the people seemed anxious to get too close.

The soldiers gathered the horses from the hitching post and everyone mounted up. A tremendous weight lifted from Chayan's shoulders as rode beyond the crowd of villagers and out of Relendel, headed west.

"You did well," his father said, when they had cleared the outskirts of the village.

Truth be told, it had gone better than Chayan expected. He waited until the soldiers spread out on the road and his soft voice wouldn't be easily heard. "When you first saw my mother, did you react the same way?"

"I was under an enchantment."

"I know. But beneath that, were you afraid of her?"

Where his father had always been reticent about Yslaaran with everyone else, even Chayan's grandfather, he had never held back from trying to answer any question Chayan asked about his Elven heritage.

His father shook his head. "I felt confusion at first, then an overpowering lust I couldn't control. That was all. No fear. Even the confusion faded. It seemed like all the things happening to me were perfectly normal—until the morning, anyway."

Chayan couldn't imagine what it had been like for him. His father had woken alone and naked in the Elven lands, aware of everything that had happened to him. He had escaped by following the trail of his clothes, left like signposts, into a bank of fog. Passing through it, he had looked back to see only his own snow-covered forest. The Elven lands were gone. He had never been able to find them again, though Chayan knew he had tried for years.

"I wish I'd been able to ask the people in Relendel about the Elves. They're so afraid of them. I've always hoped it meant they knew more about them." His father was the only person he knew of who had actually seen one, and Chayan had dreamed for years about coming to Relendel in hopes of finding some answers to his many questions.

"I know you wanted to. I'm glad you had the sense not to bring it up. I guess we both have questions that will never be answered."

Chayan nodded.

As a child, his father had ordered the educators, historians, and storytellers to gather all the knowledge about Elves available, to teach him. What they had compiled had been pitifully little and often conflicting, but his father had seen that he was taught all of it, good and bad. He had tempered the stories of abduction and menace with his own memories of Yslaaran's beauty and gentleness ... and the desire for her that had never left him.

"Do you still miss her?" Chayan knew very well he did and wasn't sure why he had asked. He felt himself flush and wished he could take the question back. Perhaps he'd wanted assurance that the feelings weren't fading, that someone else felt her absence in their life.

They rode in silence a few steps. Chayan thought maybe this was one question he wouldn't get an answer to when his father said quietly, "Always."

Chayan turned away from the pain he saw. The quiet, serious man next to him was the father he'd always known, but his grandfather spoke of another man, the man he'd been before he met Yslaaran, one that courted women and danced and contested in tournaments. Chayan's birth had brought fears and worries and longings that had changed him. Chayan had always felt responsible. He knew his father had hoped that Yslaaran would return again, even if it was just to see her son. Like Chayan's own wishes for this, the hope had faded with time.

He changed the subject. "Have you ever seen any sign of the Elves when you traveled through here?"

"No. I don't know of anyone who has. I've heard the same stories as you, but I don't know if there's any truth to them. Perhaps the people here have their reasons for acting like they do, or perhaps it's just a tradition of prejudice and fear that's been handed down generation to generation."

Tirren guided Midnight to the side to skirt a large, half-buried boulder in the road. He nudged the horse back and continued. "Whatever the reason, people here have always been prejudiced and suspicious, more than in San, which is further from the main routes. There are even the ruins of an ancient temple to one of the gods nearby, the only one left in the region, perhaps in the whole country. The folk hereabouts are too superstitious to take the stone from there for other uses."

"Could we see the ruins?"

"Of course. They aren't far from here, in fact. We should have plenty of time to see them and still find a safe spot to camp before dark."

Less than half a league from the village, Tirren turned their group north, up a small overgrown track. Soon after, they came to the ruins. Nothing remained except a gray perimeter of low stone that was thickly overgrown with vines, and a heavy, crude, stone altar at the far end. The rocks from the walls were scattered where they had fallen, like the bones of an old skeleton, lying in a wide, mossy circle. The stone floor had worn smooth with age, and debris cluttered the surface.

Chayan and Tirren dismounted and walked about the ruins, speculating which god it might have been dedicated to, though there were no clues to say if they were right. Chayan's fascination increased with every step, every new detail. The possibility that the Elves, or perhaps the gods themselves, may have stood here in ages past filled him with wonder.

They mounted again and rode up the track a short way more as his father had never explored past this point and Chayan wanted to see if there were other ruins. Tirren instructed the escort to wait as they wouldn't go far. They didn't find more ruins; however, they came to a small peasant hut, as surprising for its isolation as for its nearness to the temple. A man in his middle years and a younger man, little older than Chayan, were working outside on a section of stone pasture wall they were repairing. The man's wife turned their cow out into the pasture and picked up a bucket of milk. They looked up in alarmed surprise as Tirren and Chayan rode up.

Chayan saw that all three had flat-boned faces with small broad noses. Their skin was a bronze color instead of Heshan olive. Both men had dark hair to their waists, the older man's beginning to gray. The woman's hair was longer still, nearly to her thighs, and all three wore it in a single braid down the back. Chayan was educated enough to know from their appearance that they must be from Bansheen, the country across the mountains, though he had been unaware that any Bansheenan lived in Hesh, much less in Thiery.

"Good day to you," his father said. Chayan nodded in greeting. All three dropped to their knees, foreheads bowed to the ground. Chayan looked to his father in surprise.

"We are honored, Beodan, Kesum," the older man said, sitting back on his heels. Likely these people had heard that the Beodan would be visiting the area, and had correctly guessed their identity.

"Please, rise," Tirren said, seeming uncomfortable with the display of obeisance. "Are you recently come from Bansheen?" There was no other place they could be from. If there was an elsewhere across the seas, other than the Land of the Dead, none living knew of it.

"No, Beodan. I was raised in this house, as were my parents, and their great-grandparents." Some extreme circumstance must have brought their ancestors here from Bansheen. Once they had made it to this place, the future generations would have been stranded—the barriers of the sea to the south and west, the desert to the north, and the mountains to the east would be far too hazardous to attempt under normal conditions. Chayan recalled his tutor mentioning a Bansheenan noblewoman who had shipwrecked here during the Conflicts, and wondered if they might be descendants of hers.

"We would offer you refreshment, or what other humble hospitality we have, Beodan, Kesum," the woman said, standing and giving a deep bow. "What we have is yours."

Chayan found it ironic that these simple peasant folk were offering more genuine hospitality with less fear than the village officials with whom they had met. They glanced often in his direction, but the look on their faces held only awe.

"With thanks, no," his father said, obviously not wanting to take anything from poor folk.

"Do you know anything of the ruins nearby?" Chayan asked them on impulse.

"I am sorry, Kesum," the man answered, bobbing his head again. "We know nothing of the history of the temple. It was forgotten long before our ancestors arrived here." He seemed genuinely apologetic at not having more information.

Tirren took their leave of the family.

"Fortune favor you," Chayan said, as he and his father turned their horses. The family dropped to their knees, bowing their heads to the ground again.

They rode back to the waiting soldiers. The afternoon was waning to evening, the coming dusk felt more than seen, and Chayan knew his father wanted to be well down the road from Relendel before they stopped for the night.

When the Beodan and Kesum were out of sight, Rayel stood with his parents. A long and significant look passed between his mother and father. His father gathered himself with a deep breath and turned to him.

"You must leave for the School without delay. The Somiir must know of this."

Wordlessly, Rayel ran to his room where a pack lay in the corner, all the preparations for this trip readied at all times. He had never made the difficult and dangerous journey, as his father had, but he had prepared his entire life for the possibility.

His parents gathered the food and water he and the stock would need, while he grabbed up his pack and the gear around it.

He ran to the stable and readied three mounts. The skaggi were small beasts, the kind his people used in their desert land. One he saddled and two he made pack animals and, with a brief goodbye to his parents, set off north for Bansheen at the fastest pace he could sustain.

Chapter Three

Yslaaran lowered herself to the ground in the shade of an immense willow tree, her mind circling her long-laid plans and spiraling outward on the possibilities.

Few Elves were scattered about the courtyards today, but then her people were few. Little more than a hundred of the Light Elves, the Seely, had been created by the gods and in all the aeons since their creation, less than two score children had been born to them.

Yslaaran had been the first child. She was old enough that she had known the gods and had walked among the humans long ago, before the gods had deserted the Elves and the Elves had deserted the humans. She remembered it well. She missed those days, and the memories of them were bright colors in the tapestry of her thoughts today. Her mind swirled between past and present, and the threads that tied them together. The thread she wove now was that of her son.

She breathed in the calming perfume from the riot of flowers that grew in clusters everywhere, especially here on the palace lawns. In the evening, the night flowers that she loved would share their own heady scent. Looking across the rows of blooms she saw Nisseah walking toward her, his strawberry-blonde hair glinting in the sunlight. He had been in her thoughts as well.

He was dressed in soft brown breeches with a pale blue shirt that emphasized the ice-blue of his eyes. It was collarless and cuffless, and cinched with a wide belt of tooled leather. The grass swept soft under Yslaaran's sandaled feet as she stood and crossed the lawn to meet him.

He greeted her with an exaggerated courtly bow. "I was on my way to the palace for the dance. May I hope you will join me?" He took her hands and moved her easily in a few graceful dance steps.

Moving with him like this half made her wish she could go, even though music played nearly all the time. The Seely had been created to love pleasures so they could entertain the gods with their arts and their music and their dance. Resisting any pleasurable diversion was never easy.

"Maybe later, Nisseah," she said, as he released her. "I thought I would take a walk." She held his eyes to make sure he understood her unspoken meaning.

"I think you have someone you would rather see than me." He said it with mocking hurt, but his eyes flashed as bright as his smile. He did understand.

"Perhaps another will dance with you." She glanced to the queen, lounging with the king on silk pillows on the lawn not far from them. They both knew it had been the queen's nearness that made her careful.

"Ah, well to that," he said in a lower voice, "Evainya's eye seems to have fallen on Baedis instead of me, I fear."

Yslaaran nodded, accepting this hindrance to their plans. Evainya and Analoor were the only Elves considered mated, though both had frequent lovers. It would have been convenient if Nisseah had caught the queen's attention now, as he had in the past.

"Poor us," he said, teasing again. "I shall dance all alone and you shall go on unaccompanied."

"I will go with her," said a lively voice behind her.

Yslaaran had seen Uthbaraal lying in the grass and was not surprised he'd listened to their every word. Yet another reason she had been circumspect.

He came closer and bounced on his bare toes, the top of his head level with her shoulder. His energy could barely be contained when he stood still. His shining black eyes, black hair, and swarthy complexion stood out in sharp contrast to the Light Elves around him. He was dressed in brown and green, the colors most of the Dark Elves chose. His clothes were of a coarser material, as his kind cared nothing for finery, and his sleeveless shirt was belted with simple rope.

Yslaaran had always been glad the community of Dark Elves, the Unseely, chose to live apart, preferring the dark of the forests. They had been created all male and numbered far fewer than the Seely, but they had become wilder over the ages, without the guidance of the gods. They were far too mischievous to be allowed inside the palace anymore, though they moved freely about the Elven lands and came often to the court.

"As you wish," she replied to his offer.

She didn't want him along, especially not today, but she knew he wouldn't easily be dissuaded. Nisseah said nothing. The Unseely were too curious by half, but drawing attention to herself by acting reluctant would be worse than Uthbaraal going with her. And telling him no would only make him more determined.

"So I have my escort." She gave Nisseah another smile and took her leave. Uthbaraal was instantly at her side, excited without knowing their destination.

She led him across the courtyard and past the large, carved wooden doors of the palace that stood wide open, as always. The sweet sound of woodwind and stringed instruments drifted out, and dancing couples spun in and out of view. The floor of gold-veined, white marble glittered with insets of polished gems, winking at them. Uthbaraal stopped and stared, captivated by the movement perhaps, but more likely by the exquisite interior forbidden to him.

Yslaaran waited for him. It was a beautiful sight, she had to admit. A living palace, made from a stand of ancient madras trees, the columns of red trunks grown together, forming the walls. The barkless trees had been intricately carved, and the branches above woven into a roof that allowed soft sunlight to filter into the single, enormous room. The walls and alcoves were filled with aeons of artistry and gifts, both human and Elven: flower-dyed silk hangings, musical instruments of the thinnest wood, masks of gold, stone and marble carvings that a mortal king would weep to possess. She saw Uthbaraal's eyes sweep covetously over the treasures, though he had seen them thousands of times.

Two thrones stood at the back of the great room, impossible even for Yslaaran to ignore through the open doors. They were matching triumphs of craftsmanship: thin, hammered gold shaped into madras trees, the seats molded into the trunks, with golden branches and leaves arching up to form the high backs. Gems dripped like dew from each detailed leaf. Despite the splendor of the palace, though, neither the king and queen, nor any other, slept there. Yslaaran's people preferred to be out of doors, in the soft air and endless summer of their land.

Melancholy touched her for a moment at the sight of those thrones. She remembered a time when the queen and king had ruled from there. But that had been long ago. The thrones were used now only for Evainya and Analoor to rest and watch entertainments, when they could even be stirred to that much interest. Her monarchs, like many of the elder Seely, spent their time sleeping more often than not, waking to drink wine and play with their lovers. Evainya and Analoor were the oldest, the first creation of the gods; rulers over all the Elves since the beginning, and their decline saddened Yslaaran. The king's indolence had progressed more rapidly than Evainya's, though, and for that reason, Yslaaran and her companions proceeded carefully with their plans. The king may be beyond caring, but none would wish to see the queen roused to anger.

Yslaaran began walking again, past the palace and the sweeping courtyards, with Uthbaraal trailing along, talking all the while. They left the open lawns and entered the forest of beech and ash, finally passing through the woods to the very edge of their lands, to the Veil of Mists. She approached the great, gray wall rising above her, stretching up to the sky and out of sight to either side, the wall dividing the Elves from the humans.

When the gods left without a word, centuries ago, abandoning their creations like forgotten toys, Yslaaran and the other Elves had looked to their king and queen. It had been Evainya and Analoor who had decided that, as the gods had left them, so they would forsake the humans, whom the gods had charged them to aid. It was her king and queen who had created the mists that hid them from Men.

The gods had never returned to them. They had vanished across the seas, past the Land of the Dead, even beyond the awareness of the Elves. In the time since their separation, Yslaaran had watched the mortals become fearful and superstitious of her people, and the Elves grow ever more arrogant and disdainful of humans. Over time, most of the Elves had come to care little for what happened in the mortal world, except to venture contact for their own amusement, taking mortal men and women as lovers to enjoy their primitive roughness and fiery passions. As if possessing the mortals awhile could fire their own cool natures.

Yslaaran's reasons for taking the Man, Tirren, had been different.

Uthbaraal capered along the boundary, one hand invisible as he dragged it through the mists. She knew he enjoyed this place and the possibilities that lay beyond that gray wall. Especially here. Yslaaran had brought them to the origin of the veil, the spot where the mists anchored to the mortal lands. In this one place the boundary was thin, so thin that the Unseely could pass through unaided ... and on the other side of this point was always the village the humans called Relendel.

Yslaaran left Uthbaraal to cavort along the edge. She stepped into the veil, far enough that it surrounded her, but not so far that she emerged into the mortal world. The chill touch of the mist lay on her skin like cool, moist fingers, brushing at her arms and face. Uthbaraal would no longer be able to see her, nor could she be seen from the mortal side, but stood between worlds.

She had watched Chayan now and again from the mists, observing him as he grew. Sometimes she had left the veil and entered the forest where he camped alone as he learned to deal with the strong Elven blood in his half-human body. Before her son, she had never seen a halfbreed that was not a babe. She had not even been sure they survived their duality. And it had been essential to her plans that he must.

Chayan journeyed now with his father, she knew, and she had come to see how he fared. From the vantage of the mists, she needed do no more than think of them to find them. Tirren rode at the boy's side, surrounded by the warriors of his fortress. It had been some time since she had seen him, and an unexpected affection bloomed within her.

His memories of her burned like a flame inside him. She could see it in the lines of his body, feel it emanating from him like a fever. The memories had seared him to the soul, binding him to her. She regretted the pain it caused, but it couldn't be helped. That, too, had been necessary.

They approached the village of Relendel, the thing she had come to watch. Foreign emotions of fear and excitement brushed through her as he was first threatened and then accepted by the villagers seeing him for the first time. He did well. Well enough to keep her hope alive. Soon now. Soon she would do what no other had done ... she would meet her half-mortal child.

The plan had worked this far against all odds; it must succeed. For the survival of her people, it must.

Yslaaran left and headed back to the court, apparently having seen whatever she had come to see. Uthbaraal chose not to follow. He had a new focus; his purpose had been aimed at Relendel and he waited for the village of Men to grow dark and quiet. He stepped through the veil coming out, as always, in a wooded spot near the main road to the west of the village.

The path to the temple lay before him and he trotted up it soundlessly. He came to the ruins and entered where not even the foundation of the wall remained intact. The soft scurrying of night dwelling rodents under the vines drew him over to squat and poke fearlessly with his finger. Whatever creatures lay beneath wisely stayed hidden and his attention shifted from them.

He walked along the remains of the back wall, running his fingers over the rough, moist stone and dry leaves. When he came abreast of the altar, he moved to the front of it and hoisted himself up to sit, bare feet dangling. He looked about with eyes as sharp as any other creature's afoot this night, and the knowledge of millennia glimmered in his black eyes.

He liked this place. Even though this temple had been erected after the gods left, it reminded him of the older days and of Uulaten, the god of Justice and Death, who had created the Unseely to be his helpers. The temples had been an attempt of the small-minded humans to encourage the gods to walk among them again, unaware that they had left altogether. The humans were stupid about many things. Uulaten would never have required this temple that had been dedicated to him, nor the bloody sacrifices practiced here in the dark years of mankind, after the gods and the Elves deserted them.

After watching the night for a time, Uthbaraal left the temple and wandered up the road toward Relendel. Silence lay thick and heavy over the village, the timid humans thinking themselves safe behind their doors of wood. Few lights showed at this hour, though a small cottage near the dirt road held a mirrored candle in one window. Uthbaraal was as drawn to the light as the moths that beat at the partially drawn shutters. He placed his hands on the sill, uncaring of being seen, and peered in through the gap of the shutters.

A man and woman were readying for bed. Uthbaraal watched as the man climbed into the bed, naked and ugly, falling asleep almost as soon as he put his head to his pillow. The woman set dinner's pottery dishes on the pantry shelf across the room, brushed out her hair and picked up the man's clothes from the floor, laying them ready again for the next day. She blew out the remaining candle—within arm's reach of Uthbaraal—and undressed. She sat on the bed, producing a loud snort from the sleeping man and making Uthbaraal giggle.

Uthbaraal watched until they were both asleep, then gave the shutters a hard, banging rattle. The couple bolted upright in bed, staring at the window. Uthbaraal laughed loudly, a high, inhuman sound. Candles were re-lit and the couple spoke in excited whispers. Uthbaraal continued up the road.

He approached the center of town and headed for the inn, the only light in this circle of buildings, when he saw a cat on a shop doorstep drinking milk from a clay bowl. He moved to sit beside it. Stroking it with one hand, he lifted the saucer with the other and drank. The cat watched the bowl intently and licked at the remains when he set it down. Uthbaraal enjoyed the feel of the soft fur under his fingers. When the cat had finished with the bowl, it pushed its head and arched its back into his hand. He watched the cat as it moved, sliding his hand down its back and around its tail as he stroked. Suddenly he gave the tail a sharp pull, and laughed as the cat yowled and ran off, tail puffed with indignation.

At the center of the village, he passed the town well with the broad stone cobbling around the base. He ran a finger over the stone at the spot where he had left the last halfbreed girl born in the Elven lands. The Seely would hold long and elaborate celebrations for each rare Elven child born to them, yet halfbreeds were inferior and unwelcome. The distinction escaped him, but it didn't matter to him one way or the other. The Dark Elves were tasked with bringing the halfbreeds here, to this village, for the humans to raise if they cared to, and so he had. The Unseely had never been told where to bring the halfbreed babes; none had cared. So it was this place, by the well of the one village his kind could reach from the veil, where for all these centuries they had been left.

Through the windows of the lighted downstairs of the inn, Uthbaraal watched a man walking about. He moved to the window nearest the door and looked in. Four men were inside the common room, three seated at a table with the fourth pacing circles around them. One of the men at the table still wore an innkeeper's apron about his middle.

"... still don't know the how of it," the pacing man said, his arms flapping at his sides as he gestured.

"And we won't unless we ask, which we're not about to do," the innkeeper replied. "I still say the best we can do is wait and see. If they were unhappy with us we'd have known it by now. I don't think they'd have ridden all the way here and made pleasant talk and asked after local finances and bandits and all, and then ridden on if they had come to accuse us."

Uthbaraal listened with interest, his keen ears missing nothing.

"And what that it was a boy!" the pacing man said. "Only been one in my lifetime, and that was a girl-child. It's the reason we've always said the Beodan's son couldn't really be a true halfblood. I've always figured he was a bastard with features some of the throwbacks have sometimes if there's a halfblood in their ancestry. I figured that's why they kept him so quiet. I've seen him for myself now, and I don't doubt anymore, but how in all the gods' names did he get to the Hold? Why wasn't he left here like the others?"

There was a pregnant pause, as they thought or re-thought this information.

"Like I said, they must leave the halfbloods in other villages too and we just never heard of it," the youngest of the seated men said. "They probably keep quiet about it like we do."

"But why would the Beodan take him? Do you think he could be his real father?" the innkeeper asked. No one seemed to want to answer that question.

"So what do we do now if another one comes along?" said the pacing man, who was finally standing still, arms crossed, legs straddled.

The oldest man at the table answered, "We do what we've always done. We take them to the temple and leave them at the altar for the gods to decide their fate."

"And what if that's wrong? That halfblood is like to be our Bealdor someday," said the younger man.

Another silence filled the room.

"We do what we've always done," the older man said again. "We've discussed this all evening and haven't had one new idea since we started at it. This is my decision to make in the end, and that's what I say. If the halfblood is to be our Bealdor someday, so be it. There's nothing we can do about it. For now it's past time we were to our beds. We'll do no good worrying ourselves sick over matters we have no control of."

On that note of finality he stood. The rest got up as he did and made to disperse, except for the innkeeper who lived upstairs. That one looked as if he might need a good draught of wine before he would sleep.

The other three walked out the front door, passing within feet of Uthbaraal who stood quietly in the shadows, leaning casually with one leg bent, foot and back resting against the wall. He was thinking about what he had heard. He wondered what had happened to the halfbreeds he and the other Unseely had left here, if the villagers had, in turn, left them at the temple? Whatever it was, it was certain the gods had not decided their fate. The forest animals perhaps, but not the gods.

Chapter Four

D ashara's rickshaw entered the city square of Beneya. The noise of the hectic bazaar on the opposite side quickly swallowed the sound of wheels on stone paving. The rickshaw circled to the right, around the statue of Deya that dominated the center of the square. She held a sculpted infant in her hands; her arms extended in offering, her bronze eyes watching over the School. Water splashed at the statue's feet in a series of fountains, the fine mist evaporating quickly in the blistering Bansheenan heat. Though she had died long before Dashara had been born, Deya's actions had made Dashara's life here possible, a fact Dashara never failed to appreciate when she passed the statue.

She and Lashan, the head of her aleef, stepped out of the cart. Dashara tilted her head against the brightness of sun glaring off the white plaster of the large civic buildings, which stood shoulder to shoulder around the square, broken only where the four main roads entered. She ascended the wide marble steps of the School, and reflected light spangled off the beadwork on her midriff and the hem of her wide, gauzy skirt as she moved.

The cool shade of the dim front hall enveloped her as she entered the School. Though it was her day to attend the petitioners, the community room stood empty as she passed the open door and she hoped for some time to herself to do a little reading before helping those with farming troubles, weather questions, healing needs, and the host of other concerns for which people came to seek out the help of the Somiir. The question she had asked the philosopher on astronomy had been simple and the book he had given her was not, but she found she was enjoying the subject.

The sonorous drone of one of the older philosophers reached her as she went by the commoners' class, full to capacity for a lecture. The Izzat's classroom, next door, hummed with the low mumbles of white-robed men and women helping the upper-class patrons with questions or research.

One of the philosophers looked up as Dashara passed. She hurried out into the hall, intercepting Dashara while executing a quick bow. "Somiir Dashara. Good. You're here." The woman's face was flushed and she was breathless with excitement. Dashara couldn't imagine what might animate the normally composed woman so much. "We were just sending for you and Somiir Maiar. One of the aleef from Relendel has arrived! Just moments ago."

Dashara inhaled sharply. She had longed for this day, but had never expected it would come so soon. "Where is he?" she asked, glad her voice was calm. It wouldn't do to look as flustered as the philosopher.

"With Somiir Teyyas. They are waiting for you."

Dashara walked quickly to Teyyas's apartments in the back hall of the School, suppressing the urge to run. The aleef kneeling at Teyyas's door wore the same long gold robe and orange scarf of office as Lashan, and he stood and knocked gently at the door before Dashara reached him. Even Lashan's face held a rare expression of excitement as he took his place outside the door with the other aleef.

Teyyas opened the door. "Dashara, good. I am glad you were near." She stood back to welcome her in.

Anyone seeing the two half-Elven women together would think them no more than a generation apart, yet Teyyas was the eldest of the three half-Elven Somiir; one hundred and sixty-two to

Dashara's twenty-six years. She was still a breathtakingly beautiful woman, and Dashara suspected that wouldn't change for many years to come, if ever.

Teyyas's apartments were as well appointed as Dashara's own. Finely carved chairs with intricate needlework cushions dotted the sitting room and bedchamber. Delicate porcelain vases with gold leaf and brightly colored paints brimmed with fresh flowers, adorning side tables of rare, inlaid woods. Two reclining couches and a third, high-backed and soft, stood on colorful rugs. Rich paintings decorated the walls.

Amidst all the finery, a travel-worn boy of maybe twenty sat stiffly at the edge of a chair. Though he was obviously Bansheenan, in place of the robe and scarf of an aleef he wore a Heshan tunic and breeches. His clothes sported recent stains and looked stiff with dust and sweat. A brutal fatigue etched his face. Before Teyyas could introduce Dashara, the boy rose from the chair and dropped to his knees, pressing his forehead to the floor.

She greeted him warmly as he sat back on his heels. "Rayel, I am most honored to meet you at last." It had been no challenge to guess his identity. She gestured for him to stand.

"The honor is mine, Somiir Dashara," he said.

"Have you brought us word of a new babe in Relendel?"

She was faintly embarrassed at blurting out her question before Teyyas could tell her the news, but this was a special day for her. Though Dashara was the youngest of the half-Elves brought to Bansheen from Hesh, if a new babe had been found at the temple ruins, it would be her turn to travel to Thiery and bring it safely back. She would be the one, this time, to oversee their education and bring the babe from unwanted outcast to the full potential of its heritage, as had been done for her. She would raise the child like her own.

Teyyas answered for him. "His news is rather more than that, though I have not heard the entire story yet."

More than that? Dashara felt confused. She couldn't imagine news that was more important than finding another of their kind.

"Maiar has been sent for. He should be here soon. Rayel is understandably tired and has already told his story once. I think it best to wait for Maiar before asking him to begin again."

"Of course," Dashara said, trying to match Teyyas's calm, though curiosity burned like fire in her wondering if a babe had been found or not. Perhaps it had been found dead. Or murdered.

Teyyas gave her no clues, but turned to the boy who still stood next to her. "Rayel, I can ease your discomfort if you give me your permission to do so."

Rayel looked uncertain but nodded. Teyyas placed the heel of one hand on his forehead and stood quietly. If Dashara had extended her senses, she would have felt the magic working as Teyyas washed the exhaustion and soreness from his body. Rayel flexed his arms and legs when she finished, and blinked in wonder.

They all seated themselves to wait for Maiar. A tray of refreshments and hot tea sat on a low table by the couch, and Teyyas poured the tea into three delicate cups and handed one to Dashara on a saucer. Dashara tapped a finger in a quiet, rapid tempo against the cup while Teyyas made easy conversation with Rayel. She noticed the tick and forced herself to stop.

"Despite the healing, you'll need to rest soon, Rayel," Teyyas said. "Your trip must have been long and demanding."

"I reached Beneya in thirteen days, Somiir," he answered. There was no hint of bragging, though that was a remarkably short time to travel the entire length of Hesh, east across the desert, and south again, half the length of Bansheen to the capital.

"Did you find all you needed on your journey?"

"Yes, Somiir." Rayel took a little of the chilled fruit and pale yellow tea Teyyas offered, though he held them untouched in his lap. "The route I was taught served me well. Even the desert wasn't as bad as I had feared."

That wasn't saying much, Dashara thought. Most people trying to cross the desert feared to die there. "You found the spring?"

"Yes, Somiir, in the cliffs at the north end of the mountains. It still runs strong. And there were caches of food, grain, and more water buried farther on in the desert, where I was told I would find them. In Ishtin, I was given fresh supplies and new mounts for the rest of the journey."

"We are very grateful to the aleef in Ishtin for being so vigilant," Teyyas said. "They wait against hope, as we all do, for the rare arrival of one of your family."

"Would you like a room here, Rayel," Dashara asked, "or would you rather go to the queen's palace where your sisters will see you settled?"

"My sisters are well?" He looked relieved, as if he had been afraid to ask.

"Yes. They came safely through the desert two years ago and now serve among the highest-ranking aleef in the queen's household."

His face lit up at the news.

"The palace then," Teyyas said, without waiting for his answer. "They will be happy to see you."

A knock came at the door and Dashara's teacup rattled on its saucer. She chided herself for being jumpy, but the waiting had her wound as tight as a thread in a rug. The door opened and Dashara saw Rayel's awe increase as Maiar entered.

Dashara had green eyes and mahogany hair with red highlights. Teyyas had blue eyes and honey-streaked brown hair. Both of them had skin that was a pale version of the Heshan olive.

Maiar, however, was strikingly Elven, with light blue eyes and a creamy complexion. He had almost white-blonde hair worn, like the women, long and loose in the Elven way, instead of the Bansheenan fashion of a single braid. He looked a few years older than Dashara's mid-twenties, though he was three score years her elder. Dashara had been told for as long as she could remember that she was beautiful, but she had always thought Maiar the most beautiful of them all.

Rayel set his tea and food on the table and knelt again to perform obeisance. When he had finished, Dashara stood and gave Maiar a kiss on the cheek. If Teyyas was the closest thing to a mother Dashara had known, Maiar had been a father. He had raised her, fed her, been there when she cried, and overseen all her education; just as Teyyas had done for him.

When they had all settled again, Teyyas asked Rayel to tell them what had brought him from Relendel. To Dashara's utter amazement, he told a story of meeting the Beodan of Thiery and his grown, half-Elven son.

Rayel related the encounter verbatim for them, as was the habit of the aleef, while Dashara's mind reeled with questions. Rayel and his family would never mistake a child with recessive traits for direct progeny, so she was left to wonder at the strange circumstances that might have brought a half-Elven child to a ruling family in Thiery. The others must have been wondering the same.

"Rayel, have you heard anything that might explain why he wasn't left at the temple like we all were?" Teyyas asked. "How did he come to be raised by the Beodan?"

"We don't know." Rayel looked miserable at the admission and bobbed a bow from his sitting position. "I offer the humble apologies of my family that we were unaware of Somiir Chayan for so long. Relendel resents foreigners of any kind. We keep to ourselves to avoid trouble. If there was knowledge in Thiery of his heritage, we didn't hear of it. My parents and I offer ourselves up to your judgment and understand you may wish to replace our family with another."

"There is no need for apology, Rayel," Maiar said. "We would never think that you or your family failed us in any way. Of course you will not be replaced."

The integrity of any of the aleef was never questioned, nor ever needed to be. Unlike other servants, the aleef were born into service. They could leave at any time if they chose, but few ever did. They had their own culture, codes, and laws that even Dashara didn't fully understand, but they took profound pride in their duties and served only the most elite of the upper class.

"All that matters is that we are aware of him now," Teyyas added, "and we are very grateful for the difficult journey you have made to bring us this news." She glanced at the others. "This gives us much to discuss. Rayel, I doubt you will return to Hesh tomorrow, but you should be prepared to leave by the following day. It's time you rested now. I will have someone see you to the palace."

Rayel did a final obeisance, and Teyyas walked him to the door.

When she returned, the calm exterior she had shown to Rayel was gone. Her face drew tight as she took her seat on the couch. She wasted no time coming to the heart of the matter.

"That one of us must go is obvious. The Beodan's son is of our kind, and we are sworn to protect any of our heritage. With the prejudice in Thiery, he could be living in great physical danger or emotional distress. Their understanding of what he represents and what he is capable of is so small, he may have received no training in his abilities at all."

Dashara could hardly imagine the consequences of this. Teyyas turned and looked at her thoughtfully. Dashara hoped she wouldn't say what she suddenly feared she might.

"By rights this journey should be Dashara's, as Maiar and I have already been to Hesh, but the circumstances are not what any of us could have expected."

No. They couldn't take this from her. They couldn't. It had been nearly eighty years from the time Teyyas was found in the temple ruins at Relendel until Maiar's rescue there, and it had been nearly sixty between Maiar's birth and her own. There was no guarantee more infants would ever be found, but if another child was left at the temple, it could be decades from now. This may not be the hoped-for infant, but the responsibility should still be hers.

She gathered her confidence, hoping to forestall a direct edict. "True, the situation is unique," she felt pleased her voice sounded calm and reasonable, "but that would be the case regardless of who makes the trip. I would, of course, take any advice you or Maiar have to share on how to proceed, and undertake whatever you feel I must to prepare."

"Dashara, I don't want to take this opportunity from you," Teyyas sounded genuinely apologetic, "but this is a strange and dangerous situation." She set the teacup she had picked up back on the table, and shifted on the sofa to face her more directly. "When I traveled to Hesh to bring Maiar back, and when he made the journey for you, we entered and left the region quietly, with none but our own the wiser. Here, one of us will need to travel into the heart of Thiery, to the Hold itself, and converse with the local rulers. That person will represent all of us and what we can offer to a grown man, raised in circumstances at which we can only guess."

Dashara looked to Maiar for support. He studied her face, considering.

"There's so much that's unknown, Dashara," he said. "Thiery Hold may be welcoming, as the Beodan's son is a Somiir, but we have no way to know. So much will be at risk, and there could be genuine danger, both traveling through a hostile country and at the Hold itself."

Teyyas took up the argument again. "Consider that I am more than a hundred years older than you, Dashara. I may have spent only a few days in Hesh, but I have spent more time in the world. This is no longer a rescue mission, but a diplomatic one."

Teyyas was trying to convince her, not refusing her outright. Dashara understood their concerns, but her heart pounded at the thought of being denied this chance. If she let her anxiety show, she would only succeed in proving them right.

"Please consider my training over my age. Being the youngest has been an advantage. Teyyas, when Deya found you, no one knew how to proceed. The resources in the Hall of Records and Deya's dedication were all that saw you through those early years. No one with Elven blood had lived in Bansheen for centuries, and everything they tried with you was theory only. Maiar benefited from your experience and I benefited from you both. My training was far more efficient and thorough than either of yours."

She leaned forward, imploring. No, she thought, show confidence. She sat back again. "There is nothing you know about your heritage that I don't know, no ability you have manifested or controlled that I have not. And I've had diplomacy drilled into me from the start, for the same reason we all have."

Her diplomacy was one area where she had no doubts. To avoid upstaging the royal family, Somiir would not marry royals or each other, only Izzat, the highborn. Her whole life had been a balancing act of entertaining the attentions of scores of powerful and influential suitors, without inciting jealousy or violence. Of pirouetting on a pinhead to keep the high favor of the queen when the people loved and respected the Somiir more.

"I will be discreet. I won't let you down when I meet with the rulers there, and am not without the means to care for myself if the need arises. Please, don't deny me this chance."

Teyyas and Maiar exchanged a long look, but in the end the decision was Teyyas's to make. Dashara tried not to hold her breath.

"Don't be overconfident in this, Dashara," Teyyas cautioned, though gently. "Rayel described Chayan as a polite, educated man, but he may see him differently than we would. You will be alone among their many. We dare not risk more than one of us going."

Teyyas was right, this could be a difficult and dangerous trip, but the challenge sparked an excitement that ran through Dashara like heat lightening through a hot night sky. "I will be careful," she reaffirmed, the battle won.

Maiar added, "To be accepted as a delegate, you will need to adopt a more Heshan manner of dress. They are a modest people."

She thought with little enthusiasm of Rayel's heavy clothing, but she had already vowed to prepare in any way they thought necessary. The short-sleeved midriffs she and Teyyas wore would no more do in Hesh than the light skirts, slit on one side nearly to their hips. Even Maiar wore only a shirtless vest and blousy trousers, slit and loosely laced at the sides.

The change would not be an easy one. Like the others, her blood was more Elven than her body, and it burned hot under her skin. With the desert heat, it was nearly unbearable at times. The manner of dress may have developed as a way to keep cool, but it had become as much a part of the identity and appeal of the Somiir as their abilities. Dashara had dressed this way every day since leaving childhood behind.

"It will be best if you travel by night once you reach Relendel," Teyyas suggested. "The fewer people who see you, the safer you'll be. We know how suspicious Relendel is of anything Elven. It's reasonable to assume that all of Thiery, if not all of Hesh, is the same."

"I wonder how many other half-Elven children have slipped through our net?" Dashara wondered aloud. She had a sudden, horrifying image of scores of children abandoned all over Hesh, making their way alone in a world that hated them.

"We can't worry about things like that now," Maiar said gently. "It has to be enough for us to know that we will rescue any half-Elven babes left at that temple, or anywhere else that we hear of them."

Including Thiery Hold, Dashara thought. Their responsibility now included the Beodan of Thiery's grown son, Chayan.

"I'll need to meet with Queen Assia before leaving," she said. Her contact with a ruling family in Hesh demanded the queen's inclusion in these matters.

"I sent word to her when Rayel arrived," Teyyas answered. "She will no doubt be expecting one of us to come today."

They discussed the remaining details for her trip through the morning. Dashara left the School, her heart hammering with excitement and her head spinning with plans. Outside, Lashan summoned a rickshaw. While the runner sprinted to them with his cart, Dashara turned her eyes to the large statue of Deya dominating the square, holding the baby Teyyas in her arms. She studied it with renewed appreciation. The what-ifs of her birth had, of course, occurred to her before, but never with any serious notion that her life could be different than it was; as different as life must be for Chayan. A difference she would see for herself very soon.

Chapter Five

F ive days after Tirren and Chayan rode out for the Southlands, Shen left with four of his men for a fortnight patrol of northern Thiery. It was good to be traveling again after the winter layoff, and he rode with a lightness of spirit he hadn't felt in a good while. Their route took them three days east from the Hold, over a rough hunting trail, then north, below the Fangtooth Mountains, through the deep snow along the eastern border.

Shen stopped the party for the night near Wayden at a lean-to the patrols used, and the five of them crammed into the small shelter around the warmth of the fire. With the tight quarters and cold air, Shen considered leaving his chain mail on, as his men had done. He weighed the trouble of removing it against the discomfort of wearing it all night and the light snow they had ridden through earlier today that would rust the exposed bits of metal.

He sighed and stripped off his jerkin, wool shirt, and breeches to get to the chain mail shirt and chaps beneath. With the heavy layers removed, the cold seeped through his stockings and the lightly padded shirt that protected his skin from the metal. He wrapped his blanket about his shoulders and sat cross-legged by the fire, pulling the mail shirt into his lap to oil the hood and neck.

In battle practice the hood was useful, but for patrol it was just extra weight at the back of his neck, something to catch his long hair, and another part that needed care every time there was snow or rain. He worked an oil rag over the mail, listening to the murmur of Heras and Tine debating if a storm was on the way. The smell of linseed wafted up from the rag, nearly overpowering the heavy smell of smoke that swirled under the lean-to with every breeze.

Aeson's voice broke through the quiet conversation of the other men. "Has anyone ever made it past the mountains to the other country?" It was Aeson's first patrol and he'd been as excited as a pup since the day they set out.

The question didn't seem directed at anyone in particular so Shen shook his head and answered. "None to speak of. A few traders have tried the desert. From what I heard, less than a handful succeeded." He pulled the metal-banded, leather vambraces and fingerless mail gloves to his side to oil next.

"Most never returned," Seth added. He sat between Shen and Aeson whittling on a piece of wood. "The traders talk about it from time to time." He stopped work on the shapeless lump and looked Aeson in the eye. "No one knows if they're living the rich life in Bansheen, or if their bones are bleaching in the desert."

Even among the educated, little was known of Bansheen; Shen, like most Heshans, rarely gave it any thought. The steep jagged heights of the Fangtooths divided Hesh from Bansheen absolutely, even without the icy fields of snow that lay across their tops year-round. The mountain range stretched the width of the land, plunging in sheer cliffs into the ocean in the south, and dropping almost as abruptly into the sand dunes of the desert in the north. Other routes between Hesh and Bansheen were as effectively barred, with the wild sea crashing against the cliff faces of southern Hesh, and leagues of unrelieved desert to the north.

"I've never been this close to the mountains before," Aeson admitted.

"Not even hunting?" Seth asked.

"My father's men did the hunting for us."

Tine gave Heras a nudge. "So why are you sitting in a hut in the snow? You could be in your father's house sleeping next to the woodcutter's daughter instead of us."

Shen kept his head lowered to his work, smiling; they all knew how much the boy cherished being a soldier.

"Mighty few swordsmen are firstborn," Tine continued with mock seriousness. "None of us, for sure. Didn't your father find you suitable to take over his wool trade—and his wealth?"

"He wanted me to stay, but I've always wanted to be one of the swordsmen," Aeson said passionately, taking the bait. "It took me every day from ten till I was fifteen to convince my father to teach my brother the trade and let me come to the Hold."

"And is it all you thought it would be?" Seth grinned, indicating the lean-to with the knife in one hand and the wood in the other.

"It is now. This is the first time in two years I've been assigned a duty that wasn't cleaning something."

A burst of laughter filled the little shelter. Seth pushed Aeson's shoulder roughly, knocking him into Heras who was still laughing.

Aeson recovered his balance, smiling and undaunted. "So can you see Fresshe from here if the clouds lift?"

Shen remembered how full of questions he had been his first time out on patrol. "No. No more than you can see Licedes or Eropsa in the moons." Shen finished oiling the second vambrace. He set it aside and wrapped his forearms about his knees, giving Aeson his attention.

"Oh," the boy said, disappointed. "I mean, I always knew you couldn't see the Twins in the moons or Denietia in the ocean. I just thought as we ride right under Fresshe's Peak, that maybe you could see him sometimes."

"No, boy." Heras chimed in. "Men don't look on the gods anymore. Not anywhere."

"Will we see Geshne's Peak if the clouds lift enough?"

Shen shook his head. "It lies too directly behind Fresshe's. Maybe it can be seen from Lacedar, but I've never seen it from anywhere in Thiery."

When Shen had been young, the stories of Fresshe, the God of War, and his battles with his brother, Geshne, the God of Storms, were some of his favorites. Growing up in the shadow of Fresshe's Peak and suffering violent winter storms, those two had always been the most real of all the gods to him.

In their greatest battle they had torn the land in half, lifting up the immense mountain range as two fighting boys might draw a line in the sand to divide them. According to the tales, when the gods ceased to walk among Men, Fresshe had retreated into the central peak of the range overlooking Hesh, and Geshne, the peak behind it, facing Bansheen, that they would never have to look on each other again. Yet even this couldn't stop their bickering, and Geshne hurled mighty storms at Fresshe all winter, bringing them from the ocean in the west to batter mercilessly against mountains too tall for the heavy clouds to pass over.

Hesh had always endured harsh winters, with rain pounding the western two regions of Hadash and Eanor, changing to snow to the east over Thiery and Lacedar. Northern Lacedar and the coastal strip in the southern Thiery were the only exceptions, where the desert and the ocean moderated the foul weather.

Shen pushed the armor away and picked up his sword to check it for rust. Finding none, he crammed his things above his bedroll to make more room for the others and stretched out on his back with his head on his saddlebags. Aeson threw more wood on the fire and fell quiet—a rare treat for the rest of them.

Shen closed his eyes, imagining the lands beyond Thiery. He'd always enjoyed traveling, even at this time of year. If he'd been born to commoners he probably would have become a trader, just to ride beyond Thiery's borders. He might even have been one of those who risked the desert for the pure adventure of it.

His fantasy of exploring slowly merged with the soft pop and snap from the fire and the rustlings of the other men settling down for the night. Soon the muttering fire became the snap of sticks under his horse's feet and the jingle and thud of their passage as he traveled. A last brief awareness of his thoughts drifting wider and stranger as he rode under Geshne's eye through the desert land of Bansheen, and he knew he was slipping to the far side of sleep.

———— ⬦ ————

They rode west for the next two days, along the White River, which nearly overflowed its banks with spring runoff. The river, named for the ice and snow it carried from the mountains, ran east to west forming a natural border; the south bank Thiery, the north Lacedar. They traveled along a major road now, winding down out of the foothills. It soon transformed into the low, rolling hills of Panden, poignantly familiar to Shen as he rode through the country where he had grown up. From there they continued down to open land, dotted with large oak groves, as they neared Bern.

The air grew colder and Shen untied his cloak from his saddle, pulled it on, and looked again at the sky. Clouds were massing heavier as they rode out of the oaks. Still a league short of Bern, snow began to fall. The storm increased in intensity as they rode west, and Shen pulled up the hood of his cloak, bowing his head against the icy sting of the wind-driven snowflakes.

They endured a long league before he spotted the patrol hut, just east of the village, and arrived by mid-day. There was no point in trying to ride further and he called an early halt. Built a score of years ago to hold a company of twenty-five, the hut was large and comfortable for the few of them. Shen told his men to unpack for the night.

The next morning, in the wake of the storm, the sky dawned crystal blue, unmarred by clouds. The air was crisp and clear, and the snowy mountains stood out sharp and clean against the sky. Shen mounted up, enjoying the brilliance of sun on snow, though his breath came in white plumes and the chain mail burned cold where it touched his wrists and neck. The air warmed throughout the morning and the vapor of his breathing vanished, but the lungs of the great horses still blew streams of white.

"What is Hadash like?" Aeson asked, to anyone who would still answer his questions.

Shen thought the boy nothing if not eager to learn. "I don't know anyone who's really seen much of it except the traders," he said, "but it sounds much the same as Thiery. They have a Bealdor who seems a good man and we've had no trouble with them."

"Have any of the soldiers been there?" They would be riding along that border in another day or so and the boy's curiosity had probably been building all morning.

"Sometimes we've had the occasional bandit trying to get into Thiery with a bounty on his head. If they let us know to look out for them, we'll haul them back to their patrols."

Aeson looked west, as if he could see the neighboring region from here. He asked no more questions, lost in his own thoughts.

Less than two leagues past Bern, Shen noticed a set of tracks in the fresh snow, where a large, shod horse had traveled south toward the pastures. He slowed to get a better look. Stopping just in front of the tracks, he studied the trail of hoof prints first south, then north. Tine, at his left, shot him a questioning glance.

"Odd place for tracks to be crossing the road," Shen said. "North of here is just forest to the river." He rode on but noticed Heras pause behind him, looking north into the trees a long moment more.

Shen rode only a short distance more before he saw another set of tracks, this time heading north. He dismounted to look more closely at the prints. Bayone, his gray gelding, stood quietly, his nearly white coat blending with the snow, only the dark dappling over his hindquarters standing out. Shen rested one mailed hand on the heavy feathering of a foreleg and smelled the strong horse scent of wet hair as he squatted to look closer. He judged the tracks to be from the same horse as before, and recent, with no crust of ice from the night within the imprints. The bridge at Bern was the largest of the three crossings between Thiery and Lacedar and the only one nearby. The tracks formed a diagonal line from the bridge to the horse pastures.

Heras dismounted and looked at the tracks also, then north again. In his mid-forties, Heras was the oldest in Shen's patrol, average of height and powerfully stout. Shen studied the side of the man's face, clean-shaven, like all swordsmen, with heavy-boned features and a slightly flattened nose. Heras pulled his eyes from the trees and turned to Shen. "You're right. It is odd for a rider to be coming and going from the pasturelands to the woods, but nearly twenty years ago I saw it."

Shen had been young, still an uthow to Tirren, when Lacedar rustled horses from the border that year. Heras had been a soldier with the only company to catch a group of rustlers in the act and rout them, bringing the short-lived raids to an end. Shen waited for him to continue.

"I thought about it when we passed that first set of tracks. As near as I can recall, this is about where they were crossing before. Of course, just because tracks cross the road it doesn't mean they're coming from Lacedar."

"Do you remember well enough where you found those men before?"

"Yes, Kesum." Heras said. Though all swordsmen were highborn, his men gave Shen his due as commander. "There were only nine men from Lacedar and we had a full company. We killed nearly all of them, with only a couple of injured ones escaping across the bridge. We gathered up the loose horses and, as we did, we found where they had camped. As best I can remember it, these tracks are leading in the direction of that old camp."

Shen nodded. The tracks were unlikely to mean anything more than a rider taking refuge from the storm in the trees, but he felt an uncomfortable foreboding prickling at his skin. He didn't speak as he remounted and led them silently to the tree line. Tension increased among the men as they followed; like an arrow fitted and pulled, held without release.

When they reached the trees, he gestured for them all to dismount. He left Aeson and Tine to keep the horses quiet while the others followed him toward the river. Well into the trees, the tracks showed the rider had dismounted. Shen signaled Heras and Seth to wait while he crept forward. Hunting with his brothers in the hills of Panden had taught him a good deal about stealth.

The tracks led to a tall stand of oak-brush, unbroken on the nearest side. Shen moved silently to his left and skirted the bushes to the north end, where he noticed a small break. He stopped short of the opening, surprised to hear more than one man. He listened to their talk, trying to assess their numbers. They were being incautious, hardly bothering to lower their voices, assuming themselves well hidden.

"Leave that till later and get over. He wants to talk to all of us at once," a voice said, alarmingly close. The man being spoken to threw something, saddlebags perhaps, on the ground, and walked away from the edge of the brush. A moment later a deeper voice spoke. Shen heard the rustle of parchment. "Jin says that the pasture here has the closest large herd. We won't be able to get a stallion at the same time, so leave this area be for now. These horses are out in the main pasture already, and there was only one young herder with them at that time. Was he armed?"

"With only a bow that I could see, Beodan."

Shen's heart skipped a beat as his mind absorbed the implications of the title.

When the rustlers had first taken horses nearly a score of years before, it had never been determined if they were acting on their own or under orders from the Bealdor of Lacedar. It would have changed nothing; Thiery couldn't have marched on Lacedar Hold and fought them on their own ground over horse rustling. Instead, they had kept a full company stationed at Bern until it seemed clear Lacedar had been dissuaded from taking any more horses. There could be no mistake this time though; these men were here with the sanction of the Bealdor. "Beodan" would refer either to Vrenun's son, Maradon, or to one of Maradon's sons. From the maturity of the voice, Shen suspected it was Maradon himself.

"Since they're not in pens, we won't have to slow down," the Beodan continued. "Jin will be in the lead and can open the pasture gate from horseback. If we leave soon, the horses will still be grouped together eating their morning feed."

"We don't wait for cover of dark?" a new voice asked.

"No. Too difficult to get the horses through here and over the bridge in the dark if there's pursuit."

"I think a bunch of horse herders will give poor chase to us," a different man said, with a short laugh.

"It isn't your place to do the thinking though," the voice grated, "is it?"

A stretched and uncomfortable silence followed.

"We ride as if we belong until we're on them," the deep voice continued. "The area south and west of here is little traveled except by the horse owners and tenders. Now that the morning chores are done, we should encounter none but one or two herd boys. I trust you can take care of them. Does everyone understand what they are to do?" There were sounds of assent. "Then get ready to leave."

From the movements of men and horses and the voices he had heard, Shen made a rough estimate of seven to ten men. He dared not move one whit closer to gauge better and backed away from the brush, better covered now by the sounds of their breaking camp.

When he reached Seth and Heras, he took a deep breath and moved more freely. He signaled them to silence and they made their way quickly back to Tine and Aeson waiting at the tree line, east of the hoofprints left by the Lacedar soldier. Shen led them further east still, hoping their own tracks wouldn't be noticed. He allowed no questions. Once remounted, he led them for the road as fast as he dared. When they were safely away from the camp, Shen pulled up and briefed the others.

"I knew that bastard son of a pig was behind this before!" Heras swore.

Maradon had long held a reputation among the traders as a moody and difficult youth who had grown into a black-tempered man. Shen knew the stories and had no higher opinion of the man than Heras did.

He cursed under his breath. He wanted to send a message to the Chief Councilor in Bern, who could alert Erimar at Thiery Hold should they fail here, but there was no time to spare. At best they had no more than a brief lead. He turned Bayone west onto the road and led them toward the pastures at a gallop.

The first large pasture they came to had perhaps thirty-five heavy horses feeding on the hay that had been thrown to them. The tracks they had seen earlier led to this gate before blurring into the myriad other tracks along the fences. The next pasture had been divided into secure stallion paddocks with a large breeding barn at the south end. Pity, he thought, but there was no time to find out if there were any men about the barns. The manor houses were even farther to the west.

A young boy squatted, eating his breakfast, at the base of a large oak in the main pasture. His waterskin lay a few feet from him with his bow and quiver. Shen saw only one other boy, drawing water to fill a large trough for the brood mares in a set of paddocks behind the pasture.

"Heras," Shen said, "get that boy." He pointed to the one by the paddocks. "If he doesn't have a bow with him, make sure he gets one of our hunting bows. The rest of you, with me."

He made for the nearest boy, who dropped his bread and cheese as they rode down on him. Shen ordered him up behind Tine and they galloped for the only structure in the field, a long horse shelter at the east end of the pasture.

Heras joined them, the second herder on the saddle in front of him. Shen breathed a little easier. At least they had beaten the raiders here. The shelter opened to the east, its back to the brunt of the storms; inside, they were hidden from both the road and the gates.

Shen ordered one of the boys to give Aeson his rough wool cloak, then boosted the two herders to the roof of the shelter, to lie flat with their bows ready. Aeson put the cloak on and walked to the oak tree while Shen and the others watched through the slats of the shelter.

After the wild ride to be in place before Lacedar's men arrived, the waiting felt interminable, but a short while later the riders came into view around the bend of the road. Shen cursed when he saw that his guess had been wrong—there were twelve men. They rode cloaked and the horses they rode bore no trappings of Lacedar. They appeared to be nothing more than local villagers or merchants.

Shen's racing mind eased slightly as the four rearmost men stayed on the road, to act as spotters or to funnel the horses out, while the others entered the pasture. He was also reassured to see their hunting bows were still lashed behind their saddles, as he had hoped. They were expecting no resistance.

Shen's next gamble paid off as well; of the men who entered the pasture, all but one stopped within the gate while a single rider continued on to dispense with the herder. The man approached without suspicion as Aeson looked young enough to be the herd boy he pretended to be. Shen wished he could have put an experienced man in his place, and held his breath for the young swordsman.

The rider kept his right hand out of sight. Shen hoped Aeson noticed that fact as well. The man stopped his horse and leaned toward Aeson, saying something. The boy waited a breath too long; the man's near hand snaked out, grabbing Aeson by the cloak, pulling him off balance. His knife hand whipped around for Aeson's throat.

Shen clenched his fists, unable to do anything but watch as the boy struggled to get his broadsword free. Aeson jerked his head back, avoiding the knife and squirmed with more strength than the man must have expected. Twisting to his left, Aeson finally pulled his broadsword free as the man yanked at the neck of his cloak, trying to pull him close enough to cut his throat without falling off his horse. Aeson came up swinging, and the rider reeled back as the sword came at him. He struck his attacker solidly on the right side of the neck, knocking him off his horse with the blow, and fell himself as his sword stuck in the flesh and bone.

Lacedar's men exploded into action, spurring their mounts forward. Shen gave the signal and charged around the shelter. He led his men in a wide arc, keeping out of the way of the boys on the roof, who were standing now, firing arrows. Shen rode for

Aeson, giving the herd boys a clear shot at the enemy before his men engaged swords. At least one of the boys proved to be a good marksman. A Lacedar rider toppled from the saddle with an arrow through his left cheek.

The first group of Lacedar's men hadn't pulled up their mail hoods, and now had no time for it. The four men at the road, however, had thrown off their traveler's cloaks. Shen could clearly make out the narrow strip of red leather across their jerkins, signifying Lacedar swordsmen. They pulled up their hoods and rode for the fray.

Shen leaned forward in the saddle and gave Bayone his head. The gray stretched into a gallop that pounded through Shen's hips and chest. He reached Aeson just before Lacedar's men. Blood dripped from the boy's left cheekbone where the man had nicked his face instead of cutting his throat, but seemed otherwise all right. Shen cut in front of Aeson and spun Bayone to face the enemy. Tine, riding behind him, ponied Aeson's horse. He threw the boy the reins while the rest of the patrol met the rush of Lacedar's soldiers.

Shen traded heavy blows with the man in front of him. He heard more than saw Heras and Seth fighting to either side of him, the ring of metal on metal, the grunts of exertion. Two Lacedar soldiers rode past, trying to close on Aeson before he was fully astride. Shen could only hope Tine was still with him.

Another enemy soldier rode behind Shen, to flank him. Bayone kicked out hard at the man's horse, front hooves sliding in the mud and melting snow. Bayone connected and the impact jerked Shen forward, but he recovered his balance. He stabbed at the soldier and felt the sword bite through leather and skin just above the collarbone. Shen spun to face the man who had tried to flank him, but Heras had finished off his man and now traded blows with the soldier behind Shen.

The four Lacedar soldiers at the gate closed fast. They presented even less of a target to the boys on the roof with their mail hoods pulled up. Just as the thought occurred to Shen, one horse went down with an arrow though the neck and another reared and bolted when an arrow went deep into its rump. The Lacedar soldier farthest back shouted for the men to retreat to him, but those ahead either didn't hear or were committed to their course. By the time the last man entered the fighting, it was Lacedar's men who were outnumbered.

Shen moved forward to meet one of the new riders. The man swung his blade as they closed, and Shen threw his full strength into the block. The blow jarred his arm, but Shen had the greater strength and he knocked his opponent's sword arm wide, leaving room for a counter-swing that took his enemy's head cleanly from his body. The body balanced impossibly for a moment, fountaining blood. It slowly fell sideways from the horse.

Shen had heard of battle-fever, but understood it now for the first time. The head spinning from the body, the headless body on the horse; it should have shocked or revolted him, but it didn't. He felt strong. Fear and revulsion retreated deep in his skull. A wild energy gripped him. His blood pounded through his body and he wheeled his horse ready to attack or be attacked from any side.

The only enemy facing him now was the rider who had been the farthest back, the man who had called retreat. By age and description, Shen assumed it was Maradon. His horse half-reared and he shouted something Shen couldn't catch, but his rage impressed Shen even at this distance. Shen leaned forward, ready to kick Bayone to a gallop and meet the man when Tine shouted his name. He looked back to where Tine and Aeson had been fighting on the other side of the tree. Tine was afoot, walking unsteadily and leading an injured enemy soldier by the elbow. He pointed his sword behind him.

"Aeson is down. I dare not turn my back on this one to help him."

Heras and Seth had finished off their opponents and were riding down a man on foot. The man ran toward the herd with a bridle in hand, torn from the horse that had been shot in the neck.

Shen looked to Maradon, who kicked his horse into a dead gallop for the road. The soldier whose horse had been injured in the rump had the animal under precarious control and followed right behind him. Another rider came a few strides behind them. Abandoning the three with a curse, Shen wheeled his horse around and cantered past Tine to Aeson, who tried to roll to his knees and failed.

Shen threw himself from Bayone and gently helped Aeson to lie back against his legs. When he saw the boy's injuries, the horror of battle he'd repressed came home in a rush. He felt ill. A down-stroke had bitten through the jerkin and the mail at Aeson's right shoulder; the arm was still attached by only the bit of flesh below the joint. Worse still, a second stroke had taken him across the neck. His breath labored, wet and heavy with blood. Shen watched, helpless, while the last of the boy's lifeblood escaped through the gaping wounds and his heaving chest stilled.

Shen laid Aeson on the ground. Thiery had hardly known battle since the Conflicts. No one could have guessed Aeson's first patrol would be his last, but the responsibility lay heavy on Shen's shoulders. The blue leather diamond on Shen's chest had soaked red where Aeson had lain against it. He still kneeled by the boy, Tine beside him, when Seth and Heras returned with their prisoner.

"Is anyone else hurt?" Shen heard the roughness in his voice as he pulled his eyes from the boy to scan the rest of them. Tine was bleeding from his left leg but thought he could ride. No one else had suffered a major injury. "Heras, get the boys from the shed roof. Seth, fetch a blanket from Aeson's gear to wrap him in."

Two men rode at a gallop from the direction of the manor houses. Shen walked out to meet the landowners. Heras came back with the two boys riding double behind him, and they began adding their excited accounts as soon as they slipped from his horse.

Shen thanked the boys for their help, and they puffed visibly when he credited them with disabling three of the enemies.

"Please, come to the manor and let us see to your wounded," one of the men offered.

Shen's mind drifted back to Aeson, his dead body cooling on the ground. The men waited for an answer. He pulled his thoughts from the what-ifs and focused on the present.

He shook his head. "We need to ride to Bern and send word to Thiery Hold. I'd ask the favor of a spare horse though, for one of the prisoners."

"Of course." The landowner who had spoken dismounted and handed the reins of his own horse to Shen.

Checking once more on Tine's condition, Shen and the others mounted up. With their prisoners in tow, they set out for Bern.

Chapter Six

"Did I hear the south patrol return last night?" Tirren asked, standing at his father's shoulder. A detailed map of the region lay spread before them on the council table, held down with candlesticks and books.

He and Chayan had been ten days on the road and back in the Hold for only four. The visits to the remaining villages in the south had gone well; Chayan's appearance had shocked and unsettled some of the people, but there'd been no outward hostility. Tirren looked again to the map of the Midlands on the table. Chayan had been glad to return to the familiarity and security of the Hold, but the respite wouldn't last long. They were to set out again tomorrow at first light.

His father nodded absently, his finger tracing a route west of Fent to Eanor's border. "Jaron brought me the report this morning."

"Still no talk of Chayan in the Southlands?"

"Not according to the patrol." He looked over his shoulder at Tirren. "Rebellion, assassination ... those are things men will talk about in their cups among friends, not in earshot of soldiers from the Hold. I've had no word yet from the trader." Erimar turned, leaning a hip against the table. "The trader agreed to stay until he was sure, which means he's not yet. And even if his news is good, Tirren, it doesn't mean it will stay that way."

"Of course it doesn't," Tirren answered. *Gods*, his father had given him no quarter this year. "We'll have to monitor the Southlands—the whole region—for years. But, for now, it's been a successful start. Why won't you concede that? We never expected Chayan to be welcomed with open arms. This is all the beginning I'd hoped for."

Chayan had been introduced; rumors of his heritage, where they had existed, had been confirmed and word would spread. If the Southlands didn't conspire out of fear or hate, hopefully the worst of it was behind them. Once he had toured the whole region, Chayan would have the rest of Tirren's lifetime to win the people over, and the people would have just as long to accustom to the idea of a halfblood Bealdor. Acceptance wasn't going to happen in a fortnight.

Instead of conceding, his father changed the subject.

"My clerk told me the other day that Mern's daughter has often expressed her fondness for you. I thought when you get back ..." A knock came and his father shot an irritated look at the door. "Come," he said, shortly. Tirren thought the interruption couldn't have been better timed. Ban, Tirren's new uthow, opened the door. The boy looked curiously around the room then stared at the map on the table.

"What is it?" Tirren prompted.

Ten-years-old, Ban had been at the Hold for only a few months. It was always hard when an uthow came of age and moved into the barracks and Tirren had to start over with a child, especially this one. Ban was forgetful and easily distracted. The boy's attention returned to them, but he replied to Erimar. "Bealdor, a messenger has come for you."

Tirren followed Erimar down to the courtyard wondering if it was news from the trader spying for them in the south, and trying not to think the worst, like his father.

The young messenger was sweating despite the cool air. He was dusty and winded, and his horse blew in great heaving gasps, sweat dripping from its flanks. The rider obviously hadn't come from the local post.

The messenger approached Erimar, bowing as he presented the paper. "Bealdor, this was sent from Bern this morning."

At least it wasn't bad news from the Southlands, but Tirren couldn't imagine what news could be so urgent in the north. His father opened the seal and read, his expression stern. He passed the note to Tirren who recognized the neat, square writing. It was a report from Shen, describing an encounter with Lacedar's soldiers near Bern. Shen requested a relief patrol, so he could return directly to the Hold with the prisoners and his injured man.

He found it hard to believe that Lacedar had begun horse raids again, and harder to believe that Aeson was dead because of it. Tirren scanned the letter a second time and shook his head. "I'm sorry to see you proved right," he said to his father. "You've always distrusted them to stay quiet."

Erimar dismissed the messenger and took the letter back from Tirren. "What concerns me most is that Shen saw Maradon himself in the raiding party. If Vrenun sanctions his son to do this, what else might he dare?"

"Hesh has been quiet for generations," Tirren said. "Why in the name of the gods would they jeopardize the peace over horse raids?"

"Who can say with Lacedar?" Erimar crumpled the message in his fist. "Look at their history."

Tirren had been tutored on the Conflicts as a young boy, a war across the whole of Hesh a century and a half ago. The lesson was as odd and exciting as any of the tales of the gods—stories of madness, deceit, and murder in the High King's court, in what was now Lacedar. The High King had been poisoned and the heirs had killed each other off, leaving the crown uncertain. The lesser kings of the land had one after another entered into a struggle for succession until all of Hesh was at war.

In the end, after years of fighting, the armies, the crops, and the land had been so devastated that treaties were drawn declaring there would no longer be a High King, nor any kings. The four regions were established; each region to be ruled by a Bealdor, a leader of people rather than a land-hungry king. The regions had lived in peaceful isolation ever since, the people and the land slowly recovering from the toll of long years at war. The horse raids Lacedar that began twenty years ago were the closest thing to hostility Tirren had known in his lifetime.

"Find Jaron and apprise him." His father's voice cut through his thoughts. "Have him assign a full company to make haste for Bern. We'll have to keep men posted there until we're certain of quiet again—though Hessura knows when that might be if Maradon himself is leading raids."

Safely inside Lacedar's borders, Maradon at last slowed his pace. Rage still hammered in his veins. The two who had managed to escape with him had been forced to abandon their injured horse after crossing the bridge and caught up to him slowly, riding double. They wisely kept his silence.

The three of them entered the Hold courtyard, forced to ride in under the shocked stares of soldiers who had seen a dozen men ride out. The humiliation acted as a bellows for his anger.

A stableman came and stood statue-like, eyes downcast, holding his horse. Maradon flung himself from the saddle. People scattered like chickens as he walked through the courtyard and into Lacedar Hold. Bron approached him as he entered, but paused, sensing his mood. "Father ...?" he ventured.

Maradon ignored him utterly. He shouldered past him to the staircase, focused only on getting to his apartments, where he could think away from the eyes of others.

Cerendrin and one of her maids sat embroidering in the sitting room. The handmaid jumped when the door banged open and left the room before Cerendrin could dismiss her. Maradon slammed the door nearly on her skirts with a force that shook the doorframe and reverberated down the stone hall. His eyes caught Cerendrin's, silencing her before she could speak. He paced the room, coming to a stop by the window.

"Baes is dead." He spat the words like a curse.

He might as well have told her the moons had fallen from the sky. She stared at him like a half-wit, her mouth hanging open in stunned silence, unable to grasp his simple statement that their eldest son had been killed. Tears pooled in her eyes.

"How?" she whispered.

"By Thiery's hand. And I will see them pay dearly for it."

Hatred replaced his rage, filling him till he thought he might choke on it. His mind's eye saw again the face of the big soldier who had beheaded his son.

"But why? Did they betray you during the barter? I don't understand." She shook her head, her mouth still open. He turned away from the sight of her, but she continued anyway. "If they have more horses than they need, the sale would have been to their benefit. I don't understand," she said again.

He could feel her eyes on his back. Her questions would be endless. "Because they are murderous dogs!" he roared, turning to her and swiping at a small side table. It bounced, crashing to the middle of the room. Had she been closer, he would have slapped the stare off her face. Unable to stand more, he stalked into the bedchamber.

He stood at the window, fists planted on the stone sill, and stared unseeing into the courtyard below. He heard Cerendrin leave the other room, but his thoughts were already turning to the plans he must make. His father would have to be given the news soon, before another could tell him more than Maradon wished him to hear.

If only things could have been different, maybe today would never have happened.

If only his father had had the decency to die years ago as he ought. Maradon was fifty now, and had waited long years past reasonable to become Bealdor of the region. His father had been confined to his bed for the past two years, his left side shriveled, the arm and leg useless since the day he had fallen unconscious in the hall. Some days he could hardly speak sense, yet he wouldn't pass on the rule and he wouldn't die.

If only his father had been a stronger leader, taking what was Lacedar's due or, at the least, allowing Maradon to do it for him. When his father had found out about the horse raids of years ago, Vrenun had cuffed him nearly senseless. His father hadn't listened to his reasons, that the pastures in the south were too small to support enough quality horses and the pastures in the rest of the region bred inferior horses on dry and salty soil. And the inferior land would someday vanish altogether, taken by the encroaching desert. If they didn't infuse their lines with Thiery's horses, the farmers and soldiers alike would suffer. And no region would sell horses to Lacedar that they might use for their army. He could hardly credit that even his wife believed his tale of bartering with Thiery. With Vrenun in his present state, Maradon had been sure he'd get in and out of Thiery without his father being the wiser. He had been so sure of success he hadn't even taken the precaution of plain jerkins under the traveler's cloaks.

If only those whoresons hadn't laid ambush for them in the pasture this morning, he and his men would have been in and out of Thiery virtually unnoticed. Well, if they wanted to fight and die over the few horses that Lacedar was due, so be it. Thiery owned some of the richest lands in Hesh, while Lacedar possessed an ever-expanding portion of useless desert. Bern and the pastures that went with it had belonged to his family once. He vowed that one day soon they would again.

———— ⊙⟋⊙ ————

Bron stood at a loss in the entry hall. The two soldiers who had returned with his father had vanished, and no one had been able to tell him what had happened. He turned to go back outside and hunt down the men in his father's party when he heard a crash from his father's rooms. A moment later his mother came down the stairs, tears running down her cheeks. He breathed a sigh of relief to see her unharmed.

"Where is Emorelle?" she asked him quietly.

"I think she's in her room."

"And Ossar?"

He hadn't seen his younger brother all morning and told her so. He tried to ask what had happened, but she put her finger to her lips, glancing up the stairs, and motioned him to follow.

They found Emorelle sitting on her bed, tending to an injured bird in a small box. At seventeen years, she was old enough to wear her light brown hair caught up in a crocheted net. It emphasized how strongly she favored their mother's comely features and oval face. His mother sat by Emorelle on the bed and hugged her wordlessly. She began to cry again, and held out her other arm to Bron. He allowed her to hug him as well though her silence frightened him. She was always so strong; he couldn't imagine what had happened to make her act so out of character.

"Mother, please, what is it? What has happened?"

She dabbed her eyes, and sat up straighter, composing herself for them. "Something went wrong during the bartering," she began. "Your father didn't tell me what. Only that Baes has been killed."

Baes was dead? It seemed impossible. He was so strong, so bullish, so quicksilver in temper, that Bron could hardly imagine anything that *could* kill him. The second shock came a moment later, as he realized that at twenty-six he had suddenly become his father's successor. Not a fact his father was likely to be pleased about.

His mother released him and Bron shifted away. He stared at the little bird his sister had been tending while he tried to sort the jumble of thoughts in his head. He reached out and touched its feathered head with one finger.

Bron had always been glad that Baes had been born the eldest. His father had groomed Baes for the succession from birth. Even as a child, the harsh training, the insults, the temper never seemed to affect Baes. He may have been arrogant and a bully at times, but he had their father's spirit and was clearly the leader Bron and Ossar were not.

Baes had even taken after their father physically, where Bron and his little brother hadn't. Maradon had been so proud that his eldest son had inherited his black hair and eyes and ruddy complexion, while Bron and Ossar possessed the more common olive skin, lighter brown eyes, and their mother's softer features. Worse, Bron was the shortest of the three and lacked the stocky build that his father and Baes shared. In fact, there wasn't much about him that his father did like.

His mother and sister were still crying. Bron pulled his feet up on the bed and hugged his knees to his chest, suddenly very afraid for what the future held. He knew how bitter his father would be over losing Baes. He knew Maradon would never allow him to be his own kind of leader; he would expect him to live up to Baes's legacy, and Bron wondered what life would be like if he couldn't.

Chapter Seven

Excitement vied with apprehension as Dashara boarded the small cargo boat. By this evening she would be in Hesh for the first time since her infancy. The captain held out a hand as she stepped from the gangplank onto the deck. He was a short man and stocky, with a bristly black beard that contrasted his neat braid. Captain Venesha, Rayel had told her, when he secured the boat for them last night.

"Thank you for making your boat available, Captain. I am most grateful that you have postponed your own plans to help us."

Venesha let go of her hand and dropped to his knees, bowing his forehead to the deck.

"It is a great honor to have you aboard my humble boat, Somiir," he said, rising. "I wish only that I had a grander vessel that could carry you in the style you deserve."

"Allow me to introduce my party. You know Rayel, of course, from our family of aleef in Hesh. This is his new wife, Eessa. The soldiers are four of the palace guards that Queen Assia has kindly sent to see to my safety."

She introduced the men by name and rank, wishing the queen had not sent any of them. Over lunch, Assia had not only outlined her own cautions regarding Hesh, but had insisted on the escort. More would have been sent, but Dashara refused them, not wanting to appear in Thiery with anything approaching a show of force.

It had taken their group four days to travel from Beneya to Hassan, the closest of the few port cities in Bansheen. The surf here was milder here than at any point west towards Hesh, allowing for some fair-weather fishing and an occasional cargo boat heading east under a skilled captain. They had been fortunate to find passage so quickly.

"The tide has turned, Somiir," the captain said. "We can leave at once." His courteous manner never betrayed that she was asking him to take his boat beyond the western border of Bansheen along the virtually uncharted and hazardous coast of Hesh. She felt the weight of his trust, placing his life, the lives of his men, and his precious boat entirely in her hands.

She nodded her readiness, mirroring the same confidence he showed her.

Both Teyyas and Maiar had warned her about the strength of the ocean. Despite her assurances, she worried about her control in the wild seas west of here. She had only been on the ocean once, when Maiar had brought her here for training, and that had been in a calm, summer surf. The waves in Hesh could dash a boat to pieces as easily as a child could destroy a boat of twigs.

The small vessel proved to be a close fit for seven people, their mounts, and three pack animals. The skaggi had been roped off in the stern of the boat, and the rest of her party milled about on the deck. The cargo hold had already been full when the queen's senior guard appropriated the boat for their own use. With no room below-deck, everyone had to do their best to stay out of the way of the sailors. It was obvious none of her party had any familiarity with sailing. Eessa, especially, went wide-eyed at every sway and creak.

She seemed a sweet girl, no doubt recommended as a wife for Rayel by his sisters, but Dashara had seen the fidgeting and the preoccupied, worried expression when the girl thought no one was looking. Even marrying into the highest-ranking family of aleef couldn't counter the fact that Eessa was leaving all she knew to live in utter isolation in a foreign country with a man she had just met. Rayel's family performed such a unique service to the Somiir, and at such great cost to themselves, she was amazed Eessa had consented to the marriage at all. Seeing a woman enter into the family of aleef in Hesh, Dashara felt new wonder at the dedication of all the generations of Rayel's family and those who willingly married into it.

Captain Venesha bellowed orders for the sailors to cast off. It was finally real, Dashara thought. She was traveling to Hesh. Beginning now, her skills would be tested further than ever before. She would see the land of her birth, meet Chayan. But first, she had to get there.

The sail ruffled then snapped tight, as the captain steered the boat away from the dock and into deeper water, turning the prow west. The morning sun struck the burnished gold mail on the palace guards' breasts and backs, returning shafts of golden light to sparkle on the water. The mail, worn over white, lightly padded shirts was traditional, but the men looked uncomfortable in the breeches and soft shoes that replaced their normal segmented leather skirts and sandals.

Rayel still wore his Heshan clothing and Eessa had been provided with clothing appropriate to her new country. Dashara had remained in her own clothes for as long as she could, but that time was at an end. She knew Maiar had been correct—her sleeveless midriffs and gauze-thin, slit skirts would never do in Hesh.

"Captain, I should change as I may not have the chance later."

"Of course, Somiir, my cabin is at your disposal." He motioned sharply to a sailor. "Show the Somiir to my quarters. See that she has everything she needs."

The man bowed low to her and when he raised his head Dashara was surprised to see he bore a slave tattoo on his cheek. Slaves were criminals, usually men. They were generally of low character and commonly used for labor, but, occasionally, a man of high birth would be charged with a crime serious enough to bring a sentence of slavery. Men such as those fetched exorbitant purchase prices, and always from the Izzat women.

Dashara had noticed Bansheen's slave class steadily growing of late, especially since the recent fashion among the Izzat women, particularly widows, to own them. There was no code of honor toward slaves. Once made a slave there was no escape; all were marked with a tattoo on the left cheekbone, recognizable anywhere in Bansheen. She would never consider owning a slave personally, but the increase in the slave population had seemed to parallel a decrease in crime. Whatever else it might be, the threat of slavery over prison had proved a powerful deterrent.

The man led her to the captain's quarters without a word, wide-eyed at having been given the responsibility for her. She wondered if the captain was a hard man—hard on slaves at any rate.

She changed hastily from her preferred clothes into those made for this trip. At her suggestion, the seamstress had forgone the layered and high-necked fashions of Hesh for a modest, green dress with a slightly scooped neck and slit sleeves that fell away from her lower arms as she moved. Despite these small freedoms, the claustrophobia of the single-piece garment and the heavy fabric was abominably uncomfortable. The weight dragged at her as she climbed the ladder and returned to the deck.

Two men scurried past her into the rigging as the boat moved into a deeper channel. The coastline fell away. Dashara moved to the bow, flanked by Rayel and one of the palace guards. The waves tossed the boat from peak to trough, the prow splashing into each new depression with a great spray of water. The captain watched her expectantly and Dashara tried not to think how small these waves were compared to what they would soon encounter.

Her awareness of the others on the deck faded as she focused for the first time on the ocean surrounding them. Her mind quieted as she concentrated, extending all of her senses, opening to the ocean around her until she could feel individual grains of salt on her arms and face, and taste it on the air. She could smell the salt-wet feathers of the sea bird that landed on the railing behind her and clearly make out its fellows circling far ahead of the boat. Her body became attuned to the slightest motion of the waves beneath the prow. The noise of the surf filled her ears.

She focused on the elementals of Water and Air within her Elven blood, as Maiar had taught her so long ago, and recognized the ocean on a deeper level—understanding its mood, its currents, its depths. She merged with the ocean and became the cold water. Extending her will, the waves before the prow began to calm, as if lulled by her calm.

Dashara never left the bow, working her sway over the ocean with ever more influence as they progressed through increasingly restless waters. Beyond her small sphere, the violent sea roared its defiance. As the waves approached her circle of power they slowed and diminished, melting into the quiet waters around the boat. On the far side they gathered their momentum again and, white-tipped and angry, crashed their way to the rocky cliff faces. Dashara harnessed the wind filling the sails, but caused it to blow steadily west now, eliminating the need for the boat to tack with the normal gusts.

The captain stood silently next to her, mesmerized by the small area of almost flat water surrounding his boat, extending perhaps three times the boat's length in all directions. Even focused on her task as she was, Dashara could feel awe radiating from him. She knew he had never doubted her, would never have hesitated to send his boat west into the deadly seas at her request; but knowing the power of the Somiir was not the same as seeing it.

Dashara felt exhilarated. The ocean and wind pulsed through her body like blood, and she tamed them to her will, though they were never completely subdued. The wildness and violence thrummed inside her, obedient, but always searching for escape.

The strain of the constant battle wore at her over the day and the twenty-five leagues to their destination passed before sunset. Rayel pointed out a small cove at the base of one of the massive cliffs. A treacherous wall of rock jutted out from the cliff, parallel to the shore, leaving only a narrow gap for the boat to thread through.

Dashara's fight with the ocean increased yet again as they drew ever closer to the great rock. Her muscles trembled with the final effort. By will alone, she flattened the fierce waves that dashed with thunderous force against the rock outcrop and the cliffs at either side of the little bay. The sailors dropped the sails and bent their backs to the oars, pulling the boat neatly through the small opening, while she forced the ocean to submit. Once past the rock, the projection protected them and Dashara swayed with relief as the magic and the struggle finally ebbed from her.

The cove was barely large enough to fit the boat but Rayel had said running aground was not a risk; like most of this section of coastline, the ocean floor met the base of the cliffs far below the surface. The sailors tossed ropes over as many rocks as possible to make the boat fast. Cork bumpers were flung from the deck over the railings to hang at the widest point of the hull. If Dashara had believed the gods still influenced anything here, she would have said they must have made this cove just for their purpose. Instead, she knew, it was the tireless diligence of the aleef first brought to Relendel who had found this safe harbor.

They disembarked by means of pulling the tie lines on one side and loosening the other side until they were snug. The cliff face they secured against had a small, exposed, and nearly flat shelf of rock at the base. It sloped gently up, ramp-like, to a set of rocky stepping-stones, naturally carved when the ocean had claimed more of the cliff face. The stone looked damp and slick. Three men held their hands out to help Dashara ashore. Normally, she could have stepped across with more ease than they had, but she felt as tired now as if she had wrestled the ocean with physical strength instead of Elven will. She gratefully accepted one of the extended hands.

The men unloaded their supplies and, with more difficulty, the animals. Dashara rested, eyes closed, on a nearby boulder. She hadn't expected the trip to be so tiring, and wondered if someone of full Elven blood would have felt any fatigue at all. When Rayel informed her that all their supplies had been unloaded, Dashara rose and sought out Venesha where he examined the mooring lines.

"Captain, would you send one discreet man with us to learn the route to Rayel's home in case you should need anything while I am gone? Rayel has assured us that the villagers here do not care to be out of doors past dark; your man will be safe returning to you later tonight."

Rayel, who had followed her, nodded. "It isn't far to the track that leads to my home, and the path skirts the village."

"Of course, Somiir," he said. Turning his head, he pointed one of his stubby fingers at his boatswain, motioning the man to him. The captain turned back to her. "We are well provisioned. We will wait here for your return."

"We should be back within half a cycle of Tlaas. If for some reason we are delayed beyond that, you should go to Rayel's home where they will have instructions for you, and money if the need arises."

The captain dropped to his knees bowing his head to the cold stone. Realizing her departure was imminent, the other boatmen did likewise. "Fortune favor you, Somiir Dashara," he said sitting back on his heels, "I will not rest well until I see you safely back."

Dashara followed Rayel, and the others fell into line as they began leading their skaggi up the narrow defile to the cliff top. The ascent would be tricky, more so with the final part made in the gloom of late twilight. Reluctantly she embraced her power again, holding a cushion of air at the ready should a person or animal slip on the wet, steep climb. She hoisted her heavy skirts to her knees and began the ascent in silence. Soon they were all standing on the overgrown trailhead at the top of the cliff. They mounted again, the sailor riding double with Rayel, and made good time along the little paths.

Dashara found it oddly disturbing to ride so near to Relendel. She knew that the Elves brought their halfblood children to the coping of the village well, and she found herself looking to the east, though she knew she wouldn't see the village from here. The reality that Elves still moved about in this country brought gooseflesh to her arms and neck. The Elven stories she had grown up with took on a sudden immediacy she had never felt before. She even extended her senses on a whim, but felt nothing around her except the human world.

When they passed the temple ruins a short time later, Dashara pulled her mount to a halt. She stared quietly through the night's shadows at the cold stone altar, and a chill climbed her spine as she looked on the grim site of her second abandonment.

Soon after passing the ancient temple, they arrived at Rayel's home. The mirrored candles, warm hearth, and joy that met their arrival made a sharp contrast to the stark ruins nearby. Rayel's parents welcomed their son with obvious relief and much excitement over his new wife. If Rayel hadn't come to Bansheen at this point in his life, it would have most likely been Dashara who traveled to Relendel to bring him a bride, but she would have seen nothing of Hesh beyond this cottage.

Once the chaos of introductions and greetings quieted the group moved inside, filling the small house nearly to bursting. Dashara had looked forward her whole life to meeting the family who had found her and risked their lives to bring the news of her to the School. Khemma, Rayel's father, had been the one to travel to Bansheen and return with Maiar. His wife, Feeah, had watched Dashara, an infant only a few days old, during his journey. Without this family, Dashara would have died on that altar.

During a lull in the conversation, she presented the gifts she had brought for the family: new cloth, Bansheenan spices and foods, and a purse of gold, as it was the obligation of the Somiir to support this family. The gold would be enough to keep them all for a generation, the longest period they would go without seeing one of the Somiir.

"I also bring a gift from the Somiir," Rayel said proudly. "Somiir Dashara gave me three stories on our journey." His parent's faces lit up. Most of the aleef chose illiteracy by tradition, to prove their trustworthiness with the most sensitive correspondence—as if any would doubt them. They, instead, kept a rich oral culture along with the talent to repeat any message or conversation verbatim. New stories were nearly as valuable as gold. "I have news from my sisters also."

Dashara excused herself to allow Rayel to talk with his family, though she truly did feel as tired as she claimed to be. She was happy to retire to the room set aside for her, always kept in readiness for one of the Somiir. Imecus, the captain of the palace guards, stationed himself outside her door for the night. Dashara folded herself gratefully into the comfortable bed, but sleep eluded her a long time. She lay staring into the darkness, wondering what the following days would bring.

———— ⟨⟩ ————

Dashara had consented to Maiar's request that they travel at night for concealment, and she waited impatiently through a long day of anticipation to be on her way. After sunset, she said her farewells and she and the four guards began their journey to the Hold. Rayel had offered to travel with her, but she declined. Had he been Heshan she may have considered it, but as he was not, there was little reason to put him at further risk. She had left her aleef behind in Bansheen for the same reason, much to Lashan's distress.

It felt odd to the point of bizarre to be sneaking through Thiery in the dark, but Rayel's family had assured her the stories of prejudice were not exaggerated. She had spent her entire life feeling honored for what she was, and it was almost more than she could grasp that the same qualities could endanger her life here.

They made good time on the open road despite the dark, though the men with her were palpably tense. Dashara, with her greater night vision, rode at the front, with the familiar moons lighting the unfamiliar landscape before her. Tlaas traveled the sky first tonight, two-thirds full, followed by the half-pie of Hrar. Silence lay unbroken over the dark buildings of the little communities they passed, and Dashara looked with interest at the quiet houses concealing their mysterious inhabitants.

The guards traveled wrapped in their new cloaks against the springtime night air. Dashara didn't feel the cold; her Elven blood always burned too warm for her human flesh, even when the moons weren't full. She wore a light cloak to quickly cover her features if necessary, but the discomfort of the cumbersome thing seemed almost not worth the slight disguise it offered.

The hoof beats of the mounts and jangle of tack were the only sound in the stillness, allowing Dashara no distraction from her thoughts, no diversion for her doubts. She had fought for this opportunity and shown a confidence she wasn't sure of, yet so much rode on the outcome. Maybe one of the other Somiir *should* have made this journey. Teyyas had been right—even if she didn't know Thiery or the ruling family here anymore than Dashara did, she still had the experience of age. But Dashara could never have turned down this chance. And now, at last, she was here; the one tasked with keeping the people with her safe, with being an ambassador in a country that hated her kind, and the one to rescue Chayan if he seemed in any danger. She had taken on the responsibility to do these things, and so somehow she would.

They traveled three consecutive nights, moving quickly and camping in the daytime well off the road, deep in the trees. Shortly before sunrise on the third night, she left the road for the small stream splashing not far from the road. The mountain run-off was too cold even for Dashara to immerse herself, but she sighed as the clear water splashed the dust of the trip from her body. And she wished yet again for her own clothing as she changed into another heavy dress, dark blue this time. Imecus, head of her guards, helped her into the awkward sidesaddle and they set out on their final leg.

A pale line of gold outlined the dusky horizon behind them, fading the stars near it. By the time the sky lightened she could see the murky gray of the storm front she had felt approaching. Dawn revealed the farmlands they traveled through, and Dashara had her first real look at the countryside of Hesh.

The land was lush, despite the greenery warring still with the last vestige of the notoriously harsh Thiery winter. No snow lay in evidence, but muddy livestock trails showed proof of recent rains or snowmelt. The spring grass had a tenuous hold on the pastures, but she could see they would soon be thickly covered. There were even small bursts of color along the road, delighting her, as flowers from wild bulbs challenged the cool spring.

The tall evergreen trees they had traveled through during the night dropped behind them, though forests were still in evidence to the east and west of the pastures. Likely this whole area had been wooded until the land had been cleared for agriculture. After a lifetime of Bansheen's arid browns, she drank in the moist smell of this land, and the vista painted in a hundred shades of green.

The morning showed more of the countryside to the company, but it also showed their group to the farmers out doing chores. Even with the farms set well back from the road, she saw people stop and stare at their odd mounts. They topped a final small rise in the road and Thiery Village appeared on the hillside ahead of them. Above it lay Thiery Hold.

The road climbed more noticeably from there, and they soon entered Thiery Village. A few people were moving about the main street already: wagons hauling wood to the bakeries and blacksmiths, farmers bringing milk and produce into town, the cobbler getting an early start. All of these stared as her group passed. Dashara kept her head lowered and her hood pulled up, thankful at last for the cloak. She could see the guards tensing under the scrutiny, and uttered a few calming words.

They passed, at last, through the village and Dashara loosed a small sigh. Only then did she raise her head and take a good look at her final destination. The Hold's heavy, gray stone rose, foreboding, high above the outer walls, impregnable against the bluff. The prospect before her exhilarated and frightened her at the same time. She reminded herself again that she was not without resources. She sincerely hoped they would be enough.

Chapter Eight

The wide gates in the outer wall stood open, welcoming, at least in appearance. Two gate guards stood at the barbican; one ran toward the Hold at the first sight of their group while the second came out to meet them. Dashara's ambassadorship with Thiery Hold was about to begin. She took a deep breath to calm the rapid beating of her heart.

The gate soldier was young—barely more than a boy—and he stared open-mouthed at her. Imecus rode forward to divert his attention. "Somiir Dashara, Chosen One of Bansheen," he pronounced, "favored by the royal court of Queen Assia, requests an audience with Somiir Chayan of Thiery Hold." The young Heshan soldier looked unsure how to answer such a greeting.

Dashara saw a crowd of common folk gathering beyond the inner gate, staring and pointing at their strange company. They parted suddenly for a tall soldier, striding through the courtyard. He surveyed their group as he passed through the barbican, and towered over the gatehouse guard when he drew near. He had longer hair than the other Heshans she had seen, with a broad, handsome face, strong features, and an easy smile despite the caution in his eyes. "What have you here, Vint?" he said to the young soldier.

"I don't know," the boy answered. "He was saying something about a queen and Kesum-Chayan."

The big soldier looked to the captain of her guard, likely assuming him the leader of the group. "I am Kesum-Shen an Haredin a Nileer es Panden. Whom do I have the pleasure of addressing?"

Dashara pushed back her hood and let her cloak fall open. His eyes swung to her.

"I am Somiir Dashara, Kesum-Shen. We have made the long journey from Bansheen as we have heard of the Beodan's son, Kesum-Chayan, who may be kin of mine." It was stretching a point, but she had decided with Teyyas and Maiar that it would be the most reassuring introduction. "My companions are four of the queen's palace guards, sent to escort me on the trip."

The soldier had been staring at her and returned to himself with a small start, giving her a courtly bow. He hardly glanced at the others as she mentioned them, though she guessed by looking at him that he might be a man rather used to being in the company of attractive women. He glanced back, seeming to calculate the knot of people that had reformed in the courtyard in his wake. "I'll take you to a place where you can wait while I notify the Bealdor of your request."

She nodded her assent and the soldier turned to give low instructions. The boy, Vint, took off at a run as Dashara and her party followed Shen through the barbican and the inner gate. The barbican was short, no more than the length of three of Hesh's large horses, but she found it a disturbing reminder of this country's violent history to ride past the portcullis and through the tunnel with its old arrow slits and murder holes. Dashara wondered dryly if perhaps they should have just sent Chayan a letter.

Curious servants, tradesmen, and soldiers crowded the courtyard. The cluster of people gave way quickly as she dismounted, but stared at her companions with amazement. When they looked at her, though, it was with undisguised fear. Having experienced nothing but a lifetime of esteem in Bansheen, the reaction tied a cold knot in the pit of her stomach.

Crowds could be dangerous and unpredictable. She had seen a crowd turn to a mob once, in the slave market. A man had been sentenced for beating his infant son to death. Before the slavers could start the bidding, the wife's family had pulled the man from the platform. The crowd had joined in and the man had been torn apart before the Somiir made it out the door of the School. She wished the memory hadn't surfaced just at this moment.

The big man barked an order to other soldiers in the courtyard. She felt a bit reassured as they pushed the onlookers back and fell in with Dashara's group. Her keen ears caught the murmured speculations—that she was Chayan's Elven mother come to reclaim him by force or another halfblood seeking refuge at the Hold, and other, even more outlandish things.

She let herself be led through a side door of the Hold to a small but comfortable anteroom. Preceded by Imecus and followed by the rest of her guards, she entered the circular, stone chamber. She felt relief at escaping the courtyard, but wondered if her situation had improved when she saw a number of soldiers gather outside the door. Kesum-Shen was apparently taking no chances.

The anteroom possessed only arrow slits for light. A narrow, uncomfortable-looking bench ran most of the way around the wall. She chose to stand, and the palace guards formed a circle around her. Their agitation seemed to be notching up proportional to the martial presence outside the door and each new slight to her station.

"Remember," she said to the captain, "we are strangers in their land and I am something they fear. It is we who need to be diplomatic, not them."

Imecus nodded. Whether he agreed or not, he would respect her commands, though the tension in the lines of his body relaxed not at all.

A few minutes later a door opened on the opposite side of the room, and more armed soldiers could be seen in the hallway. A man entered, whom she assumed by his age and bearing to be the Bealdor, with a younger man, tall and attractive, following him. The younger one reminded her of a desert cat with his lean gracefulness and quiet authority. Enough soldiers entered with them to crowd the little anteroom. It seemed that Chayan had not been invited.

The older man looked at the younger who shook his head. "It isn't her."

Dashara wondered whom they had expected to find.

The older man dipped his head to her slightly, enough to be polite without showing deference. "I am Bealdor Erimar an Pathal a Messa es Thiery." He introduced the younger man at his side as his son, the Beodan of Thiery.

Imecus moved forward to speak, but Dashara forestalled him with a gesture. She gave a small curtsy and heard an indrawn breath from one of her party at the obeisance. Even the queen received only the nod of an equal from one of the Somiir. Dashara repeated the introductions of her party that she had given at the gate.

"I have been told that you believe you may be kin of my grandson, and wish to speak with him," Erimar said.

Grandson, not ward. So the Beodan *was* his father.

"It is possible we are related, though it would be a difficult thing to verify. I do, however, come representing the Somiir—" At his blank look, she added, "the half-Elven in Bansheen—in which sense we are all kin."

"Your companions are Bansheenan, certainly, but you have the look of Hesh to you."

"Yes, Bealdor. Bansheen is our adopted country; all the Somiir are from Hesh originally."

"All? How many of you are there?"

"Three of us at present."

"Do your people have exchange with the Elves?" Tirren interjected. "With your parents perhaps?"

"No, Beodan, none of us know our Elven parents. Of course, we don't have the benefit of knowing our human parents either." She felt amazed at herself for not having considered this possibility before, and tried to phrase her next question delicately. "Do you ... does Kesum-Chayan know his mother?"

"We haven't seen her since she passed Chayan into my keeping as an infant."

"I see." A flood of questions came to her, why Chayan's mother had left her son here, why she had brought him personally, but now was not the time. She hadn't been given an invitation into the Hold proper yet, nor offered any hospitality. Judging by the Bealdor's stern expression, she thought she may never receive them.

"Somiir," Erimar said bluntly, "what is it exactly that you have made such a long and difficult journey to speak with Chayan about?"

Her answer to his question was perhaps the most important thing she would say on the entire trip. All the rest hinged on this. She composed herself and began.

"The physical and emotional difficulties of growing up with our divided heritage are not easy. Unless your son somehow escaped these discomforts, I'm sure you understand." She saw a complex set of emotions pass across Tirren's face and guessed she had not missed the mark. "Though he is grown now, and likely past the worst of it, I have been sent to see if there is anything we can offer him or you in the way of help or information. If there remains a lack of understanding or control, it could present a danger to him or those near him. Our kind are very few. I was sent simply out of concern for his well-being."

"He has always been foremost of my concerns. He need not be yours." The words were hard but Tirren's demeanor appeared protective, not aggressive, which she found encouraging.

"Of course, Beodan," she hoped she had not mis-stepped already. "We in no way seek to lay any claim to your son." Not entirely true; she knew full well she would do all she could to rescue him if Chayan seemed mistreated here. "He has been fortunate indeed to be raised with a loving parent, and I plan to return to Bansheen as soon as my visit here is concluded. I wished only to meet Chayan and to make ourselves known him. However, now that I am here, it seems that there may be much we could learn from each other."

"Perhaps," the Bealdor answered for him, with more reservation than she had hoped for. "Let us find a more suitable place to speak. Excuse me not offering you rest from your journey yet, but I think getting to know each other better first would be best."

"Of course." She wanted to breathe a great sigh of relief. If he had refused her outright, she wasn't sure what she would have done.

"Heras," Erimar said to a soldier behind him. "Ask that the Green Room be made ready and refreshments brought for our guests." He turned back to her. "Somiir, I hope now you are safely here, you will feel comfortable enough in our Hold that your soldiers wouldn't mind leaving their swords at the gatehouse."

The four guards froze, some placing hands on the hilts of the thick, curved blades at their belts, drawing a mirrored response from the Heshan soldiers.

"Of course, Bealdor," Dashara said, ignoring the tension in the room, "and as you are a gracious host, I am sure we will continue to feel safe under your protection."

The Bealdor nodded, understanding the subtle question in her voice.

At a sign from her, the guards stiffly passed their swords to the soldiers. She had warned them before arriving that this might be necessary, and that trust among strangers was earned, not given.

Erimar led them to a large, well-appointed room upholstered in shades of green where servants bustled about already. Dashara removed her cloak and took a large chair opposite Tirren, with a low table between them. Erimar seated himself on the settee at her left. Tea was served and Dashara watched in amazement as the Heshans poured cream into it.

She could never have guessed that Hesh would be such a different world. The Hold was the same cold, grey stone on the inside as the outside, primitive compared to the opulence of the palaces in Beneya. Tapestries lined the walls, as much for warmth, she supposed, as for decoration. Maces, swords, spears, and other weapons and armor—some new and some ancient and broken—hung everywhere. Based on what she could observe, culture and prosperity here appeared to have run behind Bansheen's progress.

The Hold's soldiers had been told to remain outside the room and Dashara requested the same from her guards, though the captain strongly protested the separation. A serving girl set a platter of fruit and sweetened bread on the table, keeping as far from her as possible, flashing a frightened look her direction. It was hard to believe a half-Elven boy had lived here all his life. Rayel truly had not exaggerated the Heshan's mistrust of anything Elven.

"Shen told us that the Queen of Bansheen had been mentioned," Tirren said, when they were settled. "Are you of the royal household?"

"We have the honor of high favor at court, but we are not considered members of the royal family, nor in line for the succession." She sipped her tea and found it dark and bitter. No wonder they put cream in it.

"Do you know where the Elves are or how they come and go?" Erimar asked.

"No, Bealdor, we know nothing about their land except that it is near to us somehow; but from recorded descriptions of those who have been taken there, it is no part of this world."

Tirren's face tightened and he looked down at his tea. She wondered suddenly if he had been there. He ended the hopes she had of finding out by taking the conversation another direction.

"How did the Somiir come to live in Bansheen?"

"During the time of your Conflicts, Deya Aleneh, sister to Queen Sessma, traveled to Hesh as an advisor. On her way through Thiery she found Teyyas, the first of the Somiir, abandoned for dead. She took the child with her when she returned to Bansheen."

"I remember learning about Deya," Erimar said. "One of the kings sent to Bansheen for military aid during the time of the Conflicts."

"King Jiden, in what is now Eanor. He had hoped to end the war with Bansheen's help. Queen Sessma refused to commit her people to a foreign war, despite the promises of money and lands. As a show of goodwill, though, she sent her sister, a skilled ambassador. Deya, as an impartial party, helped to negotiate the final treaties between the regions."

"But you say that Teyyas still lives," Tirren said. "That would make her more than a century and a half old."

So, he didn't even know that much about his son.

"Yes, Beodan. We don't believe any of us have inherited the Elven immortality, based on how the oldest two Somiir have matured, but judging by Teyyas's rate of aging, we have guessed at a lifespan of at least two hundred and fifty years."

He sat in stunned silence, soaking in the implications.

"It was Deya who titled Teyyas as Somiir," Dashara continued, "meaning Chosen One. And it was the people who loved her and placed her above the Izzat, our highborn."

"Your people had no trouble accepting her?" Tirren asked.

"No, Beodan. The Elves were our benefactors, as they were to your people long ago. When the gods and Elves left, neither returned to Bansheen. There were droughts and crop failures, but our warmer climate kept us from suffering the Dark Years that your country did. The old records and stories of the Elves survived those centuries intact. The people of Bansheen never saw the change in the Elves that we hear you have; they have only good memories of them, and have hoped against hope for their return. Even though Teyyas was only half-Elven, the people rejoiced at her arrival."

"If you have seen no Elves, how did Deya know how to raise her, to help her through her differences?" She saw pain in the Beodan's eyes.

"The oldest records speak much of the Elves and even mention their half-Elven progeny. There was enough information that we feel as confident as we can that Teyyas developed all her Elven talents to their fullest. When Maiar was rescued, it was Teyyas who educated him. And it was Maiar who raised and trained me. We, in turn, wish to offer our experience to Chayan, if we may."

The Beodan was undoubtedly interested, but the Bealdor seemed tense, almost angry. She wasn't sure what she had said to offend him.

"I understand how Teyyas came to be in Bansheen," he said, "but that was over a century ago. How is it you were taken there?"

"Deya asked only one thing in return from King Jiden for helping with the treaties, that he discover why Teyyas had been abandoned. His spies learned that children with Elven blood had been previously outcast in that same area where Teyyas was found. Deya left two of her party here in Hesh to watch for any other half-Elven children that might be abandoned. Teyyas has stayed in touch with their successive generations."

Tirren's expression was suddenly thoughtful. "You were all found in the same area? Where was that?"

Tirren had seen Rayel's family, and Dashara worried she had said too much. She wanted to be as honest as possible with them, but not at the risk of endangering the aleef. "We were all found in southern Thiery. We do not know how many more half-Elves may have been left elsewhere." She took another sip of the bitter tea, liking it no better the second time.

"Have any halfbloods ever been found in Bansheen?" he asked.

"No. The only evidence of Elven activity has appeared in Hesh, though we don't know why. Even our children possess no Elven qualities. The Bansheenan blood is very strong. It dominates the Heshan and Elven blood within a generation."

"You have children?" Erimar said, surprised. It was the first spark of unguarded interest he had shown.

"I have none of my own as I am not mated yet, but Teyyas has three children and Maiar has a son. For political reasons, we have sworn to take human mates, and not pair with each other, yet even diluting our Elven blood further, we are still not prolific; though more than our Elven relations are reputed to be. The children of the Somiir are considered human and are titled as Izzat." She steered the conversation back to her goal yet again. "Teyyas, Maiar, and myself were the only half-Elves known to exist until we learned of Chayan. It is why we are so eager to meet with him." She set her nearly full teacup down and smoothed her skirts. "Bealdor, Beodan, I mean no harm here. I hope you will consider the long journey I have made and allow me the honor of meeting with Kesum-Chayan."

Erimar glanced at Tirren and said, "If you will excuse us, Somiir, we need to discuss this."

"Of course," she replied with all the composure of her training, though she felt none of it. How could they deny her? But from the Bealdor's face, she saw he could. Erimar gestured for her to remain seated as they left the room. She glimpsed a large gathering of soldiers outside the door before it closed with a thud.

If she failed, she didn't know how she would face Teyyas and Maiar. They had entrusted this trip to her, and they would only have this one chance. If the Bealdor denied her request to meet Chayan, she would leave never knowing if he was mistreated here, or if he knew all he should to keep himself and those around him safe.

The woman was intriguing on so many levels: an opportunity to learn about Elves and Bansheen all at once, and the first like Chayan that Tirren had ever seen. If she could truly teach Chayan to understand himself better, to make a truce with what he was, and to make his powers safer, she would be an answer to his prayers. She could also be one more step toward Chayan inheriting the rulership of Thiery.

Despite everything she offered, Tirren felt relief escaping the room. Dashara was beautiful, more beautiful than any human woman, but it was not attraction to her that made him uncomfortable. Any man in the Hold would feel some measure of draw to her, whatever his prejudices, but they had never seen Yslaaran. Dashara's beauty, however compelling, was a pale imitation, but her Elven features, hearing her talk of Yslaaran's people—it stirred the smoldering fires within him.

Tirren worked harder than anyone knew at keeping his thoughts and feelings for Yslaaran buried. If he didn't, the longing he felt for her might eat him alive. He walked in silence behind his father and resigned himself that while Dashara was here she would be a constant and uncomfortable reminder of the only woman he wanted, and the one woman he knew he could never have.

"We can't allow this," Erimar said, once they had reached the library and closed the door.

"What?" Tirren said, jarred from his thoughts. "How can we not? You heard what she said, there are three of them and each has learned from the one before. She could be a wealth of information for Chayan, not to mention a comfort for him to meet another of his kind."

"A wealth of whatever information she chooses to provide, true or not. No. She must not be allowed to see Chayan. Who knows how subtly she could teach him, disguising one lesson for another. Even if she proved honest, her very proximity might wake more magic in him than he could control."

Erimar moved to the large desk by the window and took a seat behind it, leaving Tirren forced to sit in front of him like a pupil. "She could be here under some ploy of the Elves," Erimar continued, "or have harmful intent for Chayan for her own reasons. These 'Somiir' seem anxious that there are only three of them; she might be here to steal Chayan away to Bansheen."

"She might be here to teach him how to safeguard against his power," Tirren countered. He should have known how his father would react to her offer. An Elven woman had abducted Tirren, and Erimar had trusted nothing Elven since that day. But he had to try. "I think she is only what she says she is. Chayan would never forgive us if we sent her away without him being allowed to meet her."

"All she needs do is enspell him or us and she could do whatever she wishes. Do you think we could stand against that? You have been proof enough of our susceptibility."

A flush crept up Tirren's neck and into his cheeks. He remembered all too well how easily he had been enchanted by

Yslaaran, walking into her lands without question or resistance, desire for her his only thought. But maybe Chayan, with his Elven blood, would not be so easy to confound.

Tirren ignored his father's barb. "If they have the power to influence more than one person, she could have done that from the start and forgone the pretense of asking to see him. Besides, whatever else she may be, she is an envoy from Bansheen, the first we have ever had. Would you insult their queen?"

Perhaps if she stayed here long enough, Erimar would relent. Not that Tirren didn't have his own doubts, but the woman seemed genuine. Besides, what she might be able to offer Chayan would be worth almost any risk. "Surely you noticed the insignia on the guards' breastplates. Or do you believe that's a magical illusion too?"

"You go too far," his father warned him in a low voice. "Of course I saw. I have eyes. Had I not believed that much, I would have never let her in the gates. Bansheen is too isolated from us to cause much trouble over this, I think, but now that she is here, we must at least give a show of courtesy. She must be here the shortest time possible, though. I only brought you here to discuss how best to handle this."

"And to keep me from being alone with her?"

His father's stony face was answer enough. Tirren wanted to be angry with him, to rail at him to let go of his fears and suspicions long enough to see the potential good in this, but he couldn't. He knew those fears were grounded in the love Erimar had for him and for Chayan, and the disappointment the two of them had wrought on his plans for the region. What his father did, he did to safeguard them all, however misguided.

"You heard what Shen said about the people gathering in the courtyard," Erimar continued. "More will be arriving from town, curious about the foreigners who have come here. If rumors spread about her heritage, fear could turn the crowd to a mob. We need to increase the guard at the gates and to get her out of here as quickly as possible."

"What harm can be done already has been, whether we hide her or parade her through the village. The best possible thing we could do now is be open about her presence. Why let people guess at what she is, at her purpose here? We need to control the rumors with truth." He sat up straighter. "This isn't Relendel; this is the Hold, where Chayan grew up."

"You're not so blind as this, Tirren. Why do you play the fool now? What do you think the people would do if they learned another halfblood had come here to teach your son magic? What will her presence do to the fragile bridge of trust you have spent so many years constructing?" He shook his head. "I wish the woman had never stepped foot in Hesh."

Tirren had one chance to make his father see the good in this. She was not only accepted in her country but revered and held a high station, Chayan needed to see that such a thing was possible. "She's diplomatic, well-spoken, attractive. If a few key people here at the Hold accept her, word would spread. It could be one more step toward Chayan's acceptance as Bealdor. Jaron, Shen, the other regiment leaders—they are educated, rational men who love Chayan and could influence others. Perhaps she could meet only them?"

"She will stay as hidden as we can make her, and she will leave by the morrow. There will be no more discussion of this. Gods grant that the soldiers we sent out have found Chayan by now and he is safe in his rooms. He will stay there until she leaves."

"Yes, Bealdor." The words came hard from Tirren. As hard and angry as his father's.

Chapter Nine

C hayan drew and loosed. The arrow sunk into the large bole of the thick pine tree, three hundred paces from him. The bow seemed a better design than the others he'd made, almost what he envisioned. Perhaps if he lengthened the wood by one more finger ...

The longbows of the foot soldiers were too large to use from horseback and short hunting bows didn't have the power he wanted. He would have gladly mastered the broadsword instead, but the ache that touching metal caused him ran too deep into his bones. He'd tried to overcome it by sheer willpower once and only succeeded in finding himself too weak to lift his weapon. His rank required him to be a mounted soldier, and so he continued to work on his own solution. Besides, he enjoyed getting out of the Hold by himself for awhile. Even if the walls were nearly in sight, the forest gave him a sense of peace few other things could.

He pulled the next arrow from the ground and looked at the evergreen to the left of his last target. It would be a harder shot through the trees. He lifted the bow. He heard footsteps in woods behind him.

"There you are."

Chayan dropped the bow and turned to see Vint hurrying toward him, though still a hundred paces back.

"Here I am." He gave his standard singsong reply. Playing hide and seek as boys, Vint had always given an exasperated, "There you are," whenever he finally found Chayan. The familiar exchange made Chayan smile, but Vint didn't seem to notice.

"Half the garrison is looking for you," Vint said, breathless, jogging the last bit to him.

"Why?"

"Foreigners came this morning!" He spoke all in a rush. "The Bealdor ordered you found and kept safe till he can talk to them."

"Why would he do that?" Chayan didn't understand why there would be a need to keep him safe from messengers or a patrol. "Are they from Lacedar?"

"No. They're not from Hesh. They're from Bansheen, and there's a halfblood with them. She's a woman and she says she might be your kin."

"What?" Vint was speaking so rapidly he wasn't making any sense.

"I was on the gate when they arrived. Come on, I have orders to get you back to the Hold right away." He turned and started back.

"Is it my mother?"

Vint stopped and looked at him. His eyebrows pulled together in thought. "No. No, I don't think so. She looks like you. Well, I don't know. I've never seen a real one. But she said she was from Bansheen." He started back toward the Hold. "Come on. Hurry."

It seemed clear Vint was going to be no help. Chayan pulled the rest of his arrows from the ground and overtook Vint. Whoever the visitor was, he wasn't going to risk missing her. Vint nearly ran to keep up with his long strides.

Chayan was still in front when they went through the side gate, but Vint called him to a stop before he reached the cobbles of the courtyard.

"I wouldn't go that way."

"Why not?"

"There was kind of a crowd of people there all wanting to see the strangers and get answers if they were Elves."

Chayan's father had believed for years that the people accepted him, but he didn't see the suspicious looks he received when he was alone. Better to backtrack and take the servant's entrance near the wall.

"Where is she?" Chayan asked as they entered the Hold.

"What?" Vint looked alarmed. "No. You can't go see her. I have orders to take you to your rooms."

"I just want to have a look at her. That's all." He'd been an island in a sea of same waters for his entire life. An Elven woman, a halfblood like himself, or a messenger from his mother—he was *not* getting locked in his rooms without seeing her.

He turned toward the front hallway. His rooms were to the left and up the stairs, but the knot of soldiers down the hall to his right told him that was where he wanted to be.

"Chayan, you can't," Vint pleaded.

"I just want to see her," he said, distractedly. He had hoped for so many years for his mother to come to him. After the trip to Relendel, he had given up his fancies of finding Elves or other halfbloods. And here one had traveled to the Hold to see him. He wondered if she looked Heshan, or Bansheenan, like the family he had seen in Relendel.

Half a dozen swordsmen came to alert as Chayan approached, Shen among them. He stepped out to block Chayan from entering the room.

"Chayan, you're supposed to be in your rooms. Your grandfather wouldn't be happy if he knew you were here. Seth, Tine," he looked over his shoulder at them the two men, "go with Vint and Chayan. See Chayan safely upstairs."

"I just want to see her, Shen, then I'll go. I promise."

"I'm sorry, but I'll not cross the Bealdor on this."

Vint and Shen had been the closest people to him other than his father and grandfather. If he couldn't convince either of them, he stood no hope with the others. He saw sympathy in Shen's eyes, but resolve as well. He stared at the closed door, wondering if he dared rush it.

Shen towered like a mountain in front of him. Chayan knew it was foolish to think he could get past them all. Seth and Tine moved toward him and Vint tugged at his sleeve. His desperation escalated. A tingling began in his chest.

"Shen, please. You know what my grandfather is like. What if she leaves without me getting to meet her? Please just let me see her. Just open the door so I can see and then I'll go. She says she's kin. What if she has news from my mother?"

Seth and Tine each took one of his arms and tried to gently pull him back. He struggled against them. His light bones belied his strength. He was as strong as the two of them, and desperation made him stronger still. Chayan felt the trickle of power in his chest grow. He knew he should control it but there wasn't time to focus on it; he had to convince Shen now or never.

He felt the quiver of arrows at his hip unbuckled. Did they think he would harm them? He struggled harder to break free. He heard Shen trying to calm him, but the thought of being dragged away frightened and angered him. He felt the power surge through him like the ocean waves that crashed against the cliffs of Relendel. If they would just let him go. He just wanted to see her, talk to her for a moment.

The magic building inside him increased another notch. It pushed on his ribs, it crawled under his skin. Too late, he shifted his energy from struggling against the swordsmen to fighting down the magic. He tried to block all thought, all feeling. He fought for the image of the dark stone, willing it to encase him as he had done in Relendel, but too many things fragmented his concentration. The tingle spread down his arms, making his hands buzz. Sweat broke out on his forehead. If they would let him be, he could focus.

"Let me go," he shouted. Seth and Tine took a harder grip on him.

"Easy, Chayan," Shen said. "Just go with them for now."

The door to the room they were guarding flew open and a halfblood woman stood in the doorway. "You *will* release him," she said in a commanding tone. Four copper-skinned men tried to go around her, but she braced her hands in the doorway to stop them. Her eyes dared Seth and Tine to defy her. She had large eyes, as emerald green as Chayan's own, though hers were shot through with flecks of orange. Right now they looked to catch fire with anger.

"Get him out of here," Shen said. "Now!"

"No!" Chayan struggled harder. "No. I need to talk to her." Seth and Tine lifted him off his feet. "Did my mother send you?" he pleaded as they hauled him backwards. He twisted like an eel in their grip. His chest ached with unspent power. His body felt as if would peel open at the breastbone, and something huge and powerful would emerge.

"Why in the name of all the gods is he here!" His grandfather's deep voice rolled down the hall. "Get him to his rooms, now!"

No. Not this. There would be no other chance. He had to get to her.

Power raged through him. It exploded from him like the howling fury of the west wind in winter. Seth and Tine's grip on him tore away. Shen fell back from him like a leaf in the wind. Men went flying, tapestries and arms and armor stripped from the walls. Chayan stood in the eye of a hurricane, one about to rip free of him and bring the Hold down around their heads. He felt the stones shake beneath his feet and he didn't know how to make it stop.

Suddenly, a sense of peace wrapped around him like a cocoon. The pins and needles throughout his body ceased. All the things that had been on the verge of breaking loose gently contracted back into his body. The fear abated. A sense of well-being filled him. He hadn't been cut off from his power; not only was it present, it was a part of him like it had never been, filling him but utterly controlled. From within the safety of his cocoon he sensed the woman. Her presence shared a space inside him, like another facet of his mind, though she stood unmoving in the doorway. It should have frightened him, but it didn't. He recognized the magic in her as the same as his own, but her confidence, her control was absolute. Whatever had been happening to him, she had stopped it.

"Chayan, are you all right?" she asked gently.

"Yes. Yes," he said, shaken. Chayan looked around at the clutter of things blown off the wall, at the men around him getting back to their feet, some slowly.

"Arrest her!" Chayan turned and saw men inside the Green Room helping the Bealdor up.

"Grandfather, no." Chayan's heart leapt into his throat. How could he be blaming her? "It was me. She's the one who stopped it. She controlled it. She controls it still."

His grandfather's face burned red and his hands balled into tight, trembling fists. He glared at the woman. "You dare use your magic here, on me, on my family? If you have control of my grandson, believe me when I say that I will find a way to stop you."

Chayan felt her strength, her composure. She was the antithesis of his grandfather. He had never seen his Bealdor so frightened, so shaken; he was nearly beyond reason, lashing out indiscriminately.

Tirren pushed past Erimar, out of the room and past the guards in the hall, Heshan and Bansheenan. He reached Chayan's side, concern writ large on his face.

"That was you?" he asked softly.

"I'm sorry. I'm so sorry." Tears stung Chayan's eyes as the full impact of what he had done sank in. And, worse, what he had nearly done. "I promised it wouldn't ever happen again, but I couldn't help it. There was too much happening. It grew too strong."

Erimar looked stunned, turning from the woman to Chayan. The fear and shock and pain in his face as the words finally sunk in made Chayan wish he had never been born. Erimar looked back to the woman, his voice cold as winter ice. "This never would have happened if you hadn't come here. You will leave us. Now."

"Chayan is trying to tell us that she helped him," his father said angrily, countering his grandfather where no one else dared.

"Does she control your mind now too?" Erimar shot at Tirren. "Am I the only one left with any reason?" He swung to Dashara. "Do you or do you not control my grandson's mind?"

"No Somiir would ever control the mind of another," the woman answered slowly, heatedly.

"I asked if *you* did it."

Her guards moved with her as she stepped closer to Erimar, indignation clear in her every line. "I. Did. Not."

She clenched her skirts in her fists and met him glare for glare. Chayan thought it more than he would have been able to manage.

"The ability we have to work with Spirit was given to us by the gods to help others," she said with only slightly less anger. "It would be an offense to everything we are to use that gift to our own purposes, whether well-intentioned or not. I would *never* disobey that tenet." One hand pulled free from her skirt and she pointed an accusing finger at Erimar. "Your grandson's power was on a razor's edge of breaking free. I helped him contain it, as he was unable to. It was everything I warned you could happen without training. If there has been no catastrophe before this, it has been blind luck, and if I leave without teaching him control, you will deserve whatever happens to you."

Erimar turned to Chayan for confirmation.

"It's all true, Bealdor," Chayan said. "She isn't influencing any of us. I'd feel it. She helped me contain my power before ..." He couldn't bear to say the rest: before he hurt anyone.

Erimar looked every one of his sixty-three years. Chayan had never seen him so lost, so out of his depth. He stiffened his back. His glare struck out at everyone near, Chayan included. It settled finally on Tirren.

"I'll have no part in Chayan learning magic. Do as you will, Tirren. The consequences will be on your head, as are the consequences for all of this." He walked away from them on stiff legs, like an angry, defeated dog.

The sound of his grandfather's steps receded. Chayan stared after him wondering just how far into the past Erimar would change things if he could.

Tirren turned to Shen. "Is everyone all right?" he said, breaking the deafening silence.

Shen did a quick check of cuts and bruises. "Yes, Beodan. Well enough." Chayan closed his eyes with relief.

"Good. See the hall is cleaned up. Somiir, perhaps we should go back in here," Tirren said, indicating the Green Room again.

Tirren put a hand on Chayan's back, ushering him into the room behind the woman and her guards.

When Chayan entered, her guards dropped as one to their knees, pressing their foreheads to the floor and Chayan realized for the first time that the Bansheenan family in Relendel must have been doing obeisance to him, not to his father. The men held the position, and he realized they would not move until he released them, which he did.

His father made formal introductions and Chayan finally got his first good look at the woman. It was odd and thrilling to see his fine bone structure on another, and the pale skin, smooth, with no tracing of blue veins beneath. Her blood must be the same rose-milk color as his own.

"I have no words to express my gratitude for your help," Chayan said to her. He made himself meet her eyes to say it, shame flooding him anew.

"I'm sorry for my anger, Chayan," she said. "Never before has my temper gotten the best of me. I'm not used to having my deepest principles questioned."

Tirren said, "It is we who must apologize. My father has no trust left in him for magic, not after what happened to me. He's a good man though, and trying to do what is best for everyone. This isn't easy for him. He was only trying to protect Chayan the best he knows how."

"I understand." She sounded surprisingly sincere.

"I know we have offered you little in the way of hospitality," Tirren continued, "but my father's forbearance won't last forever. If you are not too tired, I suggest you and Chayan discuss whatever is most important for him to learn as soon as possible."

Chayan's heart leaped. She was here to teach him!

"I would like nothing better," she said, wholeheartedly.

"Will this room suffice?"

"Outdoors would be preferable, if there is a place that would be safe from the people gathering in the courtyard."

Tirren considered for a moment. "Perhaps the gardens. They're walled on all sides. I must honor my Bealdor's concerns, though. I'll stay for Chayan's lessons and we must be attended by our soldiers."

It would do, Chayan thought. Considering what the options had looked like just moments ago, it would certainly do.

Chapter Ten

D ashara felt a thrill of triumph at last seeing the boy she had gone through so much to meet. When she had heard the commotion in the hall and opened the door to see him forcibly restrained, she'd believed her worst fears had come true. Visions of him as a captive here, of her and her guards in deepest danger flitted through her mind. It was only when the Bealdor had spoken that she realized his concern for his grandson.

Tirren had introduced the boy as Chayan an Tirren a Yslaaran es Thiery. So they knew the mother's name. Dashara would have to check the Hall of Records and see if Yslaaran was mentioned in any of the ancient texts.

When Tirren opened the door to lead them out, servants were busy in the hall, setting it to rights. Chayan stared at the havoc he'd wreaked, and she wondered what thoughts occupied him. At a motion from Tirren, the soldiers guarding the door fell in with them. Dashara's palace guards came as well, bristling with tension and sticking to her like sap.

Shen, the big soldier she had met at the gate, was one of the soldiers escorting them. He gave Dashara a reassuring smile, surprising her with its friendliness. Servants here had looked more afraid of her when she was drinking tea. Considering all that had passed, this man was astonishingly relaxed in her company, far more so than the other soldiers. Chayan's father missed nothing, it seemed.

"Shen was my uthow as a boy," he said without preamble, "and with me when Chayan was brought to the Hold as an infant. He has been closer to Chayan his entire life than any other person besides my father and me. You will be safe with him and his men guarding us."

She felt safer relying on her own power, not to mention her palace guards, who might be unarmed but were by no means defenseless. Another ally was never a bad thing, though, and she returned Shen's smile.

"You said that bending a person's will to your own was anathema to the Somiir," Tirren said, slowing to walk beside her.

"It is one of our deepest beliefs. The temptation to abuse our power would be strong without that strict precept, especially before the maturity of adulthood." She glanced to Chayan to make sure he was listening. They would have precious little time, and this was a good starting place for his lessons.

"Then why do *they* do it?" Tirren asked.

"The Elves? We can't know but my personal belief is that they have lost their way over time." She glanced back at the Heshan soldiers following now at a respectful distance. She weighed the consequences then told Chayan and Tirren what she knew of the gods, of their abandonment, fully aware that the Heshans still believed the gods lived in their mountains and oceans and moons. Sketchy as the histories of that time were, it had been documented with no uncertainty.

"I wonder how much the lives of the Elves changed," she said, "without the guidance of the gods, with whom they had worked so closely." She hoped the soldiers with them hadn't overheard. She wasn't sure how devout the people of Thiery were, but she didn't need to bring any more controversy to the Hold.

Considering the revelation she had just dropped on them, Chayan asked a surprising question. "What about Licedes and

Eropsa though? If the Gods of Love aren't in the moons, then why do the moons affect me so?"

She stifled an impulse to reach out and touch him. Her heart went out to this boy who had struggled through his adolescence with no guidance, no answers.

"Much in the histories refers to the full of the moons as a time of potential fertility for the Elves. We all feel that pull when either moon is full and more strongly when both are. Whether the Elves feel it as well or not, I can't say." She shrugged slightly. "I know that you aren't alone in this. It never goes away entirely, but it becomes easier to control when you have matured. Has it been getting better?"

He nodded.

They passed a set of huge doors standing open to reveal a large hall. It was filled with tables and benches of rough, unpolished wood and a high table on a raised dais. More arms and armor hung in that room than she had seen yet, and the fireplace in the back wall looked as if it could hold most of the wood in Bansheen.

Tirren stopped abruptly, diverting her attention from the hall. He pushed aside the high collar of his shirt beneath his thick tunic. "Do you know what this is?" he asked, tipping his head to the left. "I found it after that night with her, where her lips touched my neck. It has never faded." His cheeks colored; whether it was emotion from the memory or consternation from speaking aloud of that night, she couldn't guess.

Dashara leaned forward to see the mark he showed her, like a small burn on the right side of his neck. Absorbed in the small, irregular, red blotch, she touched it gently with two fingers, her face near his cheek.

He tensed under her touch like a nervous horse. Dashara moved back immediately, unsure if her intimacy had disturbed him. She began walking again, and said conversationally, "I'm sorry that I don't know what it is, Beodan, nor have I heard any reference to such a mark, but when I return I'll ask the philosophers."

Tirren straightened his collar again and nodded. He looked as if it was the answer he had expected. She realized that Chayan wasn't the only one who had gone through a difficult time, nor was he the only one with questions.

"I always thought it was a birthmark," Chayan said quietly. Tirren said nothing more.

They traversed several hallways and Dashara repeated the history of the Somiir for Chayan as they walked. Near the kitchens, Tirren led them out through a side door. They emerged into a small garden of hedges and roses with colorful wild bulbs lining the walks, like the ones Dashara had seen below the village.

She and Chayan settled on a small stone bench. Tirren took another bench just far enough away to give the impression of privacy. Shen and her palace guards stayed in line of sight while the other soldiers scattered throughout the garden, guarding gates and doors.

This wasn't at all how she had pictured this taking place when traveling here, but Dashara wasted no time getting started. "The first thing we need to do is work on your control of your magic."

Chayan's body tensed and his breath came short, but he gave a short nod for her to continue.

Dashara met his eyes and held them. "Chayan, I know what happened in the hallway was frightening. Would that I had as long as I needed to teach you all I could, but we both know I do not. The magic in you is strong and it will grow stronger as you age. Will you trust me to guide you?"

"Yes. Show me what to do."

She admired his courage. If she had ever stood on the brink of losing herself to her power, as he had done, she wasn't sure she could soon face it again.

"I will take you through exercises I learned as a child. We will go slowly. Nothing bad will happen. I won't let it."

They began.

———— ⬥ ————

Chayan couldn't imagine anything more terrifying than learning how to use the magic within him ... except not learning to control it. He shifted on the bench to face her.

"The Light Elves, or Seely," she began, "from which we are descended, were the first creation of the gods. They were made from the three elements we can work with: Air, Water, and Spirit. These are the foundation of our power. I want you to try and connect with these elements now."

Those few words told him more than he had ever learned about his magic in his life. Fear and excitement warred within him. "Quiet your thoughts," she said. "Quiet your breathing, and listen. Focus on the breeze, on the moisture in the air, on the life here in the garden; all of it, down to the smallest creature."

He made the connection quickly, the extra perception of his senses stirring. The magic trickled through him and a light sweat coated his palms as he tried to keep it from filling him up.

"Don't fight it. You will learn that opening to your power is not the same as using it. I'll help you. I won't let it go farther than this until you are ready."

He could feel her own magic around him, like a vibration.

"You were able to do that quickly," she said. "Have used your magic often?"

"No. Hardly ever." He didn't want to tell her why. The guilt of the rare times he had used it still plagued him. "But, when I was younger, I used to camp on my own a lot. If I focused too hard on the sounds or smells around me in the night I'd feel my senses ... stretch." His father, a few lengths away, leaned forward, absorbed.

Chayan had never shared that detail with him. "My skin would tingle, like now, and I'd feel like I was balancing on the edge of suddenly understanding everything around me in some new way." He looked a question at her to see if he was making sense. He could see he was.

"Yes," Dashara said, smiling. "I believe that those who are fully Elven may always feel like that, and that the larger understanding of the world that eludes us is available to them."

Gratitude filled him. The emotion of having someone finally understand him felt almost painful, like something inside him might burst.

"Describe to me what you can discern," she said.

He closed his eyes and began. "I smell the flowers and the rain from last night more strongly; I can hear the breeze stirring the leaves of the plants."

"Can you sense the breeze, even beyond the walls of the Hold, where you can't feel it?"

"Yes," he said after a moment. He left off the formality of title as Dashara had told him it was unnecessary. To her, they were both Somiir.

"Can you sense where the next rainstorm is right now?"

"Yes," he said, amazed that he actually could. He had never pushed his weather sense too far before, too afraid of the consequences.

She began a series of exercises, first having him lightly touch each element separately with his mind, then manipulating it with a trickle of power. He learned quickly. It felt as if he knew all of this at some level and had only needed to be reminded.

They worked a long while until he stood and stretched his legs, pausing in the midst of an exercise using Spirit to coax a worm to the surface of the soil. "Why can I feel Earth, but can't touch it with my magic?"

"Our power with Spirit works with aspects of Earth, like the ability to help things grow, but the gods were the only ones who had direct power with Earth. Particularly Osessus, the Goddess of the Harvest." She stood as well. "It was from Earth that the gods made mankind. Humans were made to be the antithesis of their Elven counterparts. Soil made their blood rich and fertile, and rock made them strong and stubborn, to survive. As they are from Earth, they return quickly to it, so the gods made them vital—expressive and passionate—and prolific, that their race would continue. Fire is the other elemental that we have no part of. Not even the Seely work with it. It is solely the domain of the Unseely, the Dark Elves, and of the gods."

A thought occurred to him. "If the gods made us all, why are the Elves so different from us?"

"Besides the elements they are made of, the gods made the Elves in their own image. They share talents and qualities with the gods that humans do not. But they don't share all the qualities of the gods either. They were made to serve. The gods made them sensual, loving pleasure, so they could entertain with their beauty and their fondness for art and music and dance. A side effect of this seems it may have also made them self-indulgent and dispassionate to others."

Chayan glanced at his father. Tirren had given up the pretense to their privacy and listened intently.

"The gods had a second purpose to creating the Light Elves, which, as I'm sure your own histories tell you, was to aid the gods' next creation, Man. Working with Spirit, the Seely could calm the mind or cause forgetfulness, as well as heal illness or injury. They influenced the weather and brought health to crops and animals. Where they walked, plants grew more abundant—even Bansheen was more verdant then—and the harvests in both countries were plentiful."

Chayan reached out and brushed a jasmine vine with his fingers. A strange thought occurred to him. She must have seen it in his face.

"Your gardens are very healthy, considering the winters in Hesh," she said. "Do you spend much time here?"

He nodded, still looking at the plants, distracted. "I always prefer being outdoors."

"So do I. So do the Elves."

He looked back to her, still holding a leaf. "I might have done this?"

"We of mixed blood seem to have all the Elven talents, though in considerably less measure than those of full blood. It's why the three of us in Bansheen strive to continue the work the Elves were created to do. The most important part of our heritage is the dedication we have to helping humankind."

"What about the Dark Elves?" he asked. "Why were they created?"

"Uulaten made his own helpers from the Elemental Fire. They dispensed his justice, harried the wicked, seeded fear in the unjust, and escorted the unwilling souls to the Land of the Dead. Uulaten balanced their dire tasks by giving the Unseely an immaturity of spirit, and no morals to trouble them in their duties. From what I have read of them, they seem almost child-like, but are powerful, with no sense of right and wrong, good and evil."

"Why did the Elves leave us if they were supposed to help people?" Chayan asked. He knew she wanted him to practice, but there was so much he wanted to know. He wished she could stay for weeks, months. Forever.

"We don't know why the Elves left us anymore than we know why the gods left. Though it seems the Elves have become very callous of humans now, from the rumors we hear from Thiery's Southlands."

She sat again and patted the bench, indicating she wanted to return to the exercises. He sat, his mind spinning.

"Next, I'll guide you through opening yourself to the elements you've been working with, one at a time, and teach you how to interact safely with them. You must direct the interaction with logic, never with emotion. You must always control it, or the mindless and infinite forces of nature will control you. That's what nearly happened to you earlier today."

His cheeks burned.

She took his face in her hand, made him look at her. "Chayan, that was not your fault. I can't imagine how you have come so far with no training and have kept from harming yourself or others."

He had hurt others. The guilt beat at him.

Her eyes mined him down to his soul. He wondered if she could read his thoughts, though he doubted it; he had never done such a thing. She removed her hand and released his gaze. He was glad she didn't ask about his past. Perhaps she hadn't noticed the shame in his eyes.

"Shaping our power is dangerous, as you know. You said earlier you had seldom used your power. Would you be willing to tell me what has happened before, so I can help you learn?"

So she had seen.

His father stood nonchalantly. Without looking at Chayan, he wandered down the garden path. Chayan loved his father for his understanding. Tirren knew what Chayan had to tell her, and knew how deeply it affected him to bring it up.

He took a deep breath. "There were only two times that I know of." He stared at his hands in his lap, rubbing his thumbs together. "Once when I was young, some boys who were bullying me became frightened ... I think I did that to them but I don't know how. And ... and there was a girl, too ... later." Heat climbed his neck again and flamed in his cheeks.

"What happened with the boys?" She must have guessed this would be the easier story for him.

His father had meandered out of sight. Chayan stared at a bare rosebush across the path. "I didn't have many friends when I was young. One," he admitted, "well, other than Shen, one my age, Vint. The other boys used to call him a bastard too, even though he wasn't. They all knew his father had died when he was little.

"I got teased a lot when I was young, and they hit me sometimes when my father and tutors couldn't see, before the other children were old enough to respect my rank. Once, when Vint wasn't nearby, some of the boys drew me over to a spot at the edge of the woods outside the wall. One of them picked up a large stick. I remember thinking of my father, wishing for some way to let him know. I braced myself to fight them as best I could. The last thing I remember before it happened was a little-boy-wish that fearsome monsters would come from the woods and frighten them all away."

Chayan stood, as if he could move away from the memory. He broke a twig from a rosebush and snapped it into small sections, tossing them on the ground one by one as he spoke.

"Men arrived from the Hold when they heard the screams. My father was right behind them. He'd been inside, where he couldn't hear, but he told me later he'd suddenly become worried for me. When he went outside, he saw men running out the gate. The boys were more frightened than I've ever seen anyone."

He looked at her finally. There was sympathy in her eyes.

"I had no idea what had happened. They were seeing things that I couldn't see, things that weren't there. All I could think was that perhaps my mother had somehow come to my aid. I didn't know her, but I was near to the spot where my father first met her. When everyone arrived the boys were released from whatever visions beset them. They were tormented by terrible nightmares for weeks, some for months. A couple never really got over it."

"The people here must have been afraid of you after that."

"It was hard again for a while." He couldn't begin to tell her how hard.

"Did you continue to use that power to protect yourself?"

"No. I didn't know I'd been responsible. My father suspected, I think, but I still thought it had been my mother."

"That was fortunate," she said in a soft voice. "Power can be a seductive thing, especially if one feels isolated or ostracized. Was it long before the second incident occurred?"

She would have all of it from him. Her green eyes held his for a long moment before he began.

"When I was fourteen, I started to feel the changes ... the pull of the moons." He kicked at the ground with one toe. "It made my blood so hot that some days I thought it would turn to flame and burn me to ash. I ran a fever that caused me to sweat even in the winter, and made me dizzy." He glanced at her and then away. "My dreams were filled with the images of every lusty thing I'd ever heard soldiers talk about. My father would sit by my bed and change the cold compresses himself. He tried to help me through it all as best he could, but he didn't understand what was happening to me any better than I did.

"I finally recognized a correlation between these sensations and the waxing of the moons, and I tried to keep to my rooms when either of the moons were full. One day I left to get feathers from the woods, to work on my arrow fletchings. Gwynalyn, the daughter of the man who used to be our Master of Horse, saw me walking to the woods and followed me. She was the only girl who wasn't afraid to be around me. She was the only girl I had kissed. The only girl I have kissed." He stared at his feet, unable to meet her eyes.

"I guess I opened to my magic. I didn't know that's what I was doing at the time, but my skin tingled and my senses grew sharper. I felt like I was going to burst with all the feelings inside me." He hadn't talked about this in years, and never in such detail. The words came hard. "I wanted her, and then she came to me. She let me touch her and, when I did, I couldn't stop."

He looked at Dashara finally, the pain of the memory threatening to overwhelm him. "I didn't know that I was causing it. Truly I didn't. Not until later. I thought she wanted it as much as I did."

The truth, though, was that he'd never given her an opportunity to say if she did or not, no more than his mother had given his father a choice. Chayan hadn't even felt like himself at the time and, in a way, with what he knew now, perhaps he hadn't been. But that didn't change his actions or assuage his guilt.

"What happened to Gwynalyn?" she asked quietly.

"She said she didn't remember, but I'm not sure I believe it. I thought I'd be betrothed to her, maybe even married right away, despite our ages. I would have married her, but her father wed her to some man in the village less than a fortnight later. After that I camped alone at the full of the moons for about a year, until the fevers stopped."

Telling her all this had been hard, but his next question was harder still. "Will it always be like that?"

She took his hand and drew him back to sit on the bench, not letting go. Her warm touch felt good, reassuring.

"No. Not at all, Chayan. You had no one to guide you through that time or it would never have happened in the first place. Our desires are strong, but it need not rule you. You could take a wife now without fear of possessing her mind. In time you will be able to open yourself to the power within you when you are with a woman, and still not affect her will. It can instead become a source of even greater pleasure."

His eyes filled with tears of relief. The tension flowed out of him, like a dam breaking. Whatever the consequences to him of her visit here, this knowledge alone made it worthwhile.

They spent the rest of the day practicing with Spirit, Water, and Air until he could open fully to the magic in him without fear of losing control, and at the end of the day she showed him some healing exercises.

Taking a break from the tiring healing work, they stood and walked a bit. They wandered dirt paths between the leafless bushes and the early spring greenery.

The day was settling towards evening. His father had spent most of the afternoon near them, watching, but was standing with Imecus now, chatting about Bansheen military training. Dashara led Chayan down an adjacent path.

"Chayan," she said in a voice pitched only for his ears, "I need you to know that you are welcome in Beneya—in all of Bansheen—anytime you ever wish to come. You would be more than welcome; you would be revered and given the honor due one of your heritage. Teyyas and Maiar would greet you as kin and you could learn the histories and skills properly. You would have access to any of the considerable resources available there."

She lifted one hand, forestalling him as he made to reply. "I know your duty and your family are here, and I would never ask you to forsake those. Duty is of great importance to us, and I would have given much to have known my family. But I can hope that sometime you might wish to come to us, even for a short while, to learn more and to see the potential of a Somiir's relationship to their people."

She took his hand in both of hers, "I had hoped that perhaps if you had no pressing duty, you might have even returned with me for awhile. I imagine after the events today that your Bealdor wouldn't allow it. If, however, you feel unsafe here, I will take you with me if you wish it. No matter what anyone else says." She let the offer hang in the air between them like a question.

There was temptation, of course, but he would never betray his grandfather or his father. "I thank you for the invitation. Perhaps some other time it might be possible."

She smiled to let him know she was not offended. "It is the answer I expected, if not the one I had hoped for. If ever you decide to come, or need me for any reason, you have only to get word to the aleef in Relendel." She had already explained to him the duty of the Bansheenan family he had met while traveling with his father. "Khemma, Feeah, Rayel, and Eessa are at your service for anything, and they can contact us at need. Once you reach them, I can be here within a fortnight."

Traveling to her by sea would have been impossible for him at his skill level, even if Hesh did have boats. She warned him, though, never to try it until one of them could train him on the ocean.

"I promise I'll let them know if I need you," he said.

She let the matter drop and studied the dark clouds gathering in the west. "There's a rainstorm coming. It will be here by evening. More, I think, than I'm used to seeing in a season. The air is vibrant with it."

"I feel it," Chayan said.

She smiled.

Chapter Eleven

I t was the oddest formal dinner Shen had ever attended.
Tirren had invited Shen, along with Jaron and the two
other regiment leaders, Caine and Mathom. Jaron and Caine's
wives, Verda and Sosha, had been included as well. Dashara was the
guest of honor, but Shen thought she could hardly feel very
honored when the Bealdor sent regrets for an event in his own
Hold. An absence felt by all every time Tirren looked at his father's
empty chair. In addition, the fact that the guest of honor had
precipitated events that had nearly gotten some of them killed, left
an atmosphere in the room as heavy as a wet, wool blanket. Dashara
had also created the biggest chasm between Erimar and his son and
grandson that Shen had ever witnessed.

Dashara was certainly the center of attention, but he noticed
reactions to her that varied from Chayan's unbridled excitement, to
Caine's wife, Sosha, who gave her a rabbit-in-a-hawk's-shadow look
every time their eyes met. If Shen had been in Dashara's situation,
he wasn't at all sure how he would have handled it, but she
managed herself with composed grace and elegance.

She was seated across the table from him, to Tirren's right, in
the midst of a lively conversation with Tirren about Bansheenan
farming. Chayan sat to Shen's right, with Erimar's empty chair at
the head of the table between Chayan and Tirren. The rest of the
guests sat at the lower end of the table, talking among themselves
more than to their guest.

Dashara was poised, engaging, and diplomatic to everyone, regardless of their stiffness toward her. And she was stunning. Shen could hardly take his eyes from her.

Shen looked to Chayan and saw he hadn't been the only one staring at her. "She is beautiful, isn't she?" Shen asked him.

Chayan looked abashed at being caught. "It isn't that," he said quickly. "I mean she is, but I wasn't thinking about that." He blushed.

Chayan had been painfully shy about women ever since the incident with Gwyn. Shen wished for his sake the boy could get past it. "She's older than me anyway," Chayan continued, "and lives in Bansheen. It's just strange to see another of my kind finally. It's more like suddenly having a sister. Or a mother."

"I imagine you'll be sorry to see her go." Shen picked up his mug of hot wine and swirled it, setting the cinnamon, cloves, and citrus peel spinning.

"Yes," Chayan said, speaking in low tones even though Dashara and Tirren were still talking, "and no. My grandfather is more upset than I've ever seen him."

"Ah, well. I think that'll pass once she's gone."

"I hope so. I don't know after today, though. Letting my magic loose frightened him pretty badly."

Shen laughed. "You frightened more than just him. Give me some warning next time, all right? I'm not much used to flying, and might want to armor up before I try it again."

Shen was glad to see Chayan smile at his words. The fear and shame that plagued Chayan when he lost control had always been hard on the boy. To do it in front of so many, and so spectacularly, must have been devastating.

It was another reason Tirren had been right to have this gathering. The regiment leaders could manage the rumors and influence their men, but only if they themselves weren't frightened by the events today. They needed to see Dashara's gentleness and refined diplomacy, and to know that Chayan wasn't any different for having met her.

Tirren included Chayan in his conversation with Dashara and Shen turned to Mathom, on his left. Mathom, as usual, was entertaining those near him with a story, and Shen listened in to pick up the thread.

"The boar spun faster than a fox and knocked my spear right out of my hand," he was saying. "And there I was, armored, weaponless, and nothing but a blackthorn tree next to me. The chain mail weighed me down, the boar was jumping at my feet as I climbed, and the thorns were everywhere that the mail wasn't. I wasn't one length off the ground when a thin branch broke under my feet. I dangled there like a ripe pear while the boar made a pin-cushion of the soles of my boots." Mathom grinned that wide, amicable smile of his, making his otherwise too-long nose fit his face perfectly. Mathom was only a few years older than Shen, and Shen fondly remembered the years that Mathom had mentored him as he moved up in the ranks of swordsmen.

Shen had heard the story often, but still found it funny. Mathom was shorter than most and already his muscularity tended more to stockiness. The image of him climbing the thorn tree never failed to make him laugh. It was good that Mathom had been included tonight; he had a way of setting people at ease. Even Caine's wife, Sosha, seemed to have started to relax, though it could have been the wine. She drained the bottom of another cup as Mathom began another story.

Still chuckling, Shen turned and caught Dashara watching him, smiling. Her alien beauty shocked him like river water in winter and warmed him like the summer sun every time he looked at her. He was used to the grace and physical qualities Chayan possessed, but seeing those attributes on a woman ... it stole his breath. If Dashara was only half-Elven, Shen thought with new wonder, what must Tirren's lover have been like? No wonder the man was still besotted.

Even though the Bealdor would never have allowed a romance between Dashara and Chayan, Shen had guessed Chayan would be smitten with her. A selfish part of him was glad to learn the boy had no designs on her. Not that it mattered—she would be a world away from them all soon, as out of reach as one of the moons. But he could drink her in tonight.

Her thick hair fell down her back, long and unbound, and she wore a light orange dress that brought out the orange flecks in her astounding green eyes. The dress was close-fitting, showing every curve of her body, with sleeves slashed to the elbows. An emerald necklace dangled on the expanse of smooth, pale flesh above her breasts. He had never seen a woman still dressed who showed so much skin. It drew his imagination from the necklace on downward.

"I hear you are leaving in the morning," he said to her, trying to redirect the trail of his thoughts.

"Yes." She smiled at him again, appearing not to have noticed his wandering eyes. "The boat crew is waiting on me, and delaying their own schedule to do so. Also, I've left them at the mercy of the villagers, should they be discovered. Chayan has accomplished more in one day than I would have thought possible, and I think it best to leave soon." She didn't glance at the empty chair at the head of the table, but Shen understood well enough.

Dashara picked delicately around the venison and gravy, taking a small bite of buttered leeks. Shen had never considered before tonight that Chayan's light appetite and preference for fruits and vegetables might be more than odd habits.

"Would it not be safer for you to travel by land? Perhaps I might even be allowed to take some men and accompany you." It would give him some time alone with her, and he'd always dreamed of riding beyond Thiery's borders.

She looked pleased by the offer but declined. "Thank you, no. The boatmen have no way to get back without me, and it's safer and faster for me to travel the ocean than to cross so much of your land."

He shook his head at the concept that the ocean could be safer, but didn't argue. He was sorry that she would be leaving so soon, but resolved to enjoy the intoxication of being near her while he could.

———— ⟨∿⟩ ————

"Did I hear you are leaving us already?" Sosha's soft voice drifted up the table. It was the first thing Sosha had said to her all evening, and Dashara noted that the eagerness in her eyes contradicted the polite words.

Dashara wondered how Sosha and Verda didn't choke on the high-necked dresses they wore or suffocate under the layers. Their dresses hung straight and unadorned, with narrow sleeves ending in a point of fabric that came to the middle knuckle of their hands. A pale pattern of color woven into the fabric was all that decorated the dresses and made one woman's different from the other's. Like all women here, their hair was swept back in crocheted nets. *Interesting that style had taken hold*, Dashara thought, as she had learned that few Heshan women could grow their hair as long as most men.

"Yes, I'm afraid I must leave at first light."

"What a shame," Sosha said, with just a hint of cattiness. She waved at a passing serving girl to fill her wine cup, but Caine put a hand over her arm. Caine was taller than Mathom or Jaron and lean, perhaps five years older than the captain. He had hair almost as light brown as Chayan's, though heavily graying, and sported a broad nose that looked as if it had been broken at least once.

"You said you traveled here by boat?" Mathom asked, preventing Sosha from saying more.

"Yes." Mathom had been the most cordial to her of the men and women she had been introduced to this evening, but Dashara decided that elaborating wasn't a good idea. The startled looks she received at the simple statement of fact were enough, and they could hardly be unaware that magic was involved. "Our coast isn't as fierce as yours, and Bansheen has a fair-sized fleet of cargo boats that can run in good weather," she said, sidetracking the subject.

"Do all your cities trade goods with each other?" Jaron asked. He had been quiet most of the meal, speaking only when he had something to contribute, though sounding self-assured when he did. His wife, Verda, spoke as rarely as her husband, but with a spark in her eye that hinted at an intelligent woman with more strength than she showed in public.

"The cities are under sovereign rule, but peaceful among themselves. All have free trade." There were politics involved in free trade, though, and she laid out the advantages and disadvantages of her country's system. Jaron became animated, asking astute questions. Soon all the men were asking about Bansheen, curiosity overcoming their hesitation. Tirren, Shen, and Chayan spoke among themselves, letting the conversation flourish among the guests who had previously avoided speaking to her.

A heavy-set serving woman tried to reach between Dashara and Jaron to clear the main course, but leaned so far away from Dashara that she jostled Jaron's elbow. "Gods, woman," he muttered, "she doesn't bite." Disgruntled, he pulled plates from the middle of the table himself, so she could reach them. Dashara smiled to herself.

More servers brought bread and cheese, served with lemon-water and hot wine. The interruption effectively ended the discussion about Bansheenan commerce and conversation polarized again into a new grouping, with Tirren, Chayan, Caine, and Jaron discussing horses, and Mathom entertaining the Heshan women with another story. Dashara found she and Shen were the odd ones out.

"I've been surprised how few women live here at the Hold," Dashara observed, before the silence between them became awkward.

Shen nodded. "The Bealdor's family has been without women since Tirren's mother died, so no waiting ladies, and most of the men who live here are soldiers. The soldiers stay in garrisons and a wife would have to live in the village. Many soldiers here at the Hold never marry."

"Do you mandate that men serve in the army?"

"No. We don't need to. The foot soldiers are common men who have a better life here than they might otherwise. We turn many away. The swordsmen who live at the Hold are highborn, but usually younger sons, like myself, who've chosen to be professional soldiers." A serving girl tried to pour more mulled wine into his mug and he held up one hand to prevent her. "We've had peace since the Conflicts, so there's no point supporting a large army here at the Hold. The bulk of our swordsmen are reserves, men who live all across Thiery. Unlike the professional soldiers here, they have wives and children and trades."

The bulk of their force might be reserves, but she had been told there were over two hundred soldiers that lived at the Hold. With so many unmarried men, the serving girls must not lack for attention, and she would bet there were night-houses in the village that did a thriving business.

"I see. Do Jaron and Caine's wives live in the village then?"

"No. Officers—pretty much just the men at this table—have apartments in the Hold proper. Still, Jaron and Caine are the only ones right now who are married."

"I suspect you've been popular since your promotion then," she said with a smile.

He laughed, and even blushed lightly, confirming her guess.

"With fathers more than the ladies," he said modestly.

His looks and charisma made her doubt that, but she said nothing.

For Dashara, being courted by the Izzat was not a simple matter of finding a mate; it meant dealing with scores of potential suitors as early as puberty. As with all the Somiir, Dashara had been trained in many things during her upbringing, including the arts of being with a man. She had no trouble recognizing that the interest Shen showed her went beyond merely making her feel welcome. Despite the lines of suitors waiting for her at home, Dashara found she enjoyed Shen's company, perhaps more than she should. Still, she knew there was no point in encouraging affection she couldn't return.

"Somiir," Tirren broke in. "How early might you be ready to leave tomorrow?"

"As early as you like, Beodan. I had hoped to leave at dawn." She wasn't looking forward to traveling this land in the light of day, but she courted nearly as much danger from the Bealdor if she stayed longer, and she wanted the boat crew safely back out at sea as soon as possible.

Tirren inclined his head. "My regiment and I will escort you if you will permit us."

"I would be most grateful." Grateful hardly covered it. He may be risking his father's wrath again for her sake, but she and her guards and, by extension, the boat crew, would be much safer for his company.

"If you have other duties," Shen said to Tirren, "I'd be happy to lead the men in your place. Or take my own regiment, if you wish."

Tirren swallowed a mouthful of bread and cheese and shook his head. "There wasn't time to tell you earlier. My father has ordered you to return to Bern. Now that you've had a chance to recover from the skirmish, he wants you to command the company leaving tomorrow. You can show them where you found Maradon's men camped and anywhere else you feel needs to be especially patrolled."

Shen bowed his head to his Beodan but Dashara saw a flash of disappointment. She felt a little herself.

Conversation ebbed and flowed as a desert of peaches and clotted cream in pastry was served with tea. The group had at last opened to her and Dashara answered more questions about Bansheen, though no one broached any topic that touched on the Elves. It had probably been the reason Chayan had stayed so quiet tonight. He had been insatiable today for everything she could tell him of his Elven heritage, but he was wise enough to know this was not the place to discuss such things. He may have also realized, as she had, that speaking too much together here may distance them both from the others.

Finally, chairs were pushed back and the eating, drinking, and talking diminished. When Tirren stood, officially ending the dinner, Shen offered to walk Dashara to her room. He gave her his arm and she took it, feeling the unyielding bulk of muscle under his shirtsleeve. She was tall among human women, but came only to his shoulder. After a lifetime with the smaller Bansheenan men, she found his size and strength arousing.

Her palace guards stood outside the dining room and fell in behind them as Shen led her down the hall and up the winding flight of stone stairs. "I regret that my duty won't allow me to be a part of your escort to Relendel, Somiir." Though he had asked her to call him by name, he still used her title.

"Thank you, Shen. I would have enjoyed your company."

They arrived at her guest room and he opened the door for her. Her guards were more than used to the reaction Somiir got from admirers when at the palace, and they respectfully stood back. The captain, however, stationed himself where he could see all he needed to.

Shen entered the room ahead of her and Dashara had a moment of uncertainty, wondering how forward men might be with women here. He returned to the door and she realized he'd been checking the room for her. It was spacious, by Heshan standards, with a bed, armoire, dressing table, and fireplace, and the strange, cramped copper tub in front of the fire where she had bathed for dinner.

Finding nothing amiss, he offered his hand to lead her into the room then stepped back into the doorway. He stood close to her, close enough for her to smell his musky skin mingled with scents of soap and horse.

"Perhaps we will meet again someday," she said. "I would like to return sometime to Hesh to visit Chayan again."

"I will hope for that day." He lingered long enough that she thought he might bend to kiss her. She thought she might let him. Instead he bowed formally and left.

She missed her aleef as she struggled out of her heavy dress. More tired than she had been in a long time, Dashara climbed into the spacious, canopied bed to find an uncomfortable mattress. From the smell and feel of the thing, she had to guess it was filled with horsehair. The journey and the visit had been exhausting though, and she hadn't slept since the night before last. She fell asleep quickly, her last thoughts returning to Shen, wondering what it would have been like if he had come to her bed.

At dawn, the courtyard near the stables hummed with activity as Dashara prepared to leave. Her breath left white plumes in the cool, damp morning air. She skirted a puddle and navigated the wet cobblestones as her guards escorted her to the waiting skaggi.

The thunderstorm had ended near dawn and the clouds hung low and heavy. She felt sorry to have missed most of the storm in her deep sleep, but what she had seen had been remarkable. And she had been right in her guess; more rain than she might see at home in a season.

Chayan stood in the front door of the Hold watching her go. He hadn't been allowed to travel with her, but she had already passed on all the last-minute advice and information she could think of, and had said her goodbyes to him with a hug.

Tirren and his men were already mounted. The captain of Dashara's guards had been about to help her to her mount when the Bealdor appeared and descended the front stairs. She walked to meet him, wary.

"You did my grandson a service, helping him control his magic yesterday. I wanted to thank you before you left."

The words might have been pulled on a rope from somewhere within the depths of the man, but she bowed her head as if he had lavished her with praise. "Thank you for allowing me to spend time with him. He is a fine young man who will make a great leader here someday."

Erimar made no answer. It looked like too many thoughts swirled behind those stern brown eyes for one to win out.

"I have something for you." She went to her saddlebags and pulled out a cloth-wrapped object, the size of a man's fist. Returning, she handed it to him. "I was going to give it to your son to pass on to you. It's a gift from the queen for your hospitality."

Erimar unwrapped the cloth to reveal an exquisitely detailed carving in black stone of a hunter slaying a beast. A letter of greeting and thanks from Queen Assia accompanied it.

Erimar gave her a short bow.

Dashara made her farewells, returned to her skaggi, and mounted. She scanned the courtyard. She was just about to turn away when she saw Shen leading his horse from the stables, readying for his own trip. She felt irrationally glad to see him one last time and gave him a bright smile. He returned it with a courtly bow. She nodded farewell to the Bealdor and Chayan, and rode out the double gates of the Hold with Tirren and his men following.

Chapter Twelve

Maradon finished his review of the records the clerk had brought him, and added the sheaves of parchment to the leather folder. With a grimace at the waste of his time, he took the folder from the desk and walked from the private office, through the library and up the stairs.

With each successive turn of Hrar, he felt more foolish sitting at his father's bedside, reading the list of landowners in arrears in their taxes to him. If Vrenun understood anything that went on around him still—and Maradon doubted it very much—the likelihood that he cared was even more remote. His father's eyes had clouded with a milky film in the past week. What little strength he'd possessed this year wasted from his body with the last stone of weight he'd lost.

Maradon opened the bedchamber door. An acidic smell permeated the room, too subtle to indicate his father had pissed his bed sheets. Breakfast had been brought in a few hours ago, and Vrenun's manservant reported that he had failed to eat again. Maradon wondered if the lazy wretch had left the food here to spoil. He approached the bed but stopped part way there, sensing more than seeing the unnatural stillness. He didn't need to touch his father to know that he was dead.

He stood three paces from the bed looking at the still form with a mixture of emotions, the taxes forgotten. He'd expected this day for so long—wished for it—and now that it was here, it jarred him. The broken body on the bed was nothing but an empty vessel, his father's spirit making the long journey alone to the Land of the Dead. His father was gone. The Bealdor was dead.

Maradon laid the folder on a nearby desk. He walked to the bed and touched the back of his hand to his father's forehead. He maintained the touch longer than he needed to. Finally, he bent and pressed a light kiss to the cold skin.

He had entered the room as the Bealdor's son; he left it the ruler of Lacedar. Things would change at last.

Yslaaran stood in the Veil of Mists and watched the halfbreed woman traveling east across the ocean. This new development could pose unexpected complications to her plans, and Yslaaran sifted the possibilities and options as she left the veil and headed for the palace grounds. Entering the woods, she came across one of the Unseely, spinning a stick in a brook.

"Tcoth, find Nisseah, Isurrelte, and Eanaan. Tell them I am headed for the court and have them meet me along the way."

Tcoth looked up with a sour expression. Yslaaran waited while he balked at being told what to do, debated his options, and finally stood and turned for the palace.

"Run," she said, and he did.

By the time he was passing out of sight, his gait had changed from a reluctant trot to a sprint of joyful abandon. Difficult as the Unseely could be at times, they had been created by Uulaten to perform tasks. Doing something always entertained them more than doing nothing.

Long before Yslaaran reached the palace, the other three Seely met her in a wide glade sprinkled with colorful nasturtiums and lupine, daisies and poppies. Isurrelte sank cross-legged onto the thick grass, her gown spreading around her. Nisseah kissed

Yslaaran's hand and settled beside her. Eanaan lounged on his side, plucking at the lush green blades and flower petals.

"Why the risk of bringing the four of us together, Yslaaran?" Nisseah asked, more direct than usual.

"There is reason." She looked around casually to make sure Tcoth had not returned out of curiosity, and that no other was nearby. "We have waited for my son to grow to manhood, and into his rank over other Men before I approach him. Lately, I have felt workings of magic in his land. I went to the mists to see the source. A halfbreed woman tamed the ocean to travel from the land in the east and meet with my son."

"For what purpose?" Isurrelte asked.

"I'm not certain. While she was there Chayan lashed out at his own people. Yet when they spent time together, she seemed only to teach him the fundamentals of his magic."

Yslaaran's abilities to manipulate Air, Water, and Spirit were as much a part of her as her breath, the manifestation no more than a thought. It was a thing that had never occurred to her, that Chayan might need to be taught how to use his talents, that halfbreeds conjured their power each time they used it. The surprised looks of the others said they thought the same.

"It concerns me," Yslaaran continued, "that she should travel all the way from Geshne's province to see him. And even more that Chayan would strike out at his people when she arrived. Our plan comes near to its ripening time, but perhaps the crows eat the fruit before us."

"Before Chayan, we never gave thought to our castoff children," Eanaan said, pushing himself into a sitting position. "There is much we may not know. I hope we won't come to regret our ignorance."

"Too bad we can't see into Geshne's land," Isurrelte said. "Perhaps the halfbreed woman harbors ill will toward us for our people discarding her as a babe. If so, she may have sown those seeds in Chayan."

"She didn't that I saw, but time moves differently there. I did not see all and I dared not stay too long in the mist. We wouldn't want anyone questioning what I found so interesting there."

"Even if she didn't speak ill of us," Nisseah added, "other halfbreeds may be drawn to him also. Another one might."

Isurrelte turned to Yslaaran. "I think the time has come for you to meet with your son."

Yslaaran felt an unfamiliar anxiety. So much planning had gone into this, and she hadn't expected this day so soon. "My dilemma is the same now as when he was a child. If I go to him I might ensure his loyalty or I might set his own kind more firmly against him, should he tell them of me. And the halfbreed woman caused much unrest while there. If Chayan ruled already, or even his father, it would be different."

"Is the halfbreed woman with him still?" Nisseah asked.

"No. She sails east again as we speak."

"I agree with Isurrelte, then," he said. "You must go to the boy now. You may be able to undo harm done, if any, and gauge for yourself how he feels toward our people."

Yslaaran looked at the others. All were in agreement. "I will go to him this night then." She picked a small daisy and twirled it in her fingers as she considered new paths and accelerated plans. "Perhaps the time has come to approach more Seely as well?"

"No," Eanaan said. "If Chayan rejects you, then we have played our hand for nothing. We have waited this long, we can bide our time a bit more."

"If we didn't tell them of Chayan, though," she persisted, "if we just sought to break their lassitude, make them think about the world outside our own."

"I also say no," Isurrelte said. "We are so close. Caution is everything now. We must be sure of our plan before we risk word of it reaching the queen's ears."

Nisseah nodded in agreement. "And it will if we keep talking," he said, glancing into the trees. "We have been at this too long already." He stood and said short farewells. Eanaan joined him and the two of them headed back toward the court, sauntering casually, chatting about who they might dance with this night. Isurrelte stayed on and talked with Yslaaran about nothing in particular, for appearances only, Yslaaran knew, though she felt certain no one had been in earshot.

When Isurrelte left, Yslaaran leaned back against the barkless tree and thought about the years of groundwork she had laid. Long had she watched the human forts to find a man of rank to seduce; one of the right age and temperament. One who ruled or would come to but, as yet, had no heirs. One whom she could couple with at that rare concurrence which ensured her highest chance of fertility—the blessed night of Winterfest with both moons full in the sky. Even with all that accomplished, she had been amazed when she actually conceived.

Their plans couldn't fail now. Too much was at stake. The very existence of her race hinged on the outcome.

Chapter Thirteen

Chayan held a new candle to the old one, but thought better of it before the wick caught. He had been reading late into the night yet again, studying one of the three books Dashara had given him as a parting gift. The ancient text on the history of the Elves fascinated him, but if he didn't stop now he'd wake up face down in the book, as he'd done last night.

Chayan set the unlit candle back on his desk, but before he could remove his hand from the base, a tingle raced up his spine. He experienced the unmistakable sensation of being watched, though he knew no one could be in his room. After the past two days of practice, he extended his senses almost reflexively. Immediately, he felt the presence behind him.

The sheer power emanating from the presence provoked a cold ball of fear to form in the pit of his stomach. Magic pressed against his awareness like a physical weight. The intensity frightened and humbled him. Dashara's power had felt as different in scale as his candle would to the sun.

Chayan's breath came shallow and fast. Fear froze him with his hand still on the candle, but he had to look. He turned his head to see a woman of astonishing and exotic beauty standing by his bed. His father had described his mother so often that he had little doubt this was she. The recognition did nothing to calm his pounding heart.

"Chayan, do you know me?" Her musical voice sent a thrill through him.

"If you are my mother, lady, I know you," he managed.

"I am." She moved to the foot of his bed and sat gracefully on the cedar trunk there.

Chayan turned his chair to face her properly. Her large green eyes studied him, disquieting him further. He had so much to ask her but the hurts of a lifetime bubbled to the surface ahead of the questions. "I've waited my whole life to see you. Every day, as a child, I prayed you would come."

"Am I now come too late?" she asked evenly.

"No," he said. She was here, finally, after wishing for this moment for so long. "No. It was just when I was young, well ... things were hard."

Her power awed him, and despite their shared eye color and bone structure, her beauty was as foreign to him as his appearance must be to humans. After years of longing to meet his Elven mother, he realized now that he was as different from her as he was from the family that had raised him. A lifetime of hope fell to dust with the sudden awareness that he fit in neither world.

"Many times I saw you as you grew to your manhood, though you did not see me."

"Why did you never come to me then?"

"I had reason. You needed to live among Men, to be as one of them; to come to the rule of your father's line without people despising you for your mother's blood."

He'd been despised anyway. But perhaps she was right, it might have been worse if she'd been as close to him as he had wished. "Why now, then? I don't rule yet. I'm not even old enough to be Beodan."

"A woman came to you but late, another halfbreed. What purpose brought her here?"

Though she had asked gently, Chayan hesitated. He was unsure if his answer might bring harm to Dashara in some way.

"She heard about me. In Bansheen, the half-Elves use their powers all the time—to help people. They knew that the Heshans wouldn't know how to teach me about my magic." His mother could have taught him but she hadn't. "She showed me how to control it and how it can be used to help people." He didn't know how much Yslaaran knew about Dashara already, so he strove to be as honest as he could while still being prudent.

"Her people in the East, do they willingly take the help she offers?"

"Yes, she's highly respected in Bansheen. All the halfbloods there are."

Yslaaran pondered that a moment. "And you Chayan, would you help your people also?"

"If they would accept it from me." He shrugged, knowing it unlikely.

She smiled at him. "Then you have become more than I dared hope for. I am well pleased. Tell me, what have you been taught of our people? Do you think on us with favor?"

He relaxed a little and shifted in his chair. "My father did what he could. I was raised knowing my heritage and my father's affection for you. He's always spoken well of you. He had the historians find out what they could, but it was little and, I am learning now, much in error." He gestured to the book on his desk.

"We are forgotten so soon then?" she said.

She remained all elegant composure, like the most beautiful sculpture in the world brought to life, but sadness glinted in her eyes. After a thoughtful silence she continued, "Would you hear now why I have come to you?"

She looked at him with such piercing intensity that he suddenly felt afraid again. He nodded, not daring to speak in case she should change her mind.

"Both your father's people and mine own have undergone much change during our long years apart, though for many ages we coexisted in harmony under the gods. There are those among us who would return to the way of things before the separation of our worlds. We are few yet, but our hope is that more may join us. There is much we can do to ease the difficulty of mortal lives. For myself, it pains me to see the needless suffering, and I would come again among humans to make their lives better."

"Why tell me this?"

"The world has changed since last we walked the mortal lands freely. Your people fear us ... and not always unjustly," she gave him a sad smile. "We would have a champion, one who carries the blood but is himself Man, raised amongst Men, who will pave the way for our return."

His heart jumped at the thought that with his mother's help he could be to his people what Dashara was to hers. Her cool manner, though, brought to mind the stories, true or not, of the callousness of the Elves. Even Dashara had admitted they might have become dangerous during their isolation.

"Mother ..." the word felt odd in his mouth, "with the gods gone from this world, would any of your people seek to harm us if the Elves returned?"

"We have considered this and I do not believe so. We are your elders and betters. Many would insist on veneration, as has always been our due, especially if more Seely are to be swayed to this cause. Yet, those who would help mortals will do so of wanting to; those who disdain humans would most likely keep to our lands."

Whether or not the people of Thiery could go from fear and superstition to showing respect to the Elves was something he couldn't guess, but the thought that he might help herald in a new age was a heady thought. He reigned in his excitement before his imagination ran wild.

"If you wish to return to mankind," he said, "you'd do best to begin in Bansheen, where the halfbloods—the Somiir, they call themselves—are already accepted. You'd be revered above all there."

"The land you call Bansheen is closed to us. The barriers that Geshne raised against his brother, Fresshe, hinder us also. Blindly we must step into that country. That or travel there as the halfbreed you named Dashara traveled. It is why I gave birth to a son of this land, where we may come and go at will."

"There is so much prejudice here. I don't know if it's possible."

"I have marked your life among these people. It will take time, we know, but what is time to us? If this takes the span of your years, we will wait. If your lifetime is not enough, we will work to bring forth another of halfblood to continue what you begin. Only tell me that you are willing to undertake this, and we will provide you with all the protection and help we can." She studied him and smiled. "Perhaps when you are ruler of these men, your people will not suffer the harshness of winter, nor the uncertain harvests they do now."

Even starting the process of bridging the races would be exhilarating, but having learned from Dashara that his lifespan might be two hundred years or more he wanted to believe that he could accomplish this. After meeting Dashara, Chayan had fantasized about what it would be like if the people of Thiery loved him as the Bansheenan loved the Somiir. He imagined the ways he could help those he ruled with his newfound abilities. He'd thought it nothing more than fancy, but now ... would it be so hard to work just a little at a time to convince people that the Elves weren't evil? When he was Bealdor he would rule well and fairly, and would it not be so much easier then to convince his subjects?

"I must speak with my father and grandfather about this. My first duty is to them, but now they're aware what the Somiir do for their people, I think they'll see the good in this." In truth, he wasn't at all sure about his grandfather, but there was no need to say that now. "I know my father would be happy to see you among us. He's missed you very much. Very much." His words couldn't begin to convey his father's suffering, but Chayan thought he saw a spark of regret in her eyes.

She stood and crossed the short distance to him. Taking his head in her soft hands, she bent and placed a soft kiss on his forehead.

"Know that I hold you in my heart, and I will watch over you as I may. I will speak with you again shortly. If you have need of me, call my name each day at dawn and I will come as soon as I hear."

His mother turned and walked back to the head of the bed, where he had first seen her. He noticed for the first time the mist that clung to that corner of the room. She stepped into it, and was gone.

Yslaaran stepped between the worlds and came out again in Tirren's room. She hadn't intended to see him and it was unlike her to be impulsive. It had been the sadness in Chayan's eyes when he spoke of his father's feeling that changed her mind.

A large, canopied bed stood against the center of the back wall, the curtains pulled wide to the big posts. The man lay on his back with his head turned from her, his left arm bent above his head, the covers pushed below his chest. She set a compulsion of sleep on him so he wouldn't wake, and crossed the room to sit at his side. She had been aware of the depth of his feelings for her long before speaking with Chayan. Over the years it was not only her son that she had watched.

She looked about the room with interest. It appeared tidy, with tapestries adorning the walls and woven rugs covering the cold stone floor. His writing desk stood in the corner at the far side of the bed as did an armoire. Opposite the foot of the bed was an open doorway into his sitting room. A small opening in the wall near where she had entered led to a tiled floor with a small copper tub, and likely a garderobe beyond. To the left of the door was the hearth, the fire still burning high as if he had not long been abed.

Yslaaran studied the side of Tirren's face and neck, the lean, defined muscle of his chest. His hair spread out across his shoulder, loosed from the thong that tied the front of it during the day. He slept unclothed. Modest though they were, Heshans slept naked, believing that avoiding night sweats would keep them safe from the chills that could kill them so easily. Humans feared so many things in their frailty.

Reaching out, she brushed his cheek, feeling the light stubble of beard that males of her kind never knew. She traced her hand down his neck and rested it palm down on the center of his chest. The mark she had placed on his neck years ago remained, strawberry red, and she wondered again that she had done such a thing. It was something not done in long ages, to brand a human, that no other Seely would take them. It had been important that he not be used by another, for Chayan's sake, though the chance of that had been so small as to hardly matter.

The other thing she had done to him had been far worse. She had known that leaving his memory intact of that night with her would torment him. That his desire that would fade no more than the mark on his neck. It had been necessary though, that he remember her and hold her in his heart, so he could tell Chayan of her. It had the added benefit that he had taken no other woman to wife, one that might have produced an heir to challenge Chayan's position. Seeing him now, though, she understood fully, perhaps for the first time, why the gods had forbidden such a thing. The gods had never objected to the Seely coupling with humans, but their mandate had been that humans would be left no memory of the actual joining. All these centuries after their leaving, though, the mandates of the gods meant no more than words on the wind.

Tirren shifted in his sleep under her touch and turned his face to her. Her folk might nap for the sheer pleasure of it, but never out of physical need. For Yslaaran, sleep had always been the most endearing of the mortal vulnerabilities; that some part of each day they lapsed into this defenseless state, unconscious of the world around them.

He had aged since she had last been this close to him, but he was handsome still. Human lives may be short, but they burned so bright, and she found it strangely exhilarating to have the true love of one of these fiery mortals.

Her hand still rested on Tirren's chest and she felt the rise and fall of his breath and the steady beat of his heart. She remembered the last time she had watched him sleep, as she lay next to him in the meadow, wondering if his seed would take in her womb. She stroked his face again and desire stirred within her. She released the compunction of sleep, and under her light touch he floated toward wakefulness.

———— ⟋⟍ ————

Tirren woke knowing he'd dreamed yet again of Yslaaran; the odd spice and flower scent of her skin so vivid he still smelled it.

A hand brushed his face. The last vestige of sleep dropped from him and his eyes opened to a figure above him. He was on his elbow in an instant. His left hand grabbed the arm that touched him.

"Hush now."

He remembered Yslaaran's soft, musical voice as if he had heard it only yesterday. The firelight behind her outlined the profile he knew so clearly. She pushed gently on his chest and he lay back slowly. Realizing the grip he held on her wrist he let go, lest he hurt her. He knew he should be afraid—she had enchanted and abducted him in his youth—but he couldn't bring himself to fear her. He had owned his desire for too many years; it was no longer a thing of her making. He didn't say a word, but held his breath in case she should fade and vanish as the sensual dream had done.

She stood and untied the cord at her hips, dropping it behind her, and slid the wide neck of her gown off her shoulders. It fell like a waterfall of silk to her feet. Firelight danced on her bare skin. He hardly dared to believe as she slipped beneath the covers.

He moved over her, covering her with his body, their limbs entwining. A thousand dreams made real again, at last. The scent of her filled his nostrils as he kissed her neck and slid his lips down her chest to her perfect breasts. Her skin felt soft as down. They touched and played each other until she pulled rough groans from him. When he could stand it no more, he took her.

No human woman could begin to compare. Everything about her affected him. The smell of her, the feel of her, every graceful motion—it drove him to an extremity of passion that bordered his physical limits to bear.

He moved inside her with strong, urgent thrusts, yet it was her power that threatened to shatter something inside of him. She brought him pleasure so intense that it crossed a gray boundary into sweet pain. It burned deep inside him and set his nerves on fire. It made his heart pound with deep, heavy thuds that he felt all the way into his throat. Like that first night with her, like all his dreams, it went on until he thought he would die from it. The cry she wrenched from him at last might be the same if he had taken a mortal wound.

He felt broken and empty when it ended—and satisfied for the first time in years.

He dreaded the moment she would vanish or spell him to sleep, and he held her tightly to his body. Instead of leaving him, she lay in his arms and they talked. He stroked her hair and told her of his childhood when she asked. She spoke of the palace in her land and the gods she had known so well. After eighteen years and a son together, it was a quiet time for the two of them to come to know each other.

She asked him about Chayan, about his early years and the difficulties he had endured. Tirren felt his chest swell with emotion, telling her, at last, about their son, the sad times and the glad. It brought a sense of completeness into his heart, where he hadn't realized there had been a empty space. He fought his fatigue as long as possible, watching her in his arms by firelight and speaking softly with her. Finally, exhaustion closed his eyes.

He woke in the morning and found her gone. For a brief, mad moment he wondered if he had dreamed the encounter, as he had dreamed of her so many times over the years. The flowery scent of her skin still lingering in the room convinced him it had been real, and a long red hair on the pillow was his proof.

Chapter Fourteen

E rimar broke his fast with Chayan in the private dining room. They both waited with some impatience for Tirren to wake, but Erimar knew his party had arrived back at the Hold late in the night, returned from escorting the halfblood woman to her boat. It didn't surprise him that Tirren slept later than usual, but his anger roiled close to the surface after Chayan's news, and the meal turned silent and tense.

A servant entered the room with a fresh pot of tea.

"Tell Ban to rouse his Beodan," Erimar barked, his patience at an end.

"The Beodan is on his way," the man said, glancing back at the wooden door as it swung open.

Despite his extra sleep, Tirren still looked tired.

"I hear your trip went well," Erimar said.

Tirren sat. He nodded in response and greeted Chayan with that characteristic half smile of his, then reached for a thick slice of bread and a pot of boysenberry jam.

"There were enough of us that there was no trouble. We made it there in three days. She overnighted with the Bansheenan family in Relendel and we stayed on to guard the area. She left at dawn yesterday and we rode hard to make it back to the Hold in two days rather than spend the extra night out."

"Chayan has been waiting for you to wake. He has news for you."

Chayan had been fidgeting in anticipation since Tirren walked in. At Erimar's permission, the pent-up words tumbled out. "My mother came to me last night. She appeared in my room. She said she had wanted to wait until I was grown to meet me, so people wouldn't be more afraid of me."

"I know," Tirren replied. "I saw her last night also."

Erimar felt as if he'd been hit with a battering ram. The woman had snuck into the Hold and appeared to his grandson, and Chayan had welcomed the visit. And now Tirren showed not the slightest concern. It hadn't occurred to him that she might also go to Tirren and the oversight made him angrier still. "What did she want with you?" he demanded.

Tirren turned his tired gaze to Erimar. He said nothing. He didn't need to.

Erimar's jaw clenched. Helplessness fueled his anger. Never in his life had he been less of a ruler than when that halfblood woman, Dashara, had been here. This world of magic was a world he didn't understand. He never wanted Chayan to learn magic, but not learning it had nearly killed them. And now on the heels of the halfblood leaving, the Elven woman had returned. These women were powerful and dangerous, and he had no idea how to fight them. Especially not when his own family embraced them.

"Did she tell you what she wanted with your son?" It came out in a growl, daring Tirren to know, daring him to agree with it.

"Only that she had come to meet him," Tirren said, cautiously, as if suspecting he'd been baited. Erimar breathed a hair easier. At least Tirren seemed not to be a part of the woman's plotting.

"Tell him," Erimar said looking to Chayan.

Chayan, more contrite now, recited his conversation with Yslaaran. The boy glanced his way often, obviously hoping that Erimar would be more supportive of the proposition on hearing it a second time. Tirren's face gave nothing away, though the words must have struck home. To know after all these years why he had been abducted, why Chayan had been conceived and brought to him.

Tirren took a deep breath and let it out. "Well, that is news indeed." His eyes moved from Chayan to Erimar and away again, assessing the field of battle around the table and where the troops were positioned. "She said nothing to me of this."

"I imagine you didn't talk much," Erimar retorted. Chayan, caught between them, looked at his empty plate.

After that woman had stolen Tirren away, Erimar watched his son change from an affable and popular heir to a brooding, quiet man with a halfblood son, a child who required his constant protection. So many lines of potential for Tirren had been cut short by his obsession. It had pained Erimar year after year to see Tirren's soul tortured with the memories of the woman he could never have, and to shun relationships with human women who could never measure up. Erimar's dreams of a strong line of heirs faded into the reality of one halfblood grandson. He loved the boy, but Chayan was not the successor they needed. The Elven woman had affected all their lives, and now posed a threat to the entire region.

Tirren answered the retort in a voice tight with anger. "Actually, we did talk, though nothing of import to tell." Looking to Chayan and speaking half to himself he said, "I suppose I can understand why she left this for Chayan to tell me instead of broaching it herself."

"Father," Chayan said, "surely you can see the advantages in this, for everyone. The good that could be done. Think of what Somiir Dashara told us of life in Bansheen. Given time, people here could change, and as mother said there's no need to hurry this. Would either of you have thought I'd be accepted here had you known I would be born?"

Erimar had seen how much meeting the Somiir had changed Chayan. To realize for the first time that there were those like him who were adored by their people couldn't help but give the boy some futile hope. But Tirren surely would see that Yslaaran's involvement was another matter. Or perhaps he wouldn't. Erimar decided not to wait and see which side his son would take.

"We're not talking of Bansheen," he cut in. "We are not even talking of halfbloods. We are talking about the Elves. Powerful creatures, dangerous, whom we know pitifully little about except that they toy with mortals to their own ends."

"It seems her plans are the same as our own," Tirren said, "Wait until Chayan is older, and hope that when he comes into his rule that the people will love him. It seems like she wants to help him. Perhaps I could speak with her again when she comes next...."

Erimar's restraint burned to ashes in a hot rage. He sat forward, and slapped his hands onto the table hard enough to rattle the dishes. "By the Dead, Tirren! You of all people should condemn this. You who have twice had your will stripped from you, raped for your seed. Was she here to get another child from you?"

Rare anger flared in Tirren's eyes. "She didn't take my will last night. She didn't need to."

Chayan said very quietly, "Tlaas is dark and Hrar not yet full. She wouldn't have been able to get with child last night."

Chayan's words barely registered with Erimar. The halfblood woman had been bad enough. Now Chayan's mother was back, coupling with Tirren again—and under Erimar's own roof. Things had spiraled out of control. But, by all the gods, he could still rule his own household.

"My first duty is to the region, as yours will be Tirren, and yours Chayan. Chayan *must not* risk his acceptance as Bealdor by making himself more foreign to the people of Thiery. For the security of the realm and the protection of my people, by my will,

I will not allow the Elves to come among our people. You *will* both heed me in this."

There followed a long moment of silence in the room.

"Yes, Bealdor," Tirren said, without raising his eyes. Chayan echoed him.

———— ✦ ————

His grandfather departed, leaving Chayan to his thoughts while his father sat in stony silence. He thought about the old saying that it was a harder fall from a high place than a low one. Last night he had been riding a moon, meeting his mother at last, hearing her plans for him. This morning his grandfather had spoken more basely of her than he could have imagined.

At last his father looked his way. "Your mother has no evil intentions, Chayan," he said, his voice quiet and rough. "I feel sure of it. As surely as I feel that she didn't place that thought in me."

"I believe that, too. I could wish that grandfather had met her, then perhaps he would understand."

"I think it would change nothing, Chayan. He's right, really. Our worlds have been separated too long. We have to consider the people of the region first, and your succession. It isn't as if we suffer without the Elves, or even without a system like the Somiir have set up. Not anymore." He stood to leave but stopped and laid a gentle hand on Chayan's shoulder. "Only Jhenna can know the future. Fortune favor, things will turn out for the best."

Chayan sat alone in the dining room. Though he would never wish to hurry his grandfather's death, it didn't change the fact that Erimar was old. Despite being fit for his age, his years were numbered; his edict would end one day.

It may be that the God of Fortune—wherever he might be now—knew how this would all end, but it would do Chayan no good to pray to him. Jhenna was as long gone as the rest. Perhaps when his father was Bealdor, he would be open to taking small steps toward his mother's plans. If not, if fortune did favor him, someday he would be Bealdor. He would trust to his own judgment at that time as to what was best for his people.

If his mother could be patient, then so could he.

Chapter Fifteen

The late afternoon sun sparkled off the weapons of a hundred new men. Maradon stood above the field and watched them at practice. Someday his army would equal the glory of the old high kings' forces. Someday. Change moved slowly, too slowly, but much progress had been made at Lacedar Hold in the month since he had become Bealdor.

Jin moved between the regiment leaders, overseeing the training. Glancing up, he noticed Maradon on the low hill and started across the yard toward him. Like a dog coming to heel, Maradon thought. The idea both pleased and disgusted him. Absolute obedience was necessary, but a man needed to have a backbone too. He missed Baes anew. His son should have been the one overseeing the new soldiers.

"How many today?" he asked, as Jin reached him.

"Only two, Bealdor."

Maradon grunted. The number of new recruits had been steadily decreasing all week.

"How is the training coming? Are the pig-lovers learning anything yet?"

"Better, now that the number of new arrivals has slowed and most of the men have had at least some instruction."

"See that they keep learning. At what it costs to feed them, they had best be worth it."

He did some quick calculations in his head. Increased penalties and tithes for landowners had been his first act as Bealdor, but the money coming in wouldn't cover the cost of the army for long, especially since he'd summoned every reserve in the region to the Hold.

"What about the new swordsmen?" Maradon's second act had been to pass a law requiring one son of all highborn to join the ranks of the swordsmen. Even an only son.

"They're doing well. Many had arms training at home. All came with good horses as you commanded."

The reluctance of the landowners to send their best horses to the Hold only fueled his resolve that Lacedar needed the exceptional horses and rich pastures of northern Thiery. His father had argued that their lands and pastures were enough. Maradon had known better. The argument had been a point of bitter contention between them for years.

"How soon?"

"Another week at the earliest before the men are ready."

Maradon balled his right hand into a fist and cracked the knuckles. Finances, the slow-learning recruits and, some days, the world in general seemed out to frustrate him. He had waited his whole life for this and he didn't want to wait anymore.

"Have the men been getting their history lessons?" He had drawn up the syllabus himself. Soldiers wouldn't fight with true fervor unless they shared his goal to restore Lacedar to her past glory.

"Yes, Bealdor. Some are still unconvinced about taking Bern by force, though not overtly. I have their names from the regiment leaders."

Maradon ground his teeth against the thought that Bron might be numbered among them. Bron was too like Vrenun, weak-spirited. But he was the successor now. If Maradon must hammer Bron against the anvil of his will to shape him to be the ruler Baes would have been, he would.

"I will give you your week with them. No more. Then we ride."

He gave one last look at the training fields. Lacedar would have the element of surprise. As long as they maintained that, they could capture Bern with minimal losses. The town was pitifully unprotected, far from Thiery Hold, and the villagers would put up little, if any, fight against an army. Once they took the village they would have hostages, supplies, and cover. Thiery Hold would risk losses too great to retake it.

In one week, Bern would be his.

Tirren slid the edge of his sword across the armory's grinding stone, careful not to thin the blade. The whine of the metal on stone and the repetition of the chore allowed his mind to wander as he smoothed the small chips along the edge. Not surprisingly, it wandered to Yslaaran.

He was dreaming of her nightly again, waking sweating and hard, aching for the feel of her. Strangely, though, during the daytime, when he thought of her it was with more contentment—still mixed with desire, but different than the deep painful longing he had become accustomed to over the years. The words and genuine affection that had passed between them had acted as a salve, soothing an old and deep wound.

He slipped again into the rut of counting how many days it had been since he'd seen her, and wondering when she might come to them again. Realizing where his thoughts had drifted, he made himself stop. It had been more than a month already and, though she had promised Chayan that she would return soon, Tirren knew that time passed differently for her. One cycle of Hrar would be as nothing. His lifetime would be little more.

Tirren moved from the grinding stone to a nearby table and ran a whetstone along the blade to finish the edge. Chayan must be wondering at least as obsessively if and when she would return. His son's restraint in not having mentioned it once since the morning of the fight with Erimar surprised and impressed him.

Tirren held no illusions about a future with Yslaaran, but he hoped to see her at least once more, when she returned to talk to Chayan. He swept the stone with smooth, steady strokes, and tried not to wonder what would happen when Chayan told her of the Bealdor's decision. Likely, she would vanish until Chayan became Bealdor, after Tirren was dead and burned on his funeral bier.

Finished with the blade, he walked back to the Hold for a late breakfast. He was nearly at the door when a messenger rider arrived at a gallop through the front gate, scattering chickens and people alike in the courtyard. Tirren had been headed for a side entrance, but jogged around now to the front to meet the messenger. He felt no alarm; messengers always arrived at a gallop. At least, he felt none until he saw the expression on the rider's face.

"Ho, messenger!" Tirren hailed him, as the man called out for someone to fetch the Bealdor.

Recognizing Tirren as Beodan, the rider dismounted and pulled a rolled sheaf from his bag, thrusting it at him. "An urgent message for the Bealdor from Kesum-Aramon."

Cold swept through Tirren as he took the paper. The last message from the magistrate in Bern had been a follow-up report of the attempted horse raid that Shen's patrol had thwarted, at the cost of Aeson's life, and a request for a full company of twenty-five soldiers to remain near Bern. Shen was currently commanding the company stationed there.

Tirren told the messenger to wait and entered the Hold. He addressed the first servant he saw, a boy near to manhood, polishing the armor on the walls in a nearby room.

"Do you know where the Bealdor is?"

The boy looked up, his mouth hanging open in surprise at Tirren's tone.

"I'm here." His father's deep voice came from behind him. Tirren turned to see him striding down the hall from the library, a soldier from the battlements at his side. The soldier must have seen the messenger arrive. His father wordlessly held out his hand for the rolled sheaf and broke the seal.

Reading the missive, Erimar's face paled. "Hessura and Fresshe help us," he whispered, "Maradon has certainly wasted no time." He handed the sheaf back to Tirren. "Get Jaron, Findal, and the regiment leaders of the swordsmen," his father snapped to the soldier. "Have them meet me in the council chambers."

Tirren's gut clenched. He scanned the note he held.

Bealdor,

I write to you in great haste. A trader from Bern, peddling goods in Lacedar, has sent grave news. He was traveling from Col on the small east road, nearing the intersection of the main road to Lacedar Hold, when he topped a rise and saw the Lacedar army. They were traveling south on the main road, headed for Thiery's border.

The man sent his son overland on one of the wagon horses to bring this message. The boy was young and excitable, but by his count I believe it may be Lacedar's entire contingent of swordsmen.

I beseech you to send your soldiers as quickly as possible. The pastures of Bern have been Lacedar's target in the past and I fear for our people there, if not for Bern itself.

Your servant,

High Councilor Aramon

Tirren followed Erimar as he hurried out the doors to where the messenger stood waiting. "Quill and ink!" Erimar barked, as the man began to bend knee to him. The messenger abandoned the obeisance and ran to his saddlebags, providing writing tools and papyrus.

Erimar scratched out two quick notes and handed them to the messenger. "For the lives of our men, ride with all speed to Kesum-Shen, the commander of the company of soldiers stationed in Bern. Once delivered, take the second note to Aramon. Go, man!"

The messenger paused only to stuff the messages and writing tools back in his saddlebags. Mounting his sweat-drenched horse, he spurred the horse out the gates of the Hold. The nearest messenger post stood at the edge of Thiery Village; he wouldn't have far to go before a fresh messenger and mount were on their way to Bern.

Tirren followed Erimar to the council chambers. Chayan met them in the hallway by the stairs. "I heard a messenger had come." Chayan had taken note of every messenger to arrive since his trip to Relendel.

Tirren nodded. "Lacedar marches on us." It couldn't have been what Chayan expected to hear, and he was proud he took the news like a soldier. Chayan fell in behind them as they continued to the council room. Jaron arrived a moment later, with Caine and Mathom arriving breathless soon after.

Tirren took a seat at his father's right, and Chayan next to him, though Erimar remained standing. He gave them no time to assemble before he began. He briefed them on the message as others filed into the room and took chairs around the big, oak table, then handed the message to Jaron to read in detail.

Findal, the Captain of the Foot Soldiers entered, flushed from hurrying from the training fields. Jaron passed the note to him. Like his men, Findal was not highborn, but he had been a soldier since his youth and had learned his letters as he advanced. He sat his lanky body sideways in a chair, reading slowly. He blew on the hairs of his thick, drooping gray moustache as he finished, the moustache that had served as inspiration for the facial hair so many of the foot soldiers sported.

Erimar continued. "I have sent two messages: one to Shen in Bern and one to Bern's Councilor, Aramon. Shen has been instructed to get to the bridge and fire it, to force Lacedar's army to cross at one of the other two bridges. Traveling either east to Panden or west to Eanor's border will buy us time. Aramon's message instructs that he hide the elderly and young and get the rest together behind barricades with what weapons they have. I also instructed that if our army doesn't arrive in time, Aramon must do whatever necessary to save his people."

Tirren lowered his gaze. His father's implication of surrender was clear. Bern, like most villages, wasn't walled and wouldn't be able to hold out, even for a short time.

Jaron spoke into the heavy silence. "Even if Shen fires the bridge, the enemy may reach Bern before us."

"How quickly can you muster?" Erimar said. "When could we expect to reach Bern?"

"If enough swordsmen can be gathered to leave by afternoon and we push the horses hard, perhaps we could reach Bern in the morning. And pray to Hessura the horses and men have enough left in them for the fighting," Jaron answered.

"Why not send all the men we can right now?" Mathom interjected, looking from Erimar to Jaron.

"We dare not leave with too few or we'll make a bad situation worse," Jaron answered. "There are seventy swordsmen currently at the Hold and another eighty swordsmen near enough to Thiery Village to be able to reach us soon. We can take as many of the foot soldiers as can find mounts."

Tirren did the numbers. Of the hundred swordsmen who normally lived at the Hold, including Jaron and the regiment leaders, twenty-five were already in Bern and five more were somewhere in the Southlands on routine patrol.

Tirren's father had never made service mandatory, but he had doubled the ranks of his soldiers in the past twenty years to four regiments of fifty swordsmen each and one hundred foot soldiers. The soldiers at the Hold were expensive to keep and Tirren had wondered sometimes if there was truly need for so many when they generally did no more than assist the towns in maintaining order with the frequent presence of patrols. Thiery had been a peaceful region for generations, with no threat of invasion by sea or from Bansheen possible, but Lacedar's horse raids years ago had put Erimar on edge. He had insisted on a strong army ever since.

"I'll send the muster call out immediately," Jaron continued, "but swords from the more distant areas will be spread out on the road behind us. The trader's message didn't give us an actual count. We don't know if Maradon brought all his sword troops or only some. Or if, like us, he'll have put some foot soldiers on horses."

"Findal," Tirren said, "how many of your men have or can get horses?" Most of the foot owned no horses as they had been left with their families to work the farms.

Findal answered in a voice that seemed too gruff for such a stork-like man. "Only a small portion could lay hands on a horse by the time we leave."

"Find out from Dalwer how many mounts he can round up for you," Erimar said.

Findal stood, opened the door, and spoke with the soldier from the wall posted outside. A small contingent of uthow, boys young enough to still wear their hair cropped short, milled around as well, awaiting orders. At a gesture from the soldier one of these took off at a run to find the Master of Horse.

Jaron continued, "Even if we don't need the foot to make up our numbers, it would still help us to have some archers for a first volley, and handy in case they flank us somehow. We should bring all we can."

Erimar looked to them all in turn for further input. Tirren glanced around the table at the others. He wished he had something to add but he was as inexperienced at war as the rest of them.

"Very well. Jaron, send out the muster and get the men here ready. Tirren, you'll organize the supplies we'll need to take with us and wagons to follow with re-supplies. Caine, find Shen's second and tell him he'll lead Shen's regiment. Oversee them when your own regiment is readied."

Tirren signaled to Chayan that his place would be with him. Erimar continued, "Findal, get as many of your men together as you can. Your best archers. Haste is all; we can only pray Shen's company will receive our message in time."

───── ⟨∾⟩ ─────

Tirren saw that Jaron's estimate had been accurate; working at a fevered pitch, most of the men arriving from the outlying areas were accounted for by early afternoon. Soldiers formed up in their regiments outside the walls, readying to depart. Tirren tapped Midnight's flanks with his heels and guided him forward to the front of his own regiment.

Between Findal and Dalwer, nearly sixty of the foot soldiers had horses to ride. The swordsmen coming from farther afield would need to follow as best they could. The re-supply wagons would be the last to arrive, bringing most of the remainder of the foot soldiers with the supplies, leaving only a small contingent at the Hold. It was unlikely the extra foot would see any fighting—a prolonged battle didn't seem likely, whatever the outcome.

Without fanfare, Tirren's father rode to the front of the line and started forward. The ranks of horse soldiers fell in behind him.

The Bealdors of the land may never have known war, but the old kings had ridden light horse to battle, and his father honored that tradition now. Tirren had seen it depicted often enough in the tapestries, but seeing his father at the head of an army, helmed and on light horse, chilled him. He took consolation from the fact that his father would command from a safe vantage, and would be on a fleet horse if things went poorly.

Tirren came next in the formation, with Chayan beside him. Chayan had always been a natural hand with a horse and rode at his side with a light grace; his bow slung across his back, two full quivers at his hip and a quarterstaff through a saddle loop beneath his leg. Chayan would remain a member of Tirren's regiment until he was old enough to command his own, another small piece of mind that Tirren should be able to keep him in sight during the fighting.

The remaining column of men snaked forward. Erimar set a pace the heavier horses could maintain, but only just. Tirren urged Midnight to a slow canter and the horses behind him stretched out to match it. The ground shook with the thunder of hooves, the horses blissfully unaware of how long they would hold the punishing pace. The ranks spread out along the road behind the Bealdor, each sword regiment following a leader they could identify by their elaborate battle helms, unlike the plain chain mail hoods of the swordsmen.

Like his father's stag-horned helm, Tirren wore one he had inherited from an ancestor, its eagle's beak at his brow and the narrow, upraised wings at the sides. Before this, he had only worn the heavy thing for ceremony. He felt a strange division now, riding hard toward the border and an enemy, as if some part of his ancestor rode with him, looking out through the eyes of the eagle. An ancestor who had known a lifetime of war.

Caine came next with a helm decorated with a boar's head and tusks, his regiment behind him; Mathom followed in a helm with the top fashioned into the head and shoulders of a bear, claws rising above either side. Heras came last, leading Shen's regiment, his commander's wolf helm fastened to the saddle.

Stretched out behind the swordsmen were the sixty-odd foot soldiers led by Findal, riding their wide assortment of mounts with varied skill. Their equestrian skills non-withstanding, they were easy to pick out by their large-ringed mail shirts over the thick leather jerkins. Some had plain metal helms, many dented or worse, though most wore only thick leather caps. Tirren felt a pang of guilt at bringing the disadvantaged foot soldiers, not suited to the kind of fighting they were likely to face, but they were soldiers like the rest and this was their duty as much as it was the duty of the sword. Far behind the foot soldiers, the wagons fell out of sight in the dust of the army's pace.

Tirren thought of the ride he made from Relendel to the Hold, returning from escorting Dashara. The men had goaded each other to make the twenty-five-league ride in less than two days, and had accounted that challenging. Now they would need to cover twenty leagues or more in nearly half that time.

He only hoped they could do it or Bern would surely be lost. He dared not even think about Shen.

Chapter Sixteen

S hen rubbed at his eyes, finished the last two lines of his report, and started on the patrol schedule for the following week.

The window shutter above him hung partially opened to vent the smoke from the brazier, but open, it let enough cold air into the small hut to negate the heat. He thought about closing it, then admitted that if he put his pen down, he might not pick it up again. Paperwork had always been the most tedious aspect of command, and less pleasant still with the smoke, writing by candlelight, and the unstable surface—a board across two rickety supports. He rubbed his burning eyes again.

He guessed the hour to be past the second bell of the night, though he couldn't hear Bern's bell from the patrol hut. His second shift had arrived back recently and were milling about, changing and unpacking. Most of the other soldiers were already asleep. Shen enjoyed patrol, but being stuffed in a hut with a full company was vastly different from the traveling he loved. At least there were only five days left of their fortnight rotation before the replacement company arrived.

He looked over the previous patrol schedule and mentally shifted the men to the next rotation. Six soldiers traveling west to Eanor's border and six east to Wayden, taking two days to reach their destination and two to return. The other twelve swordsmen would stay near Bern, patrolling along the road above the horse pastures, day and night, in three rotating groups. When the soldiers returned from the borders, the two groups would switch again. Shen couldn't stomach the thought of spending all his time in the hut, and would continue riding out to the pastures with the morning group.

He set his pen down and cocked his head to the right, to the west wall of the hut, concentrating to hear over the snoring, and the soft banter and thump and rustle of the men still awake. The hut was crowded tonight; the border patrols had returned earlier this evening, so the only men out were the four on night patrol of the pastures. Still listening, he plugged the inkpot, certain he'd heard a fast-approaching horse.

Shen slid carefully out from the wobbly desk and walked outside. Summer had almost arrived, the days steadily warming and the spring rains slowing, but the nights were still brisk. His body heat dissipated in the cool air but he didn't go back for his cloak. He'd been right about the hoofbeats, and they were growing louder. The moons, both nearly two-thirds full, illuminated a lone rider approaching from the direction of Bern. As he neared, Shen recognized the light horse and tan cloak of a messenger.

He walked to meet the messenger, and was surprised when the man didn't dismount. The horse pranced as the messenger produced a rolled sheaf. "I bear a message from the Bealdor for Kesum-Shen."

"I am Shen," he said, reaching for the paper. He unrolled the sheaf and read quickly. At the arrival of a messenger, Shen had half-expected bad news, but this was worse than he could have guessed. Lacedar's army headed straight for them. Shen and his twenty-four men were all that stood between them and Bern.

"Wait here," he said to the man. "You'll come with us."

"Kesum, I cannot!" The man squirmed and his horse danced sideways, as eager to be on the way as his rider. "I have a message yet to deliver, from the Bealdor to High Councilor Aramon."

"Then send your other messenger to meet me at the edge of town on the Great Road." Two messengers were always on duty at each post, and one man would do as well as another.

"As you will, Kesum." And he was off, the horse kicking clods of earth as it sprang into a gallop back the way it had come.

Shen wanted to sit down and read the missive again, to digest it and think through the options. What he wanted made no difference; there wasn't a moment to lose. He opened the door of the hut.

"On your feet! All of you," he shouted. Those still awake turned startled glances to him; those sleeping roused. "Lacedar's army approaches."

Men jerked to their feet, grabbing clothes and gear as he barked orders for the supplies they needed to bring. By the time Shen was saddling Bayone, his swordsmen were pouring out of the hut. Once saddled and mounted, the company reached the Great Road within minutes. The relief messenger waited there for him and they wordlessly gathered him up as they rode by without slowing. Shen loosed a tight breath of relief as they cantered into town and he saw no sign of the invading army.

Aramon had already acted on the message he'd received. Lights shone through open windows and people ran through the streets, spreading the word. Shen ordered four of his men to stay and help the village prepare, then headed north for the bridge with the rest of his men and the messenger.

He rode more slowly and quietly as they approached the White River, staying well to the left of the road until the bridge came into sight. His orders had been to destroy the bridge if Lacedar's army hadn't crossed yet. He had calculated the earliest soldiers could arrive from Thiery and knew he'd be lucky if help came by dawn. If he burned the bridge now and Maradon's men were near enough to see, they could set a hard pace all the way to Panden and back and be here hours before Thiery's army could arrive. Their best advantage was that Lacedar didn't know Thiery had been warned. Shen decided to delay firing the bridge as long as possible—and the gods be with them if he proved wrong.

He turned to the messenger, a young, nervous boy looking to be in his mid-teens.

"Stay with me unless we encounter any fighting," Shen said, keeping his voice low. "At the first sign of trouble, ride south until you find the Bealdor, and tell him how things stand. If we have to engage Lacedar's army, we'll die buying what time we can, but with our numbers that won't be much. The Bealdor must know if the bridge is down and where the enemy is."

The messenger nodded, too anxious to answer.

The vegetation grew thick along the shore. Willow trees and tall shrubs thrived on the water, and large oaks and cedars filled in the gaps. Shen moved his men to the thickest part of the trees on the east side of the bridge. In a whisper, he instructed his two best scouts to ride east and west, to look for signs of Lacedar's army.

Shen dismounted from Bayone and motioned for the others to do the same. He sent word down the line to hide the horses in the trees and have two men station themselves near the bridge to watch for any sign of the enemy on the road. Having calculated the distances though, and the timing of the messages, he felt it more likely that Lacedar's army was camped nearby, resting and waiting for daylight.

He watched the quiet darkness beyond the river to a count of two hundred. Feeling as certain as he could that Lacedar had no soldiers or scouts on the road north of the bridge, he sent another two men bellying across the bridge. They carried rags with them to wrap around the supporting posts at the far end and a jug of oil to pour over the rags and boards. A final pair of soldiers did the same at this near end of the bridge. He would have preferred to wait until the scouts returned with their report, but he dared not delay readying the bridge to burn. Already he risked too much.

Shortly after the men finished with the bridge, the west scout returned like a shadow. He appeared out of the trees a hundred paces from them, leading his horse, and silently made his way to Shen.

"They are close," he said quietly, "not half a league downriver. You were right, Kesum; though I couldn't hear much with the distance and the river, or see them well for the trees over there, they seem not to be moving. There were no torches or campfires, but I could make out some horses picketed. I think they're camped there and have been for long enough to be settled in. On my way back to tell you, I spotted one of their scouts near the river and moving this way, not far from where the river turns." He indicated the distant bend in the river with a wave of his arm. Shen could see it through a thinning in the trees and the light of the moons reflected in sparkles on the water. The scout continued, "I waited for him to pass my position, then returned as quietly as possible. I didn't see him coming back again. He may be near."

Shen nodded his understanding and put a hand on the scout's shoulder. All of his company—and the still-nervous messenger—were gathered together now except for the scout that had gone east, the soldiers he had left in Bern, and the four men on their routine patrol. Leaving the men on patrol had been another calculated risk, but Shen decided better to leave them there than sending others to find them and try and bring them back without attracting attention. By now they should be nearly to the pastures, far west of here, out of danger of ambush.

Shen sent the scout back to watch Lacedar's camp and give warning if they stirred. He addressed the rest of the men in a low voice. "Sit tight and keep your horses quiet. We'll stay here unless their army moves."

They were in an area of good cover and still close enough to fire the bridge with flaming arrows if Lacedar broke camp. The horses made a large enough herd that they were unlikely to whinny at noises or at horses they might smell across the river.

The east scout returned with nothing to report. The company settled with sentries posted in all directions. The men remained alert through the long, quiet hours of the night; the palpable threat of an army camped nearly within sight proved a powerful stimulant. Shen moved like a shadow among them.

Less than a quarter of the night remained until the dawn bell, when a shout suddenly broke the silence.

"Fire the bridge!" The shout came, loud and jarring, from the scout Shen had set to watch the enemy camp. He rode toward them at a gallop, shouting at the top of his lungs.

"Fire the bridge!" Shen repeated the scout's words as an order, and men exploded into action. Arrowheads dipped into the pots of oil and were touched to the hot coals they had brought from the hut in a pot of sand. A dozen arrows hit the bridge with a sound like hail, and flames burst up from both sides. Shen heard shouting from the Lacedar camp.

Shen's scout pulled up hard, his horse half-rearing. "I'm sorry, Kesum, one of their sentries spotted me when my horse shied at a fox."

Within moments the old, dry wood of the bridge burned strongly at either end. A distant sound of fast moving horses came from across the river. Shen looked to the bridge again, willing it to burn faster.

———— ⟩⟨ ————

Maradon cuffed his scout hard across the face. None of them had suspected anyone so close to the river, but the man had been a fool to let himself be seen. Hitting the scout didn't make him feel any

better, nor did it help answer why a soldier was watching this area
in the middle of the night. Worse, his scout had seen a single man,
which meant a scout from Thiery rather than a patrol. And a scout
implied a larger force nearby.

He cursed fluently, impelling the army to break camp. Men
scattered and ran for their horses, leaving possessions strewn across
the ground. Maradon bellowed for his horse. He mounted up as
another of his scouts galloped to his side. The man's horse pranced,
and he had to shout over the clamor of breaking camp.

"Bealdor, there are flames ahead. I saw them through the trees.
Up there, by the bridge." He pulled at the reins to keep his horse
from bolting and nodded up the road.

Maradon had come here in strength. He didn't need, nor had
he wanted, the cover of night for this attack. He had planned to
ride just before dawn and take Bern at first light. Thiery's patrol
knowing about them was a complication, but if the bridge were to
be destroyed it would be far more than a complication. And he was
not a man accepting of complications.

Not waiting for the army to organize, he shouted to the soldiers
that were ready and rode like a man possessed, trying to make the
bridge in time. A small voice reasoned that it wouldn't be wise to
be separated from the bulk of his army, but anger burned him to his
bones. He raced onward.

His personal guard, on light horses like himself, surrounded
him. The rest of the men followed as well as they could, strung
out haphazardly. He saw before they reached the bridge that it had
caught already. The two ends were engulfed in flames and the near
corner listed heavily toward the river. Pulling to a halt, he shouted
an order to his guard. They continued east, past the bridge at a
gallop, never slowing. Across the river, lit by the flames he had set,
sat a large soldier on a dapple-gray horse. His long hair fluttered in
the breeze of the fire.

The soldier who had beheaded Baes.

The smell of smoke and heat of the flames washed over Shen as he sat astride Bayone, watching the bridge burn. The first of Lacedar's soldiers to appear were mounted on light horses. They continued at a gallop, past the bridge and eastward, never slowing. All but one. A man in an elk-horned helm. He stayed within the edge of the trees, well back from the river's edge and out of accurate bowshot across the dark waters. Only a foot soldier's longbow would have endangered him, and he knew it.

The flickering light of the flames played across his helm. For a moment, the reflection of the fire in the swift moving river lit the man's face and Shen thought black eyes blazed straight at him. He knew it was Maradon, even before the man's regiment leaders arrived and reigned in a semi-circle behind him.

Maradon's deep voice carried across the water above the sound of the dying bridge. "You have only delayed your death!" With a shout and a gesture, his army followed him east at a canter.

Shen released a tight breath. "Well, at least we've annoyed them," he said to the messenger at his side. He tried not to think of how close they had come to disaster. Had the bridge burned one whit slower, he and all his men would lie slaughtered on this bank now, while Lacedar's army rode over their bodies and headed for Bern. He watched the mass of Maradon's army pass through the flickering shadows of dark and light, a stream of men and beasts, looking like the legendary Wild Hunt of the Elves.

"Kesum, shouldn't we be riding for Panden?" one of his men asked.

Shen pulled his eyes away from the far shore where the last regiment still passed by with a thundering of hooves. "No. Maradon has already sent his guard on to secure that bridge. On heavy horse we couldn't hope to beat them. Even if I sent our messenger to warn Panden, Maradon's guards would be there quicker. I'd only be sending men to their deaths. Bern is his goal. The best we can do is to help Bern ready itself and pray that the Bealdor arrives soon."

Pre-dawn painted the clouds on the horizon deep orange and the rising ball of the sun washed them pale again. Shen leaned against a hay bale barricade straining to see down the road in the growing light, anxious to know which army would arrive first.

A soldier on top of Bern's two-story inn suddenly let out a shout; dust on the Great Road to the south of the village. A cheer went up from the villagers stationed with their hunting bows in every upper story window and from the villagers with cudgels and swords behind Shen's soldiers at each of the barricades.

"Go now, appraise the Bealdor," Shen told the messenger who had stayed at his side through the night.

The man leapt to his horse and jumped the low barricade. Shen called to his soldiers to ready themselves to ride.

By the time his company had mounted up and waited at the road, Shen could make out the lines of Thiery's soldiers. He saw the messenger reach the head of the column. The boy spun his horse to fall in next to the stag-helmed figure riding at the head.

The villagers gave another strong cheer as the army rode past, nearly two hundred strong, never slowing. The messenger peeled off, scattering men as he re-entered the village. "Evacuate," the messenger was shouting. "By the Bealdor's orders, everyone is to ride south to Leighton."

Shen signaled his men forward, and his company fell in at the side of the column riding past. His men found their places among the ranks as the army turned onto the narrow road heading east toward Panden. Shen cantered to the front and rode just behind Tirren in case the Beodan or the Bealdor needed to speak with him. When the army had gone perhaps half a league out of town and into open land nearing the patrol hut, Erimar threw up a hand and the column pulled to a halt.

It was the first chance Shen had to really take in the condition of the army and the horses. It shocked him. Tirren's horse was trembling, slicked so wet with sweat it might have swum here. The dust on its coat had mixed with the sweat to make mud, and thick, white froth smeared its coat wherever girth, rein, or strap touched. Tirren was in little better shape than his horse. His lips looked dry enough to crack, and dark circles beneath his eyes spoke eloquently of his soreness and fatigue.

Shen nudged his horse closer. Tirren gave him his half-smile and a satisfied nod. Shen wished he could feel a measure of pride at bringing his men alive through the night and delaying Maradon, but he felt only fear at what might yet come. Tirren hadn't seen Lacedar's army pass in the night like a black torrent, raging through the dark.

"I'm glad you arrived when you did," Shen said to him. "Even at this cost."

"I just hope our mounts will make it the rest of the way." His words came out hoarse.

Shen suspected Tirren had taken less care of himself on the ride than of Midnight.

"My father wants you." Tirren tipped his head toward Erimar and Shen turned to see the Bealdor motioning him over.

Shen approached, and Erimar stood stiffly in the stirrups, looking down the road ahead. He croaked an order to Jaron to have the men water and grain their horses as quickly as possible. Shen could see that whatever the strain on the men, it was worse on the

Bealdor, the oldest man on this field and carrying the full weight of responsibility for this day.

Erimar dismounted with difficulty and walked his horse to the river. Shen followed. He filled the Bealdor in on the events of the night, giving his best estimate of where Maradon's army might be now. Likely not far from Panden's bridge on Lacedar's side, he thought. Jaron and Tirren watered their horses on his other side, listening intently to Shen's report.

"Do we fight here?" Tirren asked his father.

"No. We ride on," Erimar said. "The closer we are to Panden when we meet, the better to drive them back over the bridge."

"Kesum," Shen heard a familiar voice behind him and turned to see Heras holding out his helm, the snarling metal wolf's head cresting it. He hadn't worn the thing since Chayan's coming-of-age day. He donned it and the reality of what they faced ahead settled on his head with a weight far heavier than the helm.

Chapter Seventeen

Tirren felt as if he had spent the sleepless night being beaten with heavy sticks. Of all the men around him, Chayan alone moved with his usual grace. He worried most about the physical punishment his father had taken, but they had no options except to ride onward. His father was right, the closer to the eastern bridge they could met Lacedar's army, the better.

The break felt far too brief to do much good. He gave Midnight a long drink at the river and a few handfuls of grain, checked his legs and feet, wrapped two swollen joints, and removed stones from his hooves. Once re-mounted, he took a mouthful of dried meat and hard bread for himself as they set out once again.

Even the best-trained horses balked at cinch straps being snugged and riders mounting again. Tirren would have felt less guilt had Midnight resisted, but the horse allowed him up easily, though he hung his head and Tirren felt his legs moving rhythmically with Midnight's deep, heaving wheezes. He would have prayed not to ride his horse to death before this ended, but there were no gods left to which he could send his prayer.

The pace remained brutal when they continued, but an air of alertness returned to the men, knowing the enemy was close. The land changed from the open pastures and small oak-covered hills to evergreen forests, heralding the foothills of the mountains. They neared Panden, and a faint hope rose in Tirren that perhaps Maradon had abandoned his mad course after the bridge was burned. At the least, maybe Lacedar hadn't pushed as hard as Thiery. If they could only reach Panden Bridge first, there would be no fighting.

His hopes were dashed a few minutes later as a cloud of dust appeared not far down the road. The rumble of hooves that had been masked by their own horses, could be heard now, as well as felt. Erimar threw up one hand, signaling a halt. Jaron turned and rode along the column, bellowing commands. Hearing his father's order to form up, Tirren made a hand signal that sent his men out in a wide formation to either side of the Bealdor.

The foot soldiers jounced past, riding to the front on their wide assortment of horses. Findal rode at their side on a badly lamed dray mare, barking orders that had his men dismounting and stringing their longbows. They lined up across the road in rows, spaced widely enough to allow the swordsmen to ride between if necessary.

The approaching army slowed. Tirren easily picked Maradon out at the front by his light horse, helm, and guard. A grim smile touched Tirren's lips, seeing the man shocked to stillness by the size of the force blocking his path. His head swung side to side as he said something to the men on either side of him. Even at this distance, Tirren could hear his muffled shouting.

The two armies were closely matched. Tirren had two hundred and fifty men at his back, but Lacedar had apparently been fortifying their ranks lately also. By his best guess, Maradon had perhaps close to three hundred soldiers with him, all swordsmen by the look of them, and mounted on heavy horse.

Chayan rode up between Tirren and Erimar, guiding his horse with his knees and holding his bow across his thighs. An arrow lay notched in the string. "I could hit him from here, Bealdor. Twenty paces closer, I could take him through the heart." Tirren knew what he said was no youthful boast.

Erimar gestured for Chayan to hold and spoke a word to his guard. He touched his horse's flanks and moved forward alone. He closed approximately a quarter of the distance to Lacedar's army and stopped. A moment later Maradon did the same, bringing the two of them within hailing distance. Erimar's voice came out hoarse and strained, but carried well enough through the quiet morning to be heard.

"You have raided our border and stolen our livestock. Now you break the peace of a hundred and a half years by bringing an army to our lands. You will not achieve your purpose here, Maradon. Our forces are here to meet you and more still come. Take your army from Thiery's soil before it runs red with your blood."

Maradon's hands clenched on the reins and his gaze swept the lines of men. His attention paused somewhere behind and left of Erimar and his face darkened further. Tirren turned to see what had caught the man's attention, but saw only Shen's regiment, spread out to his left.

"How can I be sure you won't attack our rear as we retreat?" Maradon shouted back.

"I wouldn't spend the lives of my men needlessly. But I make this offer only once. Take it while you may, and we will escort you back to the border."

Maradon turned his horse back to his lines. Tirren couldn't see any sane course of action for Lacedar except retreat, though he didn't entirely trust Maradon to sanity. Erimar rode back to his own vanguard and looked from Tirren to Jaron. He shook his head in uncertainty.

Maradon kept his back turned while he conferred with his commanders. Two peeled out and rode down either side of the column spreading orders too muffled for Tirren to hear. Maradon continued to talk with his other men at the front of the lines. At last, Maradon shot them a baleful look and turned his horse. The rest of the column fell in behind him. Tirren watched with cautious optimism as the column began to move in a wide arc.

They never completed the turn.

Understanding hit Tirren just as Maradon's front lines broke and ran for the cover of the trees along the river.

Erimar spurred his horse with a shout, and the army burst into action.

Tirren jerked Midnight to the left, trying to keep up with his father's lighter and faster horse. Gauging the distance, he saw that Lacedar would make it into the trees first, but not by enough to set even a rudimentary ambush.

His mind raced with strategy as Midnight left the road, navigating the rough ground and the deadfall. Maradon's men had also spent a sleepless night and rode tired mounts, though not as near to exhaustion as Thiery's. The trees were moderately spaced here with little undergrowth. The cover would offer the same advantage and disadvantage to both armies with one notable exception—Thiery's foot soldiers would be essentially useless. Archers would be unable to dismount and use their longbows, and if they remained mounted, their short-swords for hand-to-hand battle would be vulnerable to the swordsmen's broadswords.

Midnight stumbled over a downed log, nearly sending them both to the ground. Tirren pulled back hard on the bit, raising the horse's head enough to recover his footing. Jaron rode in front of him and their army crashed through the forest behind him, trying to cut off the enemy before they could organize. Midnight's labored heartbeat drummed against his calf.

Erimar stopped just beyond the tree line. Tirren rode past at a canter, noting the spot where his father and his guard set up their command post. Erimar would be safer here than on the field of battle, but Tirren felt a pang at leaving him with only a few men, as regiment after regiment rode past him and away.

Lacedar formed their battle lines immediately after entering the trees. Jaron pointed with his sword, sending regiments to their places and indicating Tirren was to take the far right. Shen and Mathom commanded the center regiments, and Caine the left wing. Tirren had learned battle strategy along with all his other training to be a ruler, but Jaron had made the study of war-craft his life and Tirren felt grateful to have him in charge.

Findal's gruff voice came from behind, calling all the foot to him and rallying them north, away from the lines. Tirren had no time to wonder what Findal planned. He was still swinging his men into formation when the front lines of the two armies clashed.

<hr/>

Maradon hoped the forest would be enough to incapacitate Thiery's damn foot soldiers but, even if it didn't, he knew the extra men in his sword ranks gave him the greater strength. He didn't doubt Erimar's boast that more Thiery forces were on the way, but he would never tuck tail and run while he held the advantage.

If he accomplished nothing else, he must take this opportunity to avenge Baes. He'd had seen the big, long-haired soldier at the front of Thiery's ranks. Lacedar may not get Bern today, but Thiery would bleed before he left this land.

He'd pointed out the big soldier with the wolf's head helm to his key men, as well as making sure they recognized Erimar's son and the one he guessed to be his grandson, from age, description and his position between Erimar and Tirren in the lines. If that old ass, Erimar, or his son, Tirren, found out what it felt like to lose a son, then today would be sweeter still, but if he only got one, he wanted the wolf.

He wondered again how Thiery's army had appeared here to thwart him. The only explanation he could see was that the big, son-of-a-whore soldier must have broken the covenant of the regions and crossed the border to spy on them, and then sent word to the Hold.

Maradon threaded his way to the highest ground available, his personal guard following. He knew he'd have to retreat soon, to save the strength of his army for another day, but he'd sacrifice as many men as it took to achieve at least one of his objectives.

———— ⧆ ————

The two front lines collided. The impact, horse to horse, sword to sword, jarred Tirren to his teeth. Within minutes, the forest smelled of trampled pine needles, blood, and sweat. Horses and men screamed, swords rang like bells. Perhaps the battle exercises he'd practiced since his youth helped him or perhaps men had war written on their souls, but he slashed and cut through the mayhem like everyone else. He risked a glance to his right for Chayan, worried as he couldn't use broadsword or chain mail. He worried even more when he couldn't find him.

The regiment held its ground, and some of the front lines managed to cut forward into Lacedar's ranks. The killing was bloody and awkward, utterly unlike the contests and tournaments he'd had championed at the Hold. He slashed and stabbed until his blade was red. He won his way to the right, nearer to where Chayan should be and glanced around again, still not seeing him. Three soldiers rushed him at once, driving him to the left.

Tirren had seldom practiced with multiple opponents. One mistake and he'd never see Chayan grow into his manhood. He wouldn't be around to protect his son or his father. He would never see Yslaaran again. Fear gave his arm the strength he needed.

He crippled one man quickly and inelegantly, stabbing at his hip, behind the chain mail chaps he knew lay beneath the leather. Parrying with the second soldier, Midnight balked at the press of horses and men. The big horse reared—bringing Tirren out of sword range—and smashed down on the lower legs of his opponent's horse, causing it to fall to a knee and throw the rider.

Tirren spurred Midnight, intending to trample the man, but the third soldier landed a blow past his guard. He deflected it with a desperate up-thrust. The enemy's sword caught one of the high wings on Tirren's helm, striking the helm from his head with a snap of the leather chin strap, wrenching his neck viciously. He fought for his balance and brought his blade down, cleaving the man's right shoulder at the neck. Two more men rode toward him, but he spotted Thiery's blue diamond on their chests, men from his regiment fighting to his side.

He looked for Chayan again and spotted him finally, not far to his right. Chayan rode with his knees, using his modified bow, each arrow finding a target. As Tirren watched, a knot of men rushed Chayan, trying to get inside his range. He spurred Midnight forward, but another Lacedar soldier cut him off. He caught a glimpse of Chayan slinging the bow over his shoulder and laying about him with his quarterstaff—another weapon not meant for use from horseback.

Tirren dispatched his opponent, as his second in command killed one of the men surrounding Chayan. Chayan unhorsed the other three, losing only the end of his quarterstaff to a sword blow. His mount, Star, leapt into a clear space and Chayan took up his bow again. As long as his back was protected and he had arrows left, no one would get near him again.

Looking ahead, Tirren saw trees past the Lacedar soldiers in front of him. Trees and Thiery's foot soldiers. His regiment had cut through nearly to Lacedar's rear line and Findal's men trapped them from the rear. Findal must have led his men to the river, then east, flanking both armies of swordsmen. The foot soldiers' numbers looked diminished, but they still posed a substantial threat. The rear of Lacedar's army tried to push into Thiery's forces, but arrows rained down on their backs. They found themselves unable to face both attacks at once.

The battle surged and Tirren with it. They swirled among Lacedar's thin rear line and Thiery's foot soldiers. With the swordsmen helping now, some of the foot soldiers shimmied up trees to pick off soldiers who drifted from the fray, though their longbows looked awkward in the branches. The rest followed Findal, mounting up and working in pairs with their short-swords at the rear of the battle.

Men lay dead everywhere. The stink of offal and dying men and beasts filled Tirren's nostrils. He caught a Lacedar soldier under the chin with his sword point, and pushed the man from his horse. Over the horse's back, he caught sight of Shen.

Tirren relied on skills learned in his sword-drills and tournaments and Chayan fought with a cool precision and an exceptional eye. Shen was laying about him with all his prodigious strength. As Tirren watched, he swept a man from his mount even though his blade landed broadside. Soldiers whirled between them again, and the last sight Tirren had of Shen was of his friend dispatching another opponent as three soldiers wearing Thiery's blue diamond charged to his side.

Sweat ran like a river under Tirren's padding. He gauged which of the two Lacedar soldiers rushing him looked weaker when a horn sounded three short blasts. Focused so long on block, parry, and cut, the sound took a moment to register. As it echoed in his ears, he realized it had been Lacedar's call for retreat.

The battle was over. All across the field, Lacedar swordsmen spun their horses and abandoned the fight.

"Hold!" Jaron's voice carried above the remaining skirmishes and thunder of running horses. Tirren tried to wrap his mind around the concept that he could stop fighting. He let his arms fall to his sides and realized for the first time how fiercely they burned. He sat unmoving, relishing the sensation of not coming under attack for the first time in what felt like a very long time. He echoed Jaron's order. The retreating enemy galloped through Thiery's ranks unmolested.

A hoarse cheer went up from the army as Lacedar abandoned the field. Jaron shouted another command. His throat sounded painfully raw. Tirren and the rest followed him off the field to Erimar, who rode out to meet them. Fatigue, more intense than any Tirren had experienced in his life, flooded into his body as the last of the battle madness ebbed out.

"Leave the foot soldiers here to tend to the injured," Erimar shouted to Findal. "Have them disarm and guard Lacedar's injured. Swords, follow Lacedar's army to make certain they cross the bridge and do no harm to Panden."

Less than one bell later Tirren returned from Panden, having seen the dust of Maradon's retreat into Lacedar. He felt so exhausted he could hardly stay in his saddle and knew it must pale to what Midnight felt as the big-hearted horse limped and stumbled under him.

The surviving foot soldiers had brought the injured from both armies out of the trees onto the grass. With the assistance of the additional soldiers who had been steadily arriving from all over Thiery, the prisoners had been grouped together and the dead had been gathered—Lacedar's fallen on one side of the road and Thiery's on the other. They would take the Lacedar prisoners back to the Hold to ransom them back to their families.

The swordsmen rejoined the foot soldiers, the regiments re-formed, and men were counted. Erimar's expression grew stony as he looked at the number of dead wearing Thiery's insignia. Nearly a full regiment, many of them the foot soldiers.

Tirren searched for Shen, not finding him. He asked Heras, Shen's second.

"Kesum-Shen is the only man I know of unaccounted for," Heras said, looking as worried as Tirren felt. "His mount was found at the river. Someone said he saw Shen knocked unconscious, but three Thiery soldiers dragged him onto a horse and got him off the field to safety. We're still looking for the men who rescued him."

The battle was nothing but a blur of faces, though Tirren remembered seeing three men riding toward Shen. Trying to recall their faces, he couldn't place any of them. Tirren clung to the hope that if Shen had been bested, he'd been taken alive and would be ransomed back to them.

Litters were made for the injured that didn't fit in the wagons, while the horses that had survived both the ride and the battle were at last allowed to rest and graze. Tirren walked Midnight far enough into the cold river to cover the horse's legs above the knees and cool the swollen joints and sore feet. When the army was at last ready to move again, Tirren, tired as the rest, mounted up. They rode east, back to Panden—the nearest town where they could organize and recuperate—while messengers headed for Bern and Thiery Hold with news of the battle.

The re-supply wagons arrived the following mid-day, and it was another day still before horses and men were ready to travel again for those who could. Tirren had received a report on their first day in Panden. A quarter of the horses had died or foundered so badly they had to be put down. Seventeen men would stay in Panden, too injured to travel to the Hold.

The following day, the horses and men that were hale enough to travel set out, leaving behind a fresh company of reserves to patrol the border from the Fangtooths to Eanor. Also left behind, Tirren thought as he turned Midnight west, were the funeral pyres of their dead. And, somewhere out there, Shen.

Chapter Eighteen

A horse moved beneath Shen's thighs, coarse hair rubbed his face. He tried to draw a full breath and found it difficult. That and a myriad other discomforts pushed him to further awareness. Shen opened his eyes to slits. His first coherent thought was to wonder why his horse's mane was black. Sunlight burned bright shafts of pain into his head and he closed his eyes again.

He wanted to sleep but questions tickled at him, pestered him, buzzed around him like a fly in his face. Why had he been sleeping while riding? Why wasn't he riding Bayone? The quicksand miring his brain loosed its grip a little more.

Memory of the battle rushed back in.

Shen jerked up in panic. Blinding pain shot through his skull. His stomach heaved. He vomited a small amount of yellow liquid, leaving a trail of mucous in the horse's mane.

"He's coming around again." The voice behind him announced his status to others.

Shen noted the sound of many horses on the road. He didn't remember coming around before, but he understood now where he must be.

He'd discovered on his attempt to sit up that his arms and legs were bound—his wrists about the horse's neck and his ankles by a cord beneath the horse's belly. He rested against the horse's neck again. The smell of bile in the mane made him gag, but nothing more came up.

When his stomach quieted and the lancing headache receded, he slowly opened his eyes, careful not to lift his head. Looking down the length of his left arm he could see the cord about his wrist, with nothing more in his view than the dirt road and the black legs with hairy white fetlocks on the horse he rode. His hands had been bound with a short rope that wouldn't have allowed him to sit upright even if his headache had allowed it.

Shen tried gently tipping his chin up. The pain behind his eyes returned, but with less ferocity this time. He rode near to the head of Lacedar's army, led by the man riding in front of him. The soldier, a hard-faced man, probably only a little older than himself, looked back. He grinned when their eyes met. There was nothing friendly in the smile.

The warm and bright day added to Shen's nausea. The sun stood not quite overhead and he guessed it to be a little past mid-day. He assumed it must still be the day of the battle—if he'd been unconscious more than a day and a night, he likely never would have woken again. The column moved north at an easy pace, so they must be on Lacedar soil. At least Maradon hadn't accomplished his goal. If he had, the army wouldn't be on the move, they'd be in Bern.

Fully aware now, Shen could almost wish he wasn't. With the headache and nausea acknowledged, he mentally checked the rest of his body and found no part of him that didn't hurt. The events of the night and the exertion of the battle, followed by an afternoon of immobilization, had stiffened every muscle and joint in his body. Even his crotch felt bruised and sore from riding bent forward. The pommel of the saddle pushed into his gut and made breathing difficult. His hands felt thick and useless, swollen from hanging for so long in the constriction of his bonds.

Shen wished his hands could be free at least long enough to probe the injury at his left temple, where dried blood seemed the most likely cause of his stiff, matted hair pulling at the skin. His throat burned with thirst and he needed food for strength, having eaten little since mid-day yesterday, though the thought of eating threatened to make him heave again. He might have asked to sit upright but felt too unsure of his stomach and his head to try yet. Instead, he closed his eyes and wished for the luxury of unconsciousness again.

He dozed fitfully until the army halted near sunset and the absence of motion woke him. Opening his eyes, he saw men dismounting and setting up camp. The hard-faced man who had led Shen's horse approached with two other soldiers. Shen realized that the three wore the blue diamond of Thiery on their jerkins. His mind reeled at the thought of traitors.

One man looked vaguely familiar, but Shen couldn't place him. He looked a little older than Hard Face and sported a bruise on his cheek. Shen dubbed him Big Bruise. The third was a short fellow with bad breath. Bad Breath and Hard Face were completely unfamiliar. If they were part of Thiery's army, they must be reserves.

Bad Breath pulled a dagger and cut the cords that bound Shen's hands and feet while the other two stood by with swords drawn. Shen wanted to tell them it was absurd to guard him like this when he would account himself lucky if he could stand on his own feet unaided. He didn't have the chance to say anything. A groan escaped, instead, when his arms swung apart and again when his legs moved, lighting a burning fire in his knees and shoulders.

"Get down," Bad Breath ordered.

When he didn't move quickly enough, Bad Breath and Big Bruise grabbed him roughly by his jerkin and pulled him from his horse.

"Gods, he's heavy!"

Unable to hold his falling weight, they both moved clear and let him hit the ground. Shen struggled to maintain consciousness but the earth under him spun.

"You needn't tell me," Hard Face said. "I'm the one had to pull the bastard over my horse in the middle of a battle."

"Gods, what a plan," Big Bruise said. "I can't believe we even got one of them."

One of them? Shen wondered, trying to slide his hands under his chest to push himself up.

"I've never seen you move so fast as you did trying to get that jerkin off that dead kid," Hard Face said, punching Big Bruise lightly in the arm. He laughed.

It all came back to Shen.

He had slashed his blade at a man he didn't know when the blue diamond of Thiery registered. He'd nearly lost his balance trying to stop the swing. Suddenly he'd been surrounded by men in Thiery blue. They wore ribbons of cloth on their forearms—the same ribbons these three still wore. Before he had time to wonder about the ribbons, Big Bruise had struck Shen in the left temple with the flat of his blade. It was the last thing he remembered of the battle.

Bad Breath gave Shen a half-hearted kick in the hip. "Get up, you son of a whore!"

They grabbed his arms and hauled at him. His chest was half off the ground when a pair of black boots entered his vision and he was dropped face down in the dirt again. The rocky earth knocked a heavy grunt from him.

"Make very certain he doesn't die," a deep voice said.

Shen craned his head up and looked into Maradon's black eyes. He was relieved to hear that Maradon, at least, would hold to the old standards of protecting highborn prisoners; only sensible if they wanted a good ransom for him.

Maradon stared down at him a long moment. Shen saw the tightening of his face, the narrowing of his eyes a second too late. He tried to roll to the side but his reactions were too slow. Maradon kicked him hard in the jaw, throwing Shen to his back. The Bealdor of Lacedar spat in his face.

The sky whirled and Shen's stomach whirled with it, but before he could move, Maradon kicked him in the ribs. He kicked him again harder. Then harder still. Hearing his rib break sickened Shen more than the pain.

"Bealdor," Hard Face said nervously, "you'll kill him yourself if you keep on."

Maradon turned on him and the man took a quick step back. "Shut your mouth or you'll be next!" Maradon roared, but the kicks stopped. With the coiled violence of a cyclone he stormed back the way he had come.

Shen rolled to his side again and retched. He cried at the pain that tore through his chest, but his stomach continued to spasm. The muscles in his jaw cramped when he vomited, and he wondered distantly if Maradon had broken his jaw as well.

"Get up!" Hard Face shouted. Tension and anger colored his voice, and he no doubt regretted his intervention, though Shen held no illusions the man had cared anything for protecting him, he'd only been helping Maradon regain control of his anger before he killed his prisoner and blamed them later. Hard Face pulled a boot back, ready to kick Shen himself, but kicked at the tree above his head instead.

Shen wiped his mouth onto his shoulder and tried to wipe the spit from his cheek. He rolled to his knees with a groan. Hands grabbed his arms and hauled at him. "You'll wish you were dead before all is done," Hard Face hissed.

"Not very bright to kill the Bealdor's son then let yourself fall prisoner to him," Big Bruise added.

They got him to his feet and Shen's vision tunneled for a moment. He couldn't inhale and his rib grated at every movement. He worked his feet back under him and the blackness receded, but he walked unsteadily, despite the two soldiers holding him up. Blood returned to his limbs, and his stiff joints loosened a fraction. What Big Bruise said sunk in.

"It was a battle," Shen said, his voice rough from thirst and pain. His jaw ached when he talked. "I killed who was in front of me, like every man on the field did."

"Not today, you stupid bastard," Big Bruise said. "At the horse pastures."

Shen remembered the two men he had killed in the skirmish in the pasture five weeks ago. Suddenly the pieces fell into place. The head leaving the shoulders of the young man he had cut down. Maradon's horse rearing, the Bealdor shouting something incoherent. The look he'd received from Maradon that day, as he had last night, and as he had just done again. A cold arrow of fear lanced through him, flaring down from his breastbone, and stopping deep in his gut. He wondered if he would indeed wish himself dead before long.

His guards led him to a small creek where the horses had been led to water. With this new information, Shen placed the familiarity of Big Bruise as one of the two prisoners his men had captured that day in the pastures and ransomed back to Lacedar.

At the creek, Bad Breath told him to strip down to his padded shirt and wool stockings. He finally lost patience with his broken rib and his clumsy attempts to remove his jerkin and pulled a long-bladed knife from his belt. Bad Breath cut his jerkin off, then helped him with his chain mail. They took his mail shirt, chaps, and gloves, but his boots and breeches were returned. His belt knife had been missing when he first regained consciousness.

They took care of his needs with the same pragmatic approach they might for their livestock. He was allowed to drink from the creek, and one of the men roughly washed his head wound. The water he drank and the dunking they gave his head in the cold water lessened the throbbing of his headache and the pain in his jaw, but bending over caused a pain like fire in his right side. Weakness and dizziness plagued him whenever he moved his head, but his joints were flexing more easily. On the return to camp only Bad Breath held his arm, while the other two followed. Any idea he may have had of escape had shattered along with his rib.

They pushed him to the ground in the center of the camp so that he landed with his back to a tree. Hard Face pulled lengths of cord from beneath his jerkin—probably the same cords that had bound him earlier to the horse. Shen winced at the thought of being tied again. Hard Face secured his hands in front of him and tied his ankles together. Bad Breath left and returned shortly with a wooden bowl and a tin mug. Setting the bowl down in front of him, he pushed the mug into Shen's hands.

The mug burned hot against his palms with his hands tied so tightly together. The liquid cooled quickly though, and Shen savored what warmth he could as the sun set and the wetness of his hair and padded shirt increased the chill. The drink was some vile tasting tea that they hadn't bothered to sweeten with honey. The bitterness didn't sit well in his stomach, but he recognized the taste of the herb, one that would help reduce swelling inside his skull and elsewhere.

When he finished the tea, he was given the bowl. It contained only the broth of the soup the others ate. Whether it was an act of cruelty, to keep him hungry, or consideration for his head wound and nausea, the broth settled his stomach and renewed him. They retied his hands behind his back. He gingerly lay down to sleep on his good side, feeling encouraged to note a little of his strength returning.

In the morning Shen found his joint and muscle stiffness had returned with a vengeance, worse for having slept bound and without a blanket. His jaw had swollen in the night, his head pounded, and every breath seemed agony. Once they had him up and walking, the kinks worked loose enough that he could move on his own—even his jaw loosened—but the pain in his side and head continued, unrelenting.

The men who guarded him through the night had been replaced at dawn with the original three from yesterday, still wearing the Thiery jerkins. He'd heard their names the previous day, but preferred to continue thinking of them as Hard Face, Bad Breath, and Big Bruise. In short order they saw to his morning needs and gave him more of the bitter tea. The anticipation of having to ride with his broken rib made for a new torment but, after breaking his fast, one of his guards surprised him by wrapping a cloth tightly about his chest before they re-bound his hands behind his back and hoisted him onto the black mare.

They tied his ankles together under the horse but they left him sitting up this time, and he found the binding around his chest helped ease his breathing and ease his pain a bit. When he coughed and spat, Shen was relieved to see no blood.

The day was nearly cloudless again, the sky the hazy blue of early summer. Shen had never been to Lacedar before and he looked about with interest as they rode. The landscape they passed looked similar to Thiery, though drier for the season and with less undergrowth. The wooded areas were comprised primarily of evergreens, occasionally opening onto valleys dotted with farmland and villages. The land became more arid as the day progressed, and rock outcroppings, juniper, and sage began to replace the evergreens.

Shen felt Maradon's dark eyes on him at the mid-day break, though the man didn't approach him again. A part of Shen wanted to meet those black eyes, to return the challenging, hateful stare. The wiser part of him kept his eyes lowered.

"Too bad we didn't get the others." His guards were nearby, eating jerky and bread though they offered him nothing. Shen closed his eyes, pretending not to listen. "It would have been something to be bringing the Bealdor of Thiery's son and grandson back with us instead of this ass." Shen didn't need to see Bad Breath to know the man gestured at him.

"I'm glad we got the one we did," Big Bruise said around a mouthful of the dried meat. "He took me to their Hold trussed up like a Winterfest goose. Besides, he's the one the Bealdor wanted most. We'll pay enough for not getting the others—be thankful we have him."

So, they had gone after Tirren and Chayan as well. Shen smiled a grim satisfaction at their failure.

━━━━━━ ⟋⟍ ━━━━━━

They reached Lacedar Hold late in the afternoon. Like Thiery Hold, it had been built into the side of a tall bluff, making it approachable from only one direction. The Hold loomed over Shen, larger and heavier than Thiery's. The old dwelling of the high kings. For all its size though, it lacked grandeur, and looked gloomy as it leaned its heavy, dun-colored bulk out from the cliffs behind it.

Shen managed to keep his feet under him this time as they pulled him from his horse and roughly ushered him to a small set of steps near the side of the Hold. The steps descended steeply down to a heavy wooden door. A foot soldier standing guard unlocked and opened the door. Shen stepped into a narrow hallway of cool stone.

His guard prodded him down the hall to a door at his left, then unlocked the door and pushed him over the stone threshold into an open dungeon. It was lit by one tiny, barred window high on the south wall at ground level. Three men sat on the stone floor. Two sat close together, the other sat against the opposite wall and stood warily as Shen and his guards entered.

Shen's eyes were drawn to the ceiling where basket chains hung, a man-shaped set of iron bands, designed to hold a person immobile while his body wasted of thirst and hunger until death and time rotted the body to the bones. Shen couldn't decide if it was a good sign or a bad that the basket hung empty.

He paused, looking about him, and a sword jabbed him in the back. The point left a stinging cut under his right shoulder blade. He looked back at the soldier who had pushed him and the man jerked his chin toward a small, dark opening in the far wall, narrower than Shen's shoulders. Shen moved toward it with trepidation, wishing his hands were free to feel his way when the murky darkness enveloped him as he squeezed into the tunnel.

Within a few steps he hit a blank wall and was roughly turned and shoved to his right where he tripped over a short metal threshold, bumped his head on the ceiling, and came to an abrupt stop at another wall. He was ordered to stand still with his chest to the wall while his hands were cut free. The guard backed up and a wooden door he must have passed through slammed shut behind him, locking with a rusty clank.

It didn't take much time to explore the boundaries of his confinement. He was in a small oubliette, too low for him to stand up straight. Standing in the center, he could reach from the door to the back wall and from side to side. There were no provisions for sanitation, no blanket against the cold, and not enough room to lie stretched out on the dirt floor. A small metal grille in the door and the pale light of the dungeon around the corner of the tunnel gave a thin edge to his sight. What had seemed utter blackness for the first few minutes resolved into dusky darkness. He held his right side and gingerly sat down to wait, wondering what might come next.

The God of Fortune had always been kind to him. He'd been born to a good family, tall and strong even as a boy, the uthow to Thiery's Beodan, a regiment leader at a young age. He'd enjoyed soldiering and women and life. He was in his prime and he'd never contemplated death, not really, not even during the two recent skirmishes. Not until now. In the darkness and solitude, the basket chains haunted his mind's eye. He dropped his head and said a prayer to Jhenna, asking to return to his favor, though it looked too late for that now. He should have prayed to the gods more often when things were still good.

A short time later he heard the distant sound of the small swinging plate at the bottom of the main dungeon door and something sliding across the stone floor, followed by a thump and slosh of a clay water jug. He heard the three men scrabbling to get to the food, fighting to get their share—or more than their share. There came a short bark of warning and it seemed one man had cowed the others into waiting for their portion.

No food or water arrived for Shen. He remembered Maradon's words though, that he was to be kept alive. He held hard to those words in the dark, not willing to believe that his life would end by wasting away in a tiny oubliette.

"You in there, are you alive?"

The voice outside the grille woke Shen. He had fallen into a light sleep, sitting up against the back wall. He didn't think he'd been asleep long. It might be evening now, perhaps night.

"I am," Shen replied.

"You're a swordsman?" The voice was deep, conversational.

"Yes."

"What brought you to this?"

Shen shrugged to himself. "Being a soldier."

"Did you disobey the Bealdor?"

"Maradon isn't my Bealdor, Erimar of Thiery is."

"Ah, you were captured in the battle. I thought I didn't recognize you, but then there have been a lot of new soldiers."

"And you?"

Shen heard the man slide down to sit against the wall. "I'm also a swordsman, of Lacedar. Was," he corrected himself with a chuckle.

"How did you come to be a prisoner?"

"I thought invading Thiery a poor reason to risk my skin. I was overheard saying so. Not treason, mind. I didn't seek to subvert, only expressed my opinion unwisely, with too much ale in my belly. As has often been the case."

"How long have you been here?"

"A week or so, I think."

"And the others?"

"Common bandits. They were here when I was brought in."

"What is your sentence?" Shen asked.

"Sentence?" He grunted. "I was neither tried nor sentenced. I was publicly flogged, and I assumed I'd be put to death. I've heard the Bealdor even whipped his own son for similar doubts. I figured the battle plans kept everyone so busy, they forgot to kill me. When they returned, I began to wonder if they might release me after all, but now I'm not so sure. Do you know your fate, swordsman?"

"I had hoped to be ransomed back to Thiery, but I think now that won't be the case. I've learned your Bealdor harbors a very personal resentment for me. Why do you ask? Have you heard something?"

"I heard the guards talking tonight, saying they'd be rid of us all tomorrow. It piqued my curiosity and I thought perhaps you knew what they meant. They said they were sending us all, to make it worth the trip. Apparently my fate is now tied to yours." There was a scrape of leather against stone as he shifted against the wall. "I didn't much care for the flogging, but I get the feeling it might prove the least of my troubles." Shen heard the man push himself up. "I suppose we'll find out soon enough." His footsteps receded.

Worth the trip. Shen felt a grim hope ignite. If they were to travel, it might be his saving grace. He would have been unable to escape torture or execution in these dungeons, but if he had time to recover, if he was taken elsewhere with fewer guards, his strength and fighting skills may yet serve him well.

He thought on it a long while, but the stress of the past three days wore at him. Despite the headache and rib pain, the nausea and the discomfort, he curled on the stinking dirt floor and slept deeply.

--- ⟨∾⟩ ---

The turning of a key in the lock brought Shen suddenly awake. He could see the faint outline of the grille in the door and guessed it to be morning. The door swung back and his light-sensitive eyes made out the pale shimmer of steel and the outline of men. He was ordered to stand with his face to the rear wall.

He felt dizzy when he stood. His head had bothered him less during the night but it ached again now from thirst and hunger. At least when he'd examined the wound at his temple last night, he'd found the cut not too bad. His rib still pained him but the wrap around his chest was still tight enough to give the broken rib some support.

He heard the sound of metal rattling as he stood facing the back wall, head bowed against the low ceiling. More than one man crowded into the oubliette with him and a cold steel collar snapped and locked around his neck, catching some of his hair in the joint at the back. A chain hung down his chest from a loop in the center of the collar. His guards wrapped another chain snugly about his waist and hooked it so it wouldn't pull free. They placed linked manacles on his wrists next. The guard at his right turned him, and ran the chain from the collar through an iron loop between the manacles and attached it to the waist chain with a lock. Shen's hands were in front of him and could slide on the vertical chain from his groin to his face, but he couldn't move his arms away from his body nor could he separate his wrists. Efficient, he thought. He'd be able to hold reins, cup or bowl, feed himself, piss on his own without being released, and perhaps lower and raise his drawers, but he'd be capable of precious little else.

His guards guided him out the tunnel and he squeezed his eyes shut against the dim light of the dungeon. When he opened them again, he noted that the other prisoners were also being gathered up and chained in a similar fashion. One watched him with an unreadable, measuring expression; a sturdy man of middle years with the bloated features of a heavy drinker. No doubt the swordsman who had spoken with him last night.

Shen stood still as the other prisoners were escorted out first, then stumbled forward when shoved from behind. They emerged at the top of the steps outside and he squinted again. The day shone bright and harsh and he felt a heavy breeze from the west. The wind whipped his long hair, which had hung loose like a commoner's since the soldiers washed the wound at his temple two days ago.

The four prisoners were ushered to the front of the Hold where Maradon stood in the courtyard talking with a thin, greasy-looking man in common clothes. Behind the little man, three packhorses and six mounts stood tied. Only two of the mounts were saddled or bridled. Waterskins and a few personal supplies had been tied to the two saddles. A large, broken-faced man stood with the horses.

Shen had seen more of Maradon than he wanted to, but had never yet been able to study him at close range. He could now. The man wore a fine black tunic, bordered with gold and crimson, with a crimson shirt beneath, black breeches, and the same black boots that had broken Shen's rib. He was of average height but his barrel chest and sturdy figure made him look larger. Like the highborn of Thiery, he was clean-shaven, but instead of Heshan brown, his hair and eyes were as black as ink.

Maradon handed the little man a fat purse of coin. "That's near a half year's wages for most traders, Kassor. You stand to do as well again if they all get there alive." The man started to speak but Maradon overrode him. "And Kassor ... know that if this one," Maradon thrust a finger straight at Shen's chest without looking his way, "does not reach his destination, a worse fate than his own will await you. He is the only one that matters. The rest are extra for your trouble."

"Of course, Bealdor." Kassor bowed deeply. "I live to serve."

Dismissed, Kassor walked to Shen. He dwarfed the scrawny man and looked down into the trader's thin, pinched face, a long hooked nose taking up most of it. Kassor looked up like a ferret sizing up a mountain lion, then glanced to Maradon's guards holding the other three prisoners. "Put them on those horses." He indicated the ones he meant, then he called over the rough-looking man. "Cor, chain this one's hands behind his back."

The man pulled a master key from his pocket. Cor stood nearly as tall as Shen, but with a great, bulging belly that hung over the top of his breeches and a heavy, round face. He grabbed Shen's manacled hands and grinned, showing a yellowed snaggletooth in his lower jaw that jutted into the space where an upper tooth had gone missing.

He unlocked the manacles and pulled them free of the chain they floated on. Jerking his wrists behind his back, Cor held them both with one meaty hand. He stood close, turning the tight collar so the vertical chain hung down his back, scraping the skin on Shen's neck and ripping out the few hairs that had caught. Cor secured Shen's hands behind him. Shen felt the sweat on the man's warm skin, and his foul odor overpowered Shen's own smell. At least he didn't stink by choice, he thought.

Cor swung Shen around by one elbow and he found himself face to face with Maradon.

"Our basket chains haven't been used in a century," he said, "but I thought about opening them for you. I thought about many things." Maradon took a step closer, looking up into Shen's eyes. "The last sight I had of my eldest son was of him lying on Thiery soil in two pieces."

Shen had seen Maradon's temper and knew the man had little control over it. It made him unpredictable. The trip could be delayed or cancelled even now. Basket chains, evisceration, blinding with hot pokers, flaying, all these things and more had been done in the time before the Conflicts.

"I saw you across the river two nights ago," Maradon continued. "I prayed then to Fresshe for you to be delivered to me. And here you are. In the end, though, I decided anything I did to you would be too short a time for you to suffer for the things you have done to me." The hatred flared in his eyes, just as it had just before he had broken Shen's rib. Maradon's hands clenched into fists and Shen braced himself.

The man turned suddenly and walked two steps away, tension in every line of his body. His last words came to Shen on the wind.

"May you never know a day of happiness again, you bitch's whelp." He strode off.

Shen felt a moment's relief followed by a looming sense of larger dread.

In short order the prisoners were mounted single file, ready to travel. Kassor rode at the head of the procession followed by the two bandits. The Lacedar swordsman came next, Shen behind him, and Cor brought up the rear, leading the packhorses. A long rope ran from the saddle of Kassor's horse, through a loop on the halters of the prisoner's horses and tied off to Cor's saddle.

Kassor kicked his horse to a walk and the rest moved forward one by one. The prisoners rode bareback, though Shen was the only one whose arms had been secured behind his back. The weight of his chains dragged at him and he gripped with his legs as his horse started moving. He passed into the shadow of the barbican, headed toward his unknown fate.

Shen wondered if he really might have seen his last happy day.

Chapter Nineteen

Yslaaran was the last to arrive.

She had chosen the meadow again for their meeting, well away from the palace grounds or the deep forest where the Unseely spent most of their time. Nisseah, Isurrelte, and Eanaan sat on the grass, Nisseah casually flirting with Isurrelte, smiling as he placed small blue flowers in her thick blonde hair.

Yslaaran glanced about before crossing the meadow. She had waited a prudent time after her visit with Chayan to have this meeting, but caution was becoming a habit.

Eanaan stood and gave her his hand. Taking it, she sank to the deep grass, sitting to face them all. He stretched out next to her, propped on one elbow.

She began without preamble and recounted her conversation with Chayan.

"It is good that the boy is willing," Isurrelte said when Yslaaran finished.

"The boy may be willing, but the grandsire rules him," Yslaaran replied. "I fear that one will remain unconvinced."

"And what of the boy's father," Eanaan asked, "will he support the plan?"

"I spoke with him also and I believe he will." She had not wanted to tell them about seeing Tirren, but she would tell them what she must. "He loves his son and wants him to rule when his time comes."

"I looked for you the night you went to talk with the boy," Nisseah said. His blue eyes danced and his mouth crooked in a knowing smile. "I did not find you. Did you keep longer council with the boy or with the man?"

Her silence gave him his answer. She should have known she could keep nothing from Nisseah.

Isurrelte gave her a long, appraising look. "Best not to control his mind too often. Chayan may detect the influence now that he knows somewhat about his power."

"The man's mind is untouched," Yslaaran said without inflection. The others looked surprised. It was not a thing done among them to take a mortal without also enchanting the mind. Clouding the mind eased the intensity for the mortal—just as stealing the memory saved them from yearning. Even she didn't quite understand why she had chosen to do neither of those things.

Yslaaran felt a pang of regret again, like a thin needle pushed into her belly. She had used him like a tool that first time, taking him, and then leaving him the memory of it for her own purposes. Half of Tirren's short life had been spent suffering unresolved longing. It had been necessary; she knew it then and she knew it now. But this last time, had any of that been necessary?

"I learned a new thing while I was there," she said, cutting off her unaccustomed introspection. "War is brewing among mankind again. Tirren worries much about it. We must be patient while this new conflict resolves. The boy will be loyal to his grandsire during this time, and his grandsire harder still toward potential enemies."

Isurrelte shifted, "What if it comes to war? How far do we go to protect our plans?"

"If we seek to return to the old ways," Nisseah answered, sitting forward and wrapping his arms around his knees, "then we must follow the old rules. We may counsel, but we may not interfere."

"We must protect my son," Yslaaran said, with more heat than she had meant to.

"Yslaaran," he said gently, "we seek to help mankind, not to become their gods."

"I am aware of that," she said, regaining her composure. "I don't mean that we should control the affairs of men or fight their fights. I simply mean that we must counsel wisely, with an eye to what is best for all."

Eanaan stroked his chin with one thumb. "You should keep a close eye on this brewing war. We can decide the best course as the situation develops. Men are fickle. The conflict may never come to pass."

His comment rang true. There was no need to decide this minute how far they would go. If Chayan's fate was to die in one of these squabbles that mankind perpetuated, she knew she mustn't intervene. Short of that, though, "help" held a wide berth for interpretation.

"I will go again soon to see if the conflict escalates still. I would also be interested to know if Chayan has had any further contact from the halfbreeds in the east. It would be interesting to speak with one of them if they return."

The others agreed with her. With nothing more to discuss, they stood to leave. None of them wished to be seen together more often than necessary. They had far to go before their plan came to fruition. Too many of the Elves had turned a hard heart toward mankind to risk the plan being exposed prematurely. They would have to present it convincingly, with all obstacles already conquered.

After the other Seely left, Yslaaran's thoughts slipped back to Tirren. She could feel the depth of his feeling as intimately as if she could touch it with her hands. When they had first loved, when their son had been conceived, she had possessed his mind for the act, made him want her. This last time she had not. Knowing his love for her, she'd wanted to experience the full fire of his passion. She wanted to be the first to know how it felt, and she had not paused to consider what she asked of him.

Pleasure and pain had burned so bright in him that it threatened to leave him no more than ashes inside—but he had been strong. Perhaps humans could adapt with time. Perhaps he had been stronger for living with his memories. Given the choice, she felt sure it was what he would have wanted. Taking him unchanged, uncontrolled, was certainly what she had wanted.

Admitting that was hard. She would have to keep a close watch on her course with Tirren. If her intentions to help mankind were genuine, she must be careful not show the arrogance and hedonism she criticized in her people. Or had she already? She shook her head. She was charting new territory on more fronts than those she had expected.

If her reflections brought no answers, maybe her actions would. She stood, planning to head back to the court, but stopped when she saw movement at the edge of the forest. Uthbaraal walked out of the trees and into the meadow. He threw himself to his stomach on the grass in front of her. "Beauteous Yslaaran, why do you idle here lonely and thoughtful so far from the palace?"

Yslaaran looked at him closely, wondering how long he had been nearby, but saw no more mischief in his eyes than usual.

"To gain a measure of peace," she said pointedly.

Uthbaraal laughed and rolled onto his back, plucking at a blade of grass. He pushed himself to his elbows and studied her. "And have you found it?" He looked almost serious for once.

She measured him again, finding no clues in his black eyes. Misgivings twisted in her stomach. Perhaps there *was* a new edge to his mischief today.

"I am less like to now with you here to plague me." She started walking. "Come, you can sing me a rhyme as we walk, and I will be lonely and thoughtful no more."

He rose gracefully, and obliged her with his sweet tenor voice as they headed for the Seely court.

Chapter Twenty

The weather had turned hot earlier than usual this year in Lacedar and the air in the great hall felt stifling. The heat made Maradon think of the desert to the north and the dry pastures to the south. He tossed his fork to his plate, no longer hungry.

Cerendrin looked up. She had been speaking with the children about plans for the Feast of Summer the following day. Maradon couldn't care less. He'd been over it a thousand times in his mind and still couldn't see how he had been anticipated by Thiery's army. In the month since the battle he'd scoured his ranks and his household for any hint of a spy and had found no conclusive proof. After a month of investigations, the people now showed deference and fear to such excess that it had become impossible to tell the guilty from the cowardly.

Cerendrin spoke, thinking she had his attention at last. "The contests that you're judging begin at the last bell of the day. Would you like the feast served at mid-day or earlier?"

"I won't be judging the contests tomorrow. Bron will do that for me."

Bron looked up in surprise.

Maradon met his eyes, studied them again. He had never suspected Bron had been the traitor; he doubted him to have the guts to betray him, especially after the whipping he'd received for questioning the plan to take Bern. Maradon had meted out the punishment himself, in private and with a short crop, not a whip as rumor had it. He had to be tough with Bron, tough enough that he could replace Baes. Bron understood that. No, he felt sure it hadn't been Bron.

"What takes you from us at festival?" Cerendrin asked. She asked her question so softly that it was a moment before he registered it.

"The turning of the sun is too potent to waste in play. It's a day the gods attend to us. I leave tomorrow with a few of my men to make a sacrifice to Fresshe. I'll spend the day in prayer, in the old way."

Tributes had not been made to the gods for centuries but, if he could ensure favor with the God of War, he may yet see the High Kingship restored to his Hold. He would do anything in his power to make that happen. His resentment of Thiery had grown by bounds this past month; taking their northern village and pastures was no longer enough.

Not only had Thiery thwarted his plans this time, but twice now. If it was not a spy undermining him, then perhaps Fresshe had forsaken them. Perhaps a Lacedar king long ago had angered the god. Maybe that was why his ancestors had lost the throne of the High King and Maradon failed in all his ambitions.

"I hope this ritual will bring you a measure of peace," Cerendrin said, not looking up. "May the gods favor it."

--- ⟋⟍ ---

The following morning the Hold hummed with activity in preparation for the festival. Maradon gave his final instructions to Cerendrin and Bron and departed with three of his men.

Neither his wife nor his son had suggested he stay, not even for his people, who would be disappointed at his absence—not even for the other gods who might feel snubbed.

Jin rode beside him and two swordsmen followed, driving a wagon. The wagon hauled, among other things, a small iron cage containing a live boar that had been trapped earlier in the week for the feast, and a large slab of stone to serve as an altar.

They traveled five leagues east before finding a meadow with the view of the Fangtooths he sought: a huge jagged mountain with twin peaks facing east and west. Fresshe's Peak, in the center of the long mountain range, stood out majestically, the snowy crown jewel of an immense jagged crown, but from here, Maradon could even see the north edge of Geshne's peak, outlined behind the rough steep sides of Fresshe's.

"Get to work on the altar," he said as he dismounted.

The three men set about hewing a juniper and making supports for the marble slab. Maradon moved apart from them and spent the time meditating, invoking Fresshe with prayer. It was early afternoon when they began, and the day burned hot and cloudless. The men stripped to their breeches and sweat dripped from them by the time the work was done.

"Bealdor, we're ready," Jin said, approaching him quietly from behind. Maradon stood stiffly, unused to spending so long on bent knees. He turned to see the finished altar resting on four wooden supports, bound juniper needles smoldering at either end of the slab.

"Get the animal."

Maradon suited up in his mail and jerkin, like his men, and donned his chain mail gloves. No domestic animal would do as a sacrifice to the God of War, and he hoped the danger involved with a live boar would please Fresshe and show his sincerity.

The men threaded two long, wooden poles through the cage and Maradon shouldered one end to help lift it from the wagon to the altar. The cage shook with the boar's charges and tusks rammed through the bars, close enough to his arms to raise the hair on them. Once the cage sat on the altar, Jin used a javelin to back the boar up until it stepped into loops of rope they had snaked behind it. Two quick jerks of the ropes pulled the loops tight around each hind leg. The men holding the ropes braced their feet and leaned back with all their weight. They had better be strong enough, Maradon thought, or he could well end up being the one sacrificed.

He opened the door of the cage and the boar went wild. It charged, lurching from side to side. The two men at the back struggled for their footing against the wild thrashing of the seventeen-stone boar, outweighing every man there. The cage rocked precariously, and the altar shuddered on its makeshift legs.

"Get the noose over it," Maradon snapped to Jin. On his second attempt, Jin dropped a wire noose attached to a stout stick over the boar's head and pulled it up tight. Maradon placed a second noose over the beast's head, the tusks grazing the underside of his protected forearm. "Let it forward."

When they had the boar free, they pushed the cage from the altar and it fell to the rocky ground with a crash. Maradon and Jin dropped their weight to pull the boar's head to the stone. The other two men worked to flip the animal on its side. The boar made one last desperate effort to free itself. Heaving with terrible strength, it gained enough purchase with a hind foot to push up. Driving forward and right it lunged straight at Maradon's head.

Maradon lost his balance. He struggled to get his feet under him again, and pulled down on the noose with all his power with his eyes a hand's length from the tusks and the animal a heartbeat from breaking free. Jin dropped to one knee for leverage. The boar wheezed against the nooses. With his right hand, Maradon grabbed the near tusk and threw himself into the boar. He forced its head down and pushed his shoulder into its side. He buried his face against the salty, musky skin, and felt the bristly hairs prickle against his cheek.

"Get the sodding feet under control!" he bellowed.

The men at the back grappled with the beast, finally getting the ropes taut again. They wrestled the boar the rest of the way onto its side. This time they secured the feet and hips properly.

Maradon held fast to the tusk, his weight against the boar, until the head had been secured as well. When he straightened, Jin stared at his chest.

"Are you all right, Bealdor?"

Maradon looked down to see a finger long tear in his jerkin. Blood seeped through the hole. Perhaps that would impress Fresshe; he could see it impressed his men.

With the animal secured, the others moved back. Maradon, still winded, moved to the side of the altar and raised his long hunting dagger. He had spent hours in prayer and there was little left to say.

"Fresshe, give me a sign that we are not cursed. Show me that I will lead my people to victory and not to defeat. Show me that your face is not turned from us, and I will bring glory to your name!"

On the heels of the last word he brought the knife down, viciously severing the front half of the boar's thick neck. The animal thrashed strongly at first, then weakly, its life's blood pumping out onto the altar and dripping to the dry ground. The breath came loud and wet through the lacerated windpipe. A moment more and all was still.

He hoped for an immediate sign to let him know his prayers and his efforts had been recognized but heard nothing but the drip of blood to the yellowing grass and the warm breeze in the meadow. Maradon tried to remain confident as the men packed up the wagon.

———— ⟨∾⟩ ————

Queen Evainya stood in the mists with Baedis, her current lover, at her side. She watched the ritual intently.

Long ago she had turned her back on this other world, not caring if she ever saw it again. That had changed when Uthbaraal told her about the very interesting conversation he'd overheard recently. Baedis had kept watch on the doings of Men for her ever since. Today he had requested she meet him at the mists.

It had been centuries since she had stepped into the Veil, yet it seemed as familiar to her as if no time had passed at all. Coming here again had been a good thing. Looking on the world of Men woke something in her that had been asleep too long.

She and Analoor had never forbidden contact with mortals. Many of the Elves had, over the aeons, enjoyed taking mortal lovers or wandering abroad in those lands for the diversions they offered, though few did so anymore. Things had taken a far different turn of late. Seely planning to return to these humans and attempting to re-establish the old ways would be bad enough. Those times were far behind them, and she would never allow them to be revived. But to plan in secret defied her authority, something that had never happened before. She planned to see that it would never happen again.

She had often taken Nisseah as a lover and felt his betrayal sharply—but Yslaaran's treachery stung even more.

Looking on the mortal world, she felt amazement at the spread of Men. She had gone too long unaware of their proliferation. Dirty and uncivilized, nothing resembled what they had been in the days of the gods, when they had been worthy of the help of her kind.

"They are a disease on the land," she said to Baedis. "They have spread to the limits of the four directions with their dwellings and farms and woodcutting, little better than the beasts they keep penned. You have done well to call me here to see this ritual. It is indeed an opportunity not to be missed." She turned to him, standing next to her in the mists and took his hand. "If they wish to war and reduce their number on the land, then perhaps we should help them to their goal. If this little king wishes a sign from Fresshe, then let us see that he receives one."

She reached her other hand behind her for Uthbaraal, whom Baedis had sent to bring her here. Uthbaraal's warm hand eagerly wrapped around hers and she brought him forward into the mists and gave them both her instructions.

Chapter Twenty-one

"**I** need water."

It took Shen two more tries to work enough spit into his throat for Kassor to notice he spoke.

The trader pulled his horse to a halt and the rest shuffled to a stop. Looking back, he fixed Shen with a long, level stare. Shen didn't care if the man was annoyed or not. He'd had little enough food and water since being captured and none at all in the oubliette. If Maradon's big plan was just to take him to the desert and leave him there to die, in his present state it wouldn't take very long. If they meant him to live, he needed food at some point and water now.

Kassor nodded to Cor who dismounted and pulled a waterskin from his saddle. Shen winced when his rib grated as he leaned down to the mouth of the bladder Cor held for him. Cor moved it back an inch, laughing when Shen leaned further. The second time he did it, Kassor snapped at him and Cor held the skin so Shen could drink.

At mid-day they stopped and dismounted. Shen's hands were moved to the front, allowing him to eat, drink, and relieve himself, like the other prisoners. He hoped they might leave him that way. They'd only ridden a few leagues and his leg and stomach muscles cramped already from constantly holding his balance. His hopes didn't last long. When the break ended, Cor twisted the metal collar on Shen's abraded skin and pulled his hands behind him again.

The rest of that day and the next two were much the same. They rode steadily northeast into progressively more arid land, moving slowly, the horses tethered together and the packhorses laden. Shen estimated they made no more than seven leagues a day. He and the other prisoners were given small meals of jerky and flatbread three times a day. At night, all the prisoners had their hands chained behind their backs and were bound at the ankles as well, allowing Kassor and Cor to sleep without need of a guard.

He quickly came to hate having his manacles adjusted. Though it was a relief to move his arms and shoulders, Cor never missed the chance to slide a meaty hand along Shen's body or stand close enough to rub his hip against Shen's. Sometimes he would whisper something vile as he leaned in close, commenting on how long it had been since he'd last had a woman but there were other ways to make do.

If Shen had shown the same presence of mind as the Lacedar swordsman—Gerrick, he had learned the man's name was—Cor might not bother harassing him. Cor had made a lewd remark to Gerrick the first day, but the swordsman had passed it off with a self-deprecating joke and Cor lost interest.

Gerrick had taken it a step further, though. The following morning, the Lacedar swordsman had mentioned to Cor, casually, that to avoid trouble, they might want to keep the Thiery prisoner separate from the bandits. When they were in the dungeon together, he said, Shen had made it clear he was not fond of commoners. Since that moment, Cor had given Shen no peace. Shen fostered a fierce hope that he and Gerrick ended up at the same destination. Unchained.

By their fourth day on the road they entered the northeastern corner of Lacedar, where even the drought-tolerant junipers could no longer survive. The short scrub, parched ground, and dry arroyos gave way to open stretches of hard-packed sand.

Shen looked about with interest at landscapes like nothing he'd ever seen before. He'd been to the southern end of the Fangtooths many times, where the mountain cliffs dropped into the sea, but this ... from here he could see the northern end of the mountain range in the dusty distance. The last few peaks decreased in height, then sank into the sands of the desert as if swallowed by it.

By late afternoon, a tiny hamlet appeared against the dry foothills. Shen had spent years studying maps and remembered that the village of Arrend lay alone and remote at the farthest corner of Lacedar. The tiny community huddled in the meager shadow of the cliffs. Ice-melt flowed down the northern side of the dwindling mountains, to form the headwaters of the Wildcat River. The river was no more than a creek here, before larger tributaries joined it further south, the direction they had come from, but it was enough to allow life in this desolate place where none should exist.

He assumed that Arrend would be his final destination, but Kassor stopped them short of the village, far from any dwellings. North and east of here the land turned to true, featureless desert. Looking out across the barren sand Shen tried to find a way to remain optimistic. Though a village might have offered him more options for escape, if they were headed to some isolated prison perhaps there would be fewer eyes to watch him and fewer men to pursue him.

Kassor dismounted only long enough to check that the prisoners were secure and help Cor redistribute the packs. They emptied three of the six packs and filled those with dozens of empty waterskins.

"Get camp set," Kassor said when they finished with the supplies. "Tie their ankles and don't feed them till I get back. Leave his hands as they are," Kassor said, jutting his chin at Shen. His small eyes drilled into Cor, "And leave him be while I'm gone." He set off for the village, towing two of the three packhorses.

"Lie on your backs," Cor barked at all the prisoners. He pulled the lengths of rope used to tie their ankles at night from his saddlebags.

Shen glanced to Kassor, receding into the distance. He wondered if he might be able to kick Cor in the face hard enough to knock him senseless, or at least disable him enough that the other prisoners could help, but Cor started with the smallest bandit first, leaving Shen for last. It had been a bad plan anyway. There would be too little he could do to save himself with his hands chained behind his back and Kassor headed for the only community for leagues in any direction. Better to wait and heal anyway, before trying anything.

Once Cor had tied his ankles, he scooted into a sitting position and sat with his back against a rock, tipping his face into the shade as best he could manage. He felt a grateful surprise that the man had, indeed, left him alone as instructed. He'd goaded Shen no more or less than the others when binding his legs.

Cor hobbled the horses and tied nosebags of grain around their heads. After that he laid out his and Kassor's personal items, separated out the night and morning's food, and redistributed the supplies to fill the remaining packs. The tasks kept him busy and Shen dozed while he could.

"You ever wrestle?"

The words woke Shen and he came alert instantly. Cor sat near him, leaning against another boulder, staring south, toward the village.

When Shen didn't answer, Cor turned to him. "You're big enough, like me."

He was nothing like the fat, vicious bastard, he thought.

"Course that rib of yours might give you trouble now," Cor continued, looking back toward Arrend again, though the village lay obscured beyond the small rises and dips in the land. He pushed to his feet and came over to squat by Shen. It wasn't hard to guess what kind of wrestling the man intended.

Cor untied the bonds on his ankles. Shen revisited his plan to kick Cor in the face and tensed in readiness, but the man stayed too far to the side. Shen weighed his chances. Cor might be overweight, but he was strong. Shen thought of his hope for eventual escape, but he'd die fighting today if he must.

Cor stood. "Your legs are free and your horse is there." He nodded to the remaining horses, tethered not far from them. "I'll wrestle you for your freedom." He grinned, showing his yellowed snaggletooth.

Shen glanced at the other prisoners. None of the bandits were large men and none looked like fighters, but Gerrick watched with keen eyes, waiting to see which way the wind blew.

Shen sat still, not rising to the bait. Cor grabbed him by the front of his shirt and hauled him to his feet, one-handed. He stepped back, removing the knife sheathed at his belt. He tossed it well behind him.

"What'll it take to make you wrestle me?"

"My hands are chained, my rib is broken, and I have a head-injury." He wasn't lying about his head, it throbbed like it would come apart at the seams most days, especially when he bent forward or lay down. "Let my hands loose and I'll wrestle you. Or are you too scared of me to give me that much chance?"

Cor laughed and Shen's faint hope vanished. The smile faded and Cor turned serious. "I don't need your hands loose for what I want." Shen saw the decision reflected in the man's eyes, the change in attitude from baiting to resolve. Cor rushed suddenly, moving faster than a man his size should.

Shen sidestepped and twisted, but his rib kept him from turning far enough. Cor caught him on the shoulder. Shen stumbled, off balance, and Cor got behind him, sliding his arms through Shen's bound arms, and gripping him around the chest. Cor lifted him off the ground trying to throw him, but Shen kicked back hard, catching him in the shin. Cor grunted. Shen tried to head-butt the man, but he lifted Shen again and swept his legs, throwing him face-first into the sand.

Shen cried out as the mercenary landed on top of him, though most of the man's weight hit on his left side. Cor rammed a knee between Shen's legs, shoving them apart. He forced one hand under Shen's hip. He pushed the hand into his belly, trying to reach the buckles of Shen's breeches, but their combined weight was too much.

With his broken rib, Shen couldn't turn to throw the man. He waited, hoping Cor would lift his weight a little, providing enough slack in the chains for an elbow shot. Panic flooded him as Cor shifted his hips only enough to work his hand a little lower. The man's hard phallus pressed into the base of his spine and the sickening realization dawned on Shen that he might not get the chance to die fighting.

The soft thud of hooves in sand was followed by the crack of a whip splitting the air. Cor rolled off Shen with a shout.

Kassor coiled the whip for another lash.

"What are you beating me for?" Cor crabbed backward. His loose shirt covered the evidence of his intentions. "He got his legs free and made a run for the horses. I stopped him." The man looked all wounded innocence.

The nostrils of Kassor's long, hooked nose flared. His small eyes were narrowed and weighing. Shen couldn't tell whether he believed Cor or not. Apparently, it didn't matter. "If you've put his rib through his lung I'll truss you in his chains and leave you on the

Bealdor's doorstep." He turned his horse and went after the loaded pack animals that were meandering back toward the village.

Cor shot a conspiratorial grin at Shen, flashing his snaggletooth. *We got away with it*, the grin said.

———— ⟨∾⟩ ————

They mounted up and set off shortly after dawn, headed north toward the village. Cor hadn't put Shen's rib through his lung, though it burned like fire again with every step the horse took. They passed close by the village and the "prisoner parade" entertained the people here as it had in the other small villages: four men in chains, bookended by the skinny trader and the big mercenary.

Looking at the others, Shen could only imagine how he appeared. His hair had been loose in the wind and dirt for days, and for the first time in his life he sported a rough beard. His padded shirt was dirt-stained and torn in half a dozen places. The closest he had come to a bath in days was the dunking the soldiers had given his head in the creek, and the heat and his heavy clothing had added to his rank smell.

Beyond the village, the cart path they'd followed vanished altogether. Kassor headed steadily northeast, toward the terminus of the mountains, and stayed as much as possible in the blessed shadow of the cliffs. The sand grew softer beneath the horses' feet as Kassor led them east, into trackless desert.

The packs were freshly loaded, but the majority of the stores they carried were water and grain for the horses. That evening, the food and water Shen received looked about half the amount of the previous portions. Shen ate slowly, watching the sunset paint the sky a brilliant bloody-orange before fading to purple and violet. The colors of his bruises, he thought wryly.

"Will we travel at night from here?" Cor asked Kassor as he watered the horses.

"No. We'd lose a full day waiting for night. I need to see the landmarks in the day, anyway. I'll not risk traveling in the dark and missing them, not even this far west."

If they were headed east of the mountains, then either they were being left in the deep desert to die or the destination must be Bansheen. If they were headed to Bansheen, Shen couldn't begin to predict his fate or his chances of escape, if he even lived to see it. The likelihood of ever seeing Thiery again suddenly seemed very small.

The night was cooler than he would have anticipated after the sweltering day. He sat on the ground near Gerrick, preoccupied. Kassor seemed to be in a similar mindset. He had moved away from them all, and leaned against a rough boulder. He stared into the desert, as if he could see their route through the darkness.

The prisoners had spoken little to each other on the journey, usually earning a cuffing from Cor if they tried. Shen's jaw was still sore where it had been re-injured for asking Gerrick his name on the first morning. Tonight, though, the two bandits were talking in low voices while Kassor sat apart and Cor dozed nearby.

Shen didn't want to talk with Gerrick; the man was a snake and Shen didn't trust him as far as he could spit. Gerrick having seen Cor's assault yesterday didn't help either. Misplaced anger, Shen knew, but he still blamed the man, fair or not, for Cor's attentions. Gerrick had been a swordsman, though, and must have patrolled throughout Lacedar. The need for information won out over reluctance.

"Have you ever been into the desert?" he asked, softly.

"No," Gerrick answered just as quietly, still looking ahead. "No sane man would travel past Arrend."

"What about traders?"

"I've heard Kassor brag that he's crossed it twice," Gerrick answered. "He got into Maradon's favor by bringing Bansheenan gifts for him and Cerendrin. I always figured he stole them or bought them from someone else." Gerrick turned to Shen. "If he really did make it to Bansheen and back, we might have a chance of surviving a little longer."

Cor's snoring stopped abruptly. The mercenary didn't move, but Shen could see a faint shine in his open eyes by the last of the twilight. He and Gerrick fell silent. Cor grunted and got up anyway, gathering a jar of ointment and some rope. He approached the two of them and dropped the items on the ground. Grabbing Shen by an elbow, he pulled him to his feet and chained his hands behind him for the night.

"Time everyone gets some sleep. Tomorrow'll be a long day."

Having Cor anywhere near him knotted Shen's gut, but he'd found things went better when he hid the revulsion. Kassor's order that he allow no one's wounds to fester had proved yet another excuse for Cor to lay hands on him, but Shen stood quietly while Cor put the salve on his wrists and neck where the skin had scraped raw and bloody. Finished with that, Cor pulled up Shen's padded shirt and unwound the cloth binding his ribs, as it loosened each day with riding. He re-wrapped his ribs, leaning into him and reaching around his body more than necessary. Standing at Shen's left elbow, he tied off the wrap and glanced at Kassor on Shen's other side. The trader sat apart still, his back to the camp, staring into the desert. Cor slid his hand between Shen's legs and cupped his crotch.

He grinned, watching for Shen's reaction. Shen forced his muscles to relax. He stared at the horizon, striving for an expression of bored impatience as if at a childish behavior. Cor shoved Shen to the ground and tied his feet tighter than usual before moving on to Gerrick's bonds.

Shen woke to a sound during the night, a meaty rhythmic noise in the dark. Since all the prisoners slept with their hands bound behind them, it didn't leave many options. He tried not to listen, but the quiet desert offered little diversion. He rolled to his other side and tried to go back to sleep. He drifted off to thoughts of escape, to what might happen if someday he met Cor as a free man with his body healed and his hands unbound.

The horses struggled the next day, progressing slowly and sweating with the effort of trudging through the deep, soft sand. Though Kassor hugged the shade of the rocky hills to their right, once the sun reached its zenith, it beat down mercilessly on them. Shen hung his head to avoid the direct glare and wished for the lighter clothing the others wore.

The day passed in silent misery with two short stops to water the horses. The prisoners were watered as well, though not fed or allowed to dismount. For once, Shen didn't mind not eating; he had no appetite with the heat for anything but water.

When they'd first left Lacedar Hold, Shen had assumed the prisoner's horses were unsaddled and unbridled to make escape more difficult. Now he thought it had been more for the benefit of the animals. He could see that the difficulty of traveling in the desert wasn't the frailty of the people, but the vulnerability of the horses, on which all their lives depended. Horses that could each drink nearly the weight of a man per day under this heat and exertion. He wondered how many greedy traders had died out here trying to force wagons across the sand.

Shen suffered a dozen discomforts over the course of the long day: the sweat from his horse finally soaked through the thick leather of his breeches, adding chaffing at his inner thighs to the worsening abrasions at his neck and wrists; muscle fatigue and soreness assailed him from riding bareback three days with his hands chained behind his back; his energy leeched from him, evaporating in the relentless heat like the moisture from his drying face and lips. Hunger and thirst, though, dominated all else.

Sometime in the mid-afternoon, Shen felt his horse make a right turn. He lifted his head and looked around. With the monotonous plodding and relentless heat, he hadn't even noticed that they had passed the last of the hills. The short, broken ends of the mountains looked back at him, their granite roughness shimmering in the afternoon sun. The cliffs, rising perhaps fifty lengths above him, looked as if the gods had tired of slowly diminishing the height of the mountains, easing them down to the desert, and had broken them off suddenly, like a man might break a loaf of bread. Kassor stared at the cliffs as well, searching them more frequently as they traveled north, until he called a halt near sunset.

The next morning Shen watched as Kassor and Cor repacked the horses. There seemed to be plenty of food and grain, more than two men would need to get back to Arrend, but the water had run dangerously low. The resupply in Arrend had been less than two full days ago, yet with the weight the packhorses could carry through the deep sand and the amount of water nine horses consumed, it wouldn't last more than another day, no matter how strictly they rationed.

Looking north and east, Shen saw shadeless desert stretching ahead as far as he could see. Shen saw no option except that he and the other prisoners were being taken far enough from Arrend to have no chance to make it back on foot, while Kassor and Cor rode back on the last of the water. If they were stranding them out here, they'd have to do it soon.

To Shen's surprise, they continued to ride north. By noon, Kassor slowed their pace to a crawl, studying the cliffs to his right with growing intensity. He looked back along their length frequently. Shen looked too, wondering what he hoped to see. A trail to a hermitage? A shortcut trail into Bansheen?

He dozed fitfully as he rode, seeking the oblivion of sleep from his myriad torments and finding it easy to drift off in his weakened state. He woke suddenly to a loud, wordless shout from Kassor, like a raven finding a shiny prize. The little man twisted in his saddle and grinned back at Cor, the most emotion Shen had ever from the trader.

"I remembered," Kassor said, his voice cracking with dryness. "I remembered, and it is still here." Cor mustered only enough energy to nod in approval. He'd been unusually quiet and matter-of-fact the past two days, deferential to Kassor's tense mood and finally giving Shen some respite.

Kassor dismounted and scrambled with surprising agility a short way up the cliff. He reached a narrow shelf, and Shen noticed a dark stain on the rock there. Water. Of course, though the spring above him vanished even before reaching the base of the cliff.

"Bring them up," Kassor croaked. The little man knelt and took a long drink.

The other men grabbed their horses' manes, slid off, and scurried to the rocks. Shen, with his hands behind him, crooked one leg over the mare's neck and waited for Cor to help him down. Kassor had forbidden him to dismount alone so his rib wouldn't shift and kill him. Another clue he wouldn't be left in the desert to die that Shen's mind had been too sluggish to piece together.

Cor helped him down, too heat-stressed to bother harassing him, and Shen too weak to care. Eager to get to the water, Shen struggled to climb the narrow path up the sloping base of rock with his hands behind his back. His foot slipped and he smashed one knee into the rock, and had to pitch forward onto his shoulder to keep from falling backward. Cor, climbing behind him, huffed what Shen assumed to be a dry-throated laugh.

He pushed himself to his feet and finished the climb to the shelf of rock where the others sat. From here he could see that the spring appeared through a crack in the rock above, pooled in the shallow concave at his feet, and vanished again into another crevice below. He dropped to his knees and drank deeply from the tiny, gritty seep. Water had never tasted so good.

Shen rested there with the others while Cor filled and refilled a water bucket for the horses and replenished all the waterskins. The spring ran at a slow trickle, but Kassor seemed in no hurry now and Shen relished the time, sitting in the shade with a belly full of water. Kassor seemed in rare high spirits when they finally remounted and rode past the northern end of the cliffs and over the invisible border into Bansheen.

———————— ⟨⟩ ————————

Less than two days from the spring they arrived at their first town. Ishtin, Shen heard Kassor call it. As in Arrend, Cor and the prisoners stayed outside the village, while Kassor rode in alone to buy supplies. Between the gloom of evening and the distance they kept from the village, Shen learned little more of it than its name.

When they continued the next morning, they traveled a small but well-made road. Kassor took them around the town rather than through it. Shen absorbed all he could of the little he saw, studying the plant life, the dress of the people, and the plaster-like walls of the small un-timbered homes.

He appreciated the austere beauty of the whitewashed buildings in contrast to the brightly colored garments of the people. The other prisoners gaped at the people and their mounts they passed, but Shen had already seen the Bansheenan palace guards when Dashara came to the Hold, and the skaggi they had ridden. He worked to remember every word she had said about Bansheen and the capital city where she lived, Beneya. Thinking of her, faint hope grew again.

They passed other communities over the next few days, widely spaced by leagues of flat desert between, but each one larger in size than the previous. Each time, he wondered if they might be entering Beneya, though they continued through each without stopping.

The changing and foreign landscape of Bansheen fascinated him. Trees seemed to come in only a few varieties: a stunted, twisted evergreen with sparse needles, a short tree with feathery fingers of pale green hanging down like dried moss, or tall, scaly trees with foliage only near the top, reminding Shen of the crested storks in Thiery's rivers. Dry, prickly bushes dotted the land, and he watched a woman and child carefully harvesting dark green or gray berries from one into the baskets they carried.

The heavy storm clouds of Hesh seemed no more than harmless white fluff here, their potency spent on the other side of the mountains before reaching this side. They rode under a sky as blue and almost as hot as in the deep desert, yet, despite the arid climate, each community seemed to have small springs, which they had channeled into watercourses for crops.

The fifth day out of Ishtin they topped a small rise and Shen nearly laughed at his naiveté, that he could have thought the other towns might be this one. The mass of humanity and construction spread out below him could be nothing but Beneya, the "city" Dashara had described to him. An ancient white wall, twice head-high, surrounded the entire city, and soon it loomed above them, blocking out the hectic activity beyond.

Kassor rode up to the gate. The guards questioned him about the prisoners, and he produced the letter Maradon had given him. It seemed to satisfy them, and they waved the group through. The dialect Shen caught sounded odd, different from Dashara's cultured speech, or even that of her guards. Common speech, he guessed. Shen thought for the first time on the coincidence of shared language when the two countries of the continent were so geographically separated. Then he considered the Elven history he'd learned from Dashara and Chayan, and how connected the cultures must have been in the ancient days.

They passed through the tall gates and Shen experienced amazement anew at the size of the city. He forgot his pain and fear for the first time in many days as he took in the unfamiliar and stunning vista of a place he would never have guessed he would see. A pang of worry squirmed past his wonder as he despaired at how he would ever find Dashara in a city that spread as far as he could see.

Beneya held more greenery than he had seen yet in Bansheen, and must be rich with springs. Two hills rose out of the flat land far to the left, both well vegetated and sporting dozens of palaces as large as Thiery Hold dotting their sides. Gold leaf and colored tiles sparkled in the afternoon sun from their walls and domed roofs. The largest palace adorned the top of the nearest hill, and covered the entire summit with its walled courtyards.

"By the Dead!" Shen heard Gerrick exclaim in front of him. The man turned his head to crane first one direction then another.

Kassor rode down the small hill, pulling the other horses along in tow. They entered the city proper, and Kassor wove his way through Beneya without hesitation or error.

The people were again dressed in colorful clothing of a light material, most favoring reds, oranges, and yellows, though Shen saw every shade of the rainbow. The dresses Dashara had worn in Thiery were modest compared to the sleeveless gowns the highborn women here wore, sleeveless and thin enough to clearly show the shape of their bodies beneath. The wealthier-looking men wore colorful, blousy shirts tucked into wide trousers with sashes about their waists and the common men wore only a bright, shirtless vest over their wide pants. They wore no stockings and the shoes were hardly shoes at all, leaving most of the foot exposed. Many of the commoners he saw were barefoot. All the people, men and women, servants and highborn, wore their black hair in a long single braid down the back—all but children, and even most of them had hair longer than Shen's.

It took a long time to thread their way through the maze of streets, but at last they entered a large square, surrounded by majestic buildings. A statue of a woman Shen guessed to be the Queen towered in the center of the square, a baby held in her hands and fountains splashing at her feet. Shen stared about, inured by now to the humiliation of riding through a town in chains, hardly noticing the Bansheenans stopping to stare back at the Heshan prisoners.

A fair on the south side of the square was doing brisk business. It looked like Thiery Village on a festival day. Musicians strolled the crowds with children trailing behind collecting coins, food vendors carried baskets of goods, and hawkers cried the skills of their various crafts. Lithe barefoot men pulled small two-wheeled carts carrying richly dressed men and women. Shen wondered if it might be a feast day in truth or if the fair occurred daily.

A building on his right drew his eye, the one the bronze statue faced. Two men climbed the wide stairs to the entrance. They wore different costumes than he had seen yet, gold robes with long orange scarves hung around their necks. The blue and green tiles around the doorway made him wonder if perhaps the building was a temple, and these men the priests.

Kassor took them diagonally across the square between the huge buildings. He moved through the city as if familiar with it, but slowed when they left the square, looking about carefully.

Unlike the all-white plaster buildings of the square, the houses and shops on the side streets were smaller with many sporting bright colors on the doors, around the windows, or, more rarely, the entire front of the buildings. Just beyond the corner of the square a large, squat building of tan-colored, heavy stone stood out for its plainness. It was shorter than the buildings to either side and guarded by a contingent of men in the same uniforms as the gate guards. Kassor sat up straighter when he spotted it and picked up their pace.

He approached the guard at the door, dismounted, and presented his letter again. The guard read it, nodded curtly, and ordered four men to take the prisoners inside.

"The slaver'll look them over once they've been properly cleaned up," the guard said. "There be a serai nearby where you may take a room." He pointed down the street. "I will tell the slaver he can find you there tomorrow."

Kassor seemed unhappy at turning his prisoners over without payment, but he smoothed the tightness out of his face and smiled and bowed to the guard. "Of course, of course." He handed him the keys to their chains. "My companion and I will enjoy the rest after our long journey. I am certain the slaver will find them all to his liking. These two especially," he waved a thin hand toward Gerrick and Shen, "they are Izzat, you know. Very valuable." He smiled and bobbed again, wringing his hands only a little.

"You just leavin' them …" Cor began.

Kassor shot him a dark look. "They will take most excellent care of them for us, Cor. Bansheenan are honest people. They understand how far we have traveled to trade our slaves here, where we may receive a fair price." He shot another ingratiating look over his shoulder at the guard and pushed Cor toward the horses, telling him to get the prisoners down from their horses.

Slavery. So that was the lifetime of unhappiness Maradon had planned. An unhappy future indeed, Shen thought.

Chapter Twenty-two

Shen was ushered into the cool, stone building along with the others. The place looked too martial and utilitarian to be the Hold of a ruler, and with military curiosity, Shen wondered if this was where the army was barracked or if a population this size required a separate force just to patrol the city.

The soldiers wore the same white shirts and gold breast and back-plates that Dashara's palace guards had worn, but with short, segmented, leather skirts instead of breeches, and those odd open shoes. Though he obviously hadn't been brought to a royal palace, Shen still searched the face of each soldier for one he might recognize. He saw none that were familiar, but registered with amazement that at least two of the armed soldiers he could see were women.

The guards led them all to a dungeon on the lower level, where two men guarded a heavy iron door, curved swords held ready. Shen was the first to enter the room and was immediately struck by two differences between this dungeon and Lacedar's: the prisoners inside were all chained to the wall and, more startling, they were all naked.

"There." The guard holding the key to their chains motioned Shen across the narrow, rectangular room to the back wall.

Shen's heart sank as he stood with his face to the wall, staring at his newest set of bonds; manacles with long chains bolted high on the wall and tacked again about elbow height. At floor level were a set of ankle irons.

The guard went to work on his current restraints and for one blessed moment Shen felt the weight of the collar, manacles, vertical chain, and waist chain drop from his body. They landed on the stone floor with a clatter. In the next moment he was turned with his back to the wall and his hands were secured to the irons bolted there. He silently thanked Hessura when they didn't clasp on the ankle chains. The key was passed to the next guard.

Facing the room now, Shen saw that they had placed the first of the Heshan bandits on the side wall to the right of the door, followed by Gerrick on the same wall. The second bandit, Shen, and a young Bansheenan barely past boyhood, were chained to the back wall with an empty space between each. Two more Bansheenan, rough looking men, were chained to the far wall. One stared back defiantly when Shen's glance passed over him.

The Bansheenan prisoners were chained by only one wrist, and Shen wondered if he was being singled out again for his size or if all the Heshans would be treated the same. He looked up at the bolts. Tacked as they were, above his head and again near his elbows, he wouldn't be able to reach any other prisoner or use the chain as a weapon, but the length should allow him to sit or to lie with his arm above him.

His musings toward possibilities of escape stopped short when the guard turned back to Shen and pulled a wicked-looking hunting dagger from his belt. Shock stunned him to stillness. He'd been ready to die many times over the past fortnight, but he wasn't prepared for it now. It didn't make sense. Why would they bring him all the way to Bansheen just to kill him?

The knife moved to his throat and he braced himself for the cut. In three quick jerks, the cloth of his padded shirt sliced open from top to bottom. His panic ebbed as the sleeves were cut next and the shirt was tossed aside for the rag it had become. His boots were pulled off and the leather breeches and leggings off as well. Despite his Heshan modesty, he was frankly glad to be rid of the filthy, sweat drenched clothing.

Looking to his right, he saw the other Heshans also had both wrists manacled and were getting the same treatment.

"It isn't wise for you to remove my clothes," he heard Gerrick say in weak protest, "you will only punish yourselves." His guard chuckled, but continued anyway.

The guards gathered the pile of rags and left. The door clanged shut behind them and Shen had his first real look around, up at the tall stone ceiling and small windows high on the wall. Unlike Hesh's dungeons though, the barred windows were many, letting in a good deal of light and fresh air. A gutter for sanitation ran around the base of the walls with an open drain at one end. The stone room felt blessedly cool after the heat outside, but enough warm air drifted in to keep Shen comfortable.

A key squealed in the lock and the door swung open again. Four common men entered, carrying two buckets each. Water sloshed over the edges as they set them down.

"Blind me for a beggar," one said looking around the room. "If we do get more before week's end, they'll have to put them with the regular prisoners."

He picked up one of the buckets and Shen closed his eyes just before the soapy water hit him. It tasted sharp and mineral in his mouth as he spat it from his lips. The man approached him with the bucket, still partially full. Shen saw the other three men giving Garrick and the bandits the same treatment.

"What happens at week's end?" Shen asked.

His head was shoved roughly down. The man ignored the question utterly. He dumped water over Shen's hair and scrubbed briefly at it, washing days of sand, dirt, and sweat out. Finished with his hair, he pulled a shaving blade and lump of soap from his belt pouch, and roughly scraped at the beard on Shen's face and neck. Shen flinched at the two cuts he received but felt more like himself when the man was done than he had for many days.

A last bucket of water was thrown at him.

The man unlocked the latch on Shen's right wrist, picked up the buckets, and left the room with the others.

Shen shook his hair out of his eyes and noted that the Bansheenan prisoners looked relatively clean and shaven as well. Their skin tones ranged through various shades of copper. The young man was so dark he was almost brown, the older man next to him was lighter, and the angry-looking man at the end somewhere in between.

"What happens at week's end?" Shen asked again, this time to the young Bansheenan on his right.

"The slave sale," he replied, as if it should have been obvious. "Once each month, if there be enough to sell." He had the same dialect and cadence as the other common men. "Do you be Heshan?"

Shen nodded.

"How came you to Bansheen?"

"Just lucky, I guess," Shen replied.

"The men who shaved us mentioned other prisoners," Gerrick said. "Not all are sold as slaves?"

The older man spoke for the first time. "Only some. The crime must be serious enough to warrant slavery and not so serious as to make them dangerous to their owners."

"Why do the guards care what we look like to a slaver?" Shen asked him.

"The prison receives a share of the sale. They will want him to accept us all."

Shen's body and hair dried quickly in the parched, desert air. The afternoon passed and light faded in the cell. Torches were lit in the hallway, their light flickering through the grill in the door. He saw the shadow on the wall of the approaching guard before the cell door creaked opened again. Two guards entered. Both carried trays of food and one had a bucket hanging from one forearm.

Shen wondered how many times a day they were going to get washed.

The Bansheen prisoners were given bowls of food, but the Heshans were ordered to stand against the walls again. The guard with the bucket started with the bandit near the door, throwing handfuls of white power on his body, front and back. Shen wanted to think he didn't actually need the delousing, but after the past couple of weeks he wasn't so sure. He braced for the ground lime—or whatever they used here—to burn. It did, at the chaffed skin of his neck, wrists, and thighs, especially.

He was handed a bowl of thin stew and a cup of water. After days of flatbread and dried meat, the stew tasted like a feast. When he finished his supper, he dozed where he sat and finally made himself as comfortable as possible, sitting with his right arm and head on his drawn-up knees, his left hand suspended above his shoulder.

———— ⟨∾⟩ ————

Shen woke in the morning to the sound of the door opening. He was lying on his side, his head pillowed on his right arm, with his left arm stretched above him. He had slept better last night, even like this, than all the nights of travel, trying to sleep with his hands chained behind him, where no position had been comfortable.

One of the common men sluiced out the gutter with water and lye and Shen was handed a breakfast of porridge made from a dark grain he didn't recognize. When the prisoners had all finished eating, the man returned.

"Stand. Raise your right arms," he instructed. He came to each prisoner and locked their free arm.

"The slaver do come today?" the young Bansheenan asked, sounding anxious.

The man nodded.

The boy's anxiety made Shen suspicious. "What happens if he doesn't want us?" he asked the guard.

"You be executed," he replied matter-of-factly, then gathered the dishes and left.

Not long after, the door was unlocked for a pot-bellied, middle-aged man. He wore rich clothing in gaudy colors, but had the rough and scarred face of a commoner. The man stepped into the room and Shen could see, to his utter humiliation, that a woman followed behind him. She was taller than the slaver but of an age with him, dressed in a fine lavender dress trimmed in gold braid.

Shen twisted in his chains before the helplessness of his situation caught up with his instincts to hide his nakedness. He jerked his arms down to cover himself with his hands but his chains didn't quite allow it, so he dropped his hands and tried to meet his embarrassment stoically. He could see that the other Heshans were doing no better. "Gods' eyes!" Gerrick swore when he saw her. He looked as mortified as Shen felt. The Bansheenan prisoners seemed to have no modesty and showed only eager anticipation.

The slaver walked around the room slowly, examining the prisoners in turn, with his wife coming behind and judging as intently. He paused at Gerrick. "You are the murderer?"

"I can be accused of many things, but murder is not among them. If you have been told so, you were misinformed. Likely it is the other Heshan there you seek," he nodded to Shen, "He was treated as a dangerous man on the journey here."

If Shen had been free, he would have punched the self-serving bastard in the mouth.

"Treason then?"

"Not treason, but perhaps some might have misinterpreted it as such."

"Hmph," the slaver grunted. His wife examined Gerrick from his eyes, to his stout ale belly, to his feet and back again to his crimson face.

"You are Izzat?" she asked.

Gerrick looked confused.

"Highborn?" she tried.

"I am," Gerrick replied, sounding prouder than his circumstances warranted.

The second bandit was examined as quickly as the first, but the slaver stopped again at Shen and scanned Kassor's letter. "You are the murderer then?"

"It wasn't murder. I'm a soldier. We were defending our herds against raiders. My enemy captured me and sent me here."

"You are a prisoner of war, then?"

"Yes."

"Good." He sounded genuinely pleased. "That is acceptable."

"I come from a good family," Shen said. "They or my Bealdor will ransom me for any price you ask."

"Even if it had been murder," the wife said, ignoring Shen's words and moving closer, "you would still have to take him. You must take all the foreigners. Not only are the Heshans unique, but two are Izzat. This one may bring the highest price we have yet seen." She trailed a finger down Shen's chest, over his hip and onto his thigh.

Shen felt the blood drain from his face and return with a flush hot as flame. He gritted his teeth and wondered how much humiliation he could endure and still live. The woman absently left her hand on his thigh as she looked about the room at the others.

Shen huffed out a sigh and his head slumped forward when she removed her hand and walked on behind her husband. They inspected the remaining prisoners before returning to the guard at the door. She nodded once to her husband.

"We will take them all," the slaver said to the guard, and left.

When they had gone, Shen raised his head and glared at Gerrick who met his look lightly.

"No harm meant," Gerrick said. "I wouldn't want to get killed for another man's crime. Maybe being a slave won't be so bad. Perhaps I'll end up a bed warmer for some old widow." The talkative Bansheenan had told them the night before that Izzat slaves were often bought by women. "So, you said the Bealdor held a personal resentment toward you. I never guessed you meant it was you who killed his eldest son." Even the two bandits stared at Shen.

Shen didn't deign to answer the man.

"Well," Gerrick said to himself. "No wonder we all ended up here."

———— ⁓❦⁓ ————

After a light mid-day meal, a guard came and placed Shen in his old chains. He was marched, still naked, from the room. The guard escorted him up the short stairs to the main level. Shen felt his nakedness with renewed humiliation and searched about for any women, thankfully seeing none.

The guard led him to a small room lit with rush-lights. The room stood nearly empty except for a small table at the side, and two tall chairs near it, pushed close together and facing each other. A large man sat in one of the chairs.

Shen eyed the instruments laid out on the side table as the guard led him to the other chair. The chain from his collar was pulled down the seat-back and secured at the base, pulling Shen's head back far enough to strain his neck muscles and make swallowing difficult. The guards left the room.

This man looked to be no soldier and Shen took a chance while he could. "I am a friend of Somiir Dashara. I need to get ..."

The man stood and hit Shen across the mouth with a heavy, backhanded blow. "That name will not be profaned by a slave!"

Unable to spit with his head so far back, Shen swallowed the blood, hoping there was no tooth with it. The man stood over him, glaring, until sure Shen wouldn't speak again. Convinced, he sat.

The man's forearms were painted in vivid designs that Shen could see disappearing under the sleeves of his cuffless shirt as he reached for items on the table. Shen's palms began to sweat when the man picked up what looked like a round cluster of needles bound together with twine at the end of a short, thin dowel. He dipped the needles in a small inkpot, staining the end of the needles blue. He sat close enough that one of his knees rested between Shen's legs. He grabbed Shen by the jaw and braced a thick thumb below his left cheekbone, bringing the needles toward Shen's eye. Shen twisted his head at the last moment and the man grabbed his chin in an iron grip and turned him back.

"What little babies you Heshans be." He poked the needles firmly into the skin below Shen's eye a few times. Still holding Shen's jaw, he set the needles down, picked up a small cloth and wiped at the area, then dipped the needles and began again.

The process went on for some time and Shen relaxed slightly, though his cheek became more sensitive and painful as the needles repeatedly pushed into the skin of his cheek. The man wiped at Shen's face a final time and sat back to examine the result. He dabbed at the area with a strong-smelling astringent that burned the irritated skin and made Shen's eyes water, then dipped a piece of cloth in a sticky gel and pressed it to his cheekbone.

The man opened the door and called for the guard who returned to escort Shen back to the dungeon. Shen didn't dare try Dashara's name again, but another thought occurred to him.

He waited until he and the guard were in a hallway alone. In a low voice, Shen said, "Tell Imecus that I am here. He will reward you for the information." The captain of the queen's guards would surely be known to all the soldiers, and Imecus would remember Shen from his trip to Thiery Hold.

The soldier stared at him, wide-eyed. They were on the steps from the main floor to the dungeon. Without a word, the soldier shoved Shen down the last two steps so hard that he fell, landing on the point of his shoulder.

"It's the truth," Shen protested, but it was no use. He struggled to his feet. Pain lanced down his arm. He licked at his lip and tasted blood. Frustration and despair welled up in him. Dashara's trip to Hesh had probably been a quiet affair. These men likely didn't even know that she or Imecus had been to Hesh. They'd have no reason to believe Shen knew either of them personally.

The guard pushed him roughly back to his place on the wall and locked him back in his chains. The rest of the Heshans were taken away, one by one, followed by the Bansheenan prisoners. Each came back with a cloth patch on their cheek.

The patches were taken off their faces the next day and Shen laughed aloud when he looked at Gerrick. It was the first time he had laughed in a long while.

"What are you laughing at, you dog?" Gerrick said sharply.

"You bear the proud mark of Thiery," Shen replied, looking about to see that they all had the same sky-blue diamond. The mark looked smaller than it had felt from the swelling on his cheek, no bigger than his thumbnail. "Is this always the mark of a slave?" Shen asked the young Bansheenan next to him.

"Yes, always," the boy replied, looking perplexed.

Shen laughed again.

Nothing else remarkable happened that day or the next. The prisoners spoke less often, and the defiant Bansheenan not at all. He had opened his mouth once to show the stump of a tongue. Whether he had been born that way or it had been a part of his punishment, Shen hadn't asked.

Shen imagined that life as a slave would be a living nightmare. Even if being highborn got him bought by some woman, he doubted "bed-warming," would be his only duty. No matter who bought him, he would still be a slave, living out his life in a foreign country. He'd never realized how much he valued his freedom until he lost it.

His thoughts ran often to Dashara. He tried to hold onto his belief that he'd find a way to get word to her someday, but thoughts that his story would never be believed or that he could be sold to someone from a distant town defeated his optimism. It wasn't only his hope of escape from slavery that made him think of her, though. He wished, not for the first time, that he had kissed her that night in the Hold.

When he wasn't thinking of Dashara, he was thinking of home. He'd often dreamed of traveling outside Thiery, but unsure now if he'd ever see his own land again, he found himself homesick. He'd lost track of the exact date, but thought Summer Festival must have happened by now. Winterfest had always been Tirren's favorite time, even before Yslaaran; he said the feasting and cheer and candelabras burning throughout the night were a bright spot in the cold season. For Shen, though, Summer Festival had always been the most joyous. Green grass, the crops coming on, and most of summer spread out ahead like an unopened gift. This would be the first year he missed the wood splitting competition since reaching his manhood. He fell asleep that night thinking of home. In his dreams, he escaped the dungeon and forgot his fears of the coming days for a little while.

Chapter Twenty-three

It was dusk in the mortal world and the purple sky had faded to colorless night. Uthbaraal stepped out of the mists behind Baedis, into the land called Lacedar. They were at the outer wall of the king's fort, just below the gate. Two riders and a wagon approached the entrance; the human king and his retinue returning home from their futile little sacrifice.

The king paused at the gate and peered down the length of the wall to where Uthbaraal and Baedis stood. He swung his horse and spurred it forward to investigate. Uthbaraal thought it funny that the king couldn't see well in the gloom and watched him strain to identify them as he approached. Even to the human's poor eyes, Baedis' pale blond hair and light skin must stand out. Uthbaraal knew that he himself would be only a shadow among shadows.

Bitter metal rasped in the silence as one of the soldiers drew his sword and Uthbaraal curled his lip at the acrid odor of steel. Fear radiated from all four humans as they made out the features of their visitors; Uthbaraal could feel the prickling of the emotion on the air as clearly as he could smell it wafting from the men. He found their fear amusing, as well.

The king held up a hand, halting the men with him.

"Maradon," Baedis said, stepping forward, "you called to Fresshe today for help and we have been sent in answer."

"Who is it that comes to me, and what honor would you?" Maradon's voice was deferential—and, Uthbaraal noticed, steady, though probably only by the force of his will. The fear had not abated one whit, though there was arrogance aplenty in the man.

"I am Baedis. My companion, Uthbaraal, and I were sent to give you guidance. Your prayers to Fresshe have been heard and we are the instruments of your answer. By accepting what we offer, you do honor to the one who has sent us."

Uthbaraal felt glad that Baedis circumvented the truth rather than telling a direct lie in Fresshe's name. Gone or not, the gods were still the gods. Like the other Elves, Uthbaraal held out hope that they would come back someday. What Baedis said worked though; the king heard what he wanted to hear.

Maradon nudged his horse closer and dismounted, motioning to his men to do the same. One of the men sketched an old, useless—and, Uthbaraal noted, incorrect—protection rune in the air as he climbed down from the wagon. A guard called in surprise from atop the wall, not having seen him and Baedis until the king spoke to them. The king barked at the man to move on.

"I'm grateful that Fresshe has heard me," the king said. "I will do all in my power to honor both you and him, and will gladly accept your guidance." There was a shiny greed in his dark eyes.

Uthbaraal held back a smile as he looked into the black eyes of the king and wondered if the man had any idea from whom he'd inherited those eyes. Strange that the Unseely traits still showed in the man's line. It had been many generations ago since Uthbaraal had last been here. One of the Seely had allowed him to come along many years before, while he wooed a young lady. Uthbaraal had gladly accepted the invitation. He hadn't intended to mate with the woman in the courtyard, but once he saw her dancing in the garden with her ladies he hadn't been able to resist. The gods hadn't been around to stop him, after all, and the Seely with him too preoccupied with his own conquest.

"Listen then to what I say," Baedis answered, breaking into Uthbaraal's memories. "Gather all the force you can—soldiers and merchants, wainwrights and blacksmiths and farmers. Make an army like in your olden days, and march on your enemy on the first day of the dark of the moons. If you do this thing, my people will be with you."

"I will do all you ask of me," the king said solemnly. "Every man who is hale enough to carry a weapon will be marching with me at the appointed time."

"Father?" A high, sweet voice came from the gate. A girl ran down the wall toward them. "Father, look. Three swordsmen gave me ribbons at the games today." Uthbaraal watched the girl run, colored streamers fluttering in one hand. She had the beauty of a flower bud on the cusp of blooming. He felt a quick lust rising in him.

Maradon cast an irritated look her way and threw up his hand, index finger raised, stopping her out of earshot. Surprise painted her face as she realized that her father and his men were not alone. Maradon, red-faced with anger or embarrassment, turned back to Baedis. He bowed, apologizing for the interruption.

Baedis continued, "Uthbaraal will be your envoy. He will guide you as you march and lead you into battle." Uthbaraal stepped forward so that Maradon could see him more clearly.

Uthbaraal had not been to Lacedar since that time long ago, but he had heard that some of the ruling class had gone mad in the generations that followed his visit. He suspected his seed to be the cause. It was one reason Uulaten hadn't allowed the Unseely to consort with humans, the dark blood ran too strongly for their little mortal minds. Uthbaraal was glad that he hadn't killed the girl, though. His deed had never been discovered by his people, and it was fun now to see his human get.

Besides, the Seely had always taken mortals. When they had still helped mankind they called it love, and when they had ceased to care about them they called it sport, but Uthbaraal's kind had been denied this pleasure. Things were different now, though. Evainya planned the destruction of the humans; what did it matter if he took one more girl? He could even take her with him, to his own land, as the Seely sometimes did.

"There is one thing more," Uthbaraal said. Baedis shot him a dark look, but Uthbaraal knew he would be unable to contradict him without affecting the illusion that they acted on orders from Fresshe. "You must give more than just a boar to prove yourself worthy of this favor. Your daughter will be required as a token," he said, glancing behind Maradon where the girl still waited.

Maradon looked caught off guard. He had been willing to pledge anything, Uthbaraal had seen it clearly in his eyes, but he hesitated at this. "Is she for sacrifice or for bride?" Maradon asked after a pause.

"Fresshe would not require that such a one be sacrificed." Uthbaraal said smoothly. "She will be cherished for her beauty and live in splendor until such time as she may be returned to you." Uthbaraal watched Maradon weigh the condition.

"I would prove myself worthy," the king said, after a shorter pause than Uthbaraal had expected. "She is yours."

Baedis shot another dark glance at Uthbaraal, then said, "Come, child." The girl, enchanted already by Baedis, walked straightaway to him.

Uthbaraal regretted Baedis's spell. He had wanted this one aware, unlike the other one he'd spelled to keep quiet. The disappointment was forgotten a moment later, and he nearly bounced with impatience and anticipation at the thought of taking the girl with him.

Baedis strode forward and stepped into the mist. Uthbaraal took the girl's hand and followed.

Chapter Twenty-four

The day of the sale came, bringing equal parts anticipation and apprehension from the prisoners. The lack of clothing, combined with the warm, dry air had healed most of Shen's chafing and wounds except for his manacled left wrist. The buckets of water and shaving blades appeared again and all of the prisoners were cleaned. The slaver had been paying for most of the men to receive extra food the past three days, though stouter Gerrick had received less than normal, much to his dismay.

The slaver and his wife returned mid-morning, followed by two of their personal slaves.

"Should we braid their hair?" the slaver asked his wife, looking at the Heshans.

She thought for a minute then shook her head. "No, leave it. The barbaric look it gives them adds to their appeal."

She went to each of them and combed out their hair, then gave them a cloth with salt and lemon to scrub their teeth.

When the slaver seemed satisfied with their appearance he pulled lengths of thin, coarsely woven linen from a bag he carried and asked a guard to unlock the right hand of each man. He passed the strips to them and, while the Heshans stood holding them uselessly in their hands, the Bansheenan began awkwardly wrapping them one-handed about their waist and loins. The man's slaves moved about the room helping. When one approached Shen, he showed him how to wrap the cloth twice just below the waist to hold it, then around the back waistband and between the legs, wrapping the excess around the front waistband. Shen had never expected to be so glad to possess a scrap of cloth.

When they'd finished, the slaver pulled a new set of manacles from another bag. The prisoners were released from the wall, one by one, and shackled together with one long chain running through the manacle loops.

"No," the slaver's wife said when the slaver passed by Shen to take the other men first. "Put him in the middle. He will sell better after the crowd is warmed up and before the serious bidders have spent their money."

Once the last man had been hooked into the chain, they were ushered out of the cell, up the stairs, and down the hall to the open front door.

"For pity's sake man, our clothes!" Gerrick begged, when he saw where they were headed.

"You have no clothes," the slaver said. "You have no possessions except what your owner chooses to give you."

"Besides," his wife said, "the buyers need to see what they are getting."

With one guard leading and one following, they passed out of the building and into the morning sun. After days in the cool stone cell, the brightness made Shen blink and the intense heat nearly suffocated him.

They were led up the street and down the backside of the bazaar where vendors and buyers alike turned to stare as they passed. A wooden platform stood at the far end of the bazaar. They were brought up onto the platform and the chain was hooked to a stout pole at either side. Prison guards took their stations at each pole, and the two personal slaves stood behind the prisoners. The slaver and his wife moved out front, speaking with the rapidly forming crowd of potential buyers, giving details about the men and answering the many questions about the Heshans.

Shen had heard that the sales began at noon. Glancing at the sun, he gauged that would still be some time from now. A large crowd began to gather—many of them Izzat women. Shen thought he'd become immune to the embarrassment of being paraded in chains, but that was before being set in front of a crowd wearing nothing but a scrap of linen, about to be sold like a bull at a fair. He was a hand taller than the next tallest prisoner, well-muscled, in the prime of life, and a highborn Heshan swordsman; to say he received the lion's share of the attention from the crowd was to say the day was warm.

Maradon had done better than he could have known. Shen hated his life and dreaded his future. He thought of Kassor and Cor. They must be on their way back to Hesh, wealthy from their sale and probably loaded with Bansheenan goods that would make them wealthier still. Shen hoped their horses died under them in the desert and they died a slow death from thirst. He hoped Maradon hanged them when they returned, to keep anyone from learning what he'd done. He hoped Kassor and Cor killed each other for their greed of money, and that Maradon's foul temper burst a vessel in his head.

When the sale finally began, the slaver stepped back up onto the platform and announced the list of prisoners, their status, their crimes, and their qualities. The wife stepped up to the other side, where she could help spot the bidders. Without further preamble, the bidding began on the tongueless Bansheenan at the west end. He sold quickly to an Izzat man.

The currency seemed to be copper, silver, and gold coin, the same as in Hesh, though Shen had no idea of the value of the coins. He gathered from the pleased face of the buyer and the sour face of the slaver that the ending bid of seven silver and two copper coins was low.

When it came to the first of the Heshan bandits, the bidding went longer and higher, ending at ninety silver coins. This seemed to please both the slaver and the Izzat couple who paid for the foreigner.

Gerrick, on Shen's left, was next. Shen felt him tense as the bidding began. The men were quickly outbid, leaving two women still vying. The final price was one gold coin and forty silver, offered by a woman at least fifteen years older than Gerrick. He got his old widow after all, Shen thought to himself. The chain slithered through Gerrick's manacles as the woman paid the slaver's wife. A moment later he was gone, without a word or a backward glance.

Shen braced himself as the slaver announced a starting bid of one gold coin for him. The bidding began furiously. Men who only wanted to buy a strong back didn't bother to bid at a price starting so high. A few vied with the women, perhaps for the uniqueness of owning a foreigner. Eventually, the bidding came down to three women, all rapidly countering each other, none relenting: one a little older than Shen, one his mother's age and one a gray-haired woman. When the oldest woman raised the bid to three gold coins, the slaver's eyes nearly popped.

A clear, authoritative voice from the back silenced the crowd. "Six gold coins."

Shen searched the crowd with his heart in his throat and hope burning him like a flame that he recognized the voice. The slaver and his wife folded and dropped their foreheads to the platform. The three Izzat women who had been bidding bowed low in acquiescence. Shen spotted Dashara at last, moving forward through the crowd. His eyes teared with relief.

Dashara nodded to a man at her heels dressed in the odd gold robe and long orange scarf that Shen had seen several times in the city. He felt the chain pull free of his manacles and the robed man handed the coins to the slaver's wife. One of the guards bowed low to Dashara and escorted Shen to her.

"Somiir, allow me to bring the man to your palace."

"That will not be necessary. Please remove his bonds." The guard hesitated only a second before releasing Shen, bowing deeply and moving off, though he watched Shen carefully from a distance.

Maybe the God of Fortune hadn't abandoned him after all. "Did Jhenna bring you to me?" Shen asked, still stunned by her sudden appearance. He hardly trusted that she was real, that she was here.

"Imecus received a message saying you were to be sold today as a slave. Neither of us truly believed it, until I saw you for myself."

He nearly laughed. So greed had inspired the prison guard to risk contacting Imecus after all.

Shen didn't want to look away from Dashara, in case she vanished as suddenly as she had appeared. His eyes took in all of her. It was considerably more than he had seen of her before. She wore a top that ended just below her breasts and a pale blue skirt with silver beading, slit from ankle to thigh up one long leg. The irony wasn't lost on him that he could be surprised at her manner of dress while standing in front of her in nothing but a strip of linen.

The gold-robed servant returned from paying for Shen. "Lashan," she said to him, "find Kesum-Shen some clothing." He bobbed a bow and moved quickly for the bazaar.

Shen smiled. "They told me that as a slave I would have no possessions except what I was given by my owner."

Dashara put a hand on his cheek and looked up into his eyes. "You are no slave. I bought your freedom, not you."

He placed his hand over hers. "You have owned me since I first saw you at the gates of the Hold."

She stroked her thumb softly across the tattoo on his cheekbone. He let go of her hand, when he saw the pity. It was too much to bear. A fortnight of anger and fear and shame bubbled close to the surface.

She dropped her hand from his face, looking uncertain, as if her touch might have offended him.

"I'm sorry," he said, unable to explain more.

Looking again at his slave mark she said, "Perhaps later you will tell me how this all came about?"

He nodded, a dozen emotions thick in his throat.

They moved off a little way from the auction. She looked back at the platform where the last Heshan was being sold. "Are there others I should bring with us?"

Shen stopped, ashamed that he hadn't thought of them before. He didn't want to put Dashara in the position of interfering with the law here, but he considered each man.

Gerrick was too much of a lying, self-serving rat to take back to Thiery and if he returned to Lacedar, Maradon would most likely kill him ... as well as find out that Shen had been rescued. Going to some old woman's bed might be the best option the man had. The bandits probably deserved whatever fate they got, and it had turned out that the young Bansheenan had gotten drunk and killed a man in anger. The other two never claimed to be innocent of whatever they had been arrested for, and they had been tried under their own laws.

"No. I suppose not," he said at last, feeling conflicted at leaving any of them to the fate he had so narrowly escaped.

Lashan returned with a pair of light brown breeches and a plain red vest. He apologized for the commoner's clothes, saying they were the largest he could find. Shen pulled them on where he stood. He snugged the drawstring of the breeches, not caring that the wide hems came above his ankles, or that the shirtless vest fit tight across his back.

Lashan procured a second cart. Dashara and Shen got in one and Lashan took the next. The sound of the auction faded as the runner pulling their cart carried them away from the bazaar.

Shen stayed quiet during most of the ride and Dashara, thankfully, didn't press him to talk. He knew he shouldn't feel uncomfortable that she had just bought him as a slave, but the last two weeks had pushed him to his limits. It would take some time to regain his equilibrium.

He looked about with increasing interest as they left the central part of the city and approached the southeast of the two hills. A group of barefoot men sat at the bottom of the hill. One jumped up and ran to their cart, taking one of the staves, another moved to the back to push. The three men moved them at a decent pace up the increasingly steep slope.

The hills looked more vegetated than the land around them, with shrubs and trees, as well as row upon row of cultivated grapevines. Water issued down the hill in man-made channels. They passed a number of elaborate palaces, growing larger as they climbed. All were of decorated whitewashed plaster and enclosed in tall, white walls. The courtyards he could see over the walls contained elaborate gardens, some with plants sculpted into geometric shapes or fantastic animals.

Near the top of the hill, the rickshaw turned into the gate of the largest palace. Green and cobalt tile surrounded the domed top and gold-leaf designs covered the doors. Shen had known the Somiir were revered in Bansheen, but seeing the deference Dashara had been shown at the auction and the palace where she lived was beyond anything he could have imagined.

The gold-robed servant that greeted them at the door seemed confused by Shen's foreign appearance, his slave mark, and his commoner's clothes. Dashara dispelled the doubt.

"Gindin, Kesum-Shen is my honored guest. Please attend him while he is here." Turning to Shen she said, "Make yourself welcome in my home. Anything you wish, ask any of the aleef and you will have it. I assume you wish to bathe and rest first, but if there is anything else you want, please ask."

"I hardly know how to begin to thank you. Know that I'll find a way to repay both your gold and your kindness."

Dashara gave him a smile that said it was nothing. "Before you rest, if you will allow it, I would like to help with your wounds."

She waited for his answer and it dawned on him that she meant to do it with magic. Shen had watched Chayan grow to manhood, felt at ease with both him and Dashara, but being at ease with the person and at ease with their magic were two different things. "Most of them have healed in the past week," he said weakly, though many obviously hadn't.

She touched the scabs on his neck. "But this," and the raw flesh on his left wrist, "and this." She touched one arm, still puffy and red where Cor had knocked Shen into a thorn plant in the first days of his journey, and higher up, the shoulder where he had landed when the guard pushed him down the stairs. She looked at his right side. "And this." Her hand slid beneath the open vest along his injured rib where the bone had healed unevenly, leaving a small bump. Her gentle touch sent a shiver through him.

"You could straighten the bone?"

"I'm sorry." She shook her head, focused on what she felt beneath her hand. "I can't shift it, but I can finish the healing so there is no pain and no likelihood of re-injury."

He wanted to say no, but she looked too sincere. Her touch felt too good. It moved him that someone wanted to take away his pain after so many had wanted to cause it. He nodded.

Without warning a breeze blew through his bones, a coolness bubbled through his blood, a spinning lightheadedness like too much heavy mead tickled his brain. He would have told her to stop if he could have caught his breath.

She removed her hand from his side and, just as suddenly, it was over. The wicked fatigue that had plagued him for more days than he could remember was gone, leaving only a natural sleepiness. The pain from his rib and chaffed thighs and sunburn, his aching muscles and myriad other hurts and cuts—gone. Pain that had been so constant he hardly noticed it anymore shouted its absence. He touched his neck and wrist; they felt as smooth as if they had never been injured.

"Do you wish refreshment before you bathe?" She spoke as if nothing had happened.

"No," he stammered, unable to frame any other response. "A bath will be most welcome."

"Gindin, show Kesum-Shen to the baths and attend him there, then see him settled in the West Room." Turning back to Shen she said, "I hope you will be able to stay long enough for me to show you some of Beneya before we see you home to Hesh." She squeezed his hand once before Gindin led him away.

Following Gindin down a series of hallways, he felt the warm damp of the baths before he saw them, but was entirely unprepared for the sight when the man opened one of the large double doors. Before him lay a tiled pool of steaming water, four times his length and nearly as wide as it was long. There was a drain at the far end, and a trough of clay tile carried steaming warm water to refill it.

He was shown how to adjust the temperature to his liking by diverting the hot water trough to a nearby drain and swinging another that carried cold spring water into the pool. Gindin suggested Shen begin and end by rinsing under a cool stream of water falling from a high trough by the wall.

When the man left, he checked to make sure he was alone before he undressed. He stepped under the stream of cool water and used the mild vinegar set out for him to wash his hair, and the rosemary and aloe to rinse it. A smooth bar of soap rested atop a small cloth. Finished, he lowered himself into the warm bath and sat on the small bench of tile. He leaned back, closed his eyes, and felt better than he had in weeks. Perhaps better than he ever had.

Shen hadn't realized that he had dozed off until Gindin gently touched his shoulder and asked if he was ready to be shown to his rooms. He handed him a large, soft towel and took a few quick measurements before they left the bath, then walked Shen to his room wrapped in nothing but the towel.

The room was almost as impressive as the bath, with a large, opulent sitting room and an enormous bedroom. He went straight to the huge bed and crawled in, declining food for sleep. He sank into the softest mattress he had ever known, covered with fine, cool sheets. It was a far cry from his straw and ticking mattress at the Hold, and farther still from the hard ground or the stone floor of the prisons.

He was asleep before Gindin left the room.

Chapter Twenty-five

*S*hen wore nothing but a scrap of cloth while the Summer Festival spun merrily around him, all of Thiery Village celebrating except for him. The pigs jostled him but they were easier to intimidate than the bulls that had been in with him earlier. "Your turn," the farmer said, and pulled him out of the pen. Bound at the wrists he was taken to the auction block. The bidding began, but a man's voice drowned out the elderly women vying for him. "Three gold coins."

Cor's voice.

Cor pushed to the front of the crowd holding Shen's old chains. Shen twisted and struggled as men he had known all his life held him and the chains were locked on. Cor flashed his snaggle-toothed grin and leaned forward to whisper in his ear.

Shen woke with a start and pulled himself free of the sheets that had wrapped about him. He didn't know where he was and looked suddenly to the other side of the bed, half expecting to see Cor. His heart beat a rapid tempo against his chest and his skin stuck to the sheets, damp with fear-sweat. The room was dark but soft light seeped in under the door. His eyes adjusted and he recognized the bedroom in Dashara's palace.

He took a long drink from a water pitcher and cup by the bed, found the garderobe, and climbed back into the sinfully soft bed. He was asleep again as soon as he lay down.

Some unknown time later, he woke again in a less murky darkness, well-rested and ravenous. He got up and pulled back the curtains of the large windows, letting in the thin light of either dawn or dusk. Dusk, he decided. A pitcher of wash-water had been left out for him next to a basin. Soap and a shaving blade lay by the basin and a fresh set of clothes had been neatly folded on a chair.

The dark blue shirt was of a material so fine it had little weight to it. He tucked it into the wide-legged, brown pants and wrapped the light blue sash about his waist. On the second try, he thought he had it tied properly. The clothes had been tailored to him. A pair of open shoes lay on the floor beneath the chair and a leather hair thong rested by a comb on the dresser.

He opened the door of the sitting room to find Gindin kneeling outside and discovered that it was evening of his second day in the palace, just past suppertime. He had slept for a day and a half. Gindin led him through the halls, sending the first servant he saw to tell Dashara and the kitchens that her guest was awake. He led the way to an informal sitting room where Dashara sat reading. Shen saw her from the hallway, curled in a chair, her legs folded to one side, the slit in the material exposing one bare leg. He thought she looked more beautiful every time he saw her.

She closed her book as he entered the room and unfolded herself from the chair, smiling warmly. He took in every detail of her, from her bare feet to the olive skin of her lean belly, from the swell of her breasts above the brief lavender top to her mahogany hair and large green eyes. As little as she wore, it was easy to imagine her in less, and he felt the stirrings of arousal.

"I'm glad to see you awake," she said. "I worried that you were unwell, but the aleef said you were sleeping deeply whenever they checked on you."

He didn't know what aleef were, but he guessed she was referring the gold-robed servants. "It feels like I hibernated more than slept, but, yes, I'm well. Better than I've been for some time."

"You must be hungry. The kitchen is preparing a meal for you."

His stomach rumbled at the thought.

Dashara led him to an informal dining room with Lashan and Gindin trailing at a distance. As soon as he took a seat the food began to arrive. Fruits and cheeses came first, some of them unfamiliar, while the smell of meat roasting in the kitchens teased him. Dashara ordered a small plate of fruit for herself to keep him from eating alone.

All of the courses were served with a pale, chilled wine that was slightly different with each food. Shen had never known anything but Hesh's strong red wine—plain in the summer, hot with spices in the winter, and heavy with sediment in all seasons.

He found himself able to eat far less than he wanted to after two weeks of light rations, but he tried a little of everything. When the dessert of iced fruit juice had been cleared, they sat drinking a mild, yellow tea. Conversation remained polite and neutral, less personal than the conversation he wanted to have. Seeing her in her element, in her power, in that outfit, he could hardly focus on anything but her. He wondered if she was betrothed. If she had a current suitor. If she was attracted to him too, or if it was just his imagination.

Over dinner, she didn't ask and he didn't tell how he had come to be sold as a slave, but he knew he owed her an explanation. Shen toyed with the small teacup, running a finger around the delicate rim, so different from the heavy pottery of Thiery.

It wasn't that he'd been taken prisoner that gnawed at him—it was the way of battle that somebody won, somebody lost. Besides, he hadn't really been bested; Lacedar had captured him with trickery. It was the rest—the fear, the humiliations, the helplessness. Not to mention that she had seen him sold like an animal. It frightened him to think of starting to talk about it in case he couldn't stop. He tipped his nearly empty teacup on its little plate and watched it rock to stillness again.

"Lacedar brought an army onto Thiery soil," he said without preamble. He looked up at her. "We met them at the border and fought. I was captured by some men pretending to be Thiery soldiers and brought to Lacedar as a prisoner. Maradon, the Bealdor there, is the one who sent me here. It turns out I killed his son in the horse raids I told you about when you visited." He picked up the cup and drained the last of the tea. It had been as brief as he could make it, and still it invoked the weeks of pain and abuse in too-vivid detail.

Her eyes studied him, doubtless seeing the things he had been unwilling to say written on his face. "I'm sorry for what you must have endured. I'm only glad that Imecus heard about you. Word would have reached me eventually that Heshans were in Beneya and I would have investigated, but at least you were spared some time in captivity."

He nodded, grateful that she asked no questions. Thinking of the slave sale, he touched his cheek with one finger. "Will this come off in time?"

Her brow furrowed in sadness, or perhaps embarrassment. She spoke matter-of-factly. "The skin has been deeply dyed. The mark is permanent, Shen."

He tried to shrug it off. After all, it was her culture that gave the mark significance, not his. "Perhaps it'll start a fashion when I get back."

He didn't want the evening to end yet and it seemed she didn't either. They moved to a sitting room, different from the one where he had seen her reading, and even more opulent than the last. He wondered how many rooms the palace contained.

They settled on soft couches opposite each other and talked a long while. Dashara spoke about Bansheen and briefed him on some of their customs. Shen told her about Yslaaran's recent visit, knowing her interest in the Elves. She asked for details that he didn't know; Tirren had been reticent, even with him. He ended up talking about his friendship with Tirren instead, and then his boyhood in Panden.

A yawn came that he couldn't stifle.

"You are tired," she said. "I'm sorry, I have kept you up late. It must be near midnight."

"I'm not sure it can be called late when I woke at dinnertime." He smiled. "I can't believe I'm sleepy again already."

She walked to the sitting room door with him. Two different gold-robed servants knelt in the hall. "Amee is the head of my nighttime aleef," Dashara said, introducing the middle-aged woman, "and Kem will be at your door throughout the night if you should require anything." The young man stood and bowed to him.

Shen suppressed a smile at the extravagance of having a servant kneeling by his door all night on the off chance he might want something. In Thiery, if the Bealdor himself wanted something in the middle of the night, he had to wake someone or get up and get it himself.

He knew he should say goodnight to Dashara, but he didn't want to. The memory came back to him of the last time he had seen her in Hesh and hadn't been forward enough to kiss her. The memory he had played so often during his captivity. He thought she returned affection for him but couldn't be sure. He didn't know the etiquette for courting here but he wasn't going to spend the rest of his life regretting missed opportunities with her.

Shen reached out and brushed her hair back from her face with one finger, watching her reaction. He didn't have to watch long. She moved into him and turned her mouth up to his. Shen slid his arms around her. The kiss was long and sweet, and finer than any of his imaginings.

They parted slowly. He smiled down at her and said goodnight ... while he still could.

When Shen awoke the next morning, Gindin knelt in the hall. He didn't know what time the servants switched shifts, but felt he had slept later than he had expected to again. He asked Gindin to show him to the bath. The clothes Gindin brought to him when he was finished were even finer than the last.

Shen fingered the light green embroidery at the ends of the dark green sleeves, marveling at the softness of the shirt. He slipped on the buckskin-colored pants with renewed appreciation for the light materials. The morning already felt as warm as a hot summer day at home. He was even finding the "sandals" comfortable, and certainly more practical in the heat than his heavy boots would have been.

When he had dressed, Gindin took him to a terrace overlooking the city where Dashara sat at a laden breakfast table. He looked at the city spread out below them and was amazed yet again by the sheer size of Beneya.

"Queen Assia has invited us to supper with her and the other Somiir before you leave." Dashara said, as Shen took a seat. "She asked when you might feel ready."

He shrugged. "I am the queen's to command." He didn't feel much like an ambassador for Thiery, sporting a slave tattoo and having arrived in their country in chains, but he couldn't very well decline.

"How much is this going to matter?" He indicated the tattoo.

"It will matter no more to the Queen or to Teyyas and Maiar than it does to me. There may be confusion at times, though, for other people." She looked apologetic. "As long as you are with me, no dishonor will come of it, but you must be careful not to try the city on your own."

An ironic turnabout. He remembered his own concerns for her when she had been in Thiery, needing protection to go among his people.

She deftly changed the topic to the history of the royal family and of the city, pointing out landmarks from their vantage. When they finished breakfast, he crossed his forearms on the table and studied her.

"Dashara," he said—she had told him last night to call her by name and she smiled now when he used it—"you've taught me some of the customs here, but you haven't told me how a man would go about courting a Somiir."

Her smile turned wicked. "Well ... the Izzat who wish favor send gifts to show their interest, often for many years before the Somiir is old enough to court. When the Somiir is grown and has moved out of the School, he or she will begin to choose from the suitors and take lovers."

She seemed not to notice that he worked to keep his face composed at the shocking confession.

"When the Somiir is old enough," she continued, "and has known the company of a variety of lovers, one will eventually capture his or her heart."

A variety of lovers. It stung. His propriety warred briefly with his feelings for her. He looked at her, really looked, and decided his propriety could meet him in the Land of the Dead. What did it matter that she wasn't a virgin—not by a long shot, by the sound of it—neither was he. If she was Heshan, that would be different, but she was like nothing he had ever known.

"And how would a man with no gifts win the heart of a Somiir?"

"It's not gifts that impress or win," she said, sitting back and toying with a piece of orange fruit on her fork. "The Izzat only do that to bring attention to themselves." She looked up at him from under long, dark lashes. "And you most assuredly have my attention."

She did feel the same. He knew it. Well, he thought he had, anyway. Shen grinned and reached across the table to her. She put her fork down and took his hand. He kissed her palm. "Then I will endeavor to be the one you choose."

"But I have already chosen." Her look left no doubt as to whom she meant.

"Then you would marry me?" He didn't doubt that he looked as surprised as he sounded.

Dashara pulled her hand away reflexively and flushed. He had misunderstood her somehow and had embarrassed them both. She recovered quickly and reached out to him again, stopping short of touching him.

"I didn't mean to mislead you, Shen. I thought you understood I was speaking of being lovers. I know little of courtships in Hesh. Forgive me." She paused, thinking through her next words. "I believe if we spent time together, I would choose you for a mate above all others. But there's too much standing in the way, Shen. You wouldn't give up Hesh and I'd never ask you to. And I have a duty to my people here. My intention, my hope, was that we could enjoy our time together while we may."

Shen nodded. He had known relationships of convenience with women before; for the first time in his life he had wanted this to be more. He hadn't thought of marriage until he said it, but now that it was said, he realized he meant it. He would never meet a woman like her again. After the brief moment of believing she wanted the same, the reality hurt more than he expected. But she was right, of course. He couldn't ask her to leave her country when she was so important here, and he couldn't give up his life in Thiery.

Or could he?

"Let's leave it in Jhenna's hands then," he said with a smile to smooth things over. The God of Fortune would see that things happened as they should.

She pursed her lips in an odd expression he found unreadable, but she said no more. They finished breakfast over safer topics. When the small talk dwindled Dashara said, "There are some things I must attend to today. I will be away part of the day, but my home is yours. Feel free to take your ease anywhere here."

"I've been inactive too long. Is there a weapon I could use and a place I might practice for awhile?"

"Of course. Gindin will fetch you something appropriate. The rear courtyard should have ample space."

Shen practiced longer than he planned. It distressed him to discover the toll the last fortnight had taken on his body. He swung the curved sword in patterns he had practiced since childhood but tired easily. His muscles ached long before they should and he couldn't seem to suck in enough air. His weakness made him angry and he pushed himself harder, hating all the events that had made him weak. His imprisonments and humiliations pushed him to work harder, Cor and Kassor and the slavers and Maradon pushed him.

At last, winded and sweating, he sat on a bench and mopped his face. He rested with his elbows on his knees, his angers and hurts soothed for the time being. Into the newly quiet space, a new irritation bubbled to the surface. He shouldn't have mentioned marriage to Dashara. Now that he had, he may have ruined everything. All he had wanted was to let her know his feelings and learn how to court her properly. How could he have known she was asking him to be her lover? He'd been a fool. Of course she couldn't marry him. They had only days together at most.

He sat back against the wall, still panting, his frustration evaporating with his sweat. The barriers and customs that divided them weren't important, and he was the idiot he was acting if he thought they were. When Dashara had left Thiery he thought he'd never see her again. Now here they were, and she had offered to be his lover. He wished they could start over. If he could, he'd agree to be with her however he could for as long as he could.

Dashara returned near suppertime. She seemed distant over dinner, more hesitant and unsure than before. He guessed with all her suitors and training and position that it wasn't like her to misstep. Shen felt a wall between them that hadn't been there earlier.

After dinner, she rose. "I have some reading I should finish tonight ..." she began.

Shen stood and moved to intercept her. He brushed a hand down her long, bare arm. "Must you?"

"Shen, I was wrong to lead you on," she started. He slid a hand behind her neck and kissed her.

"We should stop now," she whispered, her mouth still close to his, her forehead resting on his cheek. "We can't be together in the way you want, and I don't want to hurt you."

"This is the way I want to be together." He took her in his arms and kissed her again.

His tongue slid into the warmth of her mouth. His hands moved over the fiery bare skin between her top and her skirt. Her long hair tickled his forearms. She kissed him back, softly at first, hesitant. He pulled her against him and proved to her with his kiss and with his body that he harbored no reservations.

The tightness in her loosened, some decision made. She melted in to him and returned his kiss with passion. Her hands ran down the length of his back and over his hips.

He leaned back from the kiss, breathless. "I love you, Dashara. Let me show it while I still have you."

———— ⌒⌒ ————

Two nights later, Shen breathed a sigh as he and Dashara climbed into the rickshaw, relieved to leave the politics and formality and strangeness of a queen and her court behind. He thought he'd been prepared for the meeting; he was highborn after all and had lived in the Bealdor's Hold from the age of ten. He had been wrong. Queen Assia had been welcoming and gracious, but the sheer wealth of this country made Thiery look like a beggar cousin. The power and authority she wielded made him think of the old High Kings, but even their courts might have paled in comparison.

The movement of the rickshaw created a welcome breeze in the night air as they moved along the flat road between the two hills. It had been an overwhelming and exhausting evening juggling the list of customs in his head and meeting not only the queen and her consort, but Maiar and his wife, plus Teyyas and her husband. He thought of Dashara's trip to Thiery, how she had arrived uninvited to a land where halfbloods were hated. He hoped he had carried himself half as well as she had done under harder circumstances.

He opened the small silver box the queen had given him and looked again at the ring. A large red jewel dominated the center and the mark of the royal family had been worked in fine silver around it. Along with the ring, she had given Shen a promise that prisoners had never before, and would never again, be accepted from Hesh.

He was glad she would seek out and free the other Heshans. He'd thought of them often since leaving them to their fate. Even that snake, Gerrick. The three of them would live out their lives here, and if they broke Bansheenan law, any law, they would revert immediately to slave status again.

The next morning, Shen woke early from a vivid dream of the night he had set fire to Bern's bridge. He opened his eyes, not understanding the soft bed until Dashara's quiet breathing reminded him where he slept. He lay staring at the high ceiling.

He'd been as happy this past week as he could ever remember. Dashara had become his sun and moon, warming him with her presence in the day, firing his passion during the nights. He'd regained some of the weight he had lost, and with daily arms practice began to feel himself again. He'd even explored a little of the city with Dashara, and she'd taken him to see the School and the even more astounding Hall of Records.

He thought back to his dream, seeing Maradon at the river through the flames and night. For the first time in days, his mind roamed over memories of the fighting, the bloody chaos of battle, his chains, and his imprisonments. He wondered who had been raised to regiment leader to replace him when he went missing after the fight. Heras had the most experience, but had no drive to command. Perhaps Seth. Seth was younger but would be the better choice. He wondered if his men missed him. Had they mourned him briefly and moved on? Had Tirren? Had Tirren lived through the battle, or Chayan?

"You've been thoughtful this morning," Dashara said over breakfast. "Is it time for you to return home?"

Her intuition didn't surprise him. "I have little excuse to stay. I doubt my family and my Bealdor even suspect that I'm still alive. I need to get word to them." They were on the terrace, and he looked out over the city. "I have a duty to my Bealdor, and to the men under me. I don't think that Lacedar will attack again for some time, but who can say? And even if they don't, the patrols will have been stepped up. I don't know what that battle cost Thiery or who lived and who died." He looked again at her. "I can't stay, but I don't want to leave."

"And I don't want you to leave, but can't ask you to stay." She smiled as she reached out and took his hand, "We knew this would be the case, Shen. But it isn't goodbye yet. I'll travel with you to Hesh. I'd like to learn more about Yslaaran's last visit if your Bealdor will allow me to come to the Hold again. And even if he won't, well ... I'll need to travel with you on the boat anyhow."

He stood and moved to the balcony railing, leaning back against it with his hands on top of the cool, polished marble. "And what will your queen think of you coming with me? Assia made it clear to me that she wouldn't approve if I tried to woo you away to Hesh." She had been a sharply observant woman and hadn't failed to notice the looks passing between him and Dashara.

Dashara seemed surprised, then thoughtful. "I wasn't aware she'd said anything to you. I'm quite certain she wouldn't want any of the Somiir leaving permanently, but she couldn't really prevent it if we wished to go. It isn't for her, though, but for my people here, that I would only be able to stay a short while in Thiery."

"For your suitors?" The accusation in his voice hurt her; he saw it in the tightening of her eyes. It had been unfair, but he didn't apologize.

"For all my people," she answered him pointedly. "And what, if we can't be together, will you swear off women for the rest of your life?"

He folded his arms against his chest and looked down at his crossed ankles. "Perhaps," he said quietly. "I don't know," he shrugged. He brought his eyes up to meet hers. "I only know how it makes me feel to think of you in another man's arms."

She turned her head from him, looking out over the city. "And I wish no man but you."

The silence between them grew stretched and uncomfortable. He stayed leaning against the railing a moment more, neither of them looking at the other. There seemed nothing more to say and he left her there in silence while he went to her bedroom to gather his things.

The servants had already cleaned the room, made the bed, and taken the dirty clothes. Fresh sets of clothes lay folded in her wardrobe for him. He had nothing else to wear, and debated how much of the Bansheenan clothing he should take with him to get home.

He heard her enter the room. She came up behind him and gently stroked his arms.

"This isn't what I want either, Shen."

"I know," he said.

Shen turned and she moved into him. He held her, and the warmth and softness of her felt so good that he wondered if he could ever let her go. She pressed into him, fitting against his body like they were two halves of one puzzle. His arm slid across her bare waist and pulled her tighter still. He felt himself harden. He suddenly felt overwhelmed with the need to be inside her, to possess her in whatever way he could before he lost her forever. He kissed her, deeply, then swept an arm under her legs and placed her on the bed.

She reached out to him with her own need. Wrapping one hand behind his neck she pulled him to her, kissing him, greedy for him.

He took her fiercely this time and she matched him, as always. Even in this she was different than any woman he had ever known.

Chapter Twenty-six

Tirren received the message at the first bell of the evening, just before supper. He read it twice, hardly able to believe what it said. He dropped to a bench in the courtyard, leaned back against the stone of the Hold and read it again, slowly this time.

Shen was alive and well. And in Relendel.

Tirren found his father in the library. Erimar looked up over a desk littered with paperwork for the supplies that had been used or destroyed in the battle with Lacedar. Dark circles lined his eyes, his face was pale and drawn. The battle had taken a heavy toll on him, and the cough he had started this week added to Tirren's concern.

"I just received word from Shen." Tirren crossed the room to the desk and handed the message to him.

"He's alive?" Erimar said, happy surprise lifting the heavy lines of his face for what seemed the first time in weeks. He unfolded the message, his brows drawing down as he read. "The Somiir is in Thiery again?" Of all the news in the message, his father chose that fact on which to focus. "Gods be good, will we never be rid of them now?"

Tirren's chest tightened. Chayan was one of "them."

"She saved Shen from a life of slavery and brought him safely home," he said in a tight voice, taking the letter back from his father.

"If that's all she came here for, why does he seek permission to bring her to the Hold?"

Tirren must have looked as angry as he felt. Erimar held up one hand while his cough prevented him from saying more. "I'm glad that Shen lives," he said, when he could speak again, "and is back on Thiery soil. I can't say the same for that woman."

Tirren anticipated argument, anger, belligerent refusal—he got none of those things.

His father stared blankly at the far wall, then shook his head. "I pray for answers and I get Elves," Erimar said to himself.

Chayan wielding magic, Dashara, Yslaaran, the battle with Lacedar; the last few months had taken too much out of his father, drained some essential part of him. He had been so strong all of Tirren's life, and now, even though the battle had been won, his father looked defeated. Tirren took the proffered note. "We do what we can. What we can't help, we make the best of." He'd said something similar to Chayan during their trip around the region together.

Looking at his father, he had half a mind to tell him that Dashara didn't have to come, but he couldn't. Dashara should come. It was to their advantage. The more people that saw her, the less unique Chayan became. Besides, Chayan had a list of questions that had come up since she left and no way to ask her. This opportunity for him to be with one of his own kind would not come often.

Erimar shook his head again and looked at Tirren. "Even if I refuse her, she can come anyway. I can't stop her from doing what she wants anymore than I can stop Chayan's mother from blinding you to her danger and raping you. They have magic and you embrace it. How do I fight that?" He coughed again.

"You don't need to fight any of us," Tirren said softly. "Your goals for Chayan are the same as mine, the same as Yslaaran's, the same as Dashara's; that he be accepted by his people and someday come to rule them." Tirren looked down at the note he held, then glanced out the narrow leaded glass window behind his father as if seeing the larger world outside that his father couldn't. "Dashara saved Shen's life and brought him home. He would like her to come, and she is still an ambassador. As for Chayan, the changes in him have all been good since Dashara taught him about his magic and since his mother visited him." Erimar's face went dark at the mention of Yslaaran's last visit, but Tirren pressed on. "He's more confident, more optimistic. You have to have seen it. I truly believe all will be well, but if you forbid it, I'll tell Shen she's not welcome."

Erimar stared at Tirren, examining him all the way to his soul. Perhaps he was looking for signs that his mind was controlled. "The last time she was here, I did my best to protect us all and it nearly ended in disaster. I leave it in your hands, and pray to the gods you make the right choices."

Tirren hadn't yet had the stomach to tell his father what Dashara had told him. The gods were long gone. They were on their own, and always had been.

Tirren turned down the little track past the old temple to the small cottage. The tiny peasant hut before him looked too innocent a place to foster so many secrets. The soldiers he'd brought followed behind, trampling the summer grass growing in the seldom-used trail.

Dismounting, he tied Midnight to a post. The door opened before he reached it and Shen came out, bigger than life. He was strangely dressed, but Tirren could see that more than his clothes had changed. He seemed different, harder maybe or, at least, less carefree, and Tirren wondered what the last few weeks had visited on his friend. Shen smiled broadly then, dissipating the impression.

Tirren and Shen embraced in a great bear hug. A rare laugh escaped from Tirren, and he slapped Shen on the back. "Gods, you look like one of the desert tales come to life, but I'm happy to see you alive."

"I'm glad to see you too." Shen lifted Tirren off his feet before releasing him.

"What's this?" He touched the blue diamond on Shen's cheek.

Shen's smile faded, the hardness returning for a moment, then he shrugged. "It's nothing. Just a little welcoming tradition in Bansheen."

Dashara came out of the hut with the family of aleef. Her halfblood features and beauty were no less startling than the first time Tirren had met her. He greeted her and thanked her for helping Shen, and thanked Khemma, Feeah, and Rayel for housing them both.

Tirren scanned the group. "So tell me, why is every Bansheenan here dressed in Heshan clothes and you're dressed like a Bansheenan?"

Shen looked down at his attire and laughed, a sound Tirren had missed greatly this past month. "The aleef didn't have anything that would fit me. Did you bring my gear?"

"I did." Tirren grinned and motioned to one of the men. "Tine, bring his saddlebags."

Tine walked to a gray draft horse and untied the bags.

Shen's face lit up when he saw Bayone. "You found him." He went to the big grey and stroked his nose and neck. Bayone's nostrils flared and he nosed at Shen's mouth in greeting.

Tine handed Shen his saddlebags. "He was wandering by the river. We found him when we were searching the woods for you. It's good to see you back in one piece, Kesum."

"Thank you, Tine. It's good to be home."

The other men had hung back while Tirren greeted him, but they swarmed around Shen now. Tirren waited while Shen received greetings and forearm clasps from each of the soldiers.

Every man in Shen's regiment had volunteered to come on this trip, but Tirren had brought only six.

When Shen turned away from the last man his face was tight, clamped down on some strong emotion. Tirren wondered again what stories he had to tell, or if he would.

He felt the prickling sensation of being watched and turned to see a man he didn't know standing in the doorway of the hut. The man was dressed in Heshan-style breeches and a white linen shirt with no tunic over it. Tirren stared, shocked by the white-blonde hair and ice-blue eyes. For an instant, he thought him one of the Elves, but Tirren had more experience with Elves than most and he realized his mistake quickly.

"May I introduce Maiar," Dashara said. "Another of the Bansheenan Somiir." The man moved forward gracefully to meet Tirren. "Maiar, this is the Beodan of Thiery, Chayan's father, Tirren an Erimar a Balawen es Thiery."

Maiar dipped his head in a bow. "I am most honored to meet you."

Tirren said some rote formality while his mind spun down other trails. Maiar was the first halfblood male he'd ever seen besides Chayan. Tirren thought of his son as a man grown now, but he could see from Maiar how much maturity of face and body his son still lacked. He wished he had brought Chayan along, but the reason for leaving him behind was the same as last time. The same as always ... safety.

"Maiar offered to come to Hesh with us," Shen said. "If Dashara stays awhile he can take the boat back and return for her later. If her stay is short, he hoped perhaps he would have a chance to meet Chayan before they returned."

Tirren didn't want to think what bringing both Dashara and Maiar to the Hold would do to his father. "I realize this is not the courtesy you are used to," Tirren told Maiar, "but my father is not well these days. We are at war with a neighboring region and a visit from my son's mother closely followed that of Somiir Dashara. Dashara, no doubt, has told you that my father has different ideas about what is in Chayan's best interests than I do. Allow me to speak to him first. Hopefully we will be able to send for you."

Maiar bowed again. "I understand, Beodan, and had expected nothing different. I will wait here for a message from you, or leave again for Bansheen if Dashara sends me word I should go."

Maiar had been gracious, but the refusal left Tirren feeling awkward and anxious to get on the way. With nothing more that could be said or done, the party mounted-up.

Chapter Twenty-seven

Tirren received an account of all that had happened to Shen as their party rode north. His friend's brevity said as much about his experience as his words.

Finished telling all he seemed willing to say for now, Shen asked a question of his own. "The last thing I remember of the battle is being brained by three wolves in sheeps' clothing. What happened after that?"

"We arrived back one full turn of Tlaas ago," Tirren said, "after staying a few days in Panden to rest the horses and take care of the wounded. The losses were the greatest among the foot soldiers, nearly one third." Shen winced. "Losses among the sword were less. I'll show you the roster when we get back. Twelve Lacedar sword were taken prisoner and half died of their wounds before we could ransom them back. Lacedar took no prisoners that we know of other than you. We assumed you'd drowned in the river or your body was carried off by animals."

Even saying it to Shen's face, the memories returned of the moment he finally accepted the fact, called off the search parties, and rode from the border back to the Hold without him.

"Since then we've increased our patrols and brought extra reserves to the Hold. Erimar has banned our traders from going into Lacedar for fear of their safety."

"How is the Bealdor? And Chayan?"

"Chayan is fine. He fought well." Pride swelled in Tirren even now, thinking of it. "My father ..." he sighed, "he's changed, aged. The hard ride injured his hip and he's walked with a limp ever since. He started a cough about a week ago that seems to be getting worse instead of better. I try to help him but he insists on overseeing most of the tallies and accounts of the battle himself. He mourns the men we lost and worries that Lacedar will attack again. He worries about a lot of things these days."

Dashara rode at Shen's side. She listened without comment, but Tirren said no more.

Shen glanced her way, understanding, and changed to a lighter subject. "I missed the Summer Festival this year."

Tirren nodded. "The woodcutter from San won the log splitting." He suppressed a grin, waiting for Shen's reaction.

"The dead take me!" Shen spat on the ground. "I know I could have beaten him this year."

Two woodcutters, a blacksmith, and Shen had been the finalists for the past five years. Shen had never done better than third. Tirren laughed at his friend's cock-sure confidence, more glad to have him back than he could have said.

They rode back slowly, camping out two nights and staying the third at the inn in Marshe. Now that Chayan had ridden these parts without incident, Tirren wanted people to notice Dashara. Not too much, but he wasn't going to hide her either. Staying at an inn was riskier, though. She remained outside cloaked and hooded while Tirren secured the rooms. He did a quick calculation. As when Chayan stayed here, the soldiers could rotate guard over Dashara's room and the front door through the night, the rest could share a bed. "Four rooms," Tirren told the innkeeper.

"Three," Shen said, at his shoulder.

Tirren looked back at him. He'd noticed the small intimacies between Shen and Dashara, but hadn't guessed they were lovers. It made him happy for Shen, knowing his friend's infatuation for her when she visited the first time. He probably understood it better than most would, but he wondered if it was wise when they were separated by lands and cultures and blood. Loving her would be no easy thing for his friend. He hoped Shen wouldn't suffer the same pain that had shadowed so much of his own life.

When they arrived at the Hold the following day, a mass of swordsmen swarmed Shen as soon as they rode through the gates. Like Tirren, their gaze was drawn first to the tattoo on his face, but they soon ignored it and pelted him with questions about his captivity and rescue.

Erimar greeted Dashara briefly and then excused himself to speak privately with Shen. Tirren knew he intended to question him closely about Lacedar and Maradon, more interested in that than his extraordinary experience in Bansheen.

"Dashara!" Chayan came down the hall at a fast walk, trying to keep the appearance of the dignity of his station, though Tirren could see the suppressed excitement. Dashara grinned and spread her arms wide. Tirren shook his head as Chayan abandoned all formality and ran the last few steps to embrace her. He left the two of them to catch up and went to wash, change, and let the servants know to set the private dining room.

Dinner was planned to be a small affair: Dashara, Shen, Chayan, and himself. What his father might do, even Tirren couldn't guess. When he entered the dining room, his trepidations vanished. His father hadn't made another poor excuse, but attended the dinner, formally dressed and presiding at the head of the table.

As dinner progressed, the cracks of strain began to show in his father. Awkward silences, stiffness at the mention of the Somiirs' lives in Bansheen. Every time he thought Erimar might begin to relax, he would catch a furtive glare at Dashara. He'd hoped to bring up the subject of Maiar over dinner, but knew it unwise to try yet.

Chayan looked as if he could have talked all night and Tirren finally put a halt to his questions. As they all stood to leave, Chayan gave Shen a bear hug. He'd calmed down enough to give a more courtly good night to Dashara. Tirren's smile turned a little sad as he watched Shen leave hand-in-hand with Dashara. He saw the looks the servants directed at their backs, so like the years of looks and whispers he had endured with Chayan.

Over the next couple of days Dashara and Chayan spent time talking together. Tirren gave his permission to tell her of Yslaaran's visit. Shen seemed happy to be back, spending his days training with the soldiers and his nights with Dashara. Best of all, Tirren was finding himself proved right. The Hold's inhabitants accepted Dashara more and more as time passed, even his father in small measure. Being her second time here eased some of the tension, and her gentle, reassuring nature began to slowly win over everyone from soldiers to servants.

Tirren woke the next day resolved to tell his father about Maiar. He pulled on a fresh pair of stockings and grabbed his breeches hanging over a chair by the bed. It would be a harder subject to broach now that some days had passed, and he felt guilty both at withholding the information from his Bealdor and about Maiar still waiting in Relendel.

A figure suddenly stepped toward him. His head snapped up from buckling his breeches and he stumbled backward. Yslaaran stood before him. His breath came short and his heart raced as he registered it was her. She smiled at his reaction and her eyes drifted down his shirtless and barefoot body and back to his breeches, half buckled. He let her look while his breath and heart slowed.

She came closer and reached down, gently buckling the loose strap at his hip. He studied her downturned face, inhaling the spicy flower of her skin.

"I hoped perhaps you were going to unbuckle those." He arms ached to hold her. He would have except for her expression when she finished with the buckle. "But I think you are not here for loving."

"I could wish that is why I came." She stroked her hand up from the strap of his breeches over his ribs and into the coarse hair between his nipples. His breath left him in a grunt. She dropped her hand to her side and the playfulness left her face. "I am here with news. I fear that my plan has been discovered."

"What do you mean?" A cold needle pierced his guts, arousal forgotten. "Is there danger to Chayan or my people?"

"Chayan asked much the same last time we spoke. I told him what I believed then, that it was not likely. The king has never been a concern. He has been somnolent too long and cares for little but his own pleasures. The queen was the only worry, and so we have moved slowly, letting few know what we do. When Chayan was ready, we planned to win the queen to our cause. Once that was done, the others would almost certainly follow."

"What happened?"

"The queen has turned cold to me, and to others who plan with me. This in itself would be enough, but there has been another thing." He sat on the edge of the bed and waited for her to continue.

"I recently heard a rumor that a mortal girl, a princess of Lacedar, is in the forest with one of the Unseely." She sat next to him on the bed, light as a feather. "I went to their woods and saw her for myself, though I did not confront the one who took her. I think now that it is possible he overheard our plans, and word has reached the queen. If this girl truly is the daughter of your enemy, I am doubly concerned. It seems too unhappy a coincidence."

A jumble of thoughts cascaded through Tirren's mind. She had told him about the palace in her land and the king and queen, though only in passing, but this was the first mention of others planning with her. And Maradon's daughter in the Elven lands seemed beyond coincidence, indeed. Maybe his father had been right. Maybe his involvement with Yslaaran would end up bringing harm to his people.

She reached out and ran her fingers through his hair, which still hung loose about his face. The concern in her eyes mirrored his own. "Chayan is my son, and you are my lover. Know that I would do nothing wittingly to bring harm to either of you. My intent has always been to help, both your people and my own." Her hand gently stroked his jaw, caressing the roughness of his unshaven face.

"I came first to you, but will go next to your enemy's land if you wish it, to see if I may learn more. We had hoped to remain impartial in the squabbles of Men, but you must know that I would assist you and our son above all others. I will do what I must to protect Chayan's future."

The worry in him eased slightly. "Thank you for telling me this. We felt sure that Lacedar wasn't done with us anyway, but we had hoped for a longer respite. It would be good to know what Maradon is up to." He took her hand. "How long would it take you to get to Lacedar and back?"

She gave a small shrug. "A short time—even as you impatient mortals measure it." A hint of a smile played at her lips. "To go there, a single step. I will return, when I have seen all I need."

A single step to Lacedar. He couldn't wrap his mind around it. "I'll wait for you here as long as I can."

They stood and he brushed her lips with his, struggling, even now, to keep it gentle, to control his passion for her. She turned from him and stepped into a mist near his bedpost ... and was gone.

He decided that he dare not call a servant to come shave him while he waited for her. He finished dressing, tied his hair up, and sat on a chair to pull his boots on. He was stamping his foot into the second boot when she reappeared.

He stood. Even having seen her vanish in front of him, it seemed inconceivable that in the time it took him to dress she could have been there and back. "Did you go to Lacedar?"

"I did. Your enemy musters. An army of great number gathers there. Men of all stations were assembled. Most carried no real weapons and seemed untrained in the ways of war. A mounted soldier, cross with men who were not listening, said they had eight days before the dark of the moons to learn to fight. I heard no talk of my people, and I did not see the king of that fort. I heard no talk of the girl while I was there, but the queen was crying in her chambers."

Tirren dropped back into the chair. Eight days. Gods. And it sounded like Lacedar was recruiting every able-bodied man. How could they hope to raise and train a large enough army in eight days? Their losses at the last battle would be as nothing to this. "Did they see you?"

She looked at him as if he might be making a joke and smiled when she realized he wasn't. "None see me when I stand in the mists, neither your folk nor my own."

His head hurt. He dropped his face into his hands and sighed before meeting her eyes again. "I hope you realize what aid you've just given us. If Maradon is rallying his entire region to war and we had been taken unawares, Thiery would have fallen; our army would have been slaughtered and our people subjugated. We could never have known this without you."

He sighed again at the thought of bringing this news to Erimar. "I must speak with my father." Even knowing that he had to find his father and tell him without delay, Tirren found it difficult to leave Yslaaran's side. "Are you safe being away from your lands like this?"

"I should not be gone long, but time moves differently there. I will not be missed yet."

"Perhaps you could stay while I speak with him. There is one here who wished to meet you, another halfblood who came from Bansheen to see Chayan. Perhaps you could speak with her while I am away—and with Chayan if you haven't seen him yet?"

"I felt the halfbreed's presence here. I would speak with her. And my son."

"I'll send them to you."

She nodded.

Tirren opened the door and scanned the hallway for Ban. His new uthow seemed to always be hungry and never around when Tirren needed him. About to turn down the hall to Dashara's rooms, he saw Shen's door open as Shen and Dashara stepped into the hallway.

"Somiir," Tirren called to her.

Dashara greeted him good morning with a dazzling smile.

"There is someone here who would like to meet with you." His expression must have conveyed more than his words. She stiffened and said carefully, "Who?"

"Yslaaran is here. She is in my rooms. I have news I must give my father, but she's expecting you."

Shen walked hand-in-hand with Dashara to Tirren's rooms. He could feel the tension tightening all the muscles of her arm. His own anticipation was hardly less, though apprehension overshadowed it. Half-Elves were one thing, this was quite another.

He knocked on the door and entered, though there had been no answer. She stood just beyond the doorway to Tirren's bedroom.

She was dazzling. Foreign. Terrifying.

His mouth went dry despite stirrings of arousal at the sight of her, but his overwhelming emotion was one of awe; she had an authority of power and a beauty almost too terrible to look on. With Dashara at his side, Shen moved through the sitting room to the doorway of the bedroom. He had no attention to spare for Dashara's reaction. Under Yslaaran's gaze, Shen found he could force himself no farther into the room. He had never felt the slightest inkling of need to abase himself to anyone until this moment, but even though he wanted to now, his muscles wouldn't obey.

His first coherent thought was wonderment that Tirren could endure her presence—much less her intimacy—and more, that he craved it. Regardless of what Shen's body told him, he had no wish to be any closer to her than he was right now.

Dashara was no less immune to the awe of her. She pulled her hand from his and dropped to her knees, pressing her forehead to the floor, almost certainly for the first time in her life.

"You may stand," Yslaaran said in a voice like the most beautiful music he had ever heard.

"Forgive me that I do not know how to greet you properly," Dashara said. Shen took her hand to help her stand. He felt it tremble.

"I am Yslaaran." Apparently the Elves had no need of titles or surnames. "Come to me, child."

Dashara obeyed. Shen moved with her, staying at her side, though he had no idea what he might do if the woman posed any threat.

"You came here once before to see my son. Why?"

Dashara froze, taken aback by the question, but she sounded composed when she answered. "As soon as your son was made known to us, I was sent to see what help or training I might offer. We believed that, in Hesh, one of the half-Elves would not have the advantages we are privy to, and worried for his safety here."

"And do you know why Chayan was born and brought here to be raised?"

Chayan had shared his news with both Shen and Dashara. "Yes," she answered, honestly.

Before she could say more, the door opened and Chayan rushed in, breathing hard. Relief painted his face when he saw Yslaaran. He came to her and bowed his head respectfully. "Mother. I'm glad you're still here." Yslaaran kissed him lightly on the forehead.

"Tell me Chayan, what has passed between you and your grandsire since last I came?"

He looked down. "I'm sorry. He doesn't want me to be involved in your plans. My grandfather is afraid of what he doesn't understand and thinks he does what is best for the region." Shen saw the desperation in his eyes. "But we can be patient as you said. Perhaps when my father is in power, or when I am ..."

Yslaaran nodded, but before she made a reply, the hall door opened again and Tirren entered. He moved to Yslaaran's side and her eyes softened as she looked on him. Tirren seemed to see no one else in the room until he looked at Chayan, still standing next to her. Shen felt like an intruder as unspoken emotion passed from Tirren to Chayan to Yslaaran; the three of them together for the first time since Chayan's infancy. Gathering himself with a breath, Tirren spoke to Shen.

"Yslaaran has brought news. Lacedar prepares for another invasion. Their force will be larger this time."

The last battle flashed through Shen's head—images of being knocked unconscious and waking up in bonds. He wrestled the thoughts down, determined that having been a prisoner would not make him craven. "You told the Bealdor?"

Tirren nodded. "He took it with the same resolve as always where the safety of the region is concerned, but I'm afraid for him. He is not as strong as he was going into the last battle."

"What did he say about mother being here?" Chayan asked him.

"I think the news that Lacedar is preparing for a full-scale war overshadowed even that. He didn't take it well, though, that Maradon's daughter has been abducted, or the implied involvement of the Elves in this war." Tirren looked to Yslaaran. "I did stress to him more than once that you brought invaluable information to us, and are a powerful ally. I offered to have him meet you, but he said we need to confer with the captains and regiment leaders immediately. I think the emotional and political complexities of meeting you were too much for him just now. I'm sorry. Maybe later he will speak with you directly."

He looked to Shen and Chayan again. "My father is summoning the captains and regiment leaders. We are required at once." Shen waited for his Beodan to leave, but Tirren stepped closer to Yslaaran instead. He took her hand in his. "What will happen to you if you're right about your queen knowing?"

"Nothing yet, I think. If I'm right that she has somehow goaded your enemy, she may think that enough of a lesson. I should return now, though, and I must be careful. I will not be able to travel as freely as before."

"Do nothing to endanger yourself," he said. "You have given us the information we needed. Come back only when it is safe for you."

"If there is further news, my love, I will find a way to bring it to you."

"All of Thiery is in your debt."

He let go of her hand and cupped her neck gently with both of his, bringing his mouth to hers in a deep, tender kiss. Her hands slid up his back to embrace him. The sweetness and intimacy were a side of Tirren that Shen had never seen before, and he found he couldn't turn away despite Heshan customs against public affection. When Tirren released Yslaaran at last, she stepped away from him. Shen wondered if Tirren would have had the strength to do the same.

Yslaaran kissed Chayan on the cheek, then looked at Dashara. "I will speak more with this one before I leave," she said.

A fear lanced into Shen's chest at the thought of leaving her alone with this strange and powerful woman, but Dashara bowed deeply to her and answered his look of concern with a shake of her head and a smile.

"Go now. Your Bealdor waits for you. I will see you tonight."

Chapter Twenty-eight

Tirren left his Master of Supplies hard at work and crossed the courtyard to the Hold. It had been daylight for only an hour and he was already tired. He couldn't believe that the past six days had come and gone so quickly, a blur of activity, working from before dawn until late into the night. Prepared or not, tomorrow they marched north.

It still seemed strange to think that the rally call had gone out in Thiery for the second time in less than two months. This time, though, it had been for every able-bodied man, soldier or not. They had been arriving by the wagonload. In the last battle, between both armies, over four hundred had fought. This time the numbers would be far greater, as would be the deaths.

Dealing with the feeding, housing, arming, and training of so many would have been challenge enough, but masses of other details had needed his attention. His head felt over-full, like a ticking so stuffed with straw that the bits had started falling out again. Chayan helped as much as he could, but Findal had needed him more. Tirren had hardly seen Chayan in the last few days as Chayan taught archery and quarterstaff to the untrained men arriving.

Tirren weaved through the press of craftsmen as he approached the main courtyard. They had come from all over Thiery; every storage building with space left or open section of cobblestone was occupied. Even late into the night, the light of torches moved about like bright fireflies below Tirren's windows.

He found it difficult to walk through the courtyard, or anywhere, without being stopped. Just ahead the harness-maker checked straps and fittings, the cooper rolled out barrels, and the wainwright brought up wagons to be loaded. All three of them had hunted him down daily for instructions on the smallest details.

The council meeting, the last they would have before leaving, was next on Tirren's schedule. He wanted to be there early to go over the maps one more time, though he'd studied them so often he could have drawn every hill and creek in northern Thiery blindfolded. He changed direction to avoid the three tradesmen and walked around the stable toward a side door of the Hold.

The clang and roar of the armory just past the stable drew his attention. He pulled up short when he saw Dashara standing in the middle of the mayhem. She was next to the forge, ignoring the noise and the blistering heat, talking with two young men. Tirren knew the armorer well, a crusty old man. He wouldn't have expected Dashara to be allowed in there, especially with the forges at full blast. There was more work than they could finish, even with the blacksmith helping and both of their journeymen combined.

The two young men laughed at something Dashara said, and even the old armorer shot her a smile. Tirren shook his head in wonder and continued to the Hold.

She had been moving among the men, calming fears and boosting morale so subtly that he doubted any of the people suspected magic. She had sworn to him that it was a healing art, nothing more. Considering her anathema to mind control, he believed her. And whatever it was, it was helping.

He wished again that his father would accept her help. Four days in a sickbed with the cough and fever and he still refused to allow her to visit him. Even Shen had spoken with him and given testament to her healing abilities, but the stubborn old man refused to be touched by magic. It made it all the more amazing that he'd given his permission for the work Dashara did here in the courtyard; with the weight of the impending war he had finally been willing to accept any help he could get. For others anyway.

Tirren reached the Council Room to find Shen the only one there. He took a seat at the head of the table on Shen's left and leaned back. If he closed his eyes, he would fall asleep.

"How is the Bealdor today?" Shen asked.

"Better, I think." Tirren had visited him first thing in the morning to brief him. "It's hard to tell, though. The fever is less but the cough is worse. He'll be out of his sickbed before we leave regardless. I think he'd ride with us tomorrow even if his heart stopped today."

Shen huffed a short laugh. "He'll always be a strong man."

Tirren nodded, though there was no conviction behind it. The changes in his father had come too fast for him not to have his doubts. "Shen, do you know what Dashara and Yslaaran spoke of last week, after we left the room?"

"No. Not really," Shen said, sounding surprised at the question. He chewed the corner of his lip then shook his head. "We worked late into the day. I didn't see Dashara again until I went to my rooms that evening. I know I asked her what Yslaaran had wanted with her, but I don't really remember what she said. Nothing much, evidently. I had so much on my mind that I didn't think any more about it. Why do you ask? Have you seen Yslaaran again?"

"No. It's no matter."

Tirren hadn't seen Yslaaran since she had come with the news that set all this in motion. He vacillated between relief that she hadn't tried to come back and worry that something had happened to prevent her from returning. He knew so little about her lands and her people that his imagination had more than enough room to run amok, scenarios waxing darker the more he tried to shut them out.

"How does Dashara feel about staying here until we return?"

Shen's face grew serious. Apparently, Tirren hadn't been the only one worrying about his lover.

"She says her duty is to help people and we need her help. At least Maiar and the boat continue to wait for her in Relendel in case she's forced to leave while we're gone. I don't like the thought of her staying here alone, but with no men to spare to escort her back to the sea I guess it's the only option for now." He toyed with the edge of one of the rolled maps. "In a way I'm glad, though. Her leaving will come sooner than I wish." He pulled a torn corner free. "I just hope I make it back to see her again."

Tirren had mourned Shen once already. He didn't want to go through that twice, but there were no guarantees for any of them and they both knew it.

"I'll see her safely home if you can't. I promise you. And I truly believe she'll be all right here. The servants and staff do better with her every day. Who knows, once we're all gone to war they might hide under her wings like a bunch of new chicks. It's funny what vulnerability can do to people. I would never have believed she could have made so much progress in a week as she has."

A sense of optimism infused people as she moved among them, penetrating their natural fear and distrust of her. The men had begun to look forward to her visits without knowing why. He suspected her beauty didn't hurt either.

Shen nodded. He rolled the torn bit of paper between thumb and forefinger.

"I know. Not that it makes it any easier, but somehow fear of the war has changed things. One of the new foot recruits was talking this morning. He thought Chayan had magicked his quarterstaff because he used it better after Chayan demonstrated something with it. The man was carrying it with him everywhere so no one else would take it."

Tirren smiled. Could it really be that this wretched situation with Lacedar would open doors for Chayan that years of living at the Hold had not? They'd never had the chance to finish their tour of the region, but now men from every quarter of Thiery were here, and getting to know Chayan far more intimately.

The door opened and Mathom stepped in followed by Jaron and Findal. Tirren had meant to be looking at the maps. He stood and unrolled them, scanning routes one last time. Caine showed up a moment later and took his place at the table. When everyone had settled, Tirren began.

"A messenger arrived late last night with word from Greig and Lyman that they've met up near Thiery's border."

Findal blew out his moustaches in a sigh of relief.

"Not a moment too soon," Jaron said, "I'd begun to doubt they were going to make it in time."

Tirren continued. "Those two regions joining this battle should weigh the odds in our favor, even if they only bring sword."

It would have been foolish for Eanor and Hadash to refuse to join the fight. If Maradon won Thiery, it would leave him with an army that could conquer all of Hesh. Even so, it had been no sure thing they would help. The regions had been isolated ever since the Conflicts. Until the message last night, Tirren had not really trusted that they would come.

Jaron tapped the table with a finger in frustration. "They took long enough to commit. Their delay leaves us precious little margin for error."

"They'll head straight through the northwest pastures. We can use messengers to arrange a meeting place."

"Assuming we know the best place to gather our forces," Jaron replied. "We're basing much on the belief that Maradon will cross

again at Panden Bridge as Bern's hasn't been repaired. But if we
assume wrongly and they head for the west bridge ..." He rapped
the table once with his knuckle. "I suppose you've had no further
word from your informant?"

"No," Tirren said. He had told no one but his father and Shen
how Lacedar's plans and the size of their army were known. He
would let the others continue to believe the rumors that a trader
disobeying orders to stay out of Lacedar or some malcontent
citizen in Lacedar had leaked the plans. "We can't depend on
hearing any more before we engage Lacedar."

The door opened and Erimar walked in, surprising Tirren. He
was shocked at his father's appearance. His skin was pale and dry,
as if all the blood had been sucked from it. The dark circles under
his eyes were worse than ever and his hair was combed and tied
but unwashed. He walked purposefully to the table with his
pronounced limp, and he looked more skeletal than ever. Tirren
moved from Erimar's place at the head of the table. Shen and the
others shifted down.

"Bealdor, I'm sorry I began without you. I wasn't expecting
you."

"We ride tomorrow to war." Erimar's voice was raw and weak.
"This is no time for me to be abed. Already I've spent too much
time away from these preparations." A phlegmy coughing fit took
him, turning him red-faced. He pulled a handkerchief from his
sleeve and spat. Tirren waited until he recovered before bringing
him up to date.

"Jaron, how fast can we move?" Erimar said, sitting after Tirren
finished.

"If the foot can make seven leagues a day, we'd arrive in Panden
in just under four days. Findal and I have our doubts, though, that
the new men can keep such a pace and be able to fight at the end of
it." Findal nodded agreement.

"If we plan for five full days of marching," Erimar said, "the foot will be better off but we run a greater risk of meeting Maradon on our side of the river. Worse, we might be marching to Panden as they march to the crossing at Eanor's border."

"Why not just fire all the bridges and keep the bastards on their own side?" Mathom suggested.

Jaron answered him. "Runoff from ice-melt in the mountains is nearly over. We don't want to risk encouraging Lacedar to throw up a log crossing at some point we can't guess, instead of funneling over one bridge. And after our last encounter, they'll probably be prepared for the possibility. As long as we pick the right bridge, we're better off letting them believe we don't know they're coming and ambushing them as they come into Thiery at one narrow point. Also, now that Greig and Lyman are at our western border their scouts can watch for the army and send word if Maradon turns toward Eanor. The important thing is to be in place before they cross. Pity we couldn't have been ready to march today."

Erimar turned to Findal. "What is the quickest route your men can handle?"

"Captain Jaron and I have been talking about that, Bealdor," Findal answered. "We know Lacedar begins their march tomorrow and our pace should be similar to their own, excepting we have hillier ground to cover. I was telling Captain Jaron here, I believe we can save time if we march north on the Great Road towards Bern for the first day and a half, then cut over east to Panden. We can avoid the first few hills that way, though we'll still have them to deal with when we turn east. The road will also give the men a bit of time to accustom to the march before we have to go overland."

"Good," Erimar said. "Tirren has kept me briefed on the other preparations. Anything else?" No one spoke. "Best get back to it then."

They stood and dispersed. The uthow loitering outside the council room flowed to the swordsmen they served and trailed them like gooselings. Tirren and his father were left alone. Erimar coughed again, less violently this time, but still with a deep rattle.

"Father, are you sure you feel well enough to go? There's no point leading the army if you die on the road."

"I'm well enough. The fever broke last night."

Tirren put a hand on his father's forearm. It felt thin. Chayan had been working every night with Dashara on healing arts. If Erimar got any worse, perhaps he would accept Chayan's help if not Dashara's.

There was no point in arguing now. He nodded and left his father sitting alone in the room. Tirren's uthow, Ban, gave a great yawn before following him. Tirren wished he could nap and let the boy run things for awhile.

The following morning, in the wan light just before sunrise, the regiments formed up on the road in front of the Hold. Tirren took his place behind his father, with Chayan at his side. His men streamed out behind him.

Wagons rumbled as they rolled into place behind the ranks. The smell of horse and leather was thick around him and the creak and jingle of harnesses filled the air. Midnight stamped and whickered in anticipation. Tirren looked up at the clouds scudding across the sky, darker at the horizon. Gods' eyes, did it have to rain on them too?

Tirren twisted in the saddle. The swordsmen were in formation and the foot were nearly ready. The sight of the army spread out in the dim light seemed as surreal to Tirren as he knew it must feel to those men who had never seen an army assembled in all their lives.

Scanning back up the line, he saw Shen with his regiment, last in line of the sword ranks.

Tirren had seen Shen's men earlier—every one of them sported the blue diamond of Thiery on their faces, berry-stained on their left cheekbones. Shen's wolf's-head helm was clear in the dim light though his size would have given him away anyhow. He had turned in his saddle, looking back toward the Hold.

The crowd of servants, craftsmen, and families that lined the outer wall fell silent as the departure of the army became imminent. Erimar wheeled his horse to face his men. The sunrise outlined him from behind; the stag horns of his helm above his cloaked and silhouetted form made him seem like something out of the legends of the Wild Hunt.

Tension clotted the air. Tirren knew his father had wanted to address the soldiers but his voice and strength wouldn't allow it, and he hadn't asked Tirren to do it for him. Erimar spun again and waved one arm in a signal that started the army forward.

Maradon sat at the head of his force as the sun broke the skyline. A guide had been promised to him and he tried to keep his faith strong as the men waited, shifting in their saddles near him. He saw the looks that passed between some of them.

The sun crested the horizon and the glare of its might, concentrated into a narrow focus of light, blinded him. His eyes watered and men turned their heads against the brilliance. Out of that shimmering walked a lone figure, dark against the brightness. Maradon squinted, trying to see through the glare of light. The sun rose farther above the horizon, diffusing its blinding power. The figure came closer.

The emissary either covered the distance impossibly quickly or had not been as far away as he had seemed. In the space of a few minutes he stood before Maradon's horse, an impish smile curling his lips and lighting his black eyes. The horses nearest Uthbaraal sidestepped and pulled at their bits. Maradon felt a smug satisfaction. The men had been told that Fresshe's emissary would lead them to battle, but he knew few had actually believed him until now.

The Dark Elf gave a bow that looked somehow mocking with his crooked smile. "Are you ready to meet your destiny?" he asked.

"I am."

He wanted to ask for news of Emorelle, but now was not the time. Uthbaraal had promised she would be honored and cherished. He would ask casually after her, later. He couldn't afford to seem as if he didn't trust his emissary.

Looking at the creature in front of him, Maradon's confidence waivered. Surely the thing had conveyed his daughter to the god? He resolved not to worry about it. A daughter's value was to help form beneficial alliances, and whether she was meant for the envoy of a god or for the god himself, what better alliance could he have made for Lacedar?

"Emissary, lead us to Thiery's stronghold, and with Fresshe's blessing I will rule Thiery by week's end. When Hadash and Eanor bow to me as High King I will see that all the people of Hesh do honor to Fresshe as it was in the old days, and you will be revered among my people for leading us to victory."

Uthbaraal laughed a childish, gleeful laugh and said, "Then let us away." He turned and skipped easily ahead of the horses south onto the Great Road.

The cool mist enveloped Evainya as she watched the northern king's army set forth, led by Uthbaraal. The southern army had been warned and they massed as well. Evainya suspected Yslaaran was behind that, but her meddling had done nothing except to ensure that more mortals would die.

She had also seen the kings to the west combining their forces and riding to join the battle. These would need to be watched. Though it was more than she could have hoped for, to have all this province join in the war, she must take care that rumor of their coming did not cause the retreat of the northern army.

The humans were her puppets now, and she the puppeteer.

Chapter Twenty-nine

Maradon felt more relaxed than he had in months. True, he was anxious to reach Thiery and see his goals finally realized, but a servant of Fresshe led them south and victory was assured. The God of War was on his side, and this time he would smash his enemy. The validation he had sought all these years, from his father, his family, his men would soon be his. His forefathers had ruled all of Hesh; in a few days at most, he would take his place as their rightful successor.

The Dark Elf with them unsettled his men, but to Maradon Uthbaraal was tangible proof of his alliance with a god. Uthbaraal walked at his stirrup now and it seemed as good a time as any to ask after his daughter.

"Might Emorelle come visit her mother soon? Cerendrin would be much comforted if she could see the girl has been happy."

Uthbaraal looked up at him with those mischievous eyes. "Your daughter is most happy, I assure you. I saw her just last night. I think she would like to stay awhile longer."

"Of course," Maradon replied. The wicked look in the creature's eyes when he spoke of Emorelle disturbed him. He wished he hadn't asked.

"Why can't she come visit?" Bron said from behind him.

Gods' eyes, he shouldn't have said anything in the boy's hearing. Bron had pestered him almost as much this past month about

Emorelle as Cerendrin had. Maradon was not about to allow him
to cause friction with Fresshe's envoy.

"Bron, keep your mouth shut."

"I was just wondering why she can't ..."

"I said shut your mouth!" He turned far enough to see Bron's
face pale with anger. Perhaps the boy had some vinegar in him
after all. "Take your regiment to the back of the sword lines." Bron
paused, looking like he might argue. "Now, boy."

The god that Uthbaraal served protected this entire army; a
confrontation could get them all killed. Bron wheeled his horse
angrily and motioned for his regiment to follow. Uthbaraal
grinned.

"We must make better time today," the Dark Elf at his side said.

"Why? The foot need to pace themselves."

"These are the instructions I received when I returned last
night. I don't question the one I serve. Do you?"

"Of course not. But we have the element of surprise. Why do
we need to push the men?"

"I will pass on your questions tonight. Perhaps you will get an
answer."

"No, no," Maradon said quickly, though he didn't like being
kept in the dark. "I don't question Fresshe. We will do as you say."

Giggling, Uthbaraal moved out in front of Maradon's guard
and set a pace that the marching regiments could barely hold,
especially the new men. The army pushed forward at the difficult
pace the rest of that day and into the next.

Early in the afternoon, the White River came into view from
the top of a small rise. The trees grew thicker near the water, hiding
the village of Panden beyond. Uthbaraal capered with barely
controlled excitement at the sight of Thiery's border.

"Come, come," he waved the men forward as he trotted to the
bridge.

Maradon's goal suddenly seemed truly within his grasp. Eventually a messenger rider would get word of the invasion to Thiery Hold and their little contingent of soldiers would be sent out. An invading army would not pass unnoticed, but he could sack and control these small villages in the meantime.

Maradon led his vanguard across the bridge and down the road far enough to rest while the remainder of his army funneled across and fanned out again into formation behind him. His eyes narrowed as he studied the buildings ahead. He felt the emptiness of the village before he saw it. Shop doors hung half open, a doll lay in the dirt road, farther on a shirt and a hat. It disconcerted him more to see that Uthbaraal looked surprised as well.

He sent a handful of soldiers into the nearest buildings to search for anyone hiding within. The soldiers returned, indicating no one had been found. He could see the questions and doubts rising in his soldiers. Maradon's face heated and he lashed out at his guide.

"What is the meaning of this? Do you play games? Does Fresshe seek to torment me?" His horse danced under him at his sudden movement and his anger. He jerked the reins and slapped the tails of them hard across one ear to quiet it.

Surprise or curiosity—whatever he had seen briefly on the dark creature's face—vanished in an instant, replaced with that infuriating expression that said he knew more than Maradon did.

"And what did you expect, then?" the Dark Elf said. His voice was smooth, but Maradon suspected he made up the words on the spot. "You prayed to be an instrument of the God of War. Did you think to march through this land taking whatever you wished? Not so. You have spoken often of your ability to vanquish your enemies and of your right to rule, but if you would be a servant of the God of War, you must prove yourself, and win what you would have."

Maradon fought to control the rage that boiled so easily in him. His horse had settled but shied again when Uthbaraal took a step closer.

"I am here with you," the creature continued, "as your guide and companion. You know me to be a sign of your alliance with powers greater than yourself. It has been promised to you that when you do meet with your enemy, there my people will be also, to ensure the outcome. Do you disbelieve so easily?"

Those black eyes radiated sincerity. Maradon felt it emanating from the thing, making it hard to disbelieve him. He fought down his anger and dropped his head in a deep bow. "Forgive my rashness, I do not doubt you. This was unexpected, that's all."

Uthbaraal smiled as if nothing had happened. Maradon felt certain he was forgiven. He ventured a question. "Can you tell me where the people have gone? Is Thiery is alerted already, or is such foreknowledge forbidden?"

As if in answer, one of the scouts who had ridden west appeared over a rise, approaching at a gallop. Maradon's personal guard reined back to give the man room as he stopped at Maradon's side in a small cloud of dust.

"Bealdor, I saw the village abandoned and rode on to make sure we didn't ride into ambush. I spotted one of their scouts galloping over a hill, headed southwest. He must have seen our army before we crossed the bridge. He didn't notice me and I followed him up onto a small rise where I could see their army. They are hidden in a fold between the next hills." The man hesitated, clearly afraid to go on. "Bealdor ... they have an army nearly the size of our own."

The scout backed his horse a step. Maradon wanted to rage, to shout at the unfairness of it all, but Uthbaraal assessed him with that mocking smile.

Maradon ground his teeth and nodded, "So be it. If this is our test, then let it come. This is what we have marched here for." He turned to Uthbaraal. "I will not doubt Fresshe's word, nor your assurance that he will send your people to help us." Raising his voice, he cried, "We ride to our destiny. For the High Kingship!"

"For the High Kingship!" the soldiers roared in waves, as the cheer spread through the army.

———— ⟨∽⟩ ————

Near the horse pastures, just west of Bern, the messenger rode at a gallop. His tan cloak streamed out behind him and dust kicked up from the hooves of his horse. His goal lay just ahead—the two Bealdors of the western regions, riding at the head of their combined armies.

Halting in front of him, the boy bowed in his saddle and extended a gloved hand holding a message. Greig, the older of the two was closest and took the missive from him. He passed it to Lyman after reading the few lines, hastily written.

Greig spoke to the guard on his right. "Tell the men to dismount, water their horses, and eat. It seems Thiery wants us to wait here for one bell to make sure Lacedar commits to the east bridge, at Panden. If we hear nothing by the next bell, we march again." The soldier rode down the lines shouting the order.

The boy nodded to the two rulers and turned his horse, his message delivered. He kicked his horse into a gallop and began to laugh. Once out of sight around a bend in the road, the boy and the horse shimmered; in their place stood Baedis, still laughing.

———— ⟨∽⟩ ————

Tirren looked up as Erimar limped over to Jaron, who was sitting on the grass fishing some food out of his packs, one of the last to eat as usual. He saw the worry in his father's face and moved to join them.

"... Hadash and Eanor's armies could make all the difference." Jaron was saying when Tirren arrived.

It was mid-afternoon. Greig and Lyman should have met them by noon. The rendezvous point was well hidden in a large, grassy bowl strung between the shoulders of three hills, but they had been hiding here since late morning. The rest had been welcome at first, but tension mounted now as nearly a full bell passed.

Chayan appeared silently at Tirren's side. "Still no word from the other two regions," Tirren told him.

The message from the two Bealdors this morning said their scouts had seen no sign of Maradon near Eanor's border. Erimar could wait no longer to commit to a course and had sent a messenger to Panden with the evacuation order.

"Gods' eyes!" Erimar swore. "What could be keeping them?" He coughed, hacking a wad of yellow phlegm from his chest and spitting it on the ground.

They all knew what could be keeping them—Eanor and Hadash may have turned back, changing their minds about joining this fight. Tirren looked west, reflexively, and saw only the empty hilltop.

"With Panden evacuated, we can afford to wait awhile longer," Jaron said. "Pushing as hard as we did, we should be well ahead of Lacedar's army."

They should be, Tirren thought, but he would feel better once the additional forces arrived. The timing was everything; Lacedar must move at a slower pace than Thiery, thinking they had the advantage of surprise, and the armies of Hadash and Eanor had to join them in time for the ambush.

"We ..." Erimar coughed violently into his mailed hand. Tirren wondered how his father had stayed on his horse for four days but, against all odds, he seemed a little stronger each day. "We can't move before Lacedar is spotted anyway," Erimar finished. "If we get to Panden before they cross, we'll be stalemated on either side of the river and they'll have the advantage if we try to cross to their side. I'll not have the bastards vanish today just to play cat and mouse for the rest of the summer. We're in as good a position now as we can hope to be to be. At least we will be if Greig and Lyman ever show up."

Tirren looked around the empty hills again. A few colorful wildflowers, some songbirds, and the horseflies pestering them were the only signs of life other than their own army. He was turning back to his father when the north scout suddenly appeared at the top of the hill, riding at a dead run.

"They're here!" he shouted as soon as he was close enough to be heard. Tirren saw the scout's head swing side to side, looking for the Bealdor and making for him at a gallop when he spotted Erimar.

"They were on the rise north of the river, but they were moving fast," the scout panted. "They may already have crossed the bridge."

Why would Lacedar be moving so fast? Did Maradon have spies in Thiery? Tirren worried how his father would take this latest blow, but Erimar's face showed the hard resolve it always had.

The soldiers had come alert when the scout galloped into camp. Jaron rode down the regiments even now, shouting orders. Erimar was helped onto his light horse by one of his guard. Tirren ran to Midnight where he'd left him staked out to graze. The sword re-formed their ranks and started eastward. The foot soldiers surged behind them, with bows, spears, and quarterstaffs; a bristling centipede moving over the meadow. The front column set as quick a pace as the foot could manage.

Thiery's army trampled a wide swath of grass to the top of the hill. Tirren willed them to move faster, but the slope was steep for the men on foot. At the crest, the village of Panden could be seen to the right. In front of him, Lacedar's army was spread out along the road, already through the village. Dust hung like a great, brown banner above the enemy force.

The sun was less than two fists from setting. It was a poor time of day to engage the enemy and the land not as level as Tirren could have hoped, but it seemed this was to be their battleground. Findal's rough voice carried all the way to the front of the lines, berating his foot soldiers to put on a last burst of speed to gain the open, flat ground below. The light clouds, hanging near the horizon ahead in an otherwise clear sky, would make for a brilliant sunset, Tirren thought. He wondered if he would live to see the sun rise again tomorrow.

Chapter Thirty

Evainya stood in the mists watching the armies approach each other. A thrill ran through her. The intensity of the emotion underscored how long it had been since she had truly felt anything.

The time had come. Closing her eyes, she envisioned the flawless horn that Acetis, the Goddess of the Hunt, had carried. With her imagination she touched her lips to that horn and blew. A clear, pure note resounded through the Elven lands. The Wild Hunt had been summoned.

It had been centuries since any had last taken their demon-form. In the days of wildness and abandon after the gods left, she had been inspired by the Unseely, the shapes they had taken for Uulaten and the work they had done. She had created the Hunt to satisfy the longing for purpose in those confusing years when they suddenly had none. The need for it had ebbed over time, as had so many other things.

She called the wind as she changed to demon-form. It blew her hair back, pulling the skin of her face tighter, and tighter still, until it molded to her skull. Her lips peeled back from her teeth in a terrible frozen grin. The skin of her face dissolved into the pale bone beneath, and her hands elongated, becoming skeletal. Her gown frayed into gray wisps that moved with a will of their own, resembling the fingers of gray mist surrounding her in the Veil. It was a glamour only, but like the donning of a mask and costume, it transformed her in a way that went deeper than mere appearance.

The steed she fashioned materialized beneath her. A great beast of a horse, black-fleshed but with a head of bleached bone, like her own. It wore an armor of black over the forehead and nose, and malevolent red eyes showed through the eyeholes. Warm steam blew from the bony nostrils, and it stamped and blew its impatience to be away, mirroring her own emotions.

The others came. Their shapes were as varied as their imaginations, all terrible to behold, but none so terrible as the Unseely, who were made for dark and fearful purposes. The Seely rode mostly horses or large stags fashioned from Spirit, but the Unseely rode the creatures they had ridden in wicked men's nightmares, fanged and clawed. Some chose not to ride, traveling instead on the wind, and taking their old demon-form of banshees, the form Uulaten had sent them in to gather the souls of the murdered and to frighten the guilty.

The excitement of the Hunt filled the air as her people responded to the call. The energy of the Unseely stretched even Evainya's power to hold them. She felt the air for Yslaaran and the others who had conspired with her, wondering if they, too, would answer the call.

Beneath her exhilaration she felt a layer of sadness. As she searched through her lands, she could sense all the ones who had not responded; the ones for whom idleness had turned to a lethargy of spirit, an inertia they could no longer overcome, not even for this. She hadn't known her people had drifted so far. The king was among them; she could see Analoor now in their bower. Seeing his decline clearly for the first time, the sorrow that stabbed at her like a knife turned to anger.

She herself had been lulled too deep, had drifted too far from what she once was, or she would never have failed to notice these changes, both in her folk and in the world of Men. She and her people might fade into nothing as mankind increased, she saw that now. It was good that Yslaaran had woken her to this, so she might eradicate the mortals before it was too late.

———⟨∾⟩———

Yslaaran sat alone not far from the palace, leaning against a large willow. For the first time in her long life she truly felt the passing of time. Once conscious of it, she couldn't seem to turn the awareness off again, and the days had dragged with terrible slowness as she wondered if the war had started among the kings. She wondered if Tirren and Chayan yet lived.

She felt more certain than ever that Uthbaraal had overheard her conversation and reported it to the queen, though she had been careful to avoid him and not ask after the human girl. Nothing overt had been said or done, but Evainya had been watching her, testing her, and she dared not go to the mists. Clearly, she and the others had underestimated the queen's response to their plan. If only they had been able to bring their plan to fruition and slowly sway the queen to their cause, she still felt sure Evainya would have seen the good in it.

A single note pierced the air and hung golden and unwavering. The Hunt.

No. Yslaaran shuddered even as her blood heated to the sound of Acetis's horn. She had ridden the Wild Hunt in those strange times before the Elves cloaked themselves behind the mists. Like most of the Seely, she had hunted only fox or deer. This Hunt would have a different quarry she knew, just as she knew she was responsible for its aim.

Despair touched her for the first time in her very long life. Her actions may have destroyed the very people she wanted to help.

She debated the best course, but knew that she dared not ignore the call. Yslaaran could only hope the others would come to the same conclusion. Assuming her demon-form of blinding white light and summoning a black steed, she fought down the urge that tugged at her to abandon herself to the Hunt in earnest.

She rode quickly to the mists, and recognized Nisseah, Eanaan, and Isurrelte along the way, also in demon-form. She was glad they had come ... and hoped they also only played at this game. Yslaaran positioned herself at the back. Nisseah joined her there, riding a great stag as tall as her horse, curved ram's horns crowning the stag's head. The current of excitement that ran through the Host was palpable. She gave Nisseah a long wordless look from the midst of her brightness. Nisseah's blood-red eyes looked back, apprehensive.

The queen sat at the front of the Host. Her pale hair, nearly colorless, had not changed, though the creamy skin of her face had torn away and her eyes of deep sky-blue were now as black as holes. Once stirred from her languor to a purpose, she was daunting, and Yslaaran could feel her mantle of absolute power, see it as an iridescence surrounding her.

Oh yes, they had indeed underestimated her.

Evainya surged forward into the mists, signaling the start of the Hunt. Creatures snarled and roared as they bounded behind her, following where she led. Yslaaran stayed at the back of the horde. When her steed entered the mist, she changed back to her natural form and chose a destination different from the others.

Dashara gave up the pretense of reading, tossed the book to the couch, and paced to the window again. Old men stood guard on the catwalks of the walls—as if they could do anything if an enemy came. They were like the boys playing in the armory at making weapons. This was who Shen had entrusted her to if she had to escape to the boat waiting at Relendel. She would be better off riding alone and looking out for herself. If any of these escorted her, she would have them to protect as well as herself.

The thoughts were petulant and not like her. It was a measure of the worry she felt for Shen and Chayan, but she needed to control it. Both armies must be approaching Thiery's northern border by now. She wouldn't know when battle started, how the people she loved were faring, and it tested her considerable ability to stay calm. She needed to focus on her own duty though, those old men—and the young boys and the wives and servants—they needed her. To protect and help; it was the duty she had been raised to perform, it was just ...

A flash of white behind her caught her eye. She stretched her senses and felt power fill the room, enough that it should have been blown her out the open window like a leaf on the wind. She spun to see Yslaaran, beautiful and poised, standing behind her. Dashara made to drop to her knees but Yslaaran stopped her with an impatient gesture.

"Come, quickly," she said.

She motioned Dashara to join her in the wisp of mist around her, and Dashara hurried to her side. Yslaaran had prepared her for this eventuality, that day they talked alone in Tirren's rooms—still, Dashara's heart pounded against her ribs. That Yslaaran had come for her meant their help was needed. It meant Shen and Chayan and the others were in trouble. Dashara wondered if Maiar had returned to Thiery yet with Teyyas. It had been eleven days. He should have been able to make the trip to Beneya and back by now.

In one dizzying, gut-twisting step they traveled to Relendel, as they had done eleven days ago when Yslaaran took her to see Maiar. At that first meeting, once Maiar and the aleef had recovered from their shock, she had sent him to Bansheen to fetch Teyyas. Yslaaran had prepared them then, saying she may need all the Somiir, and now, apparently, she did.

Dashara stood in front of the tiny hut again. The aleef, along with Teyyas and Maiar, came pouring out of the house. Teyyas and

Maiar pressed their foreheads to the ground before Yslaaran, and the aleef prostrated themselves in the dirt.

Dashara sensed Teyyas shaking with something between fear and excitement, and she empathized. When Dashara first met Yslaaran in Tirren's rooms, her senses felt concussed, as if by a physical blow. A lifetime of never feeling inferior to anyone, but in that first instant she had known the Elven woman was as far above her as she was above mortals ... more. Perhaps much more.

There had been an electric thrill of excitement, overpowering awe, fear ... and a flashing hot jealousy for Shen, whose attraction she could sense at the mere sight of Yslaaran. It had been all the more disturbing for knowing Yslaaran likely knew everything she felt.

Yslaaran spoke, shaking Dashara from the memory.

"You must come now if we are to help."

Teyyas lifted her eyes and stared at her, as if hearing Yslaaran speak made her somehow real. The aleef remained prostrated.

"We obey," Maiar said, getting to his feet and bowing when he spoke.

Yslaaran waited, though, studying them.

"You have said you would aid me if I asked. Know now that I ask more than I could have guessed. The Wild Hunt rides to meet the mortal armies. If you do this thing, you oppose the Elven Queen and virtually all of my people. Decide now. I leave immediately."

From the old writings about the Great Hunt, Dashara knew enough to fear it greatly. How the few of them might hope to stand against such power, she couldn't guess. Yslaaran by herself was enough to shake Dashara to her bones. Regardless, she would try. The Elves who still loved mankind and offered now to fight for them, who wanted to help the humans again with the power and knowledge of their ancient race, they deserved all she could give. Even to giving her life.

Dashara turned to Teyyas and Maiar. "I can't expect you to take such risk, and for a people who are not even our own. But I must do this thing."

"I also will go," Maiar said on the heels of her words.

His conviction was plain to see. He had raised Dashara after all, how could she think his values would be any different?

"As will I," echoed Teyyas.

Chapter Thirty-one

Tirren cantered past Erimar, leading his regiment down the last hill. His father's guards ranged around their Bealdor where he halted on the hillside, as did the scouts who would carry his orders to the commanders in the battle. Looking across the field, Tirren saw his father's counterpart, Maradon, likewise set, though with the disadvantage of more level ground and poorer vantage.

Jaron rode along the front line, halting Tirren's regiment along with the rest of the sword on the hill, and motioning them into formations. The foot soldiers moved at a jog, jockeying to get past the swordsmen and form archer's lines at the front. Long rows took ragged shape as the untrained farmers and laborers shifted to find their places while Lacedar's foot soldiers moved to meet them.

Findal's men formed up before Lacedar's army was fully set. The archers in front strung and pulled their longbows, releasing their arrows in unison; a hail of death and injury speeding to the fore of the enemy's ranks. A sea of shields reflected the sun off the brass and metal rivets of Lacedar's foot, half-blinding Tirren, while the arrows rained down on his enemy. Like Thiery's army, the recruits' shields were as makeshift as their weapons. The tattoo of arrows hitting wood and metal mingled with the cries of the injured and dying, as arrows found gaps in the defense and the flaws in the hastily constructed shields.

Before Thiery could fire a second volley, the Lacedar archers who had found their places loosed a return volley. The arrows pelted down, loud on the mass of shields, even where Tirren sat his horse out of arrow range, like the other swordsmen, to protect the horses. His stomach turned as he saw men fall, feathered shafts protruding from faces, arms, torsos, and legs. The screams of men he knew floated up the hill to him. The first of many this day, he thought, his guts wrenching at the sight and sound of death in front of him. Battle experience had done nothing, he found, to inure him to the brutal realities of this new day of fighting and dying.

Chayan, next to Tirren, had his bow drawn—though they were well back from their archer's line and his smaller bow should not have had enough force to reach the enemy. He fired two arrows in a lower arc than the longbow men, shooting at precise targets. Tirren didn't see if the first hit, flying with the other arrows, but the second, shot during the return volley, dropped one of Lacedar's archers.

A second round was fired by each army, felling more men on both sides. Tirren sat, watching his men die, able to do nothing. The helplessness, the anticipation, the smell of blood on the hill below him all gnawed at his nerves. After the second volley, Jaron signaled the charge. Findal echoed it and Thiery's foot soldiers surged forward, battle cries filling the unnaturally still air. Bows were shouldered and short swords and makeshift weapons drawn as they ran. Lacedar responded. The two armies met with a shuddering clash.

Tirren raised his sword. "Keep to the wing of the formation," he shouted to Chayan. He had said it before, but it bore repeating. Chayan would need more room to fight than most. He would be safer too, away from the tight press that the center would feel. They might be the last words he ever spoke to his son; he hoped they were the right ones.

Feeling strung as tight as Chayan's bow, he heeled Midnight's flanks and signaled his regiment forward. He led his men to the left to meet the western flank of Maradon's army. As they neared Lacedar's ranks, Chayan cut away from his side to the wing, and Tirren lost sight of him.

———⚬⚭⚬———

Maradon's horse pawed the ground. The din of fighting, the smell of battle, and the screams of horses and men made the mounts nervous as Maradon and his guard watched the battle from a low rise. In front of them, the ranks of soldiers flowed like thick mud, ebbing and surging in unpredictable directions. A press from Thiery's left wing suddenly moved the fighting Maradon's direction.

"Bealdor," Jin said at his side, "you should move back to the trees for your safety."

Maradon shook his head, annoyed at the distraction. He was far enough away to be out of range of any rogue archers, and where no sudden press of swordsmen would reach him before he could escape on his light horse. His confidence was proved right when the fighting shifted toward the center again a few moments later.

Uthbaraal stood at his other side, watching with interest. Occasionally he laughed that high, inhuman giggle that unsettled the men. It disconcerted Maradon too, now that they were watching men die. His men.

"Bealdor," one of his guard shouted and pointed to the west. An army flying the colors of both Hadash and Eanor appeared on the west road riding hard.

Maradon stared in uncomprehending shock.

"What is this?" he roared to Uthbaraal. He turned his horse, half hoping to trample the creature, but Uthbaraal stepped easily out of the way. "Your people are supposed to be here to guarantee our victory, but the cravens are nowhere in sight. And now, with no warning from you, the other regions ride to battle!"

Thiery's army had known of his coming yet again, and somehow Hadash and Eanor as well. This envoy at his side was no envoy at all. He must have been working with Thiery all along. Maradon's rage roared inside him until it seemed his skin couldn't hold it all in. Magical or not, powerful or not, the Dark Elf must bleed like any other. Maradon planned to find out.

He moved to swing down from his horse and beat the creature to a bloody pulp. Jin grabbed his arm. Maradon shook free and lashed his reins at Jin's face, leaving a small cut under Jin's eye and causing Maradon's horse to rear.

Uthbaraal gave him a look so dark it even penetrated Maradon's anger, chilling him with a spike of fear, but when the Dark Elf spoke, it was all deference.

"Patience, my king. They come even now. I feel them on the air. Why vanquish your enemies one by one, why not all at once?"

Maradon eyed the dark and beautiful creature at his side. His rage wrestled with his desire to believe the Elf. Eanor and Hadash flowed into Thiery's sword ranks with a distant shouting of orders. He would see soon enough if the thing at his side spoke the truth, but there was nothing to be done about it either way. This was the day he had waited for, and with or without Fresshe's help or anyone else's, he would see victory today or he would die trying.

Maradon felt a gust of wind from the east. He squinted to see beyond the eastern edge of the fighting. A dark horde appeared out of nothing, riding for the center of the battle. Could it be? Were the Elves here at Fresshe's command to see him to victory?

"Bealdor," Jin said.

Maradon glared at Jin and saw him pointing front and to the right; Jin apparently hadn't noticed the new army taking the field yet. Maradon followed his finger to see one young Thiery soldier, without even the benefit of a mail hood, riding from the western edge of the conflict at an angle toward him. He had twisted to one side in an unnatural fashion and rode at a gallop, guiding his horse with his knees. Maradon wondered distantly if it could be an injured soldier already fleeing the field. Whoever he was, it was no concern to him.

He turned his attention back to the dark mass approaching, staring to see if it truly was the envoy's people. The soldiers at the east end, closest to the new army began to scatter. He had trouble seeing from this distance and blasted poor vantage, but it looked like his men were panicking. These were their allies. He should have prepared his army better for the possibility of magical intervention. Of course, he could have done better if the gods-foresworn Uthbaraal had let him know what to expect.

As the Elven horde stormed into the battle lines, Maradon saw them clearly and realized he never could have prepared his men for this. They were terrible to look on. The power that oozed from the Dark Elf still frightened him, but over the days he had accustomed to the creature and come to see him essentially for what he was, a servant. The hoard riding toward the battle chilled him to his bones.

His ranks fared poorly—panic turned to madness. They fought blindly, against their own people as much as against the enemy. He watched as scores died. At his heel, Uthbaraal laughed. He shimmered into some unholy form.

Maradon swallowed hard on the cold reality of his betrayal.

"Sound the retreat!" he shouted to Jin.

Instead of signaling retreat, Jin's attention stayed locked the other direction. Maradon turned to see the Thiery soldier still angling for him, a hunting bow in his hands, raised and drawn. He must have been holding the bow down at his side earlier, as he rode. The soldier wasn't even past Lacedar's front lines. Even if Maradon hadn't been wearing chain mail, the lone soldier hardly posed any threat at this distance. As he watched, the madman sighted, drew, and loosed his arrow.

The speed and the deadly aim of the arrow registered too late. From the corner of his eye he saw Jin spur his mount and leap in front of him. Maradon dropped his reins and kicked his left boot from the stirrup, throwing himself to his right. He never made it off his horse.

The arrow hit him in the chest like a hard punch. The point tore through his mail and his skin. The impact knocked him backwards. His mind raced, trying to take in every sensation of this assault, to find a solution, an escape, but there was no escape left. The arrow ripped through the muscle of his heart. He felt the tip tear through the skin of his back and stop, trapped there against the chain mail and leather. Maradon knew before he hit the ground that he had been betrayed by the Elves, that his army was beaten, and that he had only moments left to live.

Chapter Thirty-two

Evainya led the Elves and their fearsome beasts onto the battlefield. She struggled to keep the Unseely in line, and to keep her people together, away from the danger the wild panic engendered. No stray sword cut or arrow must touch any of them.

She spearheaded all the powers of all the Elves, and also orchestrated their way through the fighting, turning men and their hateful metal away from her people to fight each other, clearing a swath for her people to ride. She had no intention of fighting. The fear they projected would be her people's safety and the mortals' doom. She would ensure that the humans fought until not a single one lived to see the end of this day.

Chayan watched his arrow strike Maradon cleanly in the chest. He swung his horse back toward the battle before the man fell, sure that Maradon's personal guards would chase him down. Pulling Star around, he felt a change in the air—a strange thickness. He extended his senses. The level of power he encountered nearly threw him from his horse. Visceral fear radiated out from it in waves. He felt the intent of the magic clearly, though distantly, recognizing the fear it emanated without experiencing it himself. He couldn't see the eastern end of the battle, couldn't see more than a few lengths in front for the swirling mass of soldiers, but he could have located the center of that rushing force with his eyes closed. It broke over the field like a wave.

Chayan tucked low in his saddle, his bow over his shoulder and his quarterstaff across his lap, and rode toward the center of the chaos. His line, his regiment, his father ... they all fought in the center of that darkness.

A black horse wheeled and cantered beside him. Feeling more than seeing through the glamour of brightness that burned like a malevolent sun, Chayan knew his mother. The image shimmered and she was herself, on a smaller, pure white steed. Panic bordered on madness all around them. The fighting reached a frenzied pitch as the fear the Elves wielded like a weapon took hold, and soldiers slashed and hacked at friend and foe alike.

"We must be quick if we are to save any," his mother said. She urged her horse forward and it leaped a small patch of fog as if jumping a stream. Chayan set his heels to Star, and his gelding jumped with the other horse, landing in that single movement at the southwestern edge of the fighting, well back from where they had started. Dashara stood there with two other halfbloods.

"They will instruct you. I must go now to your father." And, with that, she was gone.

--- ⊷◈⊶ ---

Tirren hadn't seen Chayan since he rode for the wing. His jaw tightened as he searched to his left for the last time. His regiment was scant lengths from engaging the enemy, and he forced his focus ahead. A moment later he was engulfed in the fighting, laying about with his sword, unable to think of anything beyond stroke and parry.

He faced one enemy after another, kill or be killed, willing himself not to look out at the field of thousands, the odds against him living until the end of the day. His right arm tired quickly from lifting mail and broadsword repeatedly. A quick block saved him from losing his hand to a downstroke. He slashed the man across the face.

Tirren turned to slice at the man closing on his left. A chill ran down his spine. A black shadow rolled across the lowering sun, turning the sky murky. His gut knotted with fear so strong it threatened to loose his bowels. The warm sweat of exertion running down his chest and back turned chill with fear.

He didn't understand how he had come to be here, armored and sword in hand, surrounded by madmen. The day, the place, the men around him—none of it was familiar. Worse, monsters out of legends, out of nightmares rode toward him, driving these men, their minions, before them. The stench of evil filled his nostrils. He must not fall to them, or death would be a welcome release when it finally came. He remembered now that he had always known they were coming; he had always feared them.

Visions of the horrors they planned beset him. Things he knew in his soul to be the truth. The men would unhorse him, bludgeon him, capture him. They would drag him screaming and pleading to their masters. The wild, inhuman things that rode the creatures would torture him, rape him, take pleasure in his pain, and their monsters would dismember him slowly, eating him alive, piece-by-piece. He couldn't run from them, he couldn't hide; he must kill to stay alive.

Enemies surrounded him, trying to get at him. Midnight plunged violently among them and Tirren swung his sword with a strength borne of absolute terror. Time had no meaning as he fought, hacking, destroying, trying to survive this nightmare alone. A brightness fell across him and he cried out in fear. He slashed wildly at it.

"Hush now," the voice said. Abruptly his blinding fear was gone, and Midnight stood trembling and sweating beneath him.

He saw the carnage around him, wrought with weapons and with bare hands, brother against brother.

"I am glad to find you still hale, my love," Yslaaran said. "You must get your people to safety. Your son and the other halfbreeds will protect them, over there." She pointed behind him. With a last look, she urged her mount forward into the belly of the chaos.

Tirren knew he had been mad as a spotted snake. His arms and chest were covered with blood. He couldn't think straight and his hands shook with the aftermath of a terror deeper and stronger than he had ever known. Yslaaran had been real, though, he could still make her out riding into the maw of the madness.

A dazed soldier bumped Midnight's hind end with his horse's shoulder. Midnight reared and rolled his eyes in fear. Tirren forced his mind to focus. Looking about, he saw the surviving men nearest him had stopped their fighting and stared about in shock. Some had tears rolling down their faces. Looking farther, he saw a dark and frightening host riding through the battle. Waves of hectic fighting raged where they passed, undulating out from that dark center like ripples in a pond. Pockets of calm, filled with frightened, confused men, like himself and those around him, dotted the path Yslaaran had taken.

The dead lying on the ground were wicked evidence of the magic that had driven this. They were no longer just casualties of war, gruesome enough, but men hacked to pieces. He pushed away the horror of not knowing what he had done in his own frenzy; he buried it as deeply as he could before it immobilized him.

More men around him lost the mad glaze in their eyes. On his second attempt, he found his voice and shouted to them to follow him. With shaking hands and haunted eyes, they turned their horses or ambled unsteadily toward him. The soldiers of Lacedar were motionless, uncertain what to do.

"This fight is no longer our own," Tirren yelled. "Get back to your homes!" He saw a purpose light in some of their eyes. They turned from the field and ran.

Tirren led the nearest group of his men to the south edge of the field, where Yslaaran had indicated. He found Chayan there with Dashara, Maiar, and another half-Elven woman tending to the soldiers who had already found their way to them.

"We can protect them from being taken by the madness again," Chayan shouted to him. "Bring us all you can."

Tirren looked to the place where his father should have been with his guard. A different sort of fear gripped him at the sight of the empty hill. He spun back to the field and rode for the patches of inactivity where Yslaaran and a few other Elven riders massed. He looked for Shen's wolf-head helm and those of the other regiment leaders, or any commanders whom the men might follow in their shaken state. He spotted Shen not too far east of his own position, in one of those patches of calm. Glad but unsurprised to see him still ahorse, Tirren made for him.

Evainya's spell of terror unraveled as she neared the far end of the field. She didn't need to feel the wind to know who had done this thing. She turned her demon steed. All across the field were areas where Yslaaran and her companions countered the chaos. To the south was an even more amazing thing—the cast-off get of her people herding the humans, trying to heal them with their feeble powers.

She looked at the field again. Less than a quarter of the mortals were dead. The few renegade Seely could never hope to succeed against the entire Elven host, but they would also know that Evainya would never expose her people to this many armed humans regaining their wits. If even one soldier loosed an arrow at her people, one of these worthless mortals could take the life of an immortal. It was more risk than she was willing to take.

Evainya had never in all her long life been thwarted, never challenged. The rage that built in her was a new thing. A shriek burned past her throat. It shook the field, knocking soldiers near her from their feet. Thrusting her skeletal hand out, she made a grabbing motion. The renegade Seely were swept from the field and into the mists, along with the rest of the Host.

Chapter Thirty-three

Black, oily smoke filled the air. A dozen fires burned corpses, and still the field was cluttered with dead. The damp cloth tied over Tirren's nose and mouth did little to block either the smell or the smoke. His eyes watered and his nose burned as he worked side-by-side with his men. Tirren didn't know if a Bealdor was supposed to do things like this or not. He didn't care. None of it felt real anyway.

The dead boy at Tirren's feet was the same age as Chayan. Tirren had known him since he was a child. Reaching down he grabbed the boy by the wrists, hoping both arms would stay on long enough to drag him to a burn pile. Like so many, the boy had been hacked at long after he received a mortal blow.

Tirren, again, shut out the memories of finding his own father. He had been identifiable only by his helm, his clothing, and his ring of office; the ring Tirren now wore on his left hand. He would never know if the madness had taken his father and sent him headlong into the fray, or if the wild fighting had washed over him and his guard, pulling them down in a deadly undertow. Perhaps his own guard had even turned on him. He dragged the bloodied boy across the field and tried to focus on nothing at all.

Erimar's pyre smoked at the edge of the field, but too many had died to honor them all. It made Tirren sick to throw the bodies of soldiers into burn piles, but hundreds were dead. Counting the soldiers from the other regions, nearly a thousand would never leave this field again.

Greig and Lymon had finished burning their dead and gathering their wounded this morning. They were on their way back to their own regions now. Lacedar's survivors had fled for their border as soon as their wits returned, leaving behind all of their dead and most of their dying.

The boy's sinews held until Tirren reached the pile, where a foot soldier grabbed the ankles and helped Tirren swing him onto the heap.

"Better light that one now. It won't burn if we add many more." Tirren heard the strain in his voice at his own words. "Start a new pile there." He pointed to the right. The man doused the bodies with oil and took flint and tinder to it as Tirren turned away from the burning, bloody stench.

The body of a Lacedar soldier lay in his way as he headed across the field in a new direction. As he stepped over the corpse, he felt a sudden urge to kick the dead man. The country had been at peace for a hundred and fifty years until Maradon stirred trouble. They should at least feel free to leave Lacedar's dead out for the carrion eaters, Maradon among them. That had been one body Tirren had been glad to find.

He had ridden, yesterday, through the silent summer twilight, to the little outcrop near the river where Chayan told him he would find Maradon. The man lay with the strong, slender shaft of Chayan's arrow buried deep in his chest, a look of frustrated surprise on his face. Tirren had been too tired and numb to feel much satisfaction at seeing him, other than the confirmation that they were finally rid of the wretched man.

Stepping now over and around more bodies, Tirren continued to make his way to the west edge of the field. Chayan was there, working with the other halfbloods near the wagons that had finally caught up with the army. Tirren squatted on his heels next to him and pulled his face-cloth down.

"How goes it?"

"We've made good headway," Chayan answered.

He was sitting on the ground, leaning against a wagon wheel. A man's head was pillowed in his lap and Chayan's hands rested at the man's temples, though Tirren knew his son wasn't idle. Chayan and the three Somiir had tirelessly healed the minds and bodies of countless men.

"I think no more will die than already have," Chayan continued. "A few need extra healing before they can travel, though, and there are many who need ... well ... the other kind of healing."

Tirren had seen plenty of them after the battle, some wandering dazed, some striking out at friends, and some just lying down, unwilling to get up again, though they had no outward injury. The terror, the horror, the brutal violence this army had witnessed; most of the survivors carried more wounds than the ones that could be seen.

He didn't know how much this magic took out of Chayan, but all four halfbloods sported dark circles under their eyes and skin paler than usual. What they did now, they had done through the night, and the journey here from the Hold and the battle must have taxed Chayan even before that. Tirren didn't want to add to his son's burdens, but he must.

"I just found Vint. I thought you should know."

Chayan looked at the face of the sleeping man in his lap. "Oh."

"I'm sorry, Chayan. He was always a good friend to you."

"I guess I pretty much knew when I couldn't find him after the battle." He kept his eyes down. "You haven't heard from mother, have you?"

"You know I'd tell you if I had."

Chayan nodded. The man stirred under Chayan's hands, his breathing deeper, more regular. He was one of Findal's foot soldiers, Tirren thought, and one who had never been particularly friendly with Chayan before.

Tirren looked to the other end of the wagon and saw Shen handing a water flask to Dashara. He had been at her side every spare moment, though he could do as little to help her as Tirren could do for Chayan.

"Don't wear yourself thin," Tirren said, putting a hand on Chayan's shoulder as he stood.

He had worried at first for Chayan—for all the halfbloods—that the fear and destruction the Elves had caused would be taken out on his son and the Somiir. In fact, just the opposite had occurred. It made an odd kind of sense. Chayan and the others had been a beacon of refuge at the battle. The mad and injured had been herded to them and the Bansheenan Somiir, along with his son, had protected and healed them. The halfbloods had been a haven from forces that mortals couldn't hope to prevail against or even understand. The work they did now only strengthened the acceptance.

Tirren pulled his face-cloth up and looked across the smoky haze of the field for Jaron. He needed to find out how soon they could return to the Hold. Leaving Chayan to his work, he headed toward the field, scanning the men. Jaron was easy to pick out even with his face covered, he was one of the few men bandaged in half a dozen places and still working. Tirren made for him, but Chayan's talk of Yslaaran haunted him as he walked.

He had seen her swept from the field, along with the other Elves that had helped her. He tried to push aside his fears for her as he had his mourning for his father. Now wasn't the time to indulge his personal sorrow. He hadn't even allowed himself tears when his father had been found, though Chayan had wept at his side.

Now that Yslaaran had been brought to mind again, he found her hard to banish. The pressures, the fears, and the losses over the last two days squeezed his emotions like a cider press, and distilled them into thoughts of the soft comfort of her. He wished with all his heart he could take her in his arms again, kiss her soft skin, lose himself for awhile in her, an experience intense enough that it might wash the bitterness of these last days from him.

———— ⬡ ————

A few days later, the head of Thiery's snaking army turned off the Great Road onto the smaller road that ran above Thiery Village. The Hold, up the hill to Chayan's right, looked solid and welcoming. It looked like home.

Villagers were lined all along the road, cheering their return, though many searched the faces of the soldiers and failed to find the ones they sought. Men peeled out of the formation and scattered to their homes, as they had been doing all along the road back. The army of more than a thousand that had set out dwindled now to less than two hundred; the surviving soldiers who lived at the Hold.

Chayan rode at the back of the column, among the injured, with Dashara, Teyyas, and Maiar. They stayed well back from the last regiment, out of the dust.

He worked as he rode, maintaining a spell of sleep on four men in the rear wagon, looking at them enviously and thinking of his bed, so close now. Over the last few days the magic he used had drained him like nothing in his life ever had before, and he'd managed nothing more than short cat-naps while riding with the injured who still required his attention. The others were no better off. Even with the extra endurance from their Elven heritage, all four of them had been taxed to the limits.

The line of cheering villagers fell behind as the column turned north again and climbed the road to the Hold. The servants, the children, and the elderly ranged along the walls and about the gates, waving ribbons and pennants and shouting to loved ones. It seemed surreal, as did everything that had happened since they'd left. It must be even more so for his father, who was entering these gates for the first time as the Bealdor.

The week after returning wasn't as restful as Chayan had hoped it would be. He assumed many of the duties of Beodan, now that his father didn't have time to see to them, even though he wouldn't officially take the title until he turned twenty. There had been meetings to attend and planning, and a short trip to Fent, the fief that would soon be his.

Teyyas, Maiar, and Dashara had all stayed on, for which Chayan was glad. He stayed up late every night talking with them, knowing Teyyas and Maiar would leave soon for Bansheen. He hadn't wanted to ask what Dashara planned. He suspected the only thing keeping them here, Teyyas and Maiar anyway, was hope that Yslaaran might return, but there had still been no word from her.

Preoccupied with thinking about his mother, Chayan turned right down the hall then realized he was heading for his old rooms and turned around to go the other way instead. He nearly bumped into Jaron's eldest daughter.

"Kesum," she said, shyly, not moving back. She looked at him from under her lashes in a way she never had before.

He gave a flustered greeting and stepped out of her way. Girls had never really been forward with him, certainly not after the incident with Gwynalyn, but this seemed to be yet another aspect of his life undergoing change.

The difference in how the soldiers saw him and his magic had been nearly instantaneous at the battle, and when the news spread that he had sought out and killed Maradon single-handedly, his status had risen yet again. Better still, the stories were spreading to every corner of the region as men travelled home. He had seen the change in the people in Fent when he was there the other day. Perhaps someday his mother's plan really would come to fruition and the people of Thiery might see him as the people of Bansheen saw the Somiir.

Chayan reached his new apartments. It was odd to be in his father's rooms, but probably not half so odd as it was for his father to have moved to the Bealdor's rooms. He had just closed the door when he heard a horse gallop into the courtyard below. Another messenger, no doubt. They had been coming and going so frequently since the battle, he hardly paid attention anymore.

Chayan went back to organizing his things. He looked around for a good spot for his books and settled on a shelf in his sitting room. He fingered the large volume Dashara had given him on her first visit. Every day he expected the Somiir to announce that they were leaving. He sighed.

There was a knock on the door and his father entered, a rolled sheaf in one hand and an odd expression on his face.

"I have something you should see."

He handed the sheaf to Chayan and walked past him to sit in a large padded chair, motioning for Chayan to take the seat near him. "It just arrived. It's from Bron in Lacedar."

Chayan's breath stopped. *Lacedar couldn't be planning more aggression. They couldn't.* He sat, finished unrolling the message, and read.

Bealdor, Kesum-Chayan,

I hope you will believe me when I say that Lacedar's invasion was none of my doing and I opposed it from the start. Like my grandfather,

Vrenun, I have never advocated breaking the hard-won peace of this country. I most sincerely wish to see good-will re-established and, more than this, would advocate a new spirit of cooperation between the regions, which I believe would be to all our good.

In light of this hope for a new relationship, I petition for your help. Thiery obviously holds some connection to the Elves as some aided your camp, and I witnessed on the field the truth of the trader's rumors that Kesum-Chayan is himself a halfblood. The Elves have abducted my sister, Emorelle, and I wish more than anything to rescue her from the Dark Elf I believe holds her captive. I know nothing of him but his name, Uthbaraal, and that he either is, or merely posed as, an emissary from Fresshe.

Though my father struck some deal with the Elves, they betrayed him, and I believe my sister is in grave danger. My father never shared with me how he came to make contact with the Elves.

I love my sister dearly and have prayed to all the gods to no avail. I beg you now, that if you hold any influence with the Elves, Lacedar would be in your debt if you could help effect her release.

I remain yours truly,

Bron, Bealdor of Lacedar

Chayan sat back, letting the words sink in before looking to his father. "It is good to hear that Bron wants peace. One less enemy to worry about would be a blessing."

Tirren nodded, looking thoughtful. "I just thought you should know."

"What will you say?"

"I will say that we're agreeable to peace if they hold to their word and cause no further trouble. As to his sister ... I will wish them well and say that we have no more influence than they."

"But mother ..." He stopped short at the pain that word brought to his father's face.

Though he had known his father was tired, he had not noticed before how shadowed his eyes were. As busy as Chayan had been, it had been worse for Tirren. He had suddenly assumed all of Erimar's normal responsibilities, and more, all the after-effects of the war. And, Chayan knew, the same worry for his mother that he had been feeling.

Chayan had begun calling her name every day at dawn, as she had once told him to do. He kept hoping as the days passed to hear some word of her. Each day that he did not brought more concern than the last. This letter could not have presented him a better opportunity to express what he'd been thinking.

"Perhaps there is a way. If I could get to the mists ..."

"No."

"But if I could, perhaps I could call mother to them, and not only find out what happened to Bron's sister, but also see if mother is all right."

His father's face was stone. "I said no, Chayan. Perhaps you failed to notice the Wild Hunt riding the battlefield, set on killing us all? Do you think you could go unnoticed to their lands? Negotiate with them? I saw your mother and the others working with her swept off the field against their will for helping us, and they with far more power than you. They could be prisoners. They could be dead," he said thickly. "I will not risk you as well."

Chayan tried another tack. "But father, their fighting was all with magic, creating fear. It didn't touch me. It didn't touch any of the Somiir. I don't think they're able to affect our minds."

"I don't care if magic directed at humans didn't affect you, it doesn't mean they can't kill you if they wish to. All of you have commented on how much more powerful Yslaaran is than you are. Four Elves worked to save us. Four. Out of what, a hundred, two hundred? You *will not* seek them out or spy on them."

His father was angry. He was frightened. He was so worried for Yslaaran he seemed in physical pain. Now was not the time to push this.

"I understand, Bealdor."

Chayan understood, but he didn't have to give up just yet. He had another idea.

———— ❧ ————

Dashara lay pressed against Shen's warmth, her head on his chest as he slept soundly beside her. She was still floating in the languorous heaviness that came after lovemaking, which they had done each night since his return to the Hold, knowing their time together to be short.

Every day she spent here, every night beside him, her love for Shen grew until she didn't know how she could bear to leave him, though she knew she must. Neither had spoken of it; when she broached the subject, he was unwilling to talk of it. So they would do this instead, live as if the day would never come, and when it did she would pack her things and go with the others without discussion, saying goodbye only when they must. And both their hearts would carry the scars of their parting for the rest of their lives.

She wished she could be like Suuda. The Sun Goddess had spent half the year in her Sun Palace in the north and half the year with a lover in a distant land to the south. Myth or truth, Dashara wished that such an arrangement could be possible for her. But the Somiir numbered so rare, the thought was unworthy of the devotion her people showed to her.

More than this kept her awake into the night, though. The proposal Chayan had brought to the three Somiir earlier today had been as staggering as the one Yslaaran had put to them before the battle. It was a hefty decision to weigh, but she may not be leaving as soon as she had thought. She debated waking Shen and telling him all. Looking at his sleeping face, she decided he didn't need more worry just yet.

Odd, that with all the history Bansheen had preserved, that it should be in this rustic, superstitious country that she would learn so much about the Elves. To behold Yslaaran, to sense the immensity of her power, hear her voice and her speech, witness her clothing, her mannerisms. And then more, to be taken into her confidence, travel with her into the mists and out again leagues distant, and there to see the terrible Wild Hunt and the four Seely who defied the Hunt for the sake of the mortals ... it was all beyond words. It had been terrifying and exhilarating.

Shen shifted in his sleep, rolling onto his side. She turned to curl against his back. In her heart she wondered if she could leave him yet anyway, or if she would look for one excuse after another not to go.

Sleep would be a long time coming tonight. Her contemplation of Chayan's proposal began again.

Chapter Thirty-four

Tirren rubbed his eyes and tried to refocus on the mounds of papers in front of him. Meetings with councilors, communications with Eanor and Hadash, paying the financial costs of the battle, resupplying ... it seemed like it would never end.

There was a knock on the library door.

"Come," he said distractedly.

The door opened and Teyyas, Maiar, Dashara, and Chayan entered. It seemed the time had come for the Somiir to return to Bansheen. He regretted the inevitable as much as Chayan must. The help they had given, the things they had taught Chayan, and the acceptance they had won with the people of Thiery, it had all been more than Tirren could have hoped for.

He stood, greeting them, and moved to the chairs by the fireplace. He gestured for them to sit. Teyyas and Dashara took the couch, Chayan the chair to Dashara's right, and Maiar chose to perch on the arm of the sofa, next to Teyyas. Arrayed opposite Tirren, the beauty of the four of them together amazed him yet again. Teyyas began, but what she said was not what he had been expecting.

"Bealdor, your son has told us of the letter you received from Bron in Lacedar."

Tirren shot a hard look at Chayan. He had been clear about his stand on this and Chayan shouldn't have shared the information with the Somiir.

"Yes, and as I have explained to Chayan already, there is nothing we can do about the situation."

"That may not be entirely true," Maiar said. He looked relaxed and elegant as always. His strongly Elven appearance still unsettled Tirren. "I would be most interested in seeing the Veil of Mists that I have read about for so long. Perhaps if we can find the mists, we can feel for the girl's presence. Yslaaran may even be able to sense us and inform us if she and the girl are well or are truly in danger."

"And perhaps if Yslaaran could sense you, others could also," Tirren retorted. "The Elves are now our proven enemies. Enemies powerful beyond anything we could hope to prevail against. It would be foolish in the extreme to poke that hornet's nest again."

He nearly choked on his words when he realized how like his father he sounded. Maybe Erimar had been right all along. Maybe Tirren had just needed the maturity and responsibility to see it.

"The Elves, sadly, have proven their harmful intent," Teyyas said, "though we saw that there are also those who wish to aid us. If the majority of them have aligned themselves against you, would you not use us while you can to discover what we may?"

Tirren had to consider what she said. He had seen what the four halfbloods were able to accomplish during and after the battle. More than he ever could have imagined. But they were halfbloods and they were only four. On top of that, one was his son and the other three were diplomats from a foreign land.

"The Elves are too dangerous. Our best chance is to wait, stay quiet, and hope they are done with us."

"And if they are not?" Dashara asked. "Bealdor, I have given this much thought and find I must agree with the others. If they were to suddenly come against you again, Chayan alone would have no chance. Now, while we are all together, is the best and only opportunity to see if we could discover any information that might be helpful to you, to Bron's sister, or to Yslaaran and her companions."

"What of the danger to you?" Tirren countered. "You have spoken often of how few you are and your obligation to your people. Why risk yourselves on this?"

Dashara answered, "We have discussed this at great length. This is no rash decision, but the truth is, even if we lost our lives in this endeavor, the aleef in Relendel will continue to look for more abandoned babes. The philosophers would raise and train the first, just as they did for Teyyas. Of course, we don't plan to take any risk so great that we will lose our lives, but as you say, the consequences are unknown. The rewards are as well, though."

She shifted forward, lacing her hands over her knees. "I have dedicated my entire life to helping those in need. We all have," she glanced at Teyyas and Maiar on her left. "The thought of the girl possibly held captive disturbs me greatly, but more than that, what if Yslaaran and her companions are in danger? If we were able to contact Yslaaran, or any of the others, and determine their well-being, then the risk would be well-justified. If we succeeded on the grandest scale, extracting Yslaaran or the other sympathetic Seely, should they be held against their will, it would be worth any risk. The benefits Yslaaran and the others could bring with their far greater power and wisdom would be worth any cost, even our lives. They have risked all to prove their allegiances to mankind. We owe this to them."

Tirren was taken aback. He wanted more than anything to find a way to contact Yslaaran, to make sure she was all right. The ties she had bound to him all those years ago pulled at his mind, his heart, his soul, until he could hardly sleep at night for fear of her safety. But he couldn't let that color his judgment. He had the entire region to consider.

"Father," Chayan spoke before Tirren could respond, "we know we are already at war with mother's people, whether we want to be or not. We both know they aren't likely to be done with us so easily, with only four defecting to our aid in the battle. Even the soldiers worry when and where they may return."

Tirren winced. He had heard the same rumors.

Chayan continued, "To hope that they forget about their enmity for us would be foolishly optimistic. They may even have designs against me personally, as this may all have begun due to mother's plans for me."

Tirren had already considered that possibility—another thought that kept him awake late into the night.

Chayan pressed on. "We just want to see if we are even capable of finding this Veil of Mists. We may not even be able to accomplish that much. But if the Somiir are willing to go with me, best the thing is done now before they go back to Bansheen."

Tirren dropped his head into his hands. Were they right? Was sitting and waiting to see if the Elves made another attempt to wipe them out really his best strategy? What if they came for Chayan, and swept him away as well? Fear mustn't make him as bull-headed as his father had been. He pushed his arguments aside and committed himself to considering all options.

Without lifting his head from his hands, he said, "Tell me in detail what you plan."

———

Tirren came back from his meeting with the council in Thiery Village to find Shen pacing in the entry hall. He spoke as soon as Tirren stepped through the front doors of the Hold.

"You must let me go with them."

Tirren didn't need to ask what he meant. Little else had been on his mind since his talk with the Somiir.

"Have you taken mid-meal yet?" Shen shook his head. "Neither have I."

Tirren led him to the great hall. It was early afternoon and most people had already eaten, leaving the room nearly empty. He chose a table away from the few people remaining, and he and Shen slid onto benches opposite each other.

"I'm surprised you didn't start by asking me why I approved such a plan."

A plump woman brought them bowls of food. When she had gone, Shen answered.

"I got quite the earful of reasons this morning why this undertaking has to take place. Every time I opened my mouth to object, in fact. But if they do this thing, you can't send them alone, without steel at their backs and men who know how to use it."

Tirren barely registered the admonition. He was glad the one thing becoming Bealdor hadn't changed was their friendship. Besides, he understood Shen's concerns all too well. Sending Chayan and the others alone chafed as roughly at him.

"An armed escort will only draw attention to what needs to be done in stealth. Who knows, our very humanness may be felt by them, where Chayan and the others may be able to pass near, or through if they must, without detection. Or so they tell me." Tirren leaned forward with his elbows on the table. "Gods, we know so confounded little! Twice today I nearly remanded my approval, but I know Chayan is right—if this thing can be done, then it has to be done now, while they're all here."

"So don't send an armed escort, send only me. You know I will protect them all with my life. If they're all preoccupied with their magics, they'll need someone at their backs who can watch out for them."

What he said struck home. Tirren had warred with his own futile desire to accompany them, but as Bealdor, it would be irresponsible. Shen was the better choice.

Shen watched him closely. "When do we leave?" he asked.

Tirren closed his eyes and shook his head. "First thing in the morning."

Chapter Thirty-five

Chayan walked out the front doors of the Hold into the pre-dawn quiet of the courtyard. His father waited there already with Teyyas and Maiar. Dashara and Shen joined them a moment later.

A wagon loaded with wood for the morning cookfires rumbled by on the road below as the last stars faded from the sky. The early start would hopefully avoid spectators and speculation that might come from anyone seeing their group leaving the Hold. Chayan hoped they would be back again before dark. He didn't want to think of where they might be otherwise.

Before the sun crested the horizon, his father led them out the side gate and into the woods to the west. Chayan inhaled the calming fragrance of pine, strong in the dawn air. After a short walk, Tirren stopped them and indicated a patch of sparse grass between the trees, no different from all the others around them. "That was where I first saw her."

Chayan had always known that his mother had appeared in these woods, but to see his father indicate the very spot conjured a vivid image of their first meeting, when Tirren would not have been so very much older than Chayan was now.

Chayan extended his senses. With the extra perception he could tell the other Somiir did the same. He felt nothing unusual in this spot, nor had he expected to. From his mother's comings and goings, it was the consensus among them that there was no "place"

354

where they would find the mists, but starting where his father had crossed into his mother's lands seemed as good a start as any. If a day of effort in this area proved fruitless, they would return in the evening and ride tomorrow for Relendel, where all of the Somiir had been left as babes.

"My mind was enchanted by this time," his father continued, "and I don't remember the exact spot where we entered her lands, but I have a clear recollection of where I came out that morning after." Yesterday, Tirren had shared with them all he could remember of the Elven lands and his experience there, in case any of it should prove to be helpful.

He walked on again a little way and they followed. "Here." He indicated another unremarkable spot in a wood that looked all alike. "This is where I came back through in the morning."

Chayan was not surprised he could be so accurate; he knew how brightly the memories of Yslaaran had burned in his father all those years before he saw her again. He wondered how often his father might have come here looking for her.

They walked to the place Tirren indicated. Chayan felt outward to the limit of his enhanced senses. Shen stood quietly behind them dressed in his swordsmen's jerkin and breeches, chain mail softly rattling beneath. He held his broadsword drawn, point down on the earth, hands resting one atop the other on the hilt. The readiness Chayan felt in him belied his easy pose.

His father spoke quietly with Shen. With his power tapped, Chayan could hear every word, feel every emotion of their discussion, though he was trying to keep his efforts focused elsewhere.

"Keep them safe," his father finished, the worry in his quiet words evident. His father didn't understand that Shen—excellent soldier that he was—was the least well-armed of them all. Dashara had argued the point already, begging that Shen not be allowed to accompany them, until his father had threatened to forbid the entire venture.

Tirren left Shen, came to Chayan, and wrapped his arms around his shoulders, giving him the kind of hug he seldom got now that he was a grown man. With one hand on the back of his head his father said into his ear, "Be careful. Do no more than absolutely necessary. Your mother is in her lands with power and allies of her own. You must see to it that you come back safe to your own lands and people." He felt the gentle kiss his father placed at his temple. He released him and turned to clasp forearms with Shen, then walked away without looking back.

Chayan knew how he'd wanted to stay with them, but another person with no Elven powers would do nothing to help their safety. His humanness could even jeopardize them more. Chayan turned back to the task at hand.

The four of them spread out slightly, searching in silence, working blind. Chayan walked a small pattern doing the only thing he could, feeling with his heightened senses for anything new, any sense of power. They continued this way while the sun rose two fists above the horizon. Maiar suddenly released his extended senses with a sigh, turned, and walked back to Shen. He sat on the ground near his feet and took a long pull from a waterskin.

Chayan and the others came over also. Shen, who hadn't shifted his stance by a hair all morning, sat as well, relaxing with them and sharing the waterskin.

"I will try the rest of today and longer if you like," Maiar said into the heavy silence, "but, truth is I can't think what more to do than I've done. And surely that has not been enough."

None of them were willing to say what Chayan knew they were all feeling—that perhaps they simply weren't equal to this task.

"Are you able to combine your efforts?" Shen asked.

"No," Dashara answered him. "We feel each other working, but we can't add our efforts together."

"What of the times you traveled with Yslaaran? Could you sense this mist then?"

Dashara had been in that Elven mist four times now: to Relendel when Yslaaran first met Maiar and back to the Hold, to Relendel again, and then on to the battle. Teyyas and Maiar had been only the once, and Chayan never, though he had seen his mother wielding her power over it. She pondered Shen's question.

"There was an overwhelming sense of power, but I think that came from Yslaaran herself." She looked at Shen with honest self-doubt in her eyes. "If that level of power is what is required to use the mists, then I have no chance of success. None of us do."

There, it was said.

"But you don't need to use the mists, only find them, right?"

His confidence in her made her smile. "True. I remember the sensation of being in that mist, though nothing I'm able to put into words."

"Was it anything like what you and Maiar did on the boat when you brought me back here?"

Chayan shifted to his left to face Dashara.

Her eyes were distant. "Not unlike it, I suppose." She chewed at her lower lip as she concentrated. "When we travel the sea, we work with Water and Air—the elements that make up mist ... natural mist, at any rate."

Chayan watched her trying to puzzle it out as she spoke. Her eyes came back to the present. "But there was more to Yslaaran's mist, there was Spirit in it too." She looked at Teyyas and Maiar, her eyes widening.

"When we calm the water and raise the wind, we summon," Teyyas said, finishing her thought. "Perhaps these mists need summoning rather than finding?" They all rose to their feet again, and Chayan saw Dashara give Shen's great arm a squeeze. There was no more guarantee that this would work than anything else this morning, but Chayan returned to the task with renewed determination.

Taking his place at the right of the line again, Chayan tried to imagine how to summon the mists. He could feel every detail around him as clearly as if he were a part of it all: the dew drying in the shade of the trees, the movements of the birds in the branches, the smell of green leaves unfolding. His skin tingled, ready to burst with the sensations that filled it.

Long minutes passed as he explored the small creek nearby, the sense of the water, the drops that splashed on the rocks and dried in the sun. He knew somehow that he did not have the power to create, but if this mist lay nearby, in whatever sense, he would strive to recognize its nature and call it to him.

Teyyas inhaled sharply at the other end of their line. He felt it. She had called it, and it lay just beyond sight. All his will went into grasping what he felt at the edge of his senses and drawing it to him, afraid it would slip away.

Suddenly it was there; a gray mist, reaching high above them, stretching from Dashara's position to Chayan's.

Shen moved swiftly to stand in front of them, sword at the ready. The group braced themselves as if the Wild Hunt might burst from the Veil, riding them down like so much wheat in the field. A long moment passed. Nothing happened. Shen slowly lowered his sword and looked back at them.

Chayan had no idea what they should do next. Though his father had described these mists as a dense fog he had passed through, Chayan had been hoping that with their powers, they may be able to look through it and see the land beyond, perhaps even great swaths of it, as if from a high vantage point. What he saw instead was no different from the low winter fogs that sometimes clung to the land, but a small patch only, as if it had drifted loose from a greater mass. A patch they could easily walk a circle around.

When his mother left his room on that first night he met her, she stepped into the small patch of mist near his bed and vanished. He knew that walking into this thin fog would not bring them to the woods they could see at either side.

The five of them moved close together, as much to take strength from each other as to discuss what to do next. They had not planned beyond trying to find the mists, but the next step seemed obvious.

"If we can't see through, then we must go through," Chayan said. "I was the one to ask for this expedition; I will go and return as quickly as I can when I have seen what lies beyond."

All of them moved to object, but Shen spoke first.

"You cannot, Chayan. You are Tirren's sole heir and he would never forgive me if I acceded to this. I have been sent to guard you. I will pass through to scout."

"Shen," Dashara began.

He smiled at her. "Don't worry, I don't plan to forfeit my life just yet. Tirren told us when he entered and left he saw no sign of anyone nearby; I will hope for the same—and if not, I have my sword, which we know from the histories, and from Chayan, is a deadly weapon for them. If I don't come back soon, return to the Hold and tell Tirren what has passed."

"No, my love." Dashara took his forearm gently as he prepared to move forward. "Your sword and your mortal blood are the very reason you should not be the one. Even our dual heritage might be enough to call attention to our presence. Still, we have more chance of escaping notice, and, should we be seen, we are better armed against them than even you."

"She's right, Kesum-Shen," Maiar said. "We should test these waters first. I will go. Long have I wondered what the land of my birth looked like; perhaps it's time I saw." Before anyone could say more, he stepped away from them and vanished into the gray mass.

Now the thing was done, they all stood stunned. A point had been passed that could not be undone. Chayan could see in their faces they all felt the weight of it. Scarcely a moment passed though, before Maiar stepped back through the mists.

"It is as the Bealdor described," he said, his face shining with emotion. "I came out in a forest, though not the evergreens in front of us now. A beech forest, easily seen into. Beyond was a meadow, beautiful ..." He appeared to be at a loss for words.

"Did you see anyone," Teyyas prompted.

"No." Maiar focused again. "There was no one about, though the trees begin again on the far side of the meadow and run thicker there, so I could see no farther. From the other side, this mist is a dense barrier, high enough to meet the sky, or blur into it, at least. It stretches away right and left as far as I could see. I sensed no summoning from that side, not as I feel ours here; perhaps it is a natural feature of their land. Passing back though that thick wall was as easy as entering this thin one."

"Then it is time to do the thing we have come for," Teyyas said. Without further discussion she gathered her skirts walked forward into the fog.

Maiar went next. Dashara and Shen were in front of Chayan and neither moved.

"Shen, it isn't safe for you to ..." Dashara began.

"I will not let you go without me." His tone required acceptance or a long and probably futile argument. Dashara sighed and they entered together.

Chayan entered last. The mist enveloped him. The fog thickened, cool and moist against his skin, surrounding him in a cocoon of soundless gray. The sensation lasted only a step before he emerged onto a carpet of thick, green grass. The tall barrier of fog that Maiar had described towered behind him.

The effect of the Elven lands hit him with unexpected force; his blood sang with the song of this place. Something deeper than his perceptions tugged at him. He felt a powerful bond to this land. The scent of flowers dotting the meadow mingled with the smells of the lush grass and the green leaves and every growing thing about him. Everything here possessed a sensual lushness, a hundredfold to what he had been feeling on the other side of that gray wall, even with his senses extended there. It threatened to engulf him in the wonder of it. He could lose himself here. Shen looked as strongly affected by this place as the others, even with his blunted senses.

The wood and the glade before them were neither fey, nor exotic, though everything cried out their difference from counterparts in the mortal world. The sun that hung just above the birch trees across the meadow struck them at a comfortable angle, warm sunlight with only the hint of a flower-scented breeze. Chayan knew that it would be the same anywhere here—always warm with no portion of the day beating heat down on them and no wind to sweep the gentle warmth away.

"We must not be seduced into tarrying overlong." Dashara's quiet words echoed his own thoughts.

"Are you well, Kesum-Shen?" Teyyas asked.

Chayan had hoped they would be immune to any effects on their minds, but knew that Shen was not. Chayan felt Dashara guarding Shen's mind even now.

"I am well."

Dashara nodded her confirmation to the rest of them.

If the fog was the boundary, then the most sensible course seemed to lie ahead, past the meadow. Chayan's mind remained clear, and he felt confident he was unlikely to get confused or lost. Even so, stories he had grown up hearing of mortals trapped for years in the Elven lands tugged at the buds of fear threatening to blossom in his mind. He looked to Shen again, raised on the same tales, but he moved ahead with a soldier's focus.

They continued through the thin trees and skirted the meadow—the meadow described as the place of his conception. A place Chayan had never thought to behold. The route they took offered little protection, but he saw no one. They were almost to the denser trees on the far side when a flash of color and movement caught Chayan's eye. A Seely woman stepped out of the woods in front of them, surveying the group. Shen moved to the fore, raising his broadsword point to her.

The woman was not one Chayan recognized from Yslaaran's companions on the battlefield. Her strawberry-blonde hair framed bright blue eyes that looked at Shen with what might be amusement or curiosity ... and changed to a look of quite another sort. Chayan sensed Shen's discomfiture as the woman appraised him from head to toe and back again. She glanced at Dashara. Chayan could sense her jealousy. Protectiveness radiated from her like heat from a forge.

"He is yours?" the woman said, her voice chiming with the same musical lilt his mother's did. "A fine and strong man he is. Fiery, too. But strange company he keeps." Her delving look took in the rest of them. "This is not the first time a comely man has been seen here in these lands, but surely it is the first for four grown halfbreeds. What is the tale in this, I wonder?"

Chayan answered, in a mostly steady voice. "We have come seeking news of my mother, Lady. I am concerned for her, and for a mortal girl brought here by one of the Unseely."

"You are Yslaaran's get then. I thought as much. Rest your arms, boy," she said with a glance at Shen, still holding his sword en garde. "I will tell you what you would know."

Shen held the sword a moment longer. Dashara nodded to him, and he dropped the point to the ground.

"The girl is not far." She indicated the woods to their left with a look. "Uthbaraal brought her here to the brook to hide her from the other Unseely. He went some time ago to the palace grounds, where the queen will not allow her. He likes to boast of his catch."

"And my mother," Chayan said, "is she well?"

"Yslaaran and the others who rebelled with her are also at the palace, a place you should not attempt," she added with a warning look to him. "There they will stay until such time as the queen decides otherwise. Her actions have cast a sad shadow on this land. Never before have we known discord. Now we face both rebellion and punishment."

Chayan's expression must have reflected his concern, as she added, "No, child, they have not been harmed, nor do I believe it would come to that. Their crime is grave, though, and it may be long before Evainya is willing to allow them to wander freely again."

Chayan knew what a "long time" might mean to the Elves, and despaired. "I thank you for the news you have given us," he managed.

"Yslaaran has always been in my heart; indeed, Eanaan, Nisseah, and Isurrelte hardly less. We are of similar spirit. Yslaaran spoke to me, not long ago, regarding our ancient duty to Men, and I was moved to hear her. It had been long since I thought on those days. The Wild Hunt, though it bore me along on the tide of it, saddened me when I saw the bloody purpose that Evainya planned. This was never meant to be our way, and I did as little harm that day as was possible."

Dashara curtsied to her. "Gracious Lady, we are foreigners in this land, where not all may be so generous to us as you have been. Our power is nothing to yours, and I would beg of you any aid that you may in good conscience give. We would see the young girl back with her people, who grieve for her, and ask you for any word you may offer for the freedom of Chayan's mother and her companions."

Chayan saw that the flattery had its effect; likely it had been longer than he could imagine since the Elven woman had heard such words, but it was not enough to make her defy her already irate queen.

"No, girl, I will do no more than I have done already, and I advise you to be gone with all haste. Your man shines like a beacon. It was that which drew me here. The queen will feel you before long, and you would not wish that. For myself, I must go before any discovers me here speaking with you."

Without another word she turned and walked back the way she had come, disappearing into the trees. Her warning ringing in his ears, Chayan felt suddenly exposed.

"We must hurry," he said.

"Your mother sounds as if she is in no immediate danger," Teyyas said, "and I would have no wish to try the palace grounds, even without the Seely woman's warning. But if the girl is nearby and alone, I think we will have no better opportunity to rescue her."

They all agreed.

"Shen," Teyyas continued, "you should wait on the other side of the Veil for us. She confirmed what we feared, that your mortal blood attracts unwanted attention."

"If she felt me, then others may have and could be on their way. I'll stay with you. Just do what you have to do quickly."

Teyyas's brows drew together in a worried frown, but she nodded sharply. "Let us not waste any more time."

They entered the birch stand and angled in the direction the Elven woman had indicated. Soon they encountered a small brook winding through the trees. Even the babble of the brook chimed more musical than any in Chayan's mortal world, the air soft and sweet with its moisture. Filtered sunlight dappled the ground and the water with bright spangles.

They followed the brook only a short way before Chayan's sharpened hearing picked up a light splashing. The Somiir heard it also and the party slowed as they approached the sound. Around the bole of a large tree, Chayan saw Emorelle, a beautiful girl, of an age with him. She had liquid brown eyes and tousled dark hair, with bits of leaves and grass in it. She was dressed in a thin, Elven gown. The scooped neck hung unevenly, dipping off one shoulder. Chayan flushed with anger.

She was sitting at the edge of the brook, letting water run from one cupped hand into the other until it spilled out, and then beginning again. When she noticed their approach, she looked up and smiled, an empty, vacuous expression.

The others stood back as Chayan approached her. He reached for Emorelle's hand, and she gave it as simply as a child might. Chayan pulled her to her feet and slipped her dress back onto her shoulder. "You must come with us now," he said gently. He glanced to the Somiir and saw the look of concentration on all their faces. He could feel them working to fathom the complex nature of the hold on her mind.

"Best we leave her untouched," Maiar said as he broke off his efforts. "She may return to normal when we leave these lands, and better to have her compliant than frightened for now."

Urgency hammered at Chayan's nerves also. Shen fell back to a rear-guard position as they hurried back the way they had come. They skirted the meadow again, looking often to the trees behind them.

They were perhaps twenty lengths from the safety of the Veil when a high, churlish voice howled in unchecked rage. "Nooooo! She is mine!"

Everything seemed to happen at once.

Chayan looked back, seeking the source of the voice and recognized the Unseely who had been at Maradon's side during the battle. He pushed Emorelle behind him, turning to meet the assault. With his raven hair and black eyes, he looked like every fearful tale Chayan had heard of Dark Elves, the one both the Elven woman and Bron had named Uthbaraal.

He must have come swiftly, almost upon them before he had spoken. Chayan felt a storm of violent power behind those black eyes. Uthbaraal couldn't color Chayan's mind with the fear he threw at them, but his own natural fear of the creature and the dark and unfamiliar force he wielded was sufficient.

"Help me," Dashara whispered to Teyyas and Maiar who flanked her. Chayan felt her struggle as she protected Shen from the terror beating at his mind. The greater power, one the Unseely had not yet unleashed, built in pressure, ready to burst over them. Chayan knew in his heart that this power would prove something even the four of them would be unable to match.

Uthbaraal reached Shen at the rear and, without sparing him a glance, ducked his blade and shoved him out of his way. The Dark Elf only came to Shen's chest, but Shen slammed to the ground with the force of the push. Uthbaraal reached for Emorelle, still holding Chayan's hand, and she moved mindlessly toward the Dark Elf. Uthbaraal showed no trace of concern, as if the five intruders were of less consequence than the grass he trampled under his bare feet. Despite the waves of power emanating from him, he seemed childish in his jealous, single-minded purpose to recover what was his. Chayan knew, though, without doubt, that once he had Emorelle back, he would unleash a power on them that would be anything but childlike.

Emorelle drifted toward Uthbaraal but Chayan refused to let go. He pulled her back. The Somiir, who had been ahead of him as they ran, turned to help. The power Chayan felt them mustering individually seemed no more than a summer breeze to the storm brewing in the Uthbaraal.

The Dark Elf's hand closed on Emorelle's sleeve. Suddenly he froze, his eyes going wide. Chayan watched in horror as the long blade of a sword pushed through Uthbaraal's chest with a wet, punching sound. The smell of flowers and spice swirled pungently on the air, then diminished. Uthbaraal had ignored Shen behind him as thoroughly as he had dismissed the rest of them. A look of utter astonishment crossed the Dark Elf's face, as if he couldn't fathom what had happened to him. He let go of Emorelle's sleeve and sank to his knees, one hand drifting to the blade of the sword protruding from his body, his dark blood flowing in a river from the wound.

"It burns," he said. He gently touched the metal edge. The weight of the sword dragged him over. He toppled slowly onto his side, the bloody froth at his lips ceasing with his breath.

The horror that had gripped them all as he died broke suddenly. Shen grabbed the hilt of his sword and yanked at it to free the blade.

"Get out of here!" he shouted.

They ran for the mists.

Chapter Thirty-six

Blighted grass covered the patch where Uthbaraal's body had been slain. Evainya had felt the bright light of his life snuffed out and she had come to the site. She stood now, looking at the yellow, burned ground where mortal had killed immortal. The earth and the breeze remembered the event. Evainya filled with despair.

The world the gods had made was unraveling. The changes were sharp on the air. Seely had rebelled against her and were being held contrary to their will; halfbreeds challenged them; and a Man had brought his steel to Elven lands and killed one who should have been eternal.

She missed the gods more now than she had in long ages. Looking at the shriveled grass, burned when Uthbaraal's body returned to the fiery element it had been created from, she wished for the days when the gods had overseen all and the Elves had basked in their presence.

Tirren allowed the silence wash over him when the telling was done. Shen clasped Dashara's hand as they sat together on the settee in the Green Room. Tirren and Chayan had taken the large chairs near the cold hearth of summer, the black stone carving that Queen Assia had sent for his father perched on the mantle. Teyyas and Maiar remained standing.

Tirren had been nearly frantic when they didn't return until late evening. The relief when they walked into the courtyard, Emorelle among them, turned to a cold pit in his stomach when he saw their faces. They related what had happened during what, for them, had taken place in the space of a morning.

"I pray that what I did was right," Shen said. He shook his head in self-doubt. "I didn't wait to see if Chayan and the Somiir could deal with the threat. If we didn't have the enmity of the Elves before, we certainly do now."

"You did more than I would have believed possible." Tirren answered, though his voice sounded hollow. "You rescued Bron's sister from those lands, obtained information about Yslaaran, and you returned safely. You have my gratitude. I don't judge the decisions you made while there."

"You did right, my love," Dashara said. "You couldn't feel the forces the Unseely was working. If he had pulled Emorelle from Chayan's hold and unleashed those powers against us, we never would have withstood it."

"She's right, Shen," Chayan added. "Your actions saved us." He turned to his father. "But Shen is also right, there are bound to be consequences."

A weighty quiet settled over the group.

Tirren considered a hard set of options, not liking any of them. To ride against the Host of Elves seemed absurd in the extreme, yet if they waited for Evainya to attack them, it could be worse. Chayan and Dashara were telling him that in a contest of magic, all four of them together would not have been equal to this one Dark Elf. If the whole Host rode against Thiery, not a soul in the region would survive.

Hard options indeed. Taking the offensive seemed hopeless, but the alternative was to wait and see if Evainya retaliated, which seemed likely. There wouldn't be time to fortify the Hold and villages. Even if they did have time, what good could fortifications do against magic? Tirren rested one elbow on the big arm of the chair and cradled his forehead. Crickets thrummed and chirped outside the windows in the otherwise quiet evening, their lives the same today as yesterday, as tomorrow. Erimar had always seemed so sure in his decisions. Tirren spent a useless wish that his father could be here now to make these choices.

"I'll have to consider this," he said, looking at them again. "I'll speak with Jaron and the other leaders in the morning."

Shen spoke up. "By morning they could be upon us. Perhaps we should prepare a force and wait at their border in case retribution is immediate. If nothing happens, we could remain camped there while the Hold lays in supplies in case of siege. At least they'll know that we're not afraid to confront them, and we've already been able to kill one of them." He looked to Dashara, as if asking if she supported his ideas. She nodded, but her face drew tight with strain.

"On the battlefield," Shen continued, "it seemed that as soon as the Elves were exposed to the slightest threat they were gone. It may give them some pause for us just to be there at their border."

Tirren nodded. "It may be so. But is there a 'border', or will our forces wait in the woods while the Host appears out of nothing into our courtyard?"

"It seems likely that they would come to the army and not to an empty Hold," Teyyas said.

"If the Somiir and I were with the soldiers," Chayan added, "I think that would ensure them coming to us, knowing now that we can enter their lands."

"And," Dashara finished, "if we camp with the soldiers but make no move to call the mists perhaps they will see that we will not broach their lands if they take no action against us."

Considering their circumstances, it was the best plan they had.

"I don't want to ask you again to risk yourselves for a country not your own," Tirren said looking to the Somiir.

"Hesh is the land of my birth," Dashara said. "And new ties bind me now as well as the old." She squeezed Shen's hand. "If Teyyas and Maiar choose not to join us in this, I believe Chayan and I could summon the mists, perhaps even one of us alone, now that we know the summoning."

"We will come," Maiar spoke for himself and Teyyas. "The stakes are the same as they were this morning, as are the reasons we must do whatever we can."

Tirren wasn't going to turn down help from anyone who could wield magic. "Very well then, and Thiery will owe you a greater debt than it already does. Shen, summon Jaron and Findal and the other regiment leaders for a briefing; we'll ride out tonight."

His duty was to protect his people, though it appeared that his last decision had done nothing but endanger them all even more. They had rescued a girl not of their region and gathered some small information about Yslaaran, and at what cost? His decision to let them go this morning had been wrong. Now, what had been a possible threat was a certain one. Any direction he turned, things looked all but hopeless.

Before the next bell, sixty swordsmen rode out the gates with Tirren at their head and Chayan and the three Somiir flanking him. Twenty of Findal's archers marched ahead of the swordsmen. Findal stayed at the Hold to organize the defense—such as it would be—for Thiery Hold and the nearby villages, should they fail.

"How is Emorelle?" Dashara asked Teyyas as they rode. Teyyas and Maiar had worked with her again while the soldiers had been mustering.

"We were able to unlock the working on her," she said. "Her healing will go well now."

"I'm glad you were able to free her from her compulsion," Tirren said. He had seen the girl when she first returned and she had been a pitiful sight. Yslaaran had enspelled him once to seduce him, but he shuddered to think what the girl had been through.

Maiar shook his head. "The complexity of the enchantment made me feel like a child. Fortunately, a child unable to weave a tapestry may still unravel one."

The all-too-apt comparison chilled Tirren.

They made camp in the same spot where Chayan and the others had entered the mists that morning. Campfires sprang up as there was no point in concealment, and Tirren ordered a heavy guard posted. He sat by a small fire, watching the woods ahead. His mind was a jumble of thoughts and fears. He questioned himself and his decision more and more as the time dragged on into the quiet night.

Dawn broke and the smells of cereal cooking on the fires drifted on the air. Tirren's head nodded as he sat on his unused bedroll. Chayan sat nearby, awake and watchful, though he had not slept either. He sprang suddenly to his feet, bringing Tirren instantly alert.

"They're coming."

Tirren didn't know if Chayan felt the mists, the Elves, or the Hunt, but he didn't pause to find out. Calling an alarm that roused the entire camp he pulled Midnight's reins free from his picket. He mounted up as a patch of gray mist formed before him. The archers quickly formed up ranks in the front. They were stringing bows and setting arrows to them while the mounted swordsmen lined up directly behind them.

Out of the mists walked three figures.

"Hold!" Tirren shouted. The sound reverberated in the still morning air. Some of the archers stood frozen, others had dropped their bows to their sides. They would have held their fire no matter what his command, he realized. Tirren could see Chayan concentrating on the archers, no doubt seeking to free their minds. His focus, though, was on the Elven woman at the left of the group. Yslaaran.

Whatever had been done to his front ranks, Tirren's mind was unaffected; he moved Midnight cautiously forward to meet the three Elves. At Yslaaran's left was a pale, beautiful woman. Where Yslaaran was all grace, this woman was all power. Tirren assumed she must be the queen, though he had not seen her except in her demon-form. At her other side was an Elven man, as beautiful in form and features as the women, resplendent in colorful silks, but the vague, distracted expression on his face detracted from his regal bearing. Tirren had trouble focusing on any but Yslaaran; the sight of her threatened to burst his heart. When the woman in the middle spoke, he pulled his attention to her.

"You have come for Yslaaran," she said.

Tirren felt the sharp stab of guilt. He had come to protect his people from attack.

"I give her the choice then," the woman continued. "She may leave her people for her lover and never return to us, or she may stay with her kind and never again see mortal lands. All of my folk will be given this same choice."

Yslaaran's face lost its perennial composure. She turned to Evainya with heartbreaking sorrow painting her beautiful features. Tirren could see the queen had not told Yslaaran her decision.

"I would not choose to be severed from my people, Evainya," Yslaaran said, "nor the land of my birth. I do not even know if we can endure it. But forbear. All could be remedied by a covenant between Mankind and the Elves. It is the way the world was meant to turn for us, that we enjoy our service as well as our pleasure." She took the queen's hand, imploring her. "You have not allowed me to speak of this. Please, allow me that much now." The queen said nothing and Yslaaran continued. "Our land shrinks of our own doing, not that of Man. Shunning our duty is what has made us less than we once were, and decadence diminishes our spirit. I know that you have begun to feel it also, now that you look. Guide our people back, please, that both races may be healed."

Evainya pulled away from Yslaaran's hand and turned from her, looking long at the Elven man at her side. Soft sounds carried loud in the silence while the fate of races hung in the balance scales: the stamp of a horse's hoof, the breeze in the pines, the creak of the saddle leather as Midnight shifted his weight under Tirren's legs.

"What you say may be true," Evainya conceded. Tirren wondered if she had been communicating somehow with the man, "or it may not be. I can no longer say if returning to the old ways would make things right, or if eliminating Mankind would be the better way. I know only that a point has been passed from which we cannot return. You are right. I felt this change even before Uthbaraal's death. Analoor and I spoke of it before we summoned you." She looked to the man at her side with sadness. Tirren could not tell if it was for the vacant look the king returned or for the things they had discussed.

She continued before Yslaaran could answer. "Even if you and the others choose to stay here with these mortals, our course is forever changed. Our halfblood issue has learned to enter our lands and burning steel has taken an immortal life from the world. The enmity between us would not end here, and I will in no way risk another of our kind."

She squeezed the king's hand, as if for the added strength for what came next.

"It is we who will go. I have been thinking lately on the gods and have decided that the time has come to follow them." Tirren saw Yslaaran's fair features wane a shade paler. "I do not know if we can find the path they took, but we will seek them beyond the

Land of the Dead. If we do not find them there, perhaps we will discover something new, and if we fade to nothing when we depart this realm, then perhaps that was to be our fate at any event."

"Evainya, no," Yslaaran pleaded. "There must be a way ..."

Evainya lifted her hand and Yslaaran fell silent. "It is decided. You have been brought here to choose, but if you would come with us then you are welcome." There was a hopeful look in the queen's face. "You are our only child. Analoor and I would miss you greatly." Tirren reeled at the realization that the king and queen were Yslaaran's natural parents.

He fought to stay silent and not sway her in this weighty choice, though the words formed in his throat. A tight band wrapped about his chest, making his breath short. Yslaaran's eyes ranged the small army of men and the Somiir, paused at Chayan to his right, and then locked onto his eyes and held them. He wondered if she saw the same pain in him that he saw in hers.

"I will stay." Her gaze dropped to the ground. Tirren loosed the breath he had held, though the ache that had pierced his heart as he waited on her choice strangely didn't lessen; he felt it just as keenly on her behalf, for what this decision cost her.

The Elven man's eyes still held the strange distant cast to them, though they seemed edged with sorrow now. Evainya looked no less wounded by Yslaaran's decision than Yslaaran herself.

"So be it. Though we leave you, we will ever love you." Her hand brushed Yslaaran's cheek and Yslaaran's tear fell on her fingers. The queen turned away. Analoor smiled gently at her but said nothing. He turned to follow Evainya into the mist.

The wisps of fog thinned and vanished. Yslaaran looked at the place they had disappeared, where now lay only the evergreen forest of Thiery and the memory of her people.

The archers and swordsmen were shaking off the immobility, staring in wonder at the events they had witnessed, absorbing the fact that they would not be facing the death they had ridden here expecting. Tirren dismounted and went to Yslaaran, taking her into his embrace wordlessly. There were no words for this moment.

The army broke camp quietly, with a hushed reverence for this momentous turning point in their world. Tirren tightened Midnight's saddle, preparing to leave, when Yslaaran touched his shoulder. She looked past him into the woods.

"Others come," she said. "Nisseah, Isurrelte, and Eanaan. Two more, also."

A few moments later five Seely approached from the woods. The shadow in Yslaaran's eyes lifted a little at the sight of them. Tirren welcomed them formally. Chayan whispered in his ear that the strawberry-blonde woman was the one who had met them in the meadow.

When all was ready for the short trip back to the Hold, a group of swordsmen led their horses to the Elves, and shyly offered them to the Seely. Tirren looked around with no little wonder at the party that rode with him at the head of the column: four half-Elves and six full Elves, Yslaaran at his side.

He harbored no fantasies about their future. He knew he would never bind his wrist to hers in a marriage ceremony. It was not her way. She would not rule at his side, nor be the Lady of the Hold, and he would age while she remained forever the same. But she had chosen to stay and that was enough.

More than enough.

Epilogue

Tirren scanned the great hall, filled near to bursting with guests. He had always enjoyed Winterfest the most of all the festivals, and this year's proved all the more joyous. After a summer of war and threat, the four regions were quiet once more.

The Harvest Festival in the fall had come at a time of many changes for Thiery, when peace was still new and tenuous. Now the people celebrated with a joy born of knowing they had prevailed. Bron had honored his vow of peace and communication between all the regions was open and frequent as it hadn't been in centuries, if ever. The fall harvest had been the best in memory and the winter milder than any he could remember.

Tirren watched as Chayan circulated among the guests. The respect the people showed to him bordered on reverence, but Chayan accepted it gracefully. Like the Somiir, he didn't exploit their regard, but treated them with genuine caring. He would make a fine Bealdor someday and Tirren believed his people would love him. One certainly loved him already; Emorelle had been on his arm all afternoon.

"They make an attractive couple."

Tirren turned to find Shen next to him, with Dashara at his side.

"Yes, they do. I only hope one of them doesn't burst into flames before the wedding date. I think it appropriate to wait for his nineteenth birthday, though. It'll give time for people's animosity to Lacedar to fade more, and for us to hammer out the details with Bron."

"I don't envy them the wait," Dashara said, with a smile for Shen. The two of them had been married only a month, and both still fairly glowed with the pleasure of it.

Tirren had been glad for them when Queen Assia had given her blessing for Dashara to stay. Bansheen had been well pleased with the way recent events turned out, too. Nisseah had expressed his desire to see Bansheen and had returned with Teyyas and Maiar, lately deciding to stay on in their country. Two more of the Seely had gone as well. Apparently the philosophers had been nearly beside themselves on meeting the Elves. Assia's blessing had negated the last of the remorse Dashara felt at staying in Hesh, and she and Shen had married immediately.

Eanaan and Isurrelte had stayed in Thiery as well and were here today for the festival, though it would have been rare for any of the Elves to miss a celebration of any magnitude. Eanaan and Isurrelte had been away from the Hold more and more, though. Now that they had committed themselves to being among humans, the sadness at the separation from their own kind had begun to heal somewhat. Recently, they seemed to be developing a wanderlust.

Tirren had sent a company of soldiers with them at first but, since the Battle of the Hunt, as it had come to be called, word had been spreading around the region of the "Four Companions," those who had opposed their own kind to save thousands of humans from slaughter. When the Companions decided to forsake their own people to stay among mortals, sharing their wisdom and assistance, word ran ahead of them like wildfire and they were welcomed wherever they traveled. Eanaan and Isurrelte were even discussing visiting other regions. In addition to their other travels, though, he knew they went often to their own land.

He remembered how relieved Yslaaran had been to find that she had been able to access the Elven lands after the rest of her people had left. Going there must be bittersweet, he knew, but it seemed to ease Yslaaran's pain of loss, nonetheless. Yslaaran often stayed the night with him but Eanaan and Isurrelte never spent the night in the Hold, though whether they returned each night to their own land or elsewhere, he couldn't say.

Tirren watched Eanaan and Isurrelte dancing now, moving with the grace of the gods across the floor, so beautiful that even those who were accustomed to seeing them stared in rapture. Earlier today they had played music and sung, sweet enough to make a man weep. Chayan and Dashara had been learning songs from them, and though they couldn't nearly match the Elves for their talents, they still put the Hold's musicians to shame.

Mathom began talking to Shen and Dashara. Tirren turned back to watch Eanaan and Isurrelte dance. It surprised him how mesmerizing they could be when, earlier today, he had held Yslaaran in his arms and danced with her.

As if summoned by his thoughts, he felt Yslaaran at his right shoulder. He knew her without turning; even without the spicy, flowery scent of her skin, he would have known her. He shifted to bring her to his side, and his eyes drank in the sight of her as if seeing her for the first time. It would ever be so for him. She would always be new, always astounding, always exciting.

He slipped his arm about her waist and watched his favorite festival of the year whirl on.

About the Author

Liz has followed her heart through a wide variety of experiences, including farming with a team of draft horses, and working as a field paramedic, Outward Bound instructor, athletic trainer, and a roller-skating waitress, among other curious career choices. She also knows more about concrete than you might suspect.

Her short stories have been published in a variety of magazines and anthologies, and she was a 2020 finalist for the WSFA Small Press Award. She's a two-time winner of the Colorado Book Award for Science Fiction and Fantasy, and her series of Perilous Gods mythology-based novels are coming soon from Solaris Nova. You can find a list of her published works and more at ldcolter(dot)com. (If you're a romance reader as well, you can also find her at elizadcollins(dot)com.)

Milton Keynes UK
Ingram Content Group UK Ltd.
UKHW040854301024
450479UK00001B/23

9 781735 354422